LOVE BUZZ

LOVE BUZZ

A Novel

Neely Tubati Alexander

HARPER PERENNIAL

NEW YORK • LONDON • TORONTO • SYDNEY • NEW DELHI • AUCKLAND

HARPER ● PERENNIAL

HarperCollins books may be purchased for educational, business, or sales promotional use. For information, please email the Special Markets Department at SPsales@harpercollins.com.

FIRST EDITION

Designed by Jen Overstreet

Library of Congress Cataloging-in-Publication Data has been applied for.

ISBN 978-0-06-329291-8 (pbk.)

23 24 25 26 27 LBC 5 4 3 2 1

For all the girls

who have held out for inconvenient love

Life is not merely a series of meaningless accidents or coincidences, but rather, it's a tapestry of events that culminate in an exquisite, sublime plan.

—Jeremy Piven as Dean Kansky, *Serendipity*

Part One

In a Room of Many

1.

Mandatory attendance at a bachelorette party in New Orleans during Mardi Gras is a special kind of torture. The bride is my cousin Coral, and though I'm happy for her (genuinely, so happy), I can't say I'm overjoyed about being a bridesmaid.

For one, Coral's new best friend and maid of honor, Melody, an attorney, seems to think we all possess the same blasé attitude she does when it comes to spending money. The truth is, despite saving almost fifty percent of my paycheck each month, I don't believe spending four hundred dollars on a chartreuse bridesmaid dress is at all reasonable.

Chartreuse. The color of tennis balls and unhealthy mucus.

But I can't say that.

Because I don't want to ruin Coral's big day—especially when there already lies so much unsaid between us. And I certainly don't want the judgy lawyer look from Melody, the person who has replaced me as best friend. So I bought the four-hundred-dollar dress. And the one-hundred-fifty-dollar shoes. But I drew the line at the two-hundred-dollar hair and makeup package for the wedding day, thus justifying Melody's disdain of me.

What I really want to say is that had Coral let *me* pick the bridesmaids' dresses, I would have opted for a more universally flattering shape of some kind, instead of the mermaid monstrosity that draws unwanted attention to my hips. But because Coral and I are not as close as we once were and my Auntie Lakshmi likely forced her to include me in the wedding party—

I can't say that either.

Instead, I'm drinking and laughing and playing games like Dick Pic Bingo (a Melody contribution to the "fun") while pretending this trip isn't thieving from my hard-earned savings.

I make a mental note to delete all the penis pics from my phone before I land back home tomorrow.

But at least it's the last night.

I've navigated my way through four days and nights of weather extremes—freezing in the morning, sweltering by mid-afternoon. I've endured the stench of mold and spilled liquor that makes me wonder if I'll still detect this city on me long after I've left. And there's been more alcohol consumption than I've had over the last year. I've already researched effective detox strategies for when I get home.

There has been some good though. I've had the opportunity to take in the French Quarter during Mardi Gras, and though the constant crowds have spotlighted how much I value personal space, this place is alive with history, excitement, and culture. I'm particularly drawn to the mysticism and folklore, stopping to admire each voodoo shop we've passed. In these sparse moments, the decaying smell of the city floats around me like a perfectly placed prop. This part has me enamored. This and the beignets.

But I'm not here on a lazy vacation where I can wander the streets and peruse the shops for hours. I can't consume slices of king cake while leisurely sipping café au lait. And I can't stand on the street corner to watch the parade floats drift by, admiring their detail and scale against the backdrop of riotous live horns. No, I'm at a bachelorette party, where my experiences are confined to the inside of every bar on Bourbon Street and the scores of girls (and guys) gone wild on the streets outside them.

On this last night of bachelorette debauchery, Melody has unilaterally proclaimed we must go out with a bang. We've all been ordered to don the most revealing outfits we've packed (mine—a pair of black leggings and a plain blush pink crop top—was not up to snuff per Melody's hypercritical glare), and we are under strict orders to collect as many beads as physically possible to bestow upon Coral at the end of the night. So far, I'm losing, with one measly purple strand handed to me by a waiter attempting to lure patrons into his bar, so it hardly counts.

So here we are, at the last bar of the last night per Melody's itinerary. She's planned every second of this trip, down to the bathroom breaks. The fact I haven't shit on command during her slotted times is probably adding to her deep distaste for me. We're at some bar with *Bourbon* in the name, just like the last three we've patroned.

A few more hours and this torture will be over. And if I can make it through this night without Coral puking on me—which has already happened twice on this trip—or me erupting on Melody, I'll consider it a win.

The five other girls are all dancing atop the bar. Melody is wearing hot-pink mesh underwear under her black leather mini skirt, and there are currently four men positioned at the bar, all staring up said skirt. I thought lawyers were supposed to be conservative. Not Melody.

Coral is wearing a bra top and holey, wide-leg jeans and is currently wobbling from her perch on the bar. I'm wondering when she will puke again because it has become a question of when, not if.

Leaning against the back wall, I watch them bend and swat each other's butts, making mental bets with myself about who will be the first to fall. I secretly hope it's Melody.

My phone buzzes. A text from my best friend, Clarence: *Two months until you are a Seattle legend! I hope you survive the night… try not to slap the Handmaid of Horror, er, maid of honor.* I breathe deep. Just what I needed, a reminder of my impending thirtieth birthday and the "Life at Thirty" feature I'm to be showcased in. I think to tell him it's technically ten weeks, but don't want to discuss it further. The sheer mention of these upcoming events sends a pulse of adrenaline through me as I type my response. *I really wish you were here. Still mad you found a way to back out.* Clarence is the only bridesman and the only member of Coral's wedding party who is not here in New Orleans. He somehow managed a "required work conference" for the same weekend. I expect receipts when I'm back.

I don't notice his approach, but suddenly there is a guy by my side trying to be heard over the music, though I can barely make out what he says.

"Chest for beads!" is what I hear.

"Excuse me?" I say, debating whether to raise my knee to his groin.

He leans in closer. "I said, are you not into flashing your chest to a room full of horny dudes for shitty plastic beads?"

I really look at him then. His warm brown hair is tamed with gel, though it appears to be just barely working, like his hair may spring from its delicate trap at any moment in all directions. His thick brows hover incredibly close to his eyes, as if they are all the same feature, giving him a brooding quality I am decidedly attracted to. My dark brows are the opposite, highly arched and meticulously sculpted; the time investment alone makes it the first feature I notice on others.

"Shitty plastic beads that are probably full of lead," I add, interest piqued.

He leans against the wall beside me, mimicking my position, then lifts his leg to place his foot against the wall behind him. As he does, the music transitions and I hear the screech of the sole of his light gray canvas shoe being ripped from the stickiness of the floor. I try not to think about what particular combination of filth has created said sticky substance below our feet.

"Yes, those." He motions his beer bottle toward me and I look down at the lone strand of shiny purple beads around my neck. "So if you didn't show your chest, dare I ask how you got 'em?"

"Who said I didn't show my chest?"

He raises his eyebrows and his cheeks glow pink and he looks for a moment like a preteen boy having a conversation about boobs. He keeps his eyebrows raised and now it feels as though he is calling my bluff.

"I didn't show my chest for them," I admit.

He releases the strain of his eyebrow ridge.

"A waiter took pity on me and my bare neck."

My words cause him to look at my neck, which makes my neck suddenly very sensitive to the air against it.

"Want me to take them off your hands? For health purposes," he asks.

"You'd have to earn them," I say. "This is Mardi Gras, after all."

He kicks himself off the wall and turns to face me. It's then I notice just how much he towers over me.

"I have to earn the shitty, lead-filled pity beads?" The corners of his mouth lift playfully.

"Well, they *are* a hot commodity." I take a sip of my watered-down vodka soda as he contemplates a response. We look at each other for a long moment, and I feel myself flush as I notice the dark speck in the green of his right iris just below the pupil. I say a secret thank-you to the manager of this bar for ensuring the lights are not so dim that I might miss this detail about him.

"Okay. What do I have to do to earn them?" He's still yelling over the music, though somehow this part sounds like a whisper in my ear.

"Show me your tits!" I yell through the megaphone I've made around my mouth with my hands. The corners of his mouth tug positively wide, leaving space between his teeth and where his mouth ends. It is perhaps the most adorable thing I have ever seen, in complete opposition with his brooding eye line. I think of videos of puppies and kittens and baby chicks rolling around together.

He sets his drink down on the table beside us, grabs the hem of his shirt with both hands, and lifts his gray Nirvana tee to his neck.

I want to respond with a catcall or whistle but am instead rendered silent as I take in his torso—tanned, lean, cut. My eyes linger on the happy trail that disappears into the waist of his jeans. *Happy trail, indeed.*

"Well deserved," I say when he releases his shirt. He positions it back in its place as I lift the string of beads over my head. I hold them out in front of me but instead of taking the strand, he bends down so I can place the beads around his neck. The soft bristle of his hair against my hand sends goose bumps up my arm. This close, I can smell his peppery cologne. Spellbound, I inhale, sure his pheromones are gripping in my nose, my throat, my lungs.

A warning sensor goes off inside me, though I fight to ignore it.

"I feel like this was all a master plan to show off that chest and stomach," I say. He smiles again, and I almost laugh at how endearing it is.

"Depends. Did you find it charming or douchey?"

"Douchey, definitely douchey."

"Okay, then definitely not planned. Not at all." He smiles again and I'm worried I'm staring at his face too much, though I can't seem to stop. "I'm Julian," he says, extending a hand.

"Serena." I move my hand toward his, realizing the odd nature of our interaction—that I've seen his bare chest before learning his name.

The second our palms meet, my nerves begin to dance and blood rockets around inside me like a thousand bouncy balls in a concrete box. The sensation makes its way down my body, settling between my legs. My eyes involuntarily flick down to the same area on him. I blame this city; all the nipples I've seen these past four days have turned me into an ogling pervert.

"Serena," he repeats, calling my eyes back to his. Our hands are still intertwined and the warmth and size of his feels like I've slid my fingers into a mitten fresh from the dryer. We have stopped the shaking motion of our hands, though they are still locked together. So now we are standing there, holding each other's hand between us, which I am sure looks quite odd should anyone be watching.

A new beat hits and the crowd screeches its approval. I look over to find Coral, Melody, and the rest of the bridesmaids gyrating on the bar with impressive force. I worry Coral may throw her back out.

"Ah, Lil Wayne, a Mardi Gras legend," I yell as "Back That Azz Up" roars around us.

"It's actually a Juvenile song featuring Lil Wayne, but Lil Wayne *is* from New Orleans, you know, so it does kinda fit."

I look up at him. "Why do you know that?"

He hangs his head as he smirks. "From my love of Lil Wayne, of course."

I look down at our hands, still connected. I can't seem to manage to pull away first. As if reading my mind, he releases my hand.

"Where are you from, Serena?" He has spoken my name twice now, each striking me like an electric current. He shoves both of his hands into his jean's front pockets, his beer bottle abandoned on the table beside us.

"Seattle," I say.

"No shit, me too."

"Really? What part?" I ask.

"Chamber Hill. What about you?"

My cheeks heat. Usually, I say Seattle because people outside of Washington only largely know Seattle. And if you say Washington, I've learned on this trip, people tend to think you mean D.C. "Technically I live in Bellevue." We live thirty minutes away from one another and somehow we're meeting at a bar in New Orleans, making it all the more exciting.

"No shit," he says again, still gazing at me. He reaches for his beer and takes a sip, licks his lips afterward, and I blush again. Or am I still blushing? Those lips of his are intensely red, like they've been stained by Hawaiian Punch.

"What are you doing at Mardi Gras, Serena?" he asks. It's like he knows I feel a rush of heat each time he says my name.

"Raging, of course. Isn't that the goal?"

He leans back against the wall, and I follow suit. His arm lightly brushes mine and I savor the soft, feathery sensation. We look out at the crowd of people, shoved in and pressing against one another. I am sure this place is breaching its maximum occupancy. This far end of the room where we stand tucked next to the emergency exit, our only salvation.

I glance over to the bar again, where Coral and the others are still putting on a show. Coral looks as though she's about ten minutes from puking. The crowd peeping up Melody's skirt has grown to seven.

"I don't know, I kinda think my goal is to be that guy." Julian leans in and points his beer bottle toward a booth in the corner and my eyes follow to the lone man seated in it. He looks to be in his late sixties, maybe early seventies. He's wearing a Tommy Bahama–type shirt unbuttoned low enough for one of his silver-haired nipples to be poking out.

First the glimpse of Julian's chest and now this. So many nipples at Mardi Gras, just not the kind I expected to see.

The man's arms are slung over the top of the booth back, and he's staring at the group of girls dancing in front of him like he's trying to decide which chocolate truffle to devour first from a big heart box.

"Oh god," is all I can offer. Julian laughs. My chest warms with satisfaction at having made him laugh. "In that case, you're gonna have to work on your chest hair situation, because from what I saw, you have a lot of catching up to do." I motion up and down him with my drink.

"And I need to go shopping. I don't own anything with flamingos on it. Or leaves. I suddenly, desperately need a shirt with flamingos and leaves."

"Maybe you can get a discount if you tell them you don't need the top half of buttons," I say.

"That's a good tip." He takes another sip from his beer, then looks at the guy in the booth once more. "Do you think the nipple out is intentional? Is this some kind of new trend I'm unaware of?"

I smile as I turn to face Julian again. "Maybe it's some kind of mating call to those young girls."

The corners of his mouth lift as he nods, still assessing the man in the booth. As he does, I steal a glimpse of his eyes again. Solid green at their edges, transitioning delicately to a light hazel toward the center. I attempt to commit them to memory. It's as though they should be held—those eyes—gripped under light, turned this way and that, to experience how they might come alive in new ways with each slight movement.

"The shame of it is that his nipple is out—like fully out this whole time—and nobody is giving him any beads. I feel bad for him." Julian leans in as he talks, the heat of his breath warming my ear.

"You could give him yours," I say, pointing to the purple strand around his neck.

"No way. I traded my body for these. It's my lead," he says, palming the beads. We both smile, though mine is decidedly inadequate compared to his.

He bumps my shoulder with his playfully. "Seriously, what are you doing here?" he asks in a way that makes me think he has decided I don't belong in this muggy bar of bad decisions. I take the tone as a compliment.

"Bachelorette party." I attempt neutrality in my tone, though I know as soon as the words escape me, I have failed.

"Wow," he says. "Please tell me those are your friends." He points his bottle to the bar top, where Coral has taken off her BRIDE sash and is flossing it between her legs.

I press my lips together. "The bride is my cousin. The rest I barely know. Please don't judge me."

"They're a lively bunch," he says, his eyes tracking to Melody, who has her leg wrapped around a column as she writhes against it.

"Yeah. What about you? What are you doing down here?"

"My buddy Kurt's birthday. He's always wanted to come to Mardi Gras. We surprised him for his thirtieth." He does a little bob and weave to see through the crowd. "I think that's him over there looking up your friend's skirt."

"So why aren't you over there with them, looking up skirts and yelling, 'Show me your tits'?"

He shrugs. "Not really my thing."

"Tits, you mean? Tits are not your thing? So, you're gay?"

"No, tits are my thing. Tits are definitely my thing." He blushes and his lips turn an even richer shade of red.

I imagine them searing to the touch.

"Those may just be the two cringiest sentences to have ever come out of my mouth," he says.

"Well then, I think you're on your way." I motion toward the guy in the booth, who's still evaluating the dancing girls.

We both sip our drinks in unison, eyeing each other as we do.

My stomach is rolling. Not in a too-many-beignets way, but rather in an unnerved, gripped sort of way. I wonder if he feels at all the same.

"What do you do in Bellevue, Serena?" he asks into the dense silence. He keeps saying my name in that amused way, like he's a toddler proud of himself for learning a new word, and it continues to get me every time.

"I'm an accountant," I tell him, wondering what his response will be. Usually, people are either impressed or bored. Or make some reference to Angela from *The Office*. He nods and smiles in an expression I choose to take as impressed. "What about you, Julian?" Now I'm saying his name in the same playful way.

"I work at a tech start-up."

I furrow my brow. "Well, that's super vague. Do you mean you run the place or order the free food and beer?"

"Are those the only two options?" he asks. "I do a little of everything."

It's decidedly not an answer.

"Well, I'm impressed you *have* a job. The only other guy I met on this trip is a 'professional surfer.'" I make air quotes.

"That can be a real job."

"Yes, it can be. But then he told me he's thirty-two, lives with his parents, and doesn't actually surf for money. So really, he's just jobless and spends his copious free time surfing."

Julian shakes his head and clenches his jaw. It's perfectly square, that jaw.

"Actually, there was a second guy. White. Blond. Wearing a shirt that said 'Gyno' with a rubber glove on it. He asked me what I was, and when I assumed he meant race rather than species, I told him Indian. He then proceeded to ask, dot or feather."

Julian cringes. "Yikes. I apologize on behalf of my gender. And race. And what the hell, on behalf of our species too."

He pulls his bottom lip into his mouth and it reemerges wet, an even deeper shade of red, shiny like a cherry nail polish.

I swallow.

"For the record, I don't live with my parents," he says. "My job pays actual money. And I don't walk around asking people what they are."

"Please tell me we're not playing Two Truths and a Lie right now."

"I swear," he says, raising his hand in a scout's honor.

"Marry me," I say. I mean it jokingly of course, and he does smile, though the corners of his features sharpen and I know I'm blushing. I feel it then, a pull in my abdomen. I'm already missing this interaction with this guy while I'm still in the middle of it.

"Cheers to that." He holds out his drink.

"Cheers," I say, clinking my glass to his bottle.

We gaze at each other like it's a game of chicken. I refuse to look away first.

"There you are!" I jerk as Melody appears by my side, dragging Coral behind her. I try to ignore the heat in my cheeks as Melody surveys Julian with a ravenous look in her eyes. She shifts her gaze up and down him several times. "And who are you, handsome?" she says in a throaty way I find obscene.

Julian looks to me as if I can save him. He's underestimating Melody. "Julian," he says, with a little wave before shoving his hands into his pockets.

Melody turns to me, though her eyes never leave Julian. "You sly fox," she says to me, still looking at him.

"Why'd you get off the bar?" I ask, desperate to separate Melody and Coral from Julian. Desperate to have him to myself again. Though I can claim no ownership over this man I've just met, I certainly can't stomach the idea of Melody swooping in and clutching him away. She's already done so with Coral.

"Coral needs to puke," Melody says, finally giving me her attention. We both look at Coral, whose skin has taken on a shade reminiscent of my bridesmaid dress. "We were on our way to the bathroom, but then I saw"—she circles her finger in the air between Julian and I—"this."

I look to Julian in a panic. He smiles, just a little, like we share a secret. I feel even closer to him than I did a half second ago.

"I'll take her!" I say, surprised by the warble in my voice.

"I've got her," Melody returns, tightening her grip around Coral's arm. "Maid of honor duties and all." I bite at the inside of my cheek. In any other scenario, I would not be vying to be the one to help someone to the bathroom to puke. But Melody is right. It is a maid of honor duty. And I should be maid of honor.

Coral lets out a desperate moan. I know her throw-up tells. The geyser in her belly has burst its way to her throat. We have less than thirty seconds before there's vomit on all our shoes.

The thought of leaving this moment with this guy—Julian—upsets me far more than it should. We've just met. Nonetheless, I feel the unease at the base of me. But Coral needs help. And it should be me who helps her. I want it to be me.

I grab Coral's arm from Melody and, before she can object, yell, "Be right back." My words are meant for Julian but I send them in his general direction without eye contact. I can't manage to look at him with Melody ogling him beside me. She puts up less of a fight than I anticipate, distracted by Julian. I get it.

He nods and smiles at me, again just a little, and I feel the warmth between my legs as I haul Coral to the ladies' room.

"I don't feel so good," Coral says, rocking her way through the door. There's a long line because of course there is and a million feelings swirl about inside me as we wait. Disgust at the thought of Coral vomiting on me again. A buzzing at my core brought on by the evening's unexpected encounter. Something like culpability for the feelings I'm having for a stranger, knowing what I have at home. But mostly, panic at the thought Julian may not be waiting out there for me when I return from this crowded den of drunken ladies doing the pee-pee dance.

2.

THE LINE MOVES AT A SNAIL'S PACE AND AS CORAL BEGINS TO RETCH, I RE-alize we need a backup plan. I shove her out of line to the corner of the black-and-white-checkered bathroom where a tall trash bin stands. She instinctively leans over it, white-knuckles the sides with all her might, and begins to hurl. I pull her hair back and tug at her BRIDE sash to keep it from falling into the line of fire as a few women in line moan in disgust. *Sorry,* I mouth to the line, though I'm certain they've encountered more icky moments at Mardi Gras than this.

It's not the first time I've held Coral's hair back as she's puked. I rub my free palm in small circles in the center of her back, think-ing of us—me thirteen, Coral a tender eleven—riding the Gravitron at Seattle Center the summer before eighth grade, well before those rides were removed to make way for expansive high-rises. Someone at my mom's office had gifted her ride tickets and it was a rare day out in the expensive world. It took Coral only one ride rotation to begin to dry heave. Somehow, she held it in until the ride stopped and I found her a secluded spot of asphalt to relieve herself three times over.

If nothing else, Coral is efficient. She finishes quickly, stands, straightens her BRIDE sash, and wipes at her mouth with the back of her hand. "Much better," she says as the color returns to her face.

"Come here." I lead her to the faucet. She scoops water in her palm and swooshes it around in her mouth.

"I love you," she says after spitting the water into the sink. She looks at me and her eyes are flooding. "You're my hold-my-hair-back-as-I-puke cousin who's more like a sister." Her shoulders drop as soon as the words leave her mouth. "Or, you used to be. Not anymore. Now you hate me." She says this last part with the vulnerability and incomprehension of a child.

My chest aches. "Coral," I say, gently stroking her arm. "I don't hate you. Let's not get into all this right now, okay? This trip is about celebrating you. Let's do that, and not worry about anything else."

She nods, eyes still filled with tears. She captures them with her forefinger as she presses it to the corners of each eye.

"Do you wanna head back to the hotel?" I ask.

She shakes her head intensely and I feel immediate, almost embarrassing relief that I don't have to leave. Not yet. Up until about fifteen minutes ago, I was counting the minutes until this trip was over. Now, I would do anything to extend this night, so long as Julian is part of it.

A trickle of guilt makes its way up my spine.

"Okay, then let's head back out?"

Coral nods and I place a hand on the small of her back as I lead her out of the restroom, trying my best to swallow all the feelings I don't want to feel right now. I don't want to think about my relationship with Coral and all its complexities. I don't want to think about my life at home. I just want to, for this night, feel good. And I know exactly where to go to find that feeling.

When I elbow my way through the crowd back to our spot in the corner, I find Julian, alone, again leaning against the wall with his one foot propped up. When he sees me, he pushes off the wall and turns to face me.

"Hi," he says, and I can't help but think his voice sounds a bit relieved that I'm back.

"Hi," I say, hoping he hears the same from me. "Melody eventually tired of you, did she?"

"Yeah, she grilled me for about thirty seconds and then a Miley song came on and she bolted back to the bar top." He motions his drink to the bar, where Coral has now also rejoined the group, looking as though she didn't just hurl in a bathroom garbage can.

"You're on a first-name basis with Miley Cyrus?"

He smirks.

"Do you wanna go outside?" I ask, desperate to avoid any more distractions or prying eyes.

"Yes, please."

As I lead him through the crushing crowd, I can't help but feel a current through me each time he bumps me from behind. The back of my arm running into his bicep. My shoulder against the soft cotton of his Nirvana T-shirt. My backside against the front of his jeans. When we reach the door, he leans forward and our faces are extremely close as he pushes the door open for me to slink through.

We step outside and though there are throngs of people out here too, it is decidedly quieter and cooler. We nestle against the side of the entrance, just beyond the mass of people in the street.

"Ah, it's a little better out here. It's just so . . . moist in there," he says, rubbing his palm against the back of his neck.

"Did you just say *moist* to me?"

"Charming or douchey?" he asks, face crinkled.

"One thousand percent douchey."

"Agreed. I'm zero for two. Why are you even still talking to me?" He looks into me and it feels like a dare of some kind.

I shrug. "You saw my other options." I motion toward the bar entrance.

"Do you mean Tommy Bahama or the bridesmaids?"

"Both."

We smile.

A large group pushes past us and Julian curves his hand around my waist to keep them from ramming me into the wall as they pass. I wonder if I will feel phantom remnants of that hand on my waistline long after we part. We instinctively scoot farther away from everyone and everything, hugging the corner of the building.

We stand there, staring at each other for a moment, his green eyes unblinking. A light wind sweeps through the breezeway and it makes my skin tingle. A crescendo of cheers erupts from the street and I look over just in time to see three women lined up in the middle of the street, shirts pulled to their shoulders, bare chests jiggling against the sticky air. If I were keeping track, I'd say those three sets push my visual breast count from this trip to triple digits.

"Why do you think flashing is a thing at Mardi Gras anyway?" I ask him.

He shrugs. "My guess? A traditional, sacred celebration overtaken by drunk, overindulgent tourists."

"A solid assumption."

In the street, the well-proportioned girls have moved on, replaced by a guy in a Viking hat (horns and all) and tighty-whities facing us, flicking his nipples and making aggressive eye contact with me. Julian steps between us to shield me from the horror. I fear I'm reaching sensory overload.

"Tourists ruin everything," I say, looking up at him.

"Agreed," he says. "To be fair, Mardi Gras is technically a celebration of Fat Tuesday, the last day to indulge before Lent." He returns to his spot beside me as the Tighty-Whitey Viking continues on his way.

"So all the beignets I've eaten these past four days are . . . ?"

"On point with the true meaning of Mardi Gras."

"Nice. Thank you for rationalizing that for me."

"A night of indulgences," he says, leaning his shoulder against the building as if the weight of his words is too much. He leans in. "You should tell me something you've never told anyone before." When I raise my eyebrows, he adds, "I want to know something no one else knows about you. For the sake of the true meaning of Mardi Gras, of course."

"I don't think that's how it works."

"Look around. There are no rules here."

I do as he suggests and look around. There's carefree abandon, good-natured recklessness, a general lack of bras. *A night of indulgences.* I'm inclined to agree.

"I want to know your deep, dark secrets," he continues, looking into me, then breathes in a barely audible tone, "Charming or douchey?"

Charming. Decidedly charming.

I don't answer.

He cocks his head to one side and folds his arm in a silent plea.

A tingle makes its way down me, from the nape of my neck to the heels of my feet. My lips part but nothing comes out.

"C'mon," he says before breaking into a smile. "Haven't you ever lied, cheat, or stolen? Helped hide a body? I promise I won't tell anyone."

When he says *stolen*, I fight off an internal flinch.

"Okay," I say.

We both straighten, preparing to unmask. And, if he's like me, he's embracing the slight terror inside him about how things have suddenly become serious.

"I have, actually. Stolen, that is." I say it in my most proud tone, recalling the only time in my life I've ever done anything that wasn't aboveboard.

"Really?" he says as if he's calling my bluff.

"Yes. Peanut M&Ms from the grocery store when I was seven."

He presses his lips together.

"It's not funny. It was traumatizing." I fight off my own smile.

"I'm sorry. Please continue." He pauses. "Please."

I enjoy the beg in his voice a little too much.

"A little boy was sitting in the cart ahead of my mom and me in the checkout line—a toddler, maybe two or three. That klepto baby reached over and grabbed a bag of peanut M&Ms from the shelf. He just sat there, holding the package in his fist so hard it puckered like a bow tie. He even shook it a few times, raising his arm up and down like it was a rattle. Nobody saw him, that brazen little brat."

Julian has that goofy grin back on his face and it encourages me to keep talking about this thing I've never told anyone.

"So I'm standing there watching his mom talk on the phone, her baby's thieving hand in possession of stolen goods, and she's completely oblivious. They went right out the door and . . . nothing. I expected to hear sirens, see red and blue alarms, watch the store's overhead lights flash, police officers surround her. But no. Nothing happened. Not a single thing."

Julian holds his grin in anticipation of what he knows comes next.

"So I look at my mom. She's unloading items onto the belt. I don't have much time to think about it. I grab a bag of peanut M&Ms—"

"Great choice. Peanut M&Ms, I mean."

"Right? So I hold it in my hand, pressed against my thigh. My heist is clearly not planned, though, because I'm wearing a dress and have no pockets, literally nowhere to hide this enormous yellow . . . thing that's crackling in my hand. So, I just press it between my palm and the side of my thigh and try to act normal."

Julian leans in.

"And then I notice the people behind us. It's this kid Aiden, a boy from my class. He was a little shit. His mom is saying hi to my mom. Aiden's staring at the contraband in my hand. That's when my mom says my name, and I'll never forget the echo of that bag of M&M's as it made contact with the linoleum. It's like a nuclear bomb had gone off at my feet."

"So, what happened next?" Julian asks when I pause.

"Aiden's mom insisted on buying the M&Ms for me. Said Aiden wanted one too and it would be a treat to let her get them both."

I don't tell Julian how I was virtually in tears. Or that my mother and I stood awkwardly after she paid for our groceries as the belt pushed Aiden's mom's items forward. How I had inspected each one, fascinated by what went into their bags. Lucky Charms. The thick toilet paper with imprints pressed into the two-ply sheets. The granola bars with chocolate chunks in them. My mom once picked up a box of the same granola bars from the shelf to evaluate. I remember holding my breath in anticipation it would end up in our cart, only for her to say, "Three ninety-nine and it only comes with six bars? Bah," before placing the box back on the shelf. And Aiden's mom didn't use a single coupon. I don't tell Julian that the next day at school, Aiden told the other kids I was a charity case. That I had to ask Clarence what Aiden's words meant. Or that after that, I tried to avoid trips to the grocery store with my mother.

Julian chuckles.

"What? I just shared the worst thing I've ever done and you're laughing."

"You didn't even steal them," he says, the corners of his eyes crinkling.

"What?"

"You didn't steal them," he repeats. "The woman—Aiden's mom—she bought them for you. The one bad thing you did, you didn't even do." He smiles like he's just witnessed a loving airport reunion.

"Okay, okay, I get it. You're not the first person to tell me I'm boring."

"You are anything but boring," he says and there's undeniable flirtation in his voice.

"Maybe safe is a better word," I say, pressing into the wall as another wave of laughing passersby flow by us.

"There's nothing wrong with that," he says. We both take a half step toward one another.

"I guess, but . . ." and in perhaps my most naked moment, I say, "maybe I need more excitement in my life." My skin burns immediately.

He smiles. "That's a pretty worthy pursuit, I'd say."

We both lean into the brick wall. I resist the urge to flap my arms to get some air to my pits. I clear my throat instead. "It's your turn," I manage.

"I was hoping you'd forget about me," he says.

"Never. Not when I just told you my worst offense."

He chuckles, seemingly at the idea that this grocery-store-heist debacle is my worst offense.

He licks his reddened lips. "Okay, it's only fair I share something back, right?"

I nod.

He looks up at the dim white awning above our heads, then back at me. "Okay. Deepest possible omission? Fully naked?" he asks and I, naturally, imagine him disrobed. I have to pinch my eyes shut to cancel myself positioned underneath him from the vision.

I nod again.

Then, he leans in, and in a whisper, his lips practically touching my ear, says, "I've never been in love before."

Before what?

He leans back against the building. "I've dated, but never had that punch-in-the-gut feeling, like . . ."

Like what? I think, hanging on his words. I want him to say *like this.* But I'm also silently begging him not to as it would be too much to handle. Not to mention completely, utterly ridiculous.

It would be crazy to say that as we gaze at each other, I feel my whole life has built to this one night, meeting this one man. But I swear to you, that's what it feels like in these few seconds. And the way he's looking at me, like I'm a riddle he's on the verge of solving, I can't help but think he feels it too.

He doesn't finish his statement. "Can I ask you something?" he says instead, intense concentration overtaking his face.

"That depends. Does it have to do with Tommy Bahama in there?"

He smiles, though it doesn't quite reach his eyes. "No, I just—"

"Julian!" someone yells from behind him. "I've been looking everywhere for you. I need your help. C'mon!"

We both look over his shoulder. The guy who called out to him has already turned his back on us and is reentering the bar. Julian looks at me, his eyes questioning. I give him a slight nod then follow him back inside. When we've pushed our way to the middle of the flailing crowd, we are joined by four other guys, two of them carrying a third between them whose eyes are rolling into the back of his head. The tips of his feet are barely sweeping the floor, and the front of his shirt is soaked. I run through a list of potential causes of his shirt situation in my head. Spilled drink. Water hose. Coral's puke. It's then I notice the two men holding him up on either side are security.

"What happened?" Julian says to the fourth, the one who came outside. For a moment I think they are both Julian. I shake my head, realizing I have perhaps had too much to drink.

"Long story, but we've gotta go." He looks at one of the guards. "Now."

One of the security guards chimes in. "Let's go," he barks at Julian.

Julian turns back to me, and I am sure the expression on my face matches his. Raised eyebrows, round eyes, a weirdly desperate twist across the mouth. The guard shoves Julian from behind and he's knocked several steps forward before disappearing into the crowd completely.

"Enjoy your lead poisoning!" I yell after him, though I can practically see my words dissipate into the air right in front of me, swooshed away by the drum of the music's beat and the stir of the chattering crowd.

I continue to stare in the direction he has gone, frozen to my spot. As much as I want to chase after him, I can't. Doing so would cross a line I shouldn't disturb, and perhaps already have.

3.

As I climb into a Lyft early the next morning, four days hungover and generally exhausted from the bachelorette festivities (and mostly Melody), I think of him.

Julian.

I think of his eyes, green with a little dark speck in the right one, just under the pupil. I think about his wide, goofy adorable smile. I think of the way my name sounded on his tongue and what it did to me. I think about his tongue, generally . . .

Melody shoves in beside me in the back seat and I fight off a groan. Coral takes the seat in front of us as the rest of the group climbs into another car. We all look and move like the walking dead with a snarl in our voices, innards mangled from too much indulgence over the last four days.

I stare at the back of Coral's head, wondering if she felt in her first encounter with her fiancé, Everett, what I felt last night with Julian. I want desperately to curl up on the little round woven rug in my childhood bedroom and talk about Everett and Julian with giddy abandon, the way we used to talk about boys. I picture the two of us there, lying on our stomachs, ankles crossed in the air behind us, our shared journal flipped open where we matched our first names with the last names of boys in our grade to test how they sounded together. The best evenings: when the WinCo ice cream was on sale, and my mom would surprise us with a tub of Neapolitan. We'd lie on that rug, tub between us, strawberry side in front of me, vanilla in front of her, our spoons connecting at the chocolate center as she told me time after time of her healthy obsession (her words) for Robbie Moynes, the curly-haired skateboarder, in the apartment just below mine.

But that was a lifetime ago.

I watch out the window as we drive away from our hotel. Driving down Royal, I catch glimpses of Bourbon Street across every intersection from our parallel street one small block over. There's an anxiety brewing inside me with every minute that ticks by. Somewhere in this city, the guy I met last night lingers. Is he still asleep? I picture him curled up under a set of crisp white sheets, six pack flexing each time he adjusts, his chestnut mane tousled. Is he lying awake in bed, thinking of me?

Outside, there's a gloomy, low-hanging mist that matches my mood. I think of the abruptness with which the interaction between Julian and I ended, leaving me feeling incomplete.

At this early morning hour, on the cusp of daybreak, the Quarter resembles a graveyard, a deserted haunt littered with evidence of last night's festivities. Abandoned beads. Mardi Gras masks. Discarded clothing. An occasional shoe. I can only imagine the narratives behind each item left behind, wondering if they are as divine as my own story from last night.

I press my forehead to the glass when we reach a familiar stretch. On the sidewalk stands a row of bronze statues of famous jazz musicians. I recognize them instantly. Coral hugged each one last night with great affection. She took a specific interest in the one on the far right and made a particularly disdainful joke about the woodwind instrument pressed to his lips before taking several selfies with it.

We definitely stumbled along this street, which means we're near the bar where I met Julian. The proximity alone makes me feel closer to him, to last night. When we drive past, it'll officially be gone. I feel the loss, preemptively running along my skin like the scrape of a razor. I know loss too well. I can't take on an evergreen version of it.

"STOP!" I scream as we roll through the green light.

The Lyft screeches to a halt in the middle of the intersection and everyone's wide eyes lay upon me. I'm impressed with the driver's rapid response, the minivan's braking system.

"What is it?" Melody says, her voice scratchy and sunken.

"I . . . I think I forgot something. In that last bar from last night. What was the name of it?" I point to the bar entrance through the intersection, though I can't seem to find a sign with the name. But it's the same dim white awning Julian and I stood beneath, huddled together while the Quarter's guests reveled around us. Same oak door he held open for me to thinly press by him.

"Something with Bourbon In It?" Coral offers, her voice crackly like she's got smoker's lung. "Bourbon Street Bar? Drink Some Bourbon? Bourbonite?"

"You're just saying random words," Melody mutters, her huge head thrown back against the headrest, eyes closed. It would be the perfect time to throat punch her, should one be looking to do such a thing.

I make eye contact with the driver in the rearview mirror. "Sir?" I plead, trying to hide my desperation. Surely, he knows the bars here, likely drops off and picks up at the same ones often.

He shrugs his indifference.

Melody, laying on the annoyance, says, "What could you have possibly forgotten?"

The man of my dreams? My good senses? One or the other, for sure.

"My purse!" I yell, making eye contact with Coral, who has turned around from the seat ahead of us.

"But you had your purse when we got back last night. You gave it to me to hold on the drive home in case I needed to puke in it."

"Oh, right." I'd momentarily forgotten that drunk puking Coral also has a pristine memory.

I look out the window, down the small block again to the entrance of the bar where I met Julian just hours before.

That's when I see him.

There's a guy in a Seahawks cap, sweatshirt, and dark green jersey shorts, pulling on the double doors of the bar. When they won't give, he places the side of his hand against his forehead and peers into the darkened bar from the dirty window. When he turns around and looks up and down the street, I know with categoric, bone-chattering certainty: it's Julian. He is burned into me with the verity of a core memory. My stomach lurches toward the car door.

A Jeep behind us honks and I physically jump. I place my hand on the handle, ready to burst from the car, to run to him and—oh, who knows what happens next exactly; I just need to get to him—but the honking driver behind us swerves and makes his way around on my side in dangerous proximity, middle finger thrust in the air out his half-down window as he does. It's decidedly too much rage for such an early morning hour.

I hesitate.

What am I doing? I am desperate, irrational, and sleep-deprived. But does any of it matter because Julian is standing there, only a few feet away. I must—

Julian is no longer there.

My eyes scramble all around, and I find him just ahead. His fingers are wrapped around the handle of the back door of his own Lyft, though he's still staring in the direction of the bar entrance.

HONK!

There is a new car behind us now, as we are still stalled in the middle of the intersection. Why are there so many cars on the road at this obscene hour?

"I have to move," our driver says, looking at me from the rearview mirror. I can't help but think he looks sympathetic, more understanding than Coral or Melody. Then again, perhaps he just doesn't want his five-star rating to suffer.

I can't let it end this way again. I at least need to get his full name.

His phone number. His date of birth and social security number. A hair sample. A drop of blood. A fingerprint. Even if I don't ever use them, I need to know I *could* talk to him again.

I reach for the handle again, but the car begins to move.

"What the—" Melody says, watching me attempt to slide open the door of the now accelerating minivan.

I think about jumping from the moving vehicle, but even I am not that dramatic. Plus, I'm not the tuck-and-roll type. I'm more of a flail-and-likely-break-something type. Our driver has pulled out of the intersection to the bike lane and flipped on his hazard lights.

I lean back, straining to see the sliver of Bourbon Street still available out my window, finding it just in time to watch Julian climb back into his Lyft.

In a split second he is gone. I fall back into my seat and avoid eye contact with Coral and Melody.

"What was that?" Melody demands, arms folded across her stomach and her right leg encroaching on me.

"I thought I saw Lil Wayne," I say, as it's the first thing that pops into my head.

Everyone continues to stare at me.

I shrug. "He's from New Orleans, you know."

As we pull away, the forklifts and bulldozers make their way up the street, clearing away all remnants of the night before, as if none of it ever happened.

4.

I HAVE A WINDOW SEAT ON THE PLANE RIDE HOME. POSITIONING MY HEAD and right shoulder against the plane's thin frame, I intend to sleep for the entirety of the five-hour flight. I close my eyes to savor the thoughts of *him* as the last thing in my mind before I doze off. There are just a few more hours to indulge in the fantasy before we touch down in Seattle and I have to push Julian out of my mind in exchange for my real life. But for now, I allow a slow spiral. I tell myself there are several logical reasons he could have been at the bar this morning. Perhaps he forgot something, like his wallet or debit card. Perhaps he did see Lil Wayne and in the throes of excitement chased him into the same bar from last night. But, at the core of me, I know the thing I'm afraid to admit out loud.

He was there looking for me.

Just as I'm picturing his adorable smile, I feel the weight of someone taking the middle seat beside me. I open one eye to find an older woman staring at me, her face beaming with unnecessary enthusiasm.

"Hi, I'm Odette," she says, hand outstretched. I hear her New Orleans accent, her pronunciations long and relaxed. I take her cold hand in mine, shake, release.

"Serena," I say, realizing how bland my name sounds from my mouth rather than Julian's.

"Well, aren't you just the cutest thing," she says before buckling her seat belt, pulling at the gray polyester strap forcefully. I look down at myself. I'm dressed in black yoga pants, a plain gray sweatshirt, and Nikes. My dark hair is in the messiest of buns, flopping about on the top of my head with every movement, thrown up in the boarding line with no mirror. I wonder if her eyesight is going.

"Thank you," I say before leaning my head back against the side of the plane.

"So, what were you doin' in N'awlins?"

I sigh, open my eyes. I have a feeling Odette will be steadfast in her mission to chat. I was grateful to be seated away from the bridal party on the plane ride home, having had my fill of them over the last few days. And, after my Bourbon Street meltdown this morning, I'm sure they are equally satisfied with the rows between us. But now, I wish I was seated next to one of them. They are all too hungover for small talk and are likely already drooling against their tray tables, which sounds divine.

Instead, I have Odette.

"A bachelorette party for my cousin," I tell her.

"Oh, wow!" She clasps her hands together. "What fun for you young gals. Was it a blast?"

I think of Julian first, which is no surprise. He is, without question, the highlight of these past four days. But then I think of Coral and how little time we've spent together over the last eight years. My stomach rumbles and I think of her and I working shifts together stocking shelves at the Auburn Fred Meyer in high school, sneaking expired boxes of SnackWell's and Hostess treats before they were tossed into the dumpsters out back. How we'd sit in our shared peeling white 1981 Toyota Corolla in the far corner of the parking lot post-shift, listening to Katy Perry's *Teenage Dream* album on repeat as we compared our haul like we'd just gone trick-or-treating. The best days included snagging anything Pepperidge Farm, which carried price tags our moms would never consider.

Despite all its downsides and as much as I hate to admit it, I am grateful for this trip, for the stolen moments with Coral that remind me of our childhood together as an inseparable pair. I think that maybe, just maybe, there's a glimmer of hope of a relationship between us again, though I'm not fully convinced I want that.

"Yes, actually, it *was* fun," I admit.

Evaluating Odette again, I find she's got loose, pruney skin and lumpy blue veins on her face and hands, the only parts of her that are visible. She's heavily clothed with a button-down blouse under a thick wool cardigan and tan chinos.

She leans toward me and talks behind her hand. "Did you show your boobs?"

I can't help but grin at Odette's use of the word *boobs*. Her face is incredibly kind, but also endearingly mischievous, I now notice.

"No, ma'am, I didn't."

"Well, that's a shame." She raises her hand to tuck a loose strand of hair behind her ear and there is a slight vibration in her movement. "I lifted my shirt plenty back in the day, down there on Bourbon Street. They used to be quite lovely. Perky little things," she says with a wink as she taps at the underneath of her right breast, causing it to jiggle.

A boxy man approaches and hovers at the end of our row, looking at his ticket, then us, then his ticket again. "That's my seat," he says to Odette in a gruff declaration that reminds me of my interactions with Melody this morning. I wonder if his timbre is also the result of Bourbon Street gluttony.

Odette and I watch as he rakes his eyes over me, sucking his bottom lip as he does. Then, he runs his tongue against the corner of his small mouth and Odette says, "Ew," as I think it.

"So sorry, but this is my granddaughter," Odette responds as a line forms in the aisle behind the man.

He continues to stare, dissatisfied with the reasoning.

"And I have incontinence," Odette says, practically shouting now. "I have to sit next to her so she knows when to rush me to the bathroom. I've got a big ole diaper on under here." She tugs at the lap of her tan pants. I press my lips together to avoid a smile.

He begrudgingly takes the aisle seat of our row and we both watch as he grunts himself into the chair, his right arm immediately in Odette's personal space, what little of it there can be in economy. He's got an unmistakable odor that wafts our way with his movement. It's that distinct, moldy smell of the city. My stomach churns and I silently curse him for giving my hangover a resurgence.

Odette turns back to me. "For fuck's sake," she whispers.

"Thank you," I whisper back. "Do you want to trade seats?"

She bats her hand at me. "No, no, dear, it's fine." She looks back over to the man in the aisle seat and then shoots me a look of annoyance before moving on, undeterred. "I'm on my way to visit my daughter in Seattle," she says. "From Baton Rouge. That's where I live."

"I'm headed home," I tell her, dazed by how somber I am about it.

The plane accelerates and we climb into the sky, the roar of the engine giving me comfort; it lulls me to calm as I stare out the window, questioning whether Julian is still down there somewhere as we rise away. There's a bit of an ache in my chest as the cars on the road become specs, then nothing at all. I absorb the growing distance from the ground, from last night.

In a delirious rush at the airport earlier, I wondered if perhaps Julian and I would end up on the same flight home if he happened to be leaving today as well. Perhaps that's why he was in an early morning Lyft of his own. However, after a scrupulous evaluation of every passenger's face in the boarding area and as I passed each row on the plane, I realized he's not here. Part of me is relieved. The part that knows I shouldn't be pining for a stranger.

After the plane levels off, I find Odette has pulled out a handful of airplane-sized alcohol bottles. Beside her, the man in the aisle seat groans, his eyes closed, his elbow pressing against Odette's thin frame. One jerk of the plane and I fear he may crack one of her undoubtedly delicate ribs.

"Here," she says, handing me a little bottle of Jack Daniel's. I debate it much less than expected. I'd sworn off alcohol for the foreseeable future the second I woke up this morning, but now I sort of want to drink with Odette on this plane.

"Thank you," I say. We both unscrew the tops of our respective bottles. She takes a small sip then immediately downs the rest.

I follow suit and finish mine as well. Without asking, she hands me another, this one Fireball, and takes a matching red-capped bottle for herself. I imagine the bottom of her purse looks like the clearance bin of a liquor store and I now wonder if she is, in fact, wearing an adult diaper to allow for five-plus hours of heavy drinking.

"Tell me, what was the best part of your trip?" she asks, her breath smelling of cinnamon smoke.

"I met a guy last night," I blurt, surprised by my willingness to share this information with a stranger on a plane. There's something to it, I realize, the ease of conversing with my airborne seatmate, knowing I'll likely never see her again. Midair, stranger by my side, I can push aside the complications that make my encounter with Julian less than pure.

Odette's eyes go wide, and she smiles exuberantly. Her teeth are so white and straight I'm pretty sure they're dentures. "Tell me everything," she says with the bat of a hand like we're old girlfriends sharing cocktails at brunch.

"He was incredible," I say and then sigh. I close my eyes for a moment to try to release his hold.

"Well then, why d'you seem sad about it?"

I open my eyes. She stares at me expectantly. Next to her, Aisle Seat grunts again and jerks in his sleep, making both Odette and I jump. I wonder if he has sleep apnea and is going to stop breathing several times throughout this plane ride.

"I didn't get his number. He didn't get mine. I didn't even get his last name. It ended quite suddenly. And I doubt I'll ever see him again." Saying it out loud sends a new wave of disappointment through me.

I think about how I just stood there last night, watching him go, frozen. And soon enough, Coral had puked again, this time on herself—and the bar and a few other patrons—and we too were being kicked out. And then somehow finding him again this morning . . .

Somewhere close by, though my nose can't determine where exactly, someone is eating tuna fish. The woman in the aisle seat across us has removed her shoes and is strumming her bare toes against the metal frame of the seat in front of her. The man in front of me reclines his seat to my lap.

I take another sip, purely for survival.

"Well, that's a shame." Odette pouts, then clasps her hands together.

I lean in, happy to talk about all things Julian. We are in the clouds, after all.

"Right? We had, like, serious, instantaneous chemistry. That doesn't happen, not to me." The weight of my words presses against me. I can't help but contemplate what it means about me, about the life this plane is taking me back to. I shake my head and finish the second bottle. Odette is an attentive server and immediately hands me another. This one is vodka. I will regret the mixing of alcohol later. I start sipping anyway.

I tell her about this morning, just a few hours ago, how I managed to lose him again.

"Life is full of near misses." She shakes her head. "Why would he be there? Back at that bar early this morning?"

"I don't know, maybe he left something there."

"Like you?"

I shake my head. "He couldn't have been there looking for me . . . could he?" The last part comes out sounding so incredibly hopeful that I'm a bit embarrassed.

"It's certainly romantic if he was!" She beams. "I've known of stranger things. What does he look like?" she asks, her eyes wide and twinkly.

The plane jumps a bit and Aisle Seat jerks with an aggressive inhale of stale air.

I tell her everything. About his Hawaiian Punch–red lips, that gorgeous, goofy smile. His abs, which she finds particularly thrilling. When I tell her how carved and contoured he was under his shirt, she actually squeals, which I find almost as adorable as Julian's smile. I tell her about our conversation, not even deterred by the fact it centered mostly around lead and tits. As I recount it all to Odette, I realize he is perhaps the most disruptively exciting thing that has ever happened to me.

"There's gotta be a way we can find him," she says, and I smile, appreciating she said *we*, like we're in this together now.

"I can't imagine how. All I know is his name is Julian, he lives on Chamber Hill, he's got the sexiest sense of humor I've ever encountered, and he's made me feel like we were meant to meet." Perhaps it's the lack of sleep or alcohol or dehydration, but I want to cry. "It's silly, so silly, that I'm even talking about this. It was a short conversation with a stranger and I'm acting like I met my soulmate. I don't even believe in soulmates."

"Perhaps you did, darlin'!" She bats my arm. "I had that feeling with my first husband when we met," Odette says, staring out the window. "He made my lady parts tickle the second I laid eyes on him. He literally took my breath away. I didn't even know that actually happened outside of the movies, you know, but it did."

"Wow," I whisper, leaning in closer as one does when secrets are being shared.

"Wow is right!" She takes a sip from her bottle. I have lost count of what number this is, for the both of us.

"His name was Marv. We met in church of all places. And you know that sayin' about a whore in church? Well, that was me, let me tell you. And he was no angel either. He could have erupted into flames upon entrance to that place, with all *his* sins, come to find out later.

"But I tell you what. I looked over and saw him in the middle of the service, as the preacher was carryin' on with some real heat on his words, gettin' into it, you know, and I saw Marv." She smiles, shakes her head. "And he's lookin' at me. He's already found me before I found him, starin' at me from across the aisle in the far end of his pew, with his jaw hangin' down to the floor. I was a dish back then." She pats my arm. "As soon as the service was over, he was by my side, talkin' me up. We strolled for hours, talkin' about everything. About who we were, who we wanted to be. He told me he had dreams of becomin' a science professor.

"I will never forget that feeling when I saw him for the first time, like I had been dreamin' my whole life and someone poured a bucket of cold water over my head to jolt me awake." She inhales sharply. "We were married two months later."

"Wow," I say again. "That's incredible."

She nods gently as she pats at my forearm some more. "It really was. We were married fourteen years. We had Greta, my daughter I'm on my way to see now. Then, he died in eighty-six in a boating accident on Lake Pontchartrain. I remarried twice more, but the feeling of that first encounter with Marv, I never had it again."

"I'm sorry," I say.

She bats her hand in the air with a limp wrist. "It was a long time ago. Nonetheless, love at first sight *can* happen, Serena. I know it firsthand."

Love.

The word overwhelms me, used in this context. I haven't allowed myself to contemplate if what happened with Julian was love at first sight.

"My mom would have said love at first sight is a farce. That it's nothing but lust," I tell Odette. My mom, if she were still here, would tell me prioritizing the pursuit of passion is frivolous and unnecessary. That I already have everything I need and my only focus should be to maintain this steady life, grow my savings for an inevitable rainy day ahead.

It's no surprise my mom was a cynic when it came to love. My father was a brief fling in her early twenties who, in the most cliché of moves, disappeared when she became pregnant. She always refused to talk about him and looked so pained whenever I asked about him that I only did so a handful of times.

On a late summer night in middle school, Coral and I overheard our moms talking and laughing in the kitchen when we were meant to be in bed. I remember vividly their gauzy pant legs and T-shirt sleeves rolled, fanning themselves with magazines against the dense evening heat on a rare ninety-degree August night. As we poked our heads around the wall, I heard Auntie Lakshmi say, "That drunken idiot sperm donor." It's the most I've ever known about who he was. After that night of watching our moms sip tequila from frozen shot glasses, rebelling against their Indian roots and cultural aversion to alcohol, Coral and I simply referred to my father as Don Julio.

"That feeling in your pants, you know the one, that's lust. But did you feel something else?" Odette asks.

I think of my hand in Julian's, the look he gave me right after he told me he'd never been in love.

I know exactly what she means. That thing that feels like my connection to everyone before him was a zigzagging, meandering line. But when I met him, it felt like a taut, straight vein from his insides to mine.

Shit.

I nod.

5.

ODETTE LEANS BACK AND LOOKS OVER AT AISLE SEAT, WHOSE ELBOW IS BA-sically in her lap. She lifts it with two hands and shoves it back at him with surprising strength. He grumbles and his eyes flicker before he settles again.

"You know, I'm turning thirty this year," I tell Odette, because, well, we're best friends who tell each other everything.

"Is that so?"

"Yes, and I thought, I don't know, I'm embarrassed to even say it out loud, but I thought—"

"You thought you'd have it all figured out by now?"

"Yes! I mean, I thought I was doing everything right. That I've made all the right choices, that my path is all carved out the way it's supposed to be. But now, I don't know if any of it makes sense if I can become this rattled by one little random encounter. Like maybe I don't have anything in order after all and my life is more of a mess than I ever realized. Is that the most pathetic thing you've ever heard?" I take note of the alcohol-induced drama in my voice.

"Close to it," she says with a chuckle. "Just kidding, dear. Not at all. We make plans and God laughs, or somethin' like that, right? If there's one thing I've learned in my life it's that thinkin' we have any say over what happens to us, that we can control any of it, that's the real farce."

I contemplate this. Coral is twenty-eight, has an impressive job, and is marrying the man of her dreams. Melody is married and a successful attorney. Not only am I the oldest bridesmaid, I'm the only one not married. *They* seem to have control over their lives. And as much as I hate admitting it, all this wedding nonsense has made me think about what *my* big day might be like, if I ever get there.

"It's not just about turning thirty in a couple months," I tell Odette. "Two days after my birthday, I'll be interviewed for the *UW Daily*, my old college newspaper, for a feature called 'Life at Thirty.' Once each quarter they publish a where-are-they-now type story, to showcase what University of Washington graduates have accomplished since being released to the wilds of adulthood."

"And you're afraid you haven't done enough," Odette says matter-of-factly.

I nod. "I wasn't chosen because I'm the *most successful* graduate to come out of the UW business school, not even close. I was chosen because the counselor I grew close to in my senior year is in charge of assisting the student editor with identifying compelling interviewees."

When my mom passed away unexpectedly after a massive heart attack during my senior year at UW, Dr. Murphy quickly became my lifeline. I agreed to the feature when I graduated eight years ago. Dr. Murphy even added it to his calendar back then, with great fanfare, scheduled eight years in advance for publication just days after I turn thirty, aligned to his already identified retirement date. It will be the final edition of the *UW Daily* that he will advise.

Dr. Murphy has always been the guy who's got it all figured out. Retire at sixty-five, then write that book he's always wanted to write. Scheduling me for his last feature was a huge act of faith in me, my future. A trust on his part and a promise I made in return to come through. I am the only student he has ever done that for. That one act solidified his belief in me when there was seemingly nobody left.

Eight years ago, it seemed like a great idea. I'd get to serve as inspiration to a new class of graduates, demonstrating how perfectly in order my life is. And a few days ago, I really thought I was, by most standards, a success story.

I've read enough of the articles leading up to my own to know some of the story will be about career—how I have applied my degree after graduation. At least I have that. But the pieces are just as much about the alumni's personal lives. If they are married, the family they are building. It's a showcase of their well-rounded, triumphant lives.

Technically, my life is in order. I have all the things it would take to make this article respectable. But suddenly all of it feels fake somehow. I'm now thinking of reaching out to Dr. Murphy to cancel the interview. Perhaps it's the alcohol; perhaps a small taste of passion has left me craving more, in all aspects of my life. I'm not sure which makes me crazier.

The plane heaves. Again, I think about Julian.

Perhaps a future with him wouldn't have lasted past those thirty minutes. Maybe the next thing out of his mouth would have been that he was just kidding earlier and he really is gay or he did walk over just to see my tits. But I need to know for sure.

"I have to find him," I proclaim.

Odette bounces her shoulders and nods her head animatedly.

I need to, if for no other reason than to assure myself this thing I felt with Julian was nothing more than alcohol-induced infatuation. If I can prove that, I can go into the interview knowing wherever I am in my life is, without a doubt, where I am meant to be.

I have ten weeks before I have to prove to the 46,000 students at UW, the even more alumni, and myself that I *am* a damn success story. A real one.

"Thank you, Odette." I cup her hands in mine. They are surprisingly cold and I'm saddened by her poor circulation.

"You will find him, dear. You will." She winks at me and I believe her. I really, really believe her.

And just when I think Odette from Baton Rouge couldn't be any more intriguing, she reaches into her bag (the one with the endless supply of mini-alcohol bottles) and pulls out a rectangular, mustard-yellow package. Peanut M&M's. I again feel like crying. I watch intently as she rips the top corner of the bag, pours three candies into her hand, then presses them into her mouth with her palm. Then, silently, she holds the bag over my lap. I raise my palm, catch four M&M's as she shakes the bag. One blue, one green, two brown. I look at Odette and see glimpses of what I could have with my mother, if she were still here. This woman next to me may just be my potty-mouthed, Southern white lady fairy godmother. Perhaps Bourbon Street really is full of magic.

We spend the remaining two hours of the flight building a plan. To be honest, Odette isn't of particular assistance in the logistics of it all. She possesses very little knowledge of social media, or the internet generally. She's also not from the Seattle area, so that doesn't help. But what she does provide is steadfast optimism and a butt-bouncing-in-her-seat enthusiasm that makes me feel like this plan to hunt down the guy I met for thirty minutes at a bar on Bourbon Street during Mardi Gras is neither pathetic nor creepy. Rather, that it is necessary.

The plane lands and not only do I have a plan, I have Odette's phone number and email address (because she prefers email over text).

"Go get your man!" she yells as we stand to exit the plane. Coral and Melody, a few rows back, look on, perplexed. We huddle together in a hug, standing sideways in our row because Aisle Seat is taking up most of the room.

At this moment, thanks to her unwavering support and endless supply of airplane bottles of alcohol and peanut M&M's, Odette from Baton Rouge is my favorite person on earth, sky included.

6.

THE BUZZ OF MY ALARM JOLTS ME AWAKE MONDAY MORNING. AFTER FOUR days of forced fun and several of Odette's airplane bottles of alcohol, there was little option but to collapse into bed when I made it back to my apartment yesterday, despite it being mid-afternoon. My suitcase sits unopened in the center of my bedroom and my phone is still filled with random Bourbon Street dick pics.

Despite this, I get to work early.

"Hi, Carl." I wave to the security guard behind the white marble desk when I enter the lobby of the downtown Bellevue high-rise.

"Serena! How was it?"

"Lots of booze, lots of puke," I tell him as I walk by, my black loafers squeaking against the freshly polished white marble.

He laughs, his belly bouncing below his white tucked-in dress shirt. There's a low barrier of entry to earning a howl from Carl, but it's as satisfying as ever to hear his laugh's grand echo in the marble lobby. I don't know if I'd recognize the ground floor of this building without Carl's hearty guffaw constantly swirling around it. I like to believe his propensity for laughter may keep him alive forever.

"As it should be, love, as it should be!" He's still laughing as I enter the bay of elevators on the opposite end of the lobby.

I survey the yellow-and-black logo in the elevator next to the button for the fourteenth floor. Watson Ackerly Pierce is a firm that carved out a niche offering both traditional accounting *and* wealth management services to its high-end clientele, earning it great prestige. The firm has largely been known by its acronym since its inception almost twenty years ago. And as of late, thanks to Cardi B, the firm shows up in a high number of Google searches. It doesn't help that our marketing materials read, *WAP: Everything You Need in One Place* and *We Clean Up Your (Financial) Messes.*

My office sits directly across from Lincoln Square in the heart of downtown Bellevue. I feel a little hopeful each time I look out the windows to see the surrounding modern buildings and constant cranes that hold the promise of something new.

The morning sky is murky, groggy as she awakens, but there are glints of blue sky and I anticipate a clear-up by the afternoon. The air, even inside my office building, is crisp and clean. I have a new appreciation for my state and its largely unsullied air after a few days away. It's hard to imagine venturing too far away from evergreens again.

Several clients have told me this city is depressing, with its gray, mopey skies. Most of those same clients have eventually abandoned the Pacific Northwest altogether for seaside homes in California or Florida. Those people, I quickly decide each time, never truly appreciated all the city becomes in summer, when boats and Seafair replace umbrellas and frowning skies. When the whole state opens up like a discarded cocoon, unleashing colorful new life.

Regardless, I usually like the gray. It's reliable.

Today, though, it feels like I've stepped back into the cave of my real life after feeling the sun on my skin for the first time.

I make my way to my desk next to the floor-to-ceiling window and take in the expansive views, imagining in the parts obstructed by fog.

Joey looks up at me from his usual morning everything bagel with strawberry cream cheese as I approach our shared cubicle.

"Morning," he says before I've sat down.

"Morning, Joey," I return, as I set my bag down on my desk. Joey

Parker sits opposite me, with a too-short wall between us so that when we're both seated facing our computers, we are sort of awkwardly staring at each other's faces. I can always see him, from the bridge of his nose up, as we work. The feng shui of it all is incredibly poor.

He stands and looks over the wall as I take my seat.

"How was it?" he asks.

"It was great."

Joey, like me, was hired at WAP right out of college, now in his ninth year with the firm.

"You seem surprisingly fresh and gleaming this morning," he says. Joey has a knack for saying strings of words that don't quite work together and it makes me occasionally wonder if English is his second language, though I know it is not. He has made his way around to my desk and has placed one butt cheek atop it, his arms folded in front of him.

"Yes, well, I was able to contain myself the last four days," I tell him.

"Did you accumulate a monolithic batch of beads while down there in N'awlins?" He says "New Orleans" with a decidedly pedestrian attempt at a southern accent.

"No. Afraid not," I tell him.

"I brought you a little something." No matter his quirks, Joey is a significant part of my life.

He stands at attention. "Oh?"

I reach into my purse and pull out the palm-sized brown cloth bag and hand it to him. "It's called a mojo bag. I think it's just stones and herbs inside, but it's supposed to bring good luck. That's what the woman at the shop told me anyway." I'm certain only tourists own these little bags, but I fell in love with the charming shop and the idea of bringing back a bit of Bourbon Street magic.

Joey closes his palm around the bag. "This is excellent. Thank you, Serena."

We stare at each other for a beat, then I begin tapping at my keyboard before he eventually takes the hint and walks back around to his desk. Normally Joey is a safe place, a consistent, comforting part of my life. Today, though, I find myself vexed by, well, my life and all its normal parts.

Not to mention, I've missed a lot these four days. Taking time off in March as an accountant is practically blasphemous. There are only a few weeks left until taxes are due and this is the height of our season. It's the equivalent of LeBron retreating to the Bahamas in mid-April as the NBA playoffs are set to begin, but with slightly lower stakes.

I practically begged my boss to let me have time off to go to the bachelorette party I didn't want to attend, telling her it was a once-in-a-lifetime trip and it would cause a familial estrangement if I didn't go, though the estrangement was already there. I'm sure Coral would have forgiven me, would have probably preferred it had I stayed back and not brought our complicated relationship to New Orleans, but Autumn Kaplan didn't need to know that.

I fake tap at the keys again, thinking about how much work I have to catch up on. My phone keeps buzzing beside me and I know without looking it's the bridesmaids group chat. The clacking back and forth never stops and I wonder if any of these women work during business hours.

I open the bridesmaids group text, entitled Happily Everett After. It's no surprise the text is from Melody. *Daily workouts starting today until the BIG day. Dress alterations are COMPLETE and SOME of us partook in too many beignets this weekend!!!*

I turn off my phone, not wanting to read the inevitable fifty or so responses to come over the next five minutes, including the separate text I expect from Clarence mocking the larger group text.

Over the wall, Joey is aggressively humming to the tune of "Lose Yourself" by Eminem. It doesn't flow naturally, his humming of rap songs, though this fact never seems to diminish his eagerness to constantly hum rap songs. And more often than not, I find myself humming along. It's kind of our thing—the white noise between work husband and wife.

Being back in the office, I know the first thing I should do is check my emails, see what I've missed. I know that's what I should do. But I don't.

Instead, I pull out the notebook from my top drawer, flip to a blank page near the back to begin writing down everything I know about Julian from Bourbon Street. He travels through my mind like a cloud billowing from a smoker's mouth, forceful yet unhurried, each memory making its unique shape known until it blends itself into my matter.

Green eyes, one speckled.

Red lips.

Barely tamed hair. I want to reach into my mind and tousle his mane, see what it looks like as it comes undone.

Before I've written a single thing, the familiar ding from my computer reminds me I have a meeting to get to.

Joey stops humming to say, "That must be the Dicksons."

My nine a.m. appointment is indeed with longtime clients Sutton and Carson Dickson. They are quite wealthy from Carson's days on Wall Street and each year there is a new home or boat or rare piece of art they spring on me as a new investment. I'm vaguely curious what it might be this year.

I sigh, shove the notebook back in my drawer.

Grabbing my laptop, I give Joey a weak smile as I head to the conference room.

"Serena!" Sutton shouts when I enter. She jumps to a stand, arms outstretched. I make my way over to her for the embrace.

Almost as reliable as the new luxurious purchases each year are Sutton's outfit choices. Today she's wearing a giraffe print silk blouse. She owns several tops in zebra and snake print, has an affinity for satiny desert animal prints generally.

"Sutton, Carson, nice to see you both," I say as I embrace her. She's got an incredibly thin waist that constantly makes me wonder how many hours a day she spends at the gym. Their home gym includes a Peloton bike, an interactive mirror, several sets of weights, a sectioned-off yoga studio, and two treadmills so they can run side by side. Despite this, they both have $564-a-month memberships to the most expensive athletic club in the area.

After the embrace, Sutton fake kisses both my cheeks because of course she does.

"Bought an Aston Martin, paid cash," Carson tells me before I've taken my seat. This is one of the only circumstances where what he says is technically not bragging because these are the details I need to do my job effectively. He enjoys this bit, that he can say these kinds of things here and not be judged for it.

"An Aston Martin, nice," I say, feigning admiration. I'm certain I couldn't choose an Aston Martin from a lineup of luxury cars. Or from a lineup of Kias, for that matter. "I guess the Bentley got lonely?" Sutton and Carson laugh and I feel like they want to pat me on my head and "You're so cute" me often. Thankfully, they refrain.

"Oh, and upgraded the boat. Named this new one *Sutton Love.* Get it? Like sudden, but it's Sutton."

"I get it," I say, forcing a smile. "Clever."

"When will you let us set you up with Craig?" Sutton asks. Usually, she waits until business is out of the way before springing this question on me. I simply roll my eyes and smile as if she is not serious and she bats her hand at me with a "*tsk*" in our little song and dance.

Craig, their thirty-nine-year-old son, is a part-time real estate investor (the family's post–Wall Street business) and data analyst of some kind. I suppose it's noble that he works when he doesn't have to, though I'm not certain if he does so because he chooses to or if his parents threaten to suspend his monthly trust fund payments if he doesn't. He still "parties like he's twenty-one," according to Sutton, and they are desperate to find a woman to pin him down. She tells me this as often as she tells me she can't stand his facial hair. Apparently me, ten years younger and with a much humbler life, is as decent a choice as any. It is not a challenge I imagine I'd particularly enjoy, pinning down the elusive Craig Dickson. They've never bothered to ask if I'm single, and I guess it's because they imagine it to be irrelevant when it comes to a catch like their trust-funded, party-hard son.

And so goes my day, my life. Every day, it's client after client who've got their financials in order, who make at least ten times what I do each year, who have multiple streams of income and toys upon toys they spend their money on.

It's a good thing, I remind myself, to get to work with wealthy clients, see how they invest. But, having to sit in meeting after meeting, listening to stories about months-long trips overseas and six-figure birthday presents, having to watch their money make more money than I do, has suddenly become grueling.

My mom and I had so little. Money was always a topic, a topline thought. Elusive. I was sick with a bad flu at the age of nine and in the wee hours of the morning, my temperature reached 104°F. The cost of the emergency room visit thrust us into months of debt. Who knew an IV of "precautionary fluids" in the ER had an equivalent cost of two months' rent? My mom added turmeric to everything after that.

My childhood is a blur of free school lunches and thrift store clothes, and sometimes I want to slap the unbothered look off Sutton and Carson Dickson's faces, though they'd likely sue me and the firm for all they could if I did, making their net worth all the more massive.

I think of my mother, the constant worry lines across her face, how she always looked tired and older than she was. How it seemed like life was meant to be hard and gotten through. Then, I started meeting people like Sutton and Carson. Their lives are full of pleasure and pursuit. Sometimes I wish I'd never met them, or people like them.

"Serena, if it were you, which would you choose?" Carson asks. He has pulled up a picture of a ridiculous pair of shoes on his phone. Gucci, I read in the corresponding description, and they have a lot going on—laced tennis shoes with four different patches of busy fabrics. After I've reviewed the picture for what he deems an ample amount of time, Carson scrolls and holds the phone to my face again. This time, it's a pair of incredibly shiny alligator print leather dress shoes that have what I can only describe as a kitten heel. I'm certain he cannot pull off either.

"Both are a statement," I say.

They laugh again.

"You know you're just going to get both," Sutton says to Carson, though she looks at me as she shakes her head like, *What am I going to do with him?* I smile at her as though I am incredibly charmed by their banter.

It's not a new thing, feeling resentment of all the lavishness around me, but I find my sensitivities heightened today. And this new-money attitude of Carson's makes me want to point out that my truly wealthy clients don't flaunt their fortune the way he does. That they, in fact, behave very much the opposite.

After three back-to-back appointments, I make it to my desk around one p.m. Joey is stationed at his desk, watching as I take my seat, humming "Rockstar" by Post Malone, though it takes me a moment to recognize the song.

He stops humming. "Is Craig still being volunteered to you on a golden platter?"

"Yes, apparently he is still single. Can't imagine why."

We exchange a knowing look.

Once Joey has returned his eyes to his computer, I pull open my desk drawer and retrieve the notebook.

The past few hours were as distracted as I have been since I met Julian. But still, when the Dicksons talked about cruising *Sutton Love* off the south of France last summer to "break 'er in," I pictured Julian sprawled across the bow of said yacht, his torso glistening in the Mediterranean sun.

When Penn Hartford, a twenty-six-year-old artist with a trust fund (my ten thirty client), told me about her new waterfront Magnolia neighborhood home, I pictured walking in the front door of that house to find Julian cooking dinner. He is shirtless in this fantasy as well.

I strain to remember him with his shirt on.

Back to the notebook.

His name is Julian, I write, then feel incredibly juvenile, like I am twelve years old writing in that diary I once shared with Coral. I refrain from drawing hearts around it. It's too bad I don't know his last name, as I can't complete this preteen work of art. No need, I am certain his surname would fit me perfectly.

He lives on Chamber Hill, I write next. This one feels less childish, as it is both factual and relevant. *He doesn't live with his parents, has a job that pays actual money, and doesn't walk around asking people if they're a dot or feather,* I recall, reminding myself that he is an adult and I am an adult and what I am doing is making a logical, adult list.

I continue.

He works at a tech company. This one's tricky because he never actually told me the name of the company or what his role is there.

"Nerds?" Joey says from over the wall.

"What?" I shove the notebook closed.

"Do you want any Nerds?" He extends a purple box of candy across the wall.

"No, thanks."

Joey shrugs. "Suit yourself," he says, pulling the box back to his side of the wall. Now all I hear are the little candies shuffling around in the box each time he picks it up. Joey consumes pounds of candy a month. His favorites range from Tootsie Pops to Twizzlers, and even those cinnamon hard candies that have stood the test of candy time. I imagine Odette keeps a bowl of these by her front door. I am in constant worry of Joey's dental health.

Now he is humming 50 Cent's "In da Club," Nerds clinking against his molars as he does.

I reopen the notebook.

He's a fan of Lil Wayne and Nirvana, I write, remembering the song and Julian's T-shirt. This point seems as though it will be of no help, but perhaps with some thought, it could be.

I sigh. *He's got incredible abs,* I want to write, but don't.

His name is Julian
He lives on Chamber Hill
He works at a tech company
He's a fan of Lil Wayne and Nirvana

That's it. That's the list. It's only four items long. I sigh again and see Joey's eyes flick up, a result of my constant sighing, I'm sure.

"Don't worry," he says, as he stands and leans over the short wall between us. "You'll catch it all up." He throws his head back, opens his mouth, and holds the box of Nerds above him. A stream of candies waterfalls into his mouth.

I give him a thin smile and then stare at my still-dark computer screen. I make it through the rest of my afternoon, attempting to ignore the growing anxiousness in my core. A few times, between meetings and when I grow too distracted to check emails, I flip to the page in the back of my notebook and review my list.

His name is Julian
He lives on Chamber Hill
He works at a tech company
He's a fan of Lil Wayne and Nirvana

Each time I review it, I feel oddly grounded—like I'm reading daily affirmations or a dead-on horoscope. And there's something else too. Each time I read it, my need to find him grows.

⊳━━━

As I ride the elevator up to my apartment at the end of my long first day back, I'm eager to get out of my work clothes and draw a bath. I'm nowhere near fully recovered from Mardi Gras, nor from Julian or the tailspin he's put me into. I fear I never will be.

When the elevator doors open, I stop mid-step. He's there smiling at me, leaning against my apartment door. My boyfriend, Danny.

7.

"Hi. What a surprise." I hug him, then give him a peck on the lips.

"I missed you." Danny smiles and I'm riddled with guilt. So. Much. Guilt. "I know you probably had a crazy day playing catch-up, so I won't stay. I just wanted to stop by, tell you I love you." He looks down. I follow his gaze to the bag on the floor by my door. He's brought me takeout from my favorite Thai restaurant from the other side of town and it's reminiscent of our early days together in college. There's clearly enough for two. It's not often we eat out anymore, so it's an unmistakable gesture of care.

The guilt lodges in my throat.

"I missed you too." I give him another kiss because I don't know what else to do. "Come in," I say as I unlock my door.

"You sure?"

I don't want to push him away. I'm dangerously good at it, generally.

"Yes, of course." I hold the door open. He picks up the bag of what I already know is two orders of pad Thai—Thai hot for me, mild for him—and follows me inside. I can't help but think—after all the Bourbon Street beignets, I should have a green juice for dinner instead of pad Thai. But I can't say that, not when he's gone to all this trouble.

"When you didn't return my texts all day, I figured the first day back was insane."

"It was." I think of the list about Julian in the notebook in the top drawer of my desk at work and wonder if he can see me blushing. "I'm so sorry for not getting back to you. Thank you for this."

He smiles, then kisses my forehead. Observing him when he steps away, I wonder if I've ever felt with Danny the rush of heat I felt with Julian just two nights ago. I shake the thought away, recognizing it as foolish and unfair.

I watch Danny as he pulls food containers out of the bag and places them on the counter. As he grabs two wine glasses from the cabinet to the right of the sink. As he chooses a bottle from the standing wine rack in the corner of my eat-in nook. How he does these things with knowing ease. *Mom loved him*, I think to myself, as I so often do. He's an integral brick in the foundation of a solid existence. What better way to ensure a life of stability—one removed from uncertainty or financial woes—than to be with a partner who values those same things.

The thrill of something new is not a justifiable reason to give up all I've built toward with Danny. He's too good. And, above all else, we found our way back together when I wouldn't have thought it possible.

As he plates the food, pours the wine, hands me one of each, I relish the small acts. Could I have a conversation with Danny about lead and tits, I wonder, as I watch him close the take-out containers. No, how uncouth. Does he enjoy a good Lil Wayne song now and then? Likely not—he's more of a One Direction guy.

We head for the couch. I can't remember the last time we sat at the table.

Danny and I have been together (the second time) for almost a year. Eleven solid months. The way we came back together was quite the opposite of how I met Julian, though it seemed to hold its own layer of fatedness nonetheless. I went to the movies alone one Saturday afternoon last spring to see the film adaptation of one of my favorite reads the previous year. It's not something I do often, go out alone. But Clarence, my usual movie date, was working and I tried to convince myself I didn't need a companion, that my own company was more than enough. But sitting in the darkened theater, looking around at the families and couples nestled together, multiple hands diving into shared tubs of popcorn, I felt more alone than I had in a long while. In moments like those, I miss my mom with the sharpness of a fresh blade.

And then, as the theater began to fill, another person entered my row. Danny. He was also alone. He gave me a knowing smile when our eyes locked, taking a seat, leaving one empty between us. At first, I was mortified, wondering if his date was using the restroom or buying an Icee and Twizzlers. But soon the previews began and no one took the seat beside him. The Danny I knew wouldn't have read a book about love, let alone gone to the theater to see its adaptation. *Perhaps he's changed*, I thought with a level of hopeful disbelief.

"Hi," he whispered to me across the open seat between us, so simply, as if there didn't exist a shared, tumultuous history.

"Hi," I whispered back. He smiled and, in the dark, his face lit up by the dancing popcorn on the screen, I saw nothing but kindness in his face. He didn't look uneasy and it didn't feel complicated, seeing him again. I saw him anew that day, seven years from the last, but also, he was comfortingly the same. He had this perfect skin (still does) that I could appreciate even in the dim light. His round brown eyes were still somehow unfathomably sparkly. The stabbing pain inside me eased a bit.

We didn't speak again during the movie; we didn't really even look at each other. About fifteen minutes into the film, though, he held his popcorn tub out over the empty seat between us and nodded his offer. I smiled my acceptance as I grabbed a handful of popcorn. We continued watching the movie in silence, taking turns reaching into the tub. When the movie ended, we had finished it all.

As the lights came up, we flowed into the group of other patrons exiting the theater, walking out side by side so naturally, it felt like it had been a date.

It all happened easily the second time around. There were no real decisions. Gravity just drove us closer together with no particular reason to argue. I knew it early on over these last several months. He's relieved to be back together. Grateful to have found me when I am whole again.

"So, tell me about the trip," he says as he lifts his first forkful of pad Thai to his mouth, plate balanced in his lap.

I take a long sip of wine. Did I cheat? Am I cheating? Nothing physical happened with Julian, of course. It was a conversation with a stranger at a bar. But it feels lead-filled-beads-in-my-stomach wrong. Especially after having shared the story of my M&M's theft, which I've never shared with anyone, including Danny. The truth is, I've barely thought about Danny in these last forty-eight hours. To be honest, I almost forgot about him completely. It's this last part that is particularly jarring.

"Melody was everything you'd imagine," I tell him. He's never met Melody, or Coral for that matter. Even in college, when Coral and I were still close, we ran out of time. They were meant to meet at the graduation ceremony I never attended. Even so, I've complained to him enough about my bachelorette duties that he has become complicit in my complaints.

"Did she decide what everyone ordered for every meal?" he asks, then sips his wine. This is something Danny is good at: commiserating. I laugh and it comes out more like a wail.

"Practically. And she really, really likes dancing on bars, I learned."

He rolls his eyes and takes another bite.

"And Coral, she puked everywhere, all the time. Including on me. Twice."

"Oh, god," he says, making a face like he may vomit. He finishes the bite with the grimace intact and takes a long sip of wine as if it can dispel the imaginary taste of throw-up from his mouth.

"I definitely missed Clarence." Clarence, Danny does know. And as my best friend, the only bridesman, and the only person who knows deeply the history of Coral and I, his presence was greatly missed.

"You know I'd rather be drinking champagne and dancing on bars than listening to Tony Robbins wannabes tell me how to engage my third eye or whatever the hell is gonna happen," Clarence had said about the local work-required leadership retreat he attended instead.

"The celebration of the city was pretty amazing though. The floats, the colors. I could have done nothing but sit on a balcony and people-watch all day. All trip, even."

"That sounds great. We should go back some time, just the two of us. So it can be an actual vacation."

I smile so I don't cringe. What is wrong with me? Why does the idea of going on vacation to New Orleans with my boyfriend make me feel like I'd be cheating on *Julian*? There is no good explanation really, other than it's *our* city: mine and Julian's.

I've done nothing wrong, I try to tell myself. Danny and I have never had the type of relationship where we can't have friends of—or conversations with—the opposite sex. Even a little harmless flirting is something we've both established as non-threatening. It's one of the things I was drawn to about Danny, that he has always been an advocate for our own independence. The guilt doesn't stem from my actions. I believe that. The guilt stems from how Julian made me feel, what our brief interaction did to me.

"Funny story," I say and then stop to gulp more wine. "On our last night, I ended up meeting someone from Seattle." I'm not sure why I'm doing this. Perhaps because I think it will serve to dissipate some of my guilt. I will no longer be lying by omission. If I tell my boyfriend about a platonic encounter, one of several anecdotes from my trip, perhaps it will lessen the grip Julian has on me.

"Oh yeah? That is funny." Danny is scrolling through his phone as he places another bite in his mouth, his plate teetering in his lap as he does.

"Yeah, he lives on Chamber Hill."

This makes Danny look up from his phone. "Oh?" is all he says.

"Yes. It was a brief conversation, but I just thought that was interesting, you know, meeting someone in New Orleans who lives so close."

Danny listens, having paused his scrolling, his eating. "Cool. So are you gonna reach out, you know, since he lives so close? Maybe we can all grab dinner or something." I know Danny has no interest in grabbing dinner with the random male stranger I met during Mardi Gras. What he really wants to know is if we traded contact information.

"Oh no, it was just a brief run-in. We didn't exchange numbers or anything." Danny's face doesn't change as he takes another forkful of pad Thai and goes back to scrolling on his phone.

"Well, that's cool," he says through his bite, then quickly moves on. "I can't imagine how much work you came back to." He *can* imagine it because Danny is also an accountant at a different firm. This was one of the things that made our recoupling easy.

Sometimes I like to pretend our firms have incredibly heated rivalries and we are star-crossed lovers, sneaking around like we're in a sexy romance novel. That when he shows up at my door, I should hurriedly rush him inside before someone sees him and finds us out. Or that we should slink into back booths in restaurants to avoid getting caught. Or, that we have hot sex atop a desk filled with late tax returns. But the reality is, Danny does government audits, which are completely different from preparing taxes for the wealthy. His job is numbers all day too; however, every once in a while he has a story to tell about an employee embezzling funds or a misappropriation that cost hundreds of thousands of taxpayer dollars. Interesting enough, though not star-crossed. We've never had hot sex on a desk. I think Danny would be too concerned about the tax return stacks getting out of order.

"Yeah, it's crazy. Luckily, Autumn took on some of my client prep, so that helped. Again, I'm sorry I didn't reach out when I got home or today. I was exhausted, then got up and went straight into the office. I've misplaced my mind, it seems." Perhaps I should suggest he help me find it in Julian's jeans pocket.

Danny grabs the remote lying on the couch cushion beside him and flips on the TV. With no discussion needed, he taps his way to episode five of the sci-fi series we started watching last week before my trip. It's another reliable component of our relationship. Danny and his love of sci-fi shows, all with Biblical words like *dominion* or *revelation* or *Babylon* in their titles. In college, he convinced me to watch six seasons of *Stargate,* at which point I began having vivid dreams about interstellar travel to various planets.

I press myself deeper into the couch cushions and he does the same from the opposite corner of the couch as we stare in unison at the TV.

I'm yawning before he has placed the first plate in the dishwasher. "I'll sleep at my place tonight so you can get a good night's rest," he says as he rinses dishes in the sink. I want to say "Great, thanks," but I feel the guilt bubble in my throat again.

"No, stay. I've missed you." And now that he is here, in my kitchen, rinsing dishes after a familiar night in, I know I *have* missed him.

"You sure?" he asks. I take a deep breath in annoyance. It's one of my pet peeves about Danny. Whenever I say something, he asks me if I'm sure, which makes me unsure. Perhaps because I'm tired, I find myself more annoyed than usual by the question.

"Yes, of course."

He smiles. "Great."

I help him clean up and we head to the bedroom. I lie in bed as he brushes his teeth, holding the present I picked out for him in New Orleans. A mojo bag, just like the one I purchased for Joey. I didn't think of it at the time, but now I wonder what it might mean that I chose the same gift for Joey, my work friend, as I did for my *boyfriend.* I can't help but reflect back on my conversation with Odette from the plane. Before the bachelorette trip, I felt pretty good about this upcoming birthday, the interview after. I have the job. I have the boyfriend. And though we are not engaged or married, it's part of our plan. We both value stability and security.

He gifted me a card two months after we got back together for no particular reason, with a quote from Antoine de Saint-Exupéry, the author of one of my favorite books, *The Little Prince*. It read: *Love does not consist of gazing at each other, but in looking outward together in the same direction.* I thought it summed us up perfectly, even then. But now I wonder if looking out in the same direction for too long made me lose track of who was standing beside me.

What I told Odette on the plane—that I thought I'd be closer to being married, to being settled into my life—I wonder why I suddenly believe I don't actually have any of it.

I now have the scariest thought of all: What if I don't want this life I've built?

When Danny exits the bathroom, I have already rolled to my side and closed my eyes, his present shoved into the drawer of my nightstand. I keep still as he climbs into bed, trying to wipe thoughts of Julian from my mind, from my guilty conscience.

8.

Before I'm out of bed Saturday morning, there's another in a long line of unanswered texts from Clarence. *What's going on with you?* the last one says, followed by a sad puppy face GIF, tears flowing down its fur.

His continual texts over the last few days have ranged from *Remember me?* to threats of divulging my juiciest secrets to anyone willing to listen. One text earlier this week: a picture of me from middle school with Coral-cut bangs and my thrift store clothes. There were no words of threat attached, but I recognize the insinuation— that this homely photo will end up on the internet if I stonewall him any longer.

I've known him long enough to know he's capable of seeing out his threat. He's got a folder in the photos app on his phone entitled *End Serena* filled with embarrassing or damning photos of me over the course of our lives. That folder includes many pictures, including one of me in the ninth grade sipping a Smirnoff Ice (which I held to my mouth but never actually sipped) in borrowed thigh-high boots and purple eyeliner on a senior basketball player's couch, and another of my faceplant making my way to the stage at high school graduation.

I sigh, feeling incredibly guilty for leaving him hanging. Guilt is my new companion. She never leaves my side.

Before I can talk myself out of it, I text him back: *Meet me here in an hour* with a location link.

Clarence, Coral, and I have been besties since childhood. My mom and Auntie Lakshmi met Clarence's mom, Marky, in the early nineties. At a bank, standing next to each other in a teller line, a Def-Leppard-tank-topped woman in front of them began yelling obscenities at the baby-faced employee when she was denied a withdrawal due to insufficient funds. Marky apparently stepped in and told the eighties-rock-band-loving woman to step aside or she'd call the police. As immigrant women who carried a baseline fear when out in the world, my mom and Auntie Lakshmi respected her gall. Each time we heard the story as kids, Marky's presence that day held some new inflated level of brazenness.

When my mom died, it was Clarence and the Clement family who fed me, dressed me. In the aftermath, it was Clarence's mom, Marky, who blew my nose and stroked my head until I fell asleep like she was caring for her own heartsick child. It's the Clements' home I've gone to for the last six Thanksgivings and Christmases. They were there for me through the loss the way my own family couldn't seem to be. Auntie Lakshmi and Coral had the business of living to get back to.

I stalled somewhere in the in between, sandwiched by the ghost of my mom and the life I was expected to build after.

"Well, well, well." He slows his stride as he approaches.

"You look nice," I say, evaluating Clarence. Per usual, at least three people take note of him as they walk by, though he is too aloof to notice. I know why they do, of course. He's well dressed, even better groomed, and has an exquisite face. Clarence has been told he resembles everyone from John Legend to a young Denzel, though the celebrity look-alike most often suggested is Michael B. Jordan. People say it as they flick their eyes over him, top to bottom, then again more slowly in unabashed admiration of his beauty.

I, on the other hand, have only ever been told I look like *that one Indian girl that was on* The Bachelor *that one time.*

We embrace and when he pulls back, I ask, "So, how was the conference? Did you in fact identify your superpower as the agenda suggested you would?"

At the mention of the conference, his face goes what I can only describe as fluffy. As he stares through me, it's clear Clarence has momentarily levitated elsewhere.

"C? You in there?" I wave my hand in front of his face. "Wait, is this a demonstration of said superpower? Did you learn how to leave your body?"

He comes to, rolls his eyes. "What? No." He shakes his head aggressively. "You'll be happy to know my only superpowers continue to be sarcasm and an invincible liver."

I narrow my brows. Clarence is keeping a secret. Disgustingly obvious distraction is his tell.

He looks around. "So, what's all the secrecy about? And why are we here?" He throws a hand up in the air and twirls it around.

I press my lips together as my heart thumps. It's fear I'm feeling. Fear of judgment from my best friend. He's one of the only people I have in my life who I trust. But, I want reactions like Odette's—squeals of delight and high-school-cheerleader-quality enthusiasm. I just don't know if I'll get that from Clarence. I decide to let him off the hook for his secret—for now—in place of my own.

"I met someone," I tell him.

Clarence scrunches his eyes even tighter. "Okay, who? Like a celebrity? Did you meet one of the Chrises? Please tell me it was Hemsworth."

"What? No. I met a guy. A non-celebrity guy."

"A guy..."

"Yes, a guy. In New Orleans."

"In New Orleans..."

I cross my arms against my chest. "Are you just going to repeat everything I say?"

"Maybe, at least until you start making sense."

"I met a guy in New Orleans on the last night of the trip. And we had this . . . this connection. It was unreal. And he lives here."

Clarence turns his body from one side to the other. "Here? In Tribute Park? Is he unhoused?"

"No, not *here* here, but somewhere on Chamber Hill. So I thought we could . . ."

"We could what? Wander around Chamber Hill and hope we randomly run into him while completely ignoring the fact that you have a boyfriend?"

My shoulders drop. "It sounded better in my head."

"So you met this guy for one night—"

"Julian. Yes."

"Damn, I knew it was a mistake to miss the bachelorette party. You lost your mind there without me. You know I need more info before I can commit to this deceit." Clarence's words come out a bit too light and I know he's in for the thrill alone. Nonetheless, I want him to know it all.

I take a deep breath, preparing myself to try to give my best friend the most reasonable explanation I can. "Somewhere over these last few days, I've decided the only way to stop thinking about him—Julian—is to find him. The lightning I felt that night we met was a combination of things, I'm sure—the music, the dim lighting, the alcohol. Not to mention the thrill of meeting someone on vacation. And, of course, the escape it gave me from bachelorette hell. Finding him and confirming the feeling between us was just a momentary, elemental-induced swirl will eliminate this . . . unsettledness inside me. At least, that's what I'm hoping for."

Clarence crosses his arms across his chest. "How poetic," he deadpans.

"We're simply exploring a new neighborhood on a beautiful spring day, a perfectly normal thing to do."

He arches an eyebrow and, again, I can sense he wants to see this through with me, though this song and dance is what he deems a necessary reaction.

"I'm well aware I'm in morally questionable territory," I offer.

"Well as long as you realize it. But if some guy can put *that* look on your face, he must be somethin'."

It's a decidedly easy let-off by Clarence. Something's turned him soft since I saw him last . . .

Clarence cocks his head in evaluation. "Is this guy another College Danny?" he asks, referencing the ease and purity of the relationship Danny and I had in our early days together. A relationship gold standard at the time, according to Clarence. According to everyone around us, really. Until my mom passed.

"No," I blurt. "College Danny never made me feel this way." There's a mound in my throat as soon as I speak the words. Clarence and I often refer to Danny as two different people. College Danny and then just Danny, representing the man I got back together with eleven months ago. Somehow, splitting him into two makes it easier to separate the hurt and complication of why we ended back then. All that stuff, that was College Danny. Not Danny *now*. Besides, I was different back then too. The untarnished, best version of myself before losing my mom.

Clarence fights the smile edging the corners of his mouth upward. "So what's the plan?"

I grab Clarence's arm and jump up and down. "Thank you!"

"If Danny finds out about any of this, I will play dumb."

"An easy feat for you."

He playfully slaps the back of my head.

I've never spent much time on Chamber Hill. Situated on the south side of Seattle, the neighborhood is known for its historic mansions and diverse cuisine. Its reputation precedes it as an around-the-world, walkable-eats epicenter of cultures that rivals the World Showcase at Epcot. Chamber Hill, more than anything, is a well-kept homage to heterogeneity. It's packed with hip bars and alleyway patios, and like many Seattle boroughs, it's eclectic and quirky—one of the last grandstands against the gentrification of the larger city, though it's quickly succumbing too.

There are laidback coffee shops everywhere I look (though this stereotype of the rest of Seattle is also true and therefore not specific to Chamber Hill). And as we stroll Tribute Park, coffees in hand, passing by a lily pad—blanketed koi pond, I decide I want to spend more time here.

The people-watching alone offers a fusion of generations and, seemingly, pedigrees. Older couples and mothers power-walking with strollers share the walkways. There's a group of women gabbing while playing dominos at a picnic table. An array of dogs stop to say hello as we cross paths. And somehow, I feel closer to the sun on this side of town, even peeling off my jacket as those elusive rays break through the clouds more mightily as the morning passes.

"So I know why we're here on a Saturday," Clarence offers when we've looped most of the park. "Danny's playing soccer . . ."

"Followed by three-dollar beers at that place on Staton."

We both nod. Clarence is now fully culpable of aiding and abetting.

We've toured most of the park and my resolve starts to thin. "Why would I think I'd find Julian aimlessly wandering the park at ten a.m. on a Saturday morning?" I kick a small rock off the paved walkway.

"What *do* you envision him doing with his weekend mornings?"

I think back to his lifted shirt. "Gym, maybe? Or at least, that's what his abs would indicate."

"You didn't tell me about the abs," Clarence muses. "What else do we know about him?"

I tell Clarence the full four-item-long list. I can see his gears turning. There's some semblance of hope with Clarence now on the trail.

As we stroll, I feel close to Julian in this neighborhood, *his* neighborhood. Daydreaming about him here feels less frivolous.

As Clarence and I continue on, I find myself doing what I haven't done in a long while: pretending I'm on the phone with my mom. I don't press the phone to my ear, but I do play out the conversation I wish I could have with her in my head.

"*Hi amma, what are you up to?*" she'd likely ask.

"*Oh, nothing. It's such a lovely morning and Danny is playing soccer, so I decided to explore Chamber Hill. I'm wandering around Tribute Park right now with Clarence and the sun is out. It's beautiful. You should join me.*" This happens frequently during these make-believe conversations, an eager invitation for her to join.

"*That sounds lovely, but I'm at work.*"

She was always at work.

"*Okay, well maybe another day.*"

"*Yes, another day,*" she'd likely say. "*And Serena?*" she'd add.

"*Yes, Mom?*"

"*I know you'll make the right choices.*"

My mother would want me to settle down with someone like Danny. Safe and dependable. The right choice. She met Danny just once, a rushed visit on campus during a lunch break from the electronics manufacturing plant front desk she worked at at the time. He offered a coffee shop visit, and my heart immediately constricted, knowing my mom would not be willing to pay for a coffee out. We sat at a table outside the Quad instead, where she grilled him about his career plans and financial philosophies. I was more surprised than anything when she hugged him tight before rushing away.

"She loved you," I told him soon after, and he smirked, though he was wholly incapable of realizing how monumental a statement it was. We had plans to all see each other again at graduation, where Coral and Auntie Lakshmi would meet him too. My mom wasn't alive to fulfill that second date.

After some time, Clarence and I head to Pine Street to grab another coffee. There's still no sign of Julian. He hasn't magically appeared in front of me the way he did in New Orleans and I have to admit I hold a smidge of resentment toward the universe for her lack of accommodation today.

Just around the corner from the coffee shop, one particular storefront catches my eye. *The Flatterie*, the sign above the door reads in wrought iron cursive set against sand-colored wood planks. The feel of it reminds me of the model homes Coral and I used to wander through in high school, pretending we were sisters looking to buy a house together, carrying on as though we could afford them.

When I step inside, I don't know where to look first. The free space on the walls is covered with painted words in the same wavy font that reminds me of dreaming. *Treat your body like it belongs to someone you love,* one reads. *In a society that profits from your self-doubt, loving yourself is a rebellious act*, reads another.

I take in the signs above the racks. *Hips*, one reads. *Butt*, says another. *Bust*, reads yet another. This place makes me think more of Coral, of our days as children and preteens when I would dress her up like a doll in meticulously curated outfits. And because we didn't have much, options were often recycled with required creativity, each outfit built with an intended activity in mind. Date night (the ones we wished to have someday): the sequined deep-red floor-length dress my auntie acquired at an upscale neighborhood yard sale and saved for Coral for a future prom (fancy, fancy date night, I suppose). My prom dress was a teal hand-me-down from one of the girls in our apartment building, still beautiful. Work outfit: black leggings with silk blouses, blazers, and heels pulled from the closet of Auntie Lakshmi, who dressed more professionally for her front office manager (receptionist) job than my mom was required to at hers. I haven't thought about that time with Coral in years. I smile, thinking about that prom dress still hanging somewhere in the back of my closet.

"Can I help you?" a woman asks and I realize I've been standing in the doorway for a good two minutes. I look around to find Clarence already exploring a table of baubles at the far end of the store. The woman is in her forties, I guess, though she may be older because she possesses this quality that makes me just know she's aging incredibly well. She has black curly hair, wild and untamed, and it makes me instinctually believe she is the same. Her skin is a perfect, deep shade of brown so even and silky it looks like a decadent bedsheet. She's wearing an amazing hot pink bohemian maxi dress that drapes her frame so well it reminds me of a perfectly hung piece of art.

"Hi. I'm just browsing," I tell her.

She grins and makes her way over. "I'm Tatiana," she says. "Welcome to The Flatterie!"

"Thank you. What is this place?" I ask and resist the urge to roll my eyes at myself. It's a store.

She smiles kindly. Her cheekbones protrude from her slender oval face at just the right angle and her teeth are perfectly straight, a bright white. Her eyes are large, almond-shaped and a glowing hazel. It's as if all of her prominent features are in competition with each other for the title of Most Beautiful.

"The goal here is to help women accentuate our best assets and take focus away from our not-so-favorite features. Basically, I want women to have a closet full of that one dress we would wear every day if we could because it just makes us look and feel so damn good! And to be able to go out into the world like that, with that level of confidence, well, just imagine what we'd be capable of." She winks seamlessly.

Her voice is weighted and singsongy all at once and I'm staring at Tatiana, feeling like I just watched her TED Talk.

As Tatiana continues, I learn The Flatterie is much more than a clothing store. Those signs above the racks serve a specific purpose. Every item on each rack is expertly picked to either "flatter" or "feature" areas of a woman's choosing.

On the *Bust* rack, tops to accentuate or "feature" a woman's chest include push-up corsets and low-cut V-necks. Tightly fitted blouses. On the other side of the rack are tops and dresses that serve to minimize or "flatter" the appearance of the same area: blouses with square necks and jazzy prints.

She asks me if there's anything I'd like to flatter or feature and I answer honestly—that I love my bust, but have a lack of adoration of my hips. I don't spend a ton of time thinking about this, the dislike of my hips that have always been slightly more robust than the rest of me, but I answer her question reflexively.

She smiles, walks to the back of the store to the *Hips* racks, pushes a few hangers along, and returns with just one item. It's a colorful dress, a brushstroke pattern of blues, grays, yellows, and greens that reminds me of a Monet. It's bold, eye-catching—nothing I would normally choose for myself. I usually stick to solids and wear a pretty basic uniform of slacks and sweaters at the firm, having long ago abandoned the excitement of flare-accentuated outfits. *Sensible purchases only*, as my mother would have warned.

"I've gotta run, I'm short-staffed, but try this on and let me know what you think." She winks and smiles and is off.

"Wow," Clarence says when he rejoins me, running his hand along the fabric. So immersed in this place, I'd almost forgotten he was with me. I'm intrigued by Tatiana's clear confidence in her selection and Clarence's reaction to it.

I try it on.

The cut of the dress is A-line, and it brings my eye up to the slight ruffle around the neckline, which I hadn't noticed until it came off the hanger. And, though it came from the *Hips* rack, its V-neck accentuates what I decisively consider to be my best physical asset. It shows off the lightest amount of cleavage, though my eye continues to be drawn back to that part of me in the mirror like it's an optical illusion of some kind. The skirt flows freely, loosely around my hips, and much of their size disappears underneath it. As I observe myself in the mirror, holding the skirt out at my sides and twisting, I silently sing Tatiana's praises.

Thinking of my bank account, I look at the price tag. It's not particularly expensive, far less costly than I would have anticipated from the expert curation, design of the store, and enhancing quality of the dress itself that could rival good plastic surgery. Still, I hesitate.

I feel the weight of my mother's hopes for me. I should have more, be saving more. I'm not like my clients, whose wealth was largely garnered via birthright. I have to work. Hard. I haven't quite figured out what number my savings account needs to hit before I am to feel fully secure; my mom never told me that part. It's one of the many questions I wish I would have asked before she left.

I gently swoosh my hips back and forth in the mirror, watching the fabric sway playfully. There is always a small loss of breath when I contemplate buying myself something I don't need. As my mom reminded me often, she didn't work as an anonymous office schlub who made pens and toilet paper magically appear to piss away what little we had. I feel her memory wince inside me each time I pull out my credit card.

As I stare at my reflection in the mirror, I tell myself this is better than satiating my tormented feelings with ice cream or alcohol. Besides, I don't have any room for new guilt today.

I take the dress to the register and hand it to Tatiana, who is thrilled at her winning selection. I reconcile the decision by telling myself I can wear it for the "Life at Thirty" feature photo. It will take up much of the front page of the paper, after all. And be shared across multiple online platforms.

As Tatiana rings up my purchase, "Wrecking Ball" begins to play on the store's speakers. I smirk and shake my head.

"What?" Clarence asks beside me.

"Nothing," I tell him, still shaking my head. "Inside joke."

The guilt re-stakes her on-demand claim on my throat as Tatiana hands me the bagged dress. I continue having to remind myself that I do, in fact, have a boyfriend. A serious one who, just a week ago, I thought I might marry. Soon. Now, I'm referring to Miley Cyrus songs as inside jokes with Julian, and I have no idea what I want.

I decide to surprise Danny with a rare night out, wearing the new Monet dress.

9.

I take Danny to the Cheesecake Factory for dinner. Hear me out, as it's a truly selfless act. Danny is a lover of chain restaurants. He appreciates the consistency, the length of the menus, the size of the portions. "If we're gonna go out, we should get our money's worth," he says virtually every time we venture beyond my apartment to eat.

I'm overdressed, though I don't care because Danny has complimented me several times already tonight and I believe him when he tells me I look beautiful in my new dress. Tatiana, who I found out during my visit is the owner of The Flatterie, was right, I think as we walk into the restaurant, and I notice some eyes flutter over my outfit—imagine what we women would be capable of if we could just go out confidently into the world.

We follow the hostess to our booth, and I swipe crumbs off the vinyl bench to avoid staining my new dress before I sit down.

"Why the special night?" he asks when the hostess leaves.

I shrug. "We should live a little. And we've not seen much of each other since I've been back from my trip." *Because I've been avoiding you so I can daydream about chasing down that guy from Bourbon Street I told you about.*

I make a mental note to try to plan more outings for us and silently hope he will take the cue to do the same. Danny smiles, places his hand atop mine across the table.

"It's nice," he says.

I squeeze his hand then release it to pick up my menu.

"You know what, next weekend we should do something we've never done before. Like go-kart racing or skydiving." I'm unsure why these are the two ideas of "fun" that first spew from my mouth. I'm so out of touch with what fun is, I can't even come up with a viable option for having it.

"*You* want to skydive?" he asks, eyebrows raised.

"I could skydive," I say like an unconvincing accountant.

"Sure, let's do it," he says, and I know he's calling my bluff.

"Great, I'll set it up," I say, calling his.

"Great," he repeats, and I wonder if I am now going to have to skydive rather than admit I'd prefer an acid-dipped fork to the eye.

I pick up my menu book again and wonder how there can be so many diverse options coming out of one kitchen. Danny's menu remains closed atop the table.

"Four-cheese pasta?" I ask, knowing we both reviewed the menu earlier in the day.

"I'm a creature of habit," he says with a smirk and a shrug. His eating habits are pretty consistent: refined carbs, cheese, alcohol. It wasn't particularly noteworthy when we were twenty-one, but now I find it limiting. After several months of dating this time around, I was able to convince him to add pad Thai to his list of acceptable foods, though minus the spice level I'd prefer. It's got to be excellent genetics that keep him svelte.

Our waitress arrives and takes our drink orders, asks if we know what we'd like to eat.

"Not quite yet," I say. She smiles and leaves. I can feel Danny watching as I flip through every page of the menu, reading every item. How am I to make a decision when the options range from Korean fried cauliflower and crab wontons to meatloaf?

"Hard time deciding what you want?" he asks after several minutes. *Indeed.*

"I'm gonna try something new," I say. "What do you think about that?"

"Go for it. But I'm craving the four-cheese pasta."

"Go for it," I say back.

I think about my time with Danny. I'm silently asking myself several questions as I stare at him.

Was it love at first sight?

It was more like calm at first sight this second go-around with us, if there's such a thing. There was a tranquility that accompanied him sitting two seats over in that dimmed theater. There was comfort sharing his popcorn in silence. I wanted to keep that feeling alive. To protect it. I still do. And before that, in college? That meeting was certainly different, and I do remember excitement. There was definitely excitement.

Do I want to marry him?

There's a big part of me that screams yes. We want the same things. He's golden-retriever loyal. And he's been good to me in these months together, I think as I look across the booth at him. His round eyes weren't lying the day we reconnected in that theater. He *is* kind. The kind of kind that, on what would have been my mom's fifty-first birthday, just a few weeks after we were back together, took me to a fancy waterfront dinner. The kind of kind that shows up at my door with my favorite takeout after I've returned home from a trip. The kind of kind that is trustworthy, reliable. Everything I thought I wanted.

Kind.

Stable.

Adds a layer of security.

Has a savings account.

I still want these things. And though it feels wrong, I can sense that I am also starting to need more. The first thing I might add to this new-needs list? Passion. The guilt bubble rises to my throat again and I give it a hard swallow.

There is an excruciating silence until the waitress returns with our drinks.

"I'll have the four-cheese pasta!" I yell when she arrives, and they both look at me like perhaps I need medical attention. I may.

"Same for me," Danny says, handing her the menu books. "I thought you wanted to try something new?" he adds after the waitress has left.

I shrug. "I changed my mind."

We sip our drinks (we've both ordered the same light-on-the-pour glass of cabernet), and this whole night is reminiscent of an awkward first date, which makes me feel even more felonious.

"You know they mark up wine like two hundred percent at restaurants?" he says, sipping.

"Yes," I offer, though he has shared this detail several times before.

The more I try to act normal, the more I don't know what to do with my hands, my face. And as I have come to expect, my brain betrays me again with its precise path to *him* every chance it gets. Sitting across from Danny, my boyfriend again of eleven good, solid months, I am thinking—*I miss the girl I was with Julian.*

Danny sips his wine and his eyes wander around the restaurant.

I've always thought the silence between us was comfortable, pleasant even. That it took depth in a relationship to be able to sit quietly and enjoy one another's noiseless presence. I still believe that, I do. Though now I also wonder if Danny and I have just run out of things to say to one another.

Our entreés arrive and Danny places the first bite in his mouth, though I am unsure of how because mine is still much too hot. He smiles at me with the contentment and enthusiasm of a first bite.

"You really do look beautiful tonight," he says after he has swallowed. "This dress is . . ." He doesn't finish his sentence but instead presses his mouth into a circle and lets out a sound like "Phew!"

The compliment warms me. This is something on the list about

Danny, should I build one. He is generous with compliments. *He is solidly good,* I remind myself, feeling the guilt associated with the need to remind myself. "Thank you, Danny. You look really handsome tonight," I tell him, determined to compliment him more often. "I was thinking I'll wear this dress for the 'Life at Thirty' feature."

"Perfect," he says.

Danny is also a UW alum who reads every "Life at Thirty" feature. Like me, he has never missed the publication. When I first saw him reading one and casually mentioned I was to be featured, his reaction was one of having just seen a movie star. And envy, I definitely sensed envy. He missed that part of my life—the part where Dr. Murphy helped me find a path forward. He didn't mean to make me feel like I didn't deserve it, I know he didn't. But when I explained the circumstances and he said, "Man, I wish I became friends with Dr. Murphy when we were in school," I wilted.

I'm grateful for the activity of eating. Danny tells me about the new audit he's leading at work and we discuss watching an episode or two of that sci-fi show when we get back to my place.

"Remember the day we went to Snoqualmie Falls a few months back?" I ask. "We had that incredible meal at Salish Lodge and then bundled up to take photos outside?"

Danny smiles and nods. "Yeah, that was a great day."

"It *was* a great day. What made you plan that day, to surprise me with it?" I ask.

"Oh, I got a gift card from Aunt Kelly for my birthday a while back. Never used it. It was going to expire."

"Oh," I say, which fittingly comes out sounding like a deflating balloon.

Danny is twisting his fork in small circles to capture a string of cheese around it. "We took some good pictures that day, I think. Send me those, will you? They will be perfect to post." He lifts another bite of pasta, strands of cheese pulling at his fork as he does. I fear what will happen if he ever becomes lactose intolerant.

"Sure," I say on an exhale. Danny and his social media. It was a trait that didn't seem to fit his personality when we first met, his internet fixation. I quickly learned though, he spends most of his time watching, reposting, and commenting on urban foraging videos. Turns out, it's a pretty content-heavy niche.

Then the thing happens that changes the course of the night. The thing I crave, but also, when it happens, immediately makes my stomach plummet to my heels.

"Julian, party of two!" the hostess yells from the front of the restaurant. In a reflexive act, I scoot out of the booth to try to catch a glimpse of the hostess stand behind me and knock my purse to the ground as I do. Out falls its contents, including my notebook, flipped open to the list about Julian; the page pressed flat from the frequency with which I've reviewed The List over the past few days. Danny is quick to the ground, scooping up items and handing them to me, the notebook last. I watch in horror as his eyes catch on the list.

"What's this?" he says, eyebrows pressed together, kind round eyes narrowed in concern.

10.

I PULL THE NOTEBOOK FROM HIS GRIP. "IT'S NOTHING. JUST NOTES ON A client."

"Bizarre client," he says, rising from the ground, round eyes bent to narrow slits.

"Psshht. Yeah!" I squeak.

"And who likes Lil Wayne anyway?"

"Ha! Nobody," I say, in an obscene display of overacting.

He gives me a bewildered look as he scoots into his side of the booth.

I've just done the thing that, up until now, I had avoided doing. I've lied to Danny. I'm someone who lies to my significant other. I cringe in disdain and self-loathing.

Danny's eyes remain narrowed, and I try to tuck Julian into the deepest well of my mind, concerned my face may somehow give away the real meaning of this list.

"Why would your client's musical preferences be something necessary to commit to paper?"

"What?" I hear Danny's question. Clearly. But I don't have an answer to give, so I take the cowardly way out and play dumb.

"Why would you write down your client's musical preferences?" Danny repeats. He's not particularly vexed. His face gives nothing other than inquisitory interest. But also, he doesn't immediately drop the subject, which sets my skin aflame.

"Oh, you know, for, like, things to connect on next time I see them. It goes a long way to remember innocuous details like that." I'm rather worried by how easily the lie comes.

Danny's eyes flicker to the notebook in my hand again. When he remains quiet, I add, "So, Mr. Dickson, how much do you love that new Lil Wayne bop that just released?" as a decidedly poor example of how I might apply this type of information.

He smiles. I forcibly exhale. "Since when would you say *bop*?" he asks playfully, interlacing his fingers atop the table and leaning forward.

I take my seat opposite him, the vinyl beneath me squeaking as I do. "You're right. That was a ridiculous example."

The hostess yells out again, "Julian, party of two!"

I feel terrible that I've just lied to Danny. I do. But this . . . coincidence, this chance, this maybe . . . I can't just let it go. Not when Julian has consumed my thoughts since we met.

"I'm gonna go to the bathroom," I say, fumbling out of the booth again. "All this cheese, you know," I say, motioning to my stomach.

"Oh, yeah. Okay." Danny watches as I exit the booth. I take a few steps and look back to find his eyes still on me, forcing me to in fact make my way to the ladies' room.

I dip behind the door, attempt to behave like a normal human as I hover behind it. Crouched, I sneak a peek of the dining room when another woman swings through the bathroom door. She eyes me, wondering what I'm doing crouching in the corner of the Cheesecake Factory bathroom. *I'm hiding from my boyfriend whilst searching for the guy from Bourbon Street,* I tell her with my eyes.

The door swings shut behind her. I steel myself, staring at the back of the bathroom door, focusing in on the ornate carving of the wood. If it's Julian—*the* Julian—out there, I have to find out, come what may. Even if it means he's not as glorious as I remember him. Even if it means having to answer to Danny.

I take a deep breath and push through the door.

In the dining room, Danny scrolls his phone with a thin strand of cheese hanging from his bottom lip that gleams in the overhead lighting like freshly spun silk. I slip past him unnoticed and head to the other side of the restaurant, searching each booth and table for Julian, Party of Two. Examining each face, I wonder who might be the second in Julian's party of two, attempting to mentally prepare myself for a host of possibilities.

And then, there, in a corner booth, is Julian. I find him, so simply, as though it's meant to be. As if he can sense my presence, my eyes on him, he looks up and we connect across the cream-tiled floor, over the burgundy-draped booths. He rises, trancelike, our eyes still locked, and I'm rooted to my spot in the middle of the dining room as he makes his way over. When he reaches me, he takes my hands in his. Mittens fresh from the dryer. Bouncy balls in a concrete box. With his slight touch, I feel it all again.

"Serena," he says, and my name from his tongue still has the same effect it did the night we met.

"Julian."

"I thought you were gone forever."

"Same," I breathe.

"Should we sit?" he asks, pointing to his corner booth.

"Yes," I say, unsure if I can form anything other than one-word sentences.

He leads me to his empty booth.

Before I can ask where his guest is, Julian has my hand in his again. "Can I please have your last name? Your phone number, date of birth, social security number? A hair sample, drop of blood, fingerprint?"

I nod, mouth open. "Yes to all of it."

"Eggroll?" he says, picking one up from the plate on the table between us.

I nod, mouth open.

He reaches across the table, presses the flaky, deep-fried good-ness to my lips. I take a bite, staring at him as I do. It's the best egg-roll I've ever tasted. It rivals a Bourbon Street beignet. I really, really love the Cheesecake Factory.

He moves the eggroll from my mouth to his, our eyes still locked, and it's essentially a kiss, him taking a bite after me, where my lips just were. He stares at me across the booth as he chews, swallows. I watch his throat bob as he does and instinctively swallow back.

"Should we head to Vegas, to that little white chapel where Joe Jonas and Sophie Turner got married? And Britney Spears, to that one guy."

"Why do you know the history of A Little White Wedding Chapel?"

"I googled it after we met." He leans in. "So?"

"Julian. We don't know each other. We met once. I don't know anything about you."

"You know everything important. You know how you felt when we met."

I lose my breath. Was that feeling enough? Enough to upend my life for?

"Serena!" The familiar voice is sharp and biting in my right ear.

I look up to find Danny hovering over the booth. He eyes me, then Julian, then our hands, intertwined across the tabletop.

Guilty heat rises to my ears and I open my eyes with a sharp in-take of air, still staring at the backside of the bathroom door. Even in my fantasy, it's a bad idea to run into Julian while out with Danny.

"Are you okay?" a woman asks from the sink, likely wonder-ing why I'm standing inches away from the bathroom door, gazing deeply at it. I turn to face her. She's wearing white Bermuda shorts, a sleeveless, palm-tree-printed collared shirt, and a visor that says *Los Angeles*. I wonder if she's just returned from a vacation.

"No. I'm okay. Thank you."

As she nods and exits, I move to the spot at the sink, staring at myself in the mirror. Fantasy Julian has evaporated. There were no eggrolls, despite the lingering taste of fry oil stuck in my cheeks. I smooth out my Monet dress.

I do make a quick sweep of the parts of the restaurant that are visible when I exit the restroom, though Real Julian is nowhere to be found. Perhaps it's for the better.

"That took a while. You okay?" Danny asks when I return to the booth. His concern only adds to my despondence.

"Yes, fine." We chew in laden silence. Cocking my head, I release my fork and stare at Danny, attempting to x-ray his insides. I don't manage to see much except cheese.

"What?" he asks self-consciously, mid-bite.

"Do you believe in soulmates?" I ask him.

"C'mon, Serena," he says. He shakes his head then goes back to chewing.

"No, I'm serious. Do you?" I lean forward, elbows on the table on either side of my plate, jaw in my hands. I expect his answer to be no. I'm pretty sure it's no. But then again, we came together again the way we did. And those first seven months together, they were as close to perfect as one can hope for. Seven months back then felt like a lifetime. Dog years.

He leans forward conspiratorially. "Serena," he says, reaching his palm out. I obediently place my hand atop his. "*You* are my soulmate." Then, he flicks my hand away and laughs. It's not malicious the way it might sound. He means it playfully, though it's clear he thinks the idea of soulmates is laughable. I tilt my head in the other direction as he picks his fork back up, wondering how well you can really know someone after seven years apart and only eleven months back together. Or, at all. I am, after all, holding a secret he has no knowledge of.

This new version of Danny, eight years later, is a completely different person than College Danny. But I can never quite pinpoint if it's him who's changed or if it's my view of him that has. No matter how hard we both try, the magic we had together before my mom died, it has morphed into something . . . else. Baggage perhaps. Or maybe it's simply the complexity of more lived time. Perhaps perfection was easier to achieve back then because we, ourselves, were closer to perfection. Before burden ruined us.

We can't exit the restaurant fast enough. I inform Danny I'm not feeling well. I blame it on all the cheese that kept me in the bathroom long enough to have an entire fantasy about running off with Julian. When I tell him I'm sure he doesn't need to stay (he asks me twice), he drops me off at the entrance of my building.

When he kisses me good night, I pay attention. I am attuned to the sensation of his lips on mine, his sage and cedarwood scent, his body heat. I feel something, I do. I feel safe and protected and loved. It's so good to feel loved.

Back inside my apartment, feeling the weight of my internal discourse, I'm desperate for inspiration.

First, I think to email Odette, but the idea of having to wait for the response (and the picture I have in my head of her likely chicken-pecking at the keys in a slowly crafted reply) is painful. I glance at the clock as the phone rings, wondering if I'm going to wake her.

"Hello there," she answers and I smile, grateful that while on the plane I typed my number into her contacts and even took a selfie from her phone for my caller ID photo.

"Odette, how are you?"

She spends the first five minutes regaling me with a list of her ailments and daughter-scheduled doctor's appointments and I realize this will likely be the introductory exchange of any future calls. I am glad to hear, though, there are no significant pressing health issues.

When she asks why I've called, I let it all out on an exhale. "I have to tell you something, Odette. I have a boyfriend. I've *had* a boyfriend for almost a year now. I had a boyfriend when I met Julian. His name is Danny." I feel like I've just confessed my sins to a priest and now wonder if I am also a whore in church like Odette once claimed to be. Somehow, I don't burst into flames right then on my linen, highly flammable couch.

"Oh please, I know that," she says. I picture her batting her hand in the air with her flimsy wrist.

"You *know*? How? I didn't tell you that on the plane."

"You didn't have to, dear. The guilt and divide were written all over your face." My mouth is open and I wonder if Odette has developed some clairvoyant skill from living so close to the voodoo of New Orleans.

"Why didn't you say anything?"

"Because, dear, you weren't ready to tell me. You wanted to gush about this new boy you met. And believe me, I was happy to talk about him. Tell me about his abs again."

Now I'm thinking about Julian's stomach, his chest. As if I needed the prompt.

"Am I crazy?" I ask.

"No, dear, you're windswept."

I contemplate this. "Does windswept mean I've lost control?"

There is rustling in the background and it sounds like Odette has ripped open a bag of chips and begun crunching away, mouth open. "No, Serena, because you never had control," she says.

Goddammit. Odette from Baton Rouge gets me better than I get myself.

"Relationships take work. There are times of drought and moments of highs and lows. But if you put in the effort, you can find your way back. But you have to want to."

"I thought you were rooting for Julian, but now it sounds like you are rooting for Danny?"

"I'm rooting for *you*, dear." More crunching. "Perhaps you need to think about why something so simple as a brief encounter could make you question so much." When I don't immediately respond, she continues. "Perhaps you aren't happy? Perhaps you didn't know you were unhappy until something made you happy."

"It's more than that. I didn't know prioritizing happiness was an option," I say.

I go quiet and Odette allows me the silence. Her words make

me think of my mom. She was a worrier. She worried, all the time, mostly it seemed, that my life would turn out the same way hers had. That I'd be alone, killing myself, literally, to survive. That I'd spend my life storing coupons and incessantly calculating costs, never able to get my footing, always struggling to stay a step ahead on a sinking sidewalk. It's like she thought a hard life was a bad chromosome she may have passed down to me.

I often wondered why she didn't just move us back to India to be closer to her parents. The only time I ever asked she simply said, "We live here." I always thought her ego wouldn't allow it, to trudge back home and have to admit defeat. In some ways, I believe she viewed it as her life's accomplishment, coming to the US, and without a man at that. I imagine she felt a responsibility to Auntie Lakshmi and Coral as well—to not leave them here alone. It's impossible not to think about what-ifs. What if she had taken me back to India? Would it have relieved some of the stress on her body, her heart, and allowed her a few more years?

My job would have pleased her. Danny most certainly pleased her. These thoughts used to give me comfort. Now they torment me. For the first time, I wonder if I have to let her desires for my life go and instead pursue the things that might make me happy, whatever those things might be.

"Thank you, Odette," I tell her.

"I don't know that I've been much help." She's made no effort to pull the phone away as she crunches.

"You have, Odette. You absolutely have."

I hang up the phone, knowing what I need to do come Monday morning.

11.

"SERENA! HOW WAS IT?" AUTUMN ASKS AS SHE WALKS PAST MY DESK Monday morning. I haven't spoken to my boss since I returned from the bachelorette trip a week ago. It's not uncommon to barely see Autumn this time of year. We've both been heads down in client meetings and tax prep.

"It was great. Thank you again for letting me take the days," I say, swiveling my chair to face her. I catch Joey's eyes over the wall as I turn.

Autumn nods and gives me her signature closed-mouth smile.

"I hate to tear you away as we're up against it, but do you think I could get some time with you today?" I look at Joey, who's staring over the wall. "Alone."

Autumn gives me a warm, thin smile. "Sure. How 'bout you join me for lunch today? In my office? I'll order something in?"

"Great, thank you," I say as Autumn hurries off in her purposeful stride.

Autumn hired me right out of college eight years ago on "potential and aptitude," as she described it. She's who I've aspired to be in my career.

Sometimes I look at her and want to dress her, the way I used to do with Coral. She's got a gorgeous figure and if it were mine, I'd highlight my hips more. If I dressed her, I'd put her in a pencil skirt with a tucked-in button-down blouse, like, every day, because it would look so flawless on her. Instead, she wears pleated, ankle-length slacks and untucked, oversized blouses. I also don't know if I've ever seen what she looks like with her hair released from its tight bun at the nape of her neck. I wonder what Tatiana at The Flatterie might choose to dress her in, and I find the idea a little thrilling.

She's only offered to join her for lunch once, on my first day with the firm eight years ago.

Now the seconds tick to noon. I've returned my notebook to its drawer—I've reviewed The List twice so far today—and have made my way to the bottom of my inbox, which relieves a pinch of my anxiety. Seeing no new emails in my inbox is deeply satisfying in a pathetic kind of way.

Joey leans over the wall. "How is Danny doing? Missed you those four days and nights you were away, I'm sure."

I press my bottom lip up. "He managed just fine."

Joey consistently finds ways to insert Danny into conversation—a constant awareness and disappointment on his end that I have a boyfriend who is not him.

He typically leaves his desk at precisely 11:45 a.m. to eat his premade salmon and rice bowl while watching FoodTok videos in the break room, but now the clock has struck 11:46 a.m. and he's made no move to shut down his station or pull out his lunch. I'm pretty sure he's going to sit there all through the lunch hour, watching Autumn's office door, waiting for me to return so he can pop up like a head from a game of Whac-A-Mole and ask, "What was that about?"

At five to, Autumn emerges with a bag from Maggiano's across the street and says, "Whenever you're ready, Serena," as she walks by. I pop out of my chair and scurry after her, closing her office door behind us and taking a seat opposite her at the round table in the corner.

She pulls two chicken chopped salads and Diet Coke cans from the bag, sets them both in the center of the table. We are silent for a few moments as we both open our containers, position our utensils and napkins.

"Any client concerns I should be aware of? Did the Dicksons try to set you up with their son again?" she asks.

"They did, but it was a tame attempt this time. I think they're giving up hope that I'm Craig's match. And no concerns, I'm all caught up."

She nods.

"So," she begins, then places a bite in her mouth, and it feels like the heaviest of cliffhangers. She swallows and continues. "I'm glad we're doing this. There are some things I'd like to chat with you about as well."

"Oh?"

She swipes at the corners of her mouth with her napkin, then replaces it in her lap. "We're just about through the busy season. And as I think more about what comes after, I wonder if you've done the same." She stares at me expectantly and I'm beginning to wonder if she can read my mind—if everyone around me is suddenly clairvoyant.

"I'm not sure what you mean exactly," I say.

Autumn smiles tightly and leans forward. "I've been wondering, Serena, if you like it here."

"If I like it here?" I repeat, raking my fork over my salad.

"Yes, I mean, do you like working here? And not just here at WAP, but generally, do you even like accounting?"

The question catches me. I've worked at WAP, for Autumn Kaplan, for eight years. She has never questioned my commitment. I'm unsettled by the direction of our conversation, concerned I may lose my nerve if I don't speak my intentions soon. "Is this because I took time off for my trip?" I ask, curling the edge of my napkin in between my thumb and forefinger in my lap. "Again, I'm sorry about the timing."

"No, no, not at all. In fact, I'm glad you finally took some time off," she says. "I've been thinking about you a lot lately. You've been here for almost eight years. That's a long time. I've raised your salary each year because of your performance, but you've never shown particular interest in taking on special projects or learning more about other positions." She sips her Diet Coke. "And please let me say, there is nothing wrong with that. Nothing at all. Joey, for example, has expressed he loves what he does and wants to stay right where he is forever. That's great for him, that he knows what he wants. And you are very good at your job; I don't want you to think I'm saying that you aren't. You very much are. Your clients love you. But you've been here since you graduated, in the same role, and I'm wondering what you might want to do from here."

"Can I ask you something?" I wipe my mouth and replace the napkin in my lap. "Why did you hire me?"

Autumn leans forward and looks at me thoughtfully. "Do you remember what you said in your interview?"

I immediately feel the urge to cry.

Autumn leans back in her chair, looks down to the ground, smiles. "I asked you what the hardest thing is you've had to overcome." Autumn pauses and the tears swell in my eyes. I don't particularly remember this question from my interview. I don't remember much from that year of my life. I was a puddle that shuttered at every nearby footstep. But the tears come nonetheless, stimulated by the sheer mention of that window of time. I can see the struggle on Autumn's face, deciding whether she should go on.

I nod, giving her permission to continue.

"You said your mom had died five months ago. And that you finished your semester, then the next one to graduate, because you didn't have any alternative. It was that or likely never finish. I thought, this is a young woman who, at a relatively young age, has risen past one of the worst things we will experience in our lives and she's here. She's resilient. This job, this career, it will be easy in comparison." Autumn stops to hand me a napkin, which I accept and blot at my eyes with, though I have one in my lap. "I've hired people before, you know, the ones with the most experience, the person who says all the right things in the interview, and more often than not,

I've ended up disappointed by them one way or another. When I've hired people like you, who've shown grit and determination in their lives, you are the ones who succeed. Every time."

I now have tears streaming down my cheeks and silently curse them when I can't seem to stop. Crying at work, is there anything more shameful? But, my interaction with Autumn at this moment feels maternal, and the longing is sharp along my spine. I feel like the baby bird in the children's book *Are You My Mother?*, desperately searching for a mother, getting it wrong each time. I think of some of my first core memories, our foursome trips to the library—Auntie Lakshmi, Coral, Mom, and I—Coral and I negotiating who'd get to take that book home, though it never mattered because it would travel back and forth between us several times before it's due-back date. We read and reread that book well past it's intended age. I feel the urge to flip its pages again now.

"If you want to keep doing what you are doing, forever even, I fully support it, Serena. But, I just wonder, if this is really what you want to be doing. You know, in your career. With your life."

It's that last little bit that strikes me like static, and I feel the rise of goose bumps on my arms, my legs.

Autumn leans in closer across the table and places her hand atop mine in a surprising gesture. "Serena, I fear you are getting the wrong idea from this conversation. I apologize if I haven't been clear. I am very happy with you here and I want to offer you a promotion. I just wanted to verify if it's something you'd in fact want."

She's right, this I was not expecting.

She continues, "It's a small one, not quite the big office position yet, but I'd like to offer you the senior accountant role. You'd largely keep your same clients but would have the opportunity to take on a few more, particularly a few of our VIPs."

I stare at Autumn, knowing I should jump at the opportunity, express gratitude, smile, and maybe even cheer. I don't do any of those things. There's a pull along the back of my neck distracting me. The pull reminding me why I asked for this meeting in the first place.

I did everything right.

I went to the four-year university. I got the practical finance degree. I was hired at a reputable firm right out of college. I got a responsible job in a responsible profession that largely withstands layoffs and economic disaster. My mom would be so proud. *She* would have pushed me to have conversations about taking on more responsibility with Autumn earlier. I hear her now, in the room with us.

"Take it, amma. Take the promotion. How exciting."

"I don't know . . ."

"What do you mean, you don't know? This is a great opportunity."

"Yes, but . . . I don't know if I want to do it. To work even harder to help other people remain wealthy. To manage their finances so they can go enjoy their lives. What if I want to enjoy mine?" The heat rises to my cheeks. I would never say such a thing to her except in death.

"You'll take it. It's the right thing to do. I want what's best for you, you know that, right? I've gotta get back to work."

Sitting in Autumn's office, triggered by her simple question, I feel like the frog in the slowly boiling pot who doesn't know it's drowning. Now I feel the wet heat.

This is no longer what I want. Or maybe it never was.

Something has happened to me since Bourbon Street, a shift I'm not quite sure how to define. It's like meeting Julian released an oil spill in me that's spreading over everything, turning it all to black.

I don't want my "Life at Thirty" article to be about my job as an accountant that I don't even particularly like.

I look at Autumn, and before my brain can stop my mouth, it says, "No. This is not what I want to be doing. In fact, the reason I wanted to meet with you today was to tell you that I think it's time I move on from WAP."

I feel like I should apologize, as I know this was probably not the right thing to say.

She leans forward, tugs at the slight roll along the front of her blouse that her movement created. "I had a feeling this was coming."

"You did?" How could she possibly when I barely knew myself?

"I've never had to ask Joey if he's happy here. It's evident he is."

My lack of passion has been apparent to others. To people I respect and value, like Autumn. And that discontent predated Julian.

She strums her fingers against the glass table. "Is there anything I can offer you to stay? I'd kick myself if I didn't at least ask. Perhaps there's a change we could make that *would* make you more content here? It's why I've offered you this promotion. But if there's something else . . ."

What could she offer me? I think about it, hard. The office next to hers is empty, though I can't imagine working at WAP and not sitting across from Joey, staring at him from the nose up. More money *would* be nice. It would allow me to inch closer to a bank account balance that makes me feel secure, whatever that number may be. I should suggest any number of things. But I don't. I don't because my mom is eight years gone and I cannot live my life for her any longer.

"I'm sorry, Autumn. You have been great to me and I so appreciate everything I've learned from you these past eight years. But I think your instinct is right. I'm just not passionate about what I'm doing here." I press my lips together, trying not to listen to the part of me screaming curse words at my unruly mouth, willing it to stop. "Should I pack my things?" I ask, because I'm unsure how this situation is meant to go.

Autumn sighs, leans back in her chair, crosses her arms in front of her. "I'd love for you to stay, but it sounds like you've made your decision. I guess we'll call this your two weeks' notice? That will get us largely through the season. Use this time to figure out what it is you want." She places her hand atop mine again and I realize I do still want to be Autumn Kaplan: smart, passionate, really good at what I do—just maybe not in accounting.

We finish our lunches with the lightness that accompanies dried tears and definite decisions, then I head back to my desk. Joey stops humming "99 Problems" and pops his head over the wall before I've sat down.

"What was that about?" he asks.

"I gave my two weeks' notice." I stare at my computer screen and feel the heat rise to my face, go down to my belly, my feet.

What have I done?

I think about storming into Autumn's office to beg for my job back, wondering if Julian has somehow twisted and stretched my brain cells and nerves beyond repair. I should tell her I'm an idiot (true) and don't know what I'm doing (also true). My body won't co-operate, though, as it stays firmly planted to my chair as if I've been tied to a cement block and thrown into the ocean. Perhaps that's why it's difficult to breathe.

I pull into the garage of my apartment building as the sky grows navy gray, take my parking spot, and sit in the dim light. Almost thirty and unemployed. I think of sitting down with that undoubt-edly baby-faced twenty-two-year-old interviewer in a few weeks and am petrified.

My life, just a few days ago, was a meticulously crafted piece of art. I've just taken a knife to it.

I have to come up with a new plan before I turn thirty in a few short weeks and before the interview. But, even more pressing, I think of how disappointed Danny is going to be when I tell him I've quit my job with no plan.

12.

I'VE ORDERED TAKEOUT FROM THE ITALIAN DINER ACROSS THE STREET FROM my building. Two glasses of wine are poured, though I've already downed most of mine. I am plating the food when the sound of the buzzer makes me jump.

"Hey, babe," Danny says when I open the door. He observes the takeout containers on my counter. "Ordering in on Monday night? And after we've just gone out? What's gotten into you?" he teases and kisses my forehead as he breezes past me and removes his jacket. He goes to the two-seater table in the kitchen nook and picks up the wine glass meant for him.

"How was your day?" I ask. I go back to plating the food for something to do with my hands.

"It was okay. I barely got up from my desk. This UnionCore audit is the worst. Jack says it may take five months to get things in order. I've never seen books that are such a mess." Somewhere along the talk of CFOs, I lose the trail of his story and do a lot of mmhmm'ing as he talks. I set the two plates on the table and sit down.

"What's the big occasion?" he asks, noting the move from our usual places in front of the TV.

I shrug. "Thought we could mix it up." He sits down in the empty chair opposite me.

"Oh, so speaking of Jack, he and Laurie got a new puppy this weekend. A Pomeranian. He showed everyone pictures of it all day like a proud dad. He even looked like a disheveled new parent who didn't get any sleep all weekend. It is a cute little thing, I have to admit. Looks like a stuffed animal." Danny smiles and shakes his head amusedly. He pulls out his phone, finds one of Jack's social media pages, and holds up a picture of the puppy for me to gush over.

"Cute," I offer, hoping this conversation does not lead where I'm afraid it may. It's not the first time Danny has gushed over a new puppy or sidewalk doggie over the last few months, hinting at a desire for a shared pet. My stomach roils.

"It got me thinking . . ."

Don't say it.

"It would be kinda nice to have a dog around."

He said it.

"You want to get a dog?"

"Maybe *we* should get a dog."

I take a long sip of wine. I like dogs, I do. Who doesn't like dogs? I think of his family's Jack Russell, Norman, who will likely croak any day now and for a moment I want to do this for him. It's a brief, fleeting moment. "We don't live together, Danny. You think it's wise to share a dog?"

"We will soon enough." He shrugs then dives into his grilled cheese sandwich. I don't tell him his order comes from the diner's kids' menu.

"I don't know, it doesn't seem like the right time for something like that," I say.

He shrugs and I'm grateful he doesn't seem particularly tied to the idea.

"What about you, how was your day?" He peels the crust from the edge of his sandwich, creates a small stack on the corner of his plate.

As I watch him eat, I try to remember the instant I decided I loved him. Was there a specific moment I looked into his round eyes, adored his perfect skin, and thought, I love this man? We threw the word around so liberally back during those seven months in college. It wasn't untrue, but also, it was too simple to be the kind of love that grows through hard things. After getting back together, when he took me to dinner on what he knew was my mom's birthday, I remember sitting across from him on that outdoor patio, golden hour light streaming across his face, thinking, I could marry this man.

I think of how we slept together that night and the taste of him was a lucid reminder of who I used to be and wished to be again. How he would whisper things like "You're so beautiful" and "I love your body" in an ongoing address of praise that made me more confident than I had ever been in bed. He said "I love you" that night, for the second first time, and as we lay in the dark, catching our breath, I said it back. And like everything else in our relationship from the moment we found each other again, we fell into whatever came next.

The next day, I shared him with my mom.

"Danny and I found our way back," I told her. I lay in bed, staring at my ceiling—this time in the light of day—thinking about Danny next to me from the night before.

"Amma, that's wonderful. Tell me everything," she would have said.

"I get why you love him," I told her confidently. *"He's incredibly kind. An accountant. He wants a family. He has a 401(k). And last night, he told me he loves me again. That perhaps he never stopped."*

"It sounds perfect. I can't wait for you to have all the things I never did. I'm so happy for you."

"Thank you, Mom. I'm happy."

"I wish I could see him. Oh shoot, gotta get back to work."

I smiled at the ceiling bitterly.

I gulp my wine. "It was a pretty eventful day, actually," I tell Danny.

"Oh?" he says through a mouthful. He wipes the grease from his fingers with his napkin.

"Yeah."

He raises his eyebrows at me expectantly.

"Yeah, so I gave my notice today." I watch him take this in, a spasm happening just behind his forehead.

"You did what? You didn't even tell me you were looking."

"I wasn't. I mean, I'm not. Not yet at least." I finish my wine and go to the kitchen counter to grab the bottle. He turns his chair to face me and as he does, it scrapes against the tile floor, producing a loud screeching sound that makes me wince. He doesn't seem to notice.

"Wait, so you don't have another job lined up?"

"No, I don't."

He's waiting for me to say more, to explain to him that this is part of a well-thought-out master plan I have yet to reveal to him. He wants me to tell him the plan. When I don't continue, he stands up.

"So, you just quit your job, with no thought? Did something happen at work? Did Joey do something?" He leans against the counter beside me, looking at me like I'm a bird that has just flown into a window. He's trying to decide if I am dead or just stunned. To be determined.

"No, of course not. Joey is harmless. Nothing happened, not like that. I decided I don't want to work there anymore. That I need to pursue something different. Something . . . more. Autumn even offered me a promotion. I said no." I say these words as if I am dictating a lunch order and my matter-of-fact tone seemingly confuses him more.

"You said no," he repeats.

"Yeah, so we decided on a two weeks' notice."

"Wow, okay. What are you gonna do?"

Crawl into a hole and die is the right response according to his facial expression.

"I'm not sure," I say. When I pictured this conversation, role-played it on the drive home, I thought I would try to reassure him. That I would say things like, *Don't worry, I'm going to figure it out* or *I'm going to jump on the job boards tomorrow.* But somehow, now that it's happening, I can't seem to offer him these reassurances. In fact, I don't really even want to.

"I can make a few introductions at my firm," he says. Danny is a problem solver, a fixer. And right now, he believes he can fix the mess I've just made of my life.

"No, no, don't do that. I'm not even sure I want to stay in accounting." I'm a bit surprised by my willingness to say this part aloud. To him of all people.

He's squinting at me as if his eyesight has gone bad. "This isn't like you, Serena. I thought you were . . ."

Intelligent, stable, not a sociopath? I silently venture a few guesses to his dysfunctional Mad Libs.

He doesn't finish the sentence. Instead, he starts a new one. "What's going on with you?"

Well, that is a very relevant question, one I haven't stopped asking myself over the last week.

"And what about the 'Life at Thirty' feature for *The Daily*?"

This last question makes my throat clench. His interest and devotion to these features, and the fact he is bringing it up now, remind me of what I already know: it's a big freakin' deal.

"Of course I've thought about it."

"Maybe you should just back out, you know, with this new development."

"Why would you say that?" I ask, trying to mask the annoyance in my tone, though I clearly fail because he's looking at me like I've just spoken another language.

"I just mean, if you aren't, you know, confident in doing it, then perhaps you shouldn't do it. There's nothing that says you can't back out."

"I made a commitment, Danny. A big one to the one person who was there for me when my mom died." I see the recoil across his body, as if he's wrapped his fingers along an electric fence. *The one person who was there for me when my mom died. And that person was not you.* "Are you afraid of the secondhand embarrassment of your association with me? Don't worry, you don't have to be in the cover photo if that's the case. I won't mention you at all if you want."

He puts his hands out in front of him like I'm a predator about to charge. "Calm down, that's not what I'm saying at all." Welp, he did it. He's said the words that instantly raise my blood pressure. *Calm down.*

"Then what are you saying?" I fold my arms in front of me and bend my knee at him. He's rarely seen me like this. I'm usually quite composed. Logical, like him. I know he values this as a trait, generally, and in me. He conveys the sentiment often.

"I was just saying, if you don't want that kind of pressure, if quitting your job is some sort of rebellion against this interview, against turning thirty, then just don't do it. I'm trying to help."

I raise my eyebrows at him. There's a shit ton to unpack in what he just said. I think of Odette at this moment. Of what she divulged on the plane. About how when she laid eyes on Marv for the first time that day in church all those years ago, it was like she had been dreaming her whole life and at that moment someone poured a bucket of cold water over her head that jolted her awake.

I feel like I'm still asleep.

Things with Danny have always been easy though. And when you grow up with a mom whose life was only ever hard, easy is not only beautiful, but it releases a sandbag from your ankle.

"Why do you want to marry me?" I eventually ask into the quiet between us.

"Why are you asking me that?" he says with a lightness in his voice, as if I am fishing for compliments and reassurance.

I am.

"I just want to know. We never really talk about it. I mean, we've talked about getting married, but never really about *why.* And we've only been back together for a year. By most standards, that's really quick to be engaged."

"That's putting the cart before the horse, don't you think? Aren't you going to wait until I ask you at least before you consider us engaged?" His words are light but there is carryover annoyance in his voice.

"Stop, you know what I mean. Why do you want to marry me?"

He furrows his brow as he evaluates me. "Because we're good together. *Perfect* together." He smiles, though it doesn't reach his eyes.

"Nothing's perfect," I say. Perhaps back then we were close, but now? Now I don't know.

"Of course not, but we fit so well. We want the same things. We have the same goals. That's what I mean. At least I thought we did."

He moves from the kitchen and leans against the back of the couch. "And my family loves you."

I met Danny's parents on what happened to be our three-month anniversary in college. They invited us over for dinner at Danny's childhood home on a Friday night and I was immediately uncomfortable. Not because of his parents; they were charmingly doting. But when we pulled up to the house and I saw two stories, double front doors, and potted topiaries up the walk, I felt immediately like the poor kid in too-tight tennis shoes.

Danny did not grow up wealthy, but solidly upper-middle-class and never wanted for anything. It has never occurred to him that a kid could have constant worry about money. Not because he is uncaring, but because he's never had to think about it.

"What are the things we want that are the same? What are the goals we have in common?" I ask.

"What is this, Serena? Did you come across some sort of compatibility test online?"

"I'm not trying to corner you, Danny. I'm simply trying to talk about us. About our lives together."

He sighs, moves to the front of the couch, and sits. I follow suit—him in his usual corner, me in mine. "Okay," he says. "We both want to get married. We both want kids. We are both at the place in our lives where we want those things soon. Which is why I'm so taken by this choice to just quit your job." I wait for him to continue, but apparently he's done. He's just staring at me with his eyebrows raised in anticipation of my approval.

"Do you believe in love at first sight?" I ask.

"Serena," is all he says. He's calm and light and stern and joking all at once in his tone and his face hints of a twisted smile.

I think about pressing, but I already know the answer. Expecting him to say something to surprise me, something different than the practical answer I anticipate from his mouth, will simply set me up for disappointment.

He must see the look of defeat on my face, because he then says, "I love you." His round eyes are so sincere, I should feel the soothing calm at my base that he typically provides. I don't.

"Now, no old Julia Roberts movies for you for a while," he says. "And I'm sure if you wake up tomorrow and decide this was all a mistake, Autumn will gladly take you back." He taps my knee twice then presses play on the next episode of that sci-fi show we've been watching.

There's too much happening inside me to focus on the show. Unease. Torment. And, of course, guilt.

"Danny," I say with the conviction of a woman who's desperate for more. "I think we should end this."

13.

DANNY SETS THE REMOTE BETWEEN US ON THE COUCH CUSHION AND SHIFTS his body toward me. "What's gotten into you?" He's agitated. I can't blame him. This is unfair. He's not the one who's changed. I have. But I care too much about Danny to drag him along while I trudge the mud conflicted.

When I don't respond, his eyes grow intense, darting around the room. I think for a moment he's looking for hidden cameras as though this is some kind of joke. When he doesn't find any, he says, "Where is this coming from, Serena? First you quit your job, now you want to break up with me? Is this some sort of post-quarter-life crisis?" He picks up his phone from his lap, which somehow bothers me like a splinter in the pad of my finger.

"I'm sorry, I just, I can't do this anymore. You haven't done anything wrong. I just need to be alone, I need to figure things out on my own."

"Did you just 'it's not you, it's me' me?" he asks, scooting closer.

"I don't mean it like that. Maybe I *am* having a life crisis of some kind."

"Serena," he says in a tone I can't help but find patronizing. "You're just scared about turning thirty, about this Udub *Daily* feature. I get it."

"What do you get?"

"I get you want to be married by the time you turn thirty. Don't worry, it's coming."

I hear an actual click in my head as I register his words. There's likely an impending engagement. A few weeks ago, it was exactly what I wanted. Now, I panic at the thought of him getting down on one knee. It makes me feel like I should be breathing into a paper bag. Or placed on a ventilator.

"Danny, that *is* what I wanted. But lately, I've been thinking, maybe I don't know what I want and that's okay, you know? To not know, to want to explore."

"You want to explore options, other people, is that it?"

"No, that's not what I mean. I just don't think wanting to get married is the same as thinking you've found The One." As soon as I speak the words, I anticipate his eye roll before it happens. He is not a believer. I get it. Neither was I.

"Why are you so caught up in soulmates and 'The One' lately?" He puts air quotes around *The One* and curls his fingers so aggressively as he does, I fear he may snap one at the joint.

I lean forward, hands turned upward in my lap, pleading. "Danny, don't you ever think perhaps there is someone better suited for you out there? Maybe someone who can make a mean grilled cheese and who loves accounting."

"Nobody loves accounting."

I fear he has missed my point. "I'm sorry," is all I can offer.

He scoots closer though still has not risen from the couch. "Are you sure this is what you want?" I sigh. All these hairline fractures I looked past have now caused a clean break.

It's the worst kind of breakup because he's done nothing wrong. There is no clear flaw in him I can point to, that I can rest my defense on. How do I tell him I just need more? I can't, not without making him feel like he's not enough.

"I was ready to propose," he says, and I have to swallow the burn in my throat.

"I know, and I'm sorry."

"No, you don't know. I have a plan. Or, *had* a plan. I was going to propose at Coral's wedding. At the reception." I want to press my hand against his mouth to force him to stop talking. Each detail he shares is like a separate clamp on my skin.

I try not to contemplate why he would choose someone else's wedding to propose. I don't mention the problematic nature of a proposal at Coral's wedding reception as it's hardly relevant now.

"I guess I'll go," he says, his voice a barely-there whisper. I don't know what to make of the fact that he didn't put up much of a fight. He has only asked me if I am sure once.

He rises from the couch and I follow him to the door, grasping the finality of the situation.

Panic rises in me again as a counterfeit future runs through my mind. There will be no wedding to Danny, there will be no kids who share our features, there will be no picture of him and I together for the "Life at Thirty" feature.

I have officially made a mess of my life, my future.

When he's in the hallway, he turns to face me again. "Are you sure this is what you want?" he asks again, and the pang of frustration I feel at the question tells me the answer is yes. He's staring at me with this baffled look and part of me wonders if he thinks I'm doing this simply to avoid admitting I don't want to go skydiving.

My lack of response is answer enough. He looks down at the ground for a long moment and then back at me with big round eyes, and I think he's going to say something profound, something romantic. That he's going to try to save our relationship, try to convince me this is all a huge mistake. I kind of want him to. To show me he is capable of a grand gesture, of making me feel what I felt with Julian because that would make my life a hell of a lot easier. But what he says instead is, "Since we may not be talking, can I get that picture of us at Snoqualmie Falls? I think it's the one I'd like to post when I announce our breakup."

I try not to deflate as his words stomp the last bit of air out of me. He is a pragmatist, after all. And he's the one with social media, not me. This is the most newsworthy event he's gotten to post about since Norman the Jack Russell got bit by a Doberman four months ago. He managed seven posts out of that situation. I can at least give him this final request.

I pull my phone from my back pocket and stand next to him as I open my photos app. We both see the most recent pictures in my feed at the same time.

A screen full of Bourbon Street dick pics.

"Are those . . ." Danny says, though mercifully, he doesn't finish his sentence.

I press the power button on my phone and the screen goes black. He stares. At the phone, then me.

I can only imagine the thoughts running through his mind as he tries to reconcile what he just saw. Does he think I've been chatting with other guys throughout our relationship, amassing dick pics along the way like trophies? Does he think I've saved a collection of dicks from the internet that I secretly use to get my rocks off when he's not around?

I'm about to explain, then, stop myself. In some self-deprecating way, I feel like I should let him have this. Let him think I've got some bizarre penis obsession. Maybe it will make his landing from this breakup softer (no pun intended).

I picture the conversation with his parents, all three of them huddled around their white marble kitchen island, as he tells them about the breakup. ". . . and she had a collection of dick pics on her phone."

"You should probably change your locks," I picture his mom saying over one of her omnipresent cheese platters.

"I'll text it to you," I tell Danny, shoving the phone into my back pocket. He nods slowly, undoubtedly wondering who exactly he's spent the last year of his life with. And he's probably wondering what other dark secrets I've been hiding.

He turns and plods down the hall.

We didn't even hug goodbye.

I watch out the hallway window as he exits the building, stopping to snap a picture of the nettles poking out from the shrubbery along the side of the building.

That's good, I think, as he replaces his phone in his pocket and disappears from view. *It's a potentially exciting find for his urban foraging content.* Perhaps he'll whip up some feel-better nettles-based pesto with his findings—enjoyed in a bowl of noodles, covered in parmesan cheese, of course.

I sit down on my couch, unsure of what to do with myself. Flipping on the TV, I shuffle to the last episode of that sci-fi show Danny and I had been watching. I remove it from my list. I don't even like sci-fi.

When enough time has passed and I know he is safely gone, I grab a coat and follow his route down the elevator, stopping at ground level. The air outside is crisp and the swirling mist sprays against my cheeks like tickles of tiny brush bristles. I walk, breathing deeply as I go. In the course of a few hours, I've managed to lose my job, my boyfriend, my entire future.

I can't help but think about my mom as I make my way down my street, the glow from the restaurants and storefronts lighting my way. I've thought about her more in these last few weeks than I have in a long while. I can't ignore the ache of disappointment I know she'd feel about these choices. It's in me like a layer of butter lining my arteries. I can't help but wonder—am I sabotaging my own life?

"I'm sorry," I tell her as I walk, wrapping my arms around my center. *"I broke up with Danny."*

"Amma, why?" she asks in breathy disbelief.

"Because marrying someone good with money isn't reason enough. I want more."

She sighs. *"What is your plan? What's next?"*

I scramble through what she might find to be acceptable answers. But I can't lie to her. Not when she's still showing up for me. *"I don't know,"* I tell her honestly.

I stop at a crosswalk and close my eyes. Losing the last man my mom met means losing her further. The damp cold nips at my skin and every noise around me fades away. The sturdiness of the night cradles me. *It's okay*, I tell myself. *I will be okay.* And I know I will. I've been through worse. There is sadness, yes, but also relief.

Before I can forget again, I pull out my phone, take a look left and right to ensure no one is around, and delete the collection of Bourbon Street dick pics.

14.

On the night of our breakup, it's Julian who comes to me in my dreams, not Danny. It's the most vivid dream I've ever known and I cannot help but think it means he is watching me somehow, trying to affirm to me that he agrees with these recent life developments. Yes, apparently, I now view Julian as my spirit guide as well as the possible love of my life.

Back to the dream.

There is no buildup. He's just there, beside me in bed, already shirtless and tangled in my taupe-colored sheets. The light outside is dim, though just bright enough that I can see his details oh so clearly. His upper body is just as I remember it, long and lean, strong and defined though not overly so. His is the body type I'd choose from a lineup every time. He's lying on his side facing me, head propped against his hand. His hair is tousled, hanging in his face, and it's as gloriously sexy undone as I had hoped. I reach up and shuffle my hand around in it and it's like I'm submerged in a pile of cotton balls.

He smiles and I am overcome with an immense amount of gratitude for the pleasure that smile brings me. I stare at it unabashedly, because it's my dream and I get to do so without consequence. That smile is just as goofy and adorable as I remember and it gives me the same flutter in my gut as when I first saw it. I never thought I'd use words like *goofy* and *adorable* and *sexy* to describe one thing, one feature, but it's appropriate when it comes to his smile that pulls away from his teeth. He releases the grin slowly and I focus in on his Hawaiian Punch–red lips. I want to drink them.

He reaches his hand forward, gently brushes a loose strand of hair behind my ear as I mimic his body position. I urge him to speak. I need to hear his voice again. I need him to come alive in another way. And, because it's my dream, he listens.

"I've missed you, Serena," he says, cupping the side of my face with his free hand. I feel the surge of it, his hand on my skin. I run my fingertips along his glorious abs, in awe of their ridges and mass. His smile is fully gone now, and he's looking at me with the intensity he had right before we were separated on Bourbon Street. Like he knows I will awaken sometime soon and this encounter too might meet a *premature* end.

He scoots closer, pressing his lips to mine, and my senses are more attuned to it than if it were a real kiss. Because in real life, there are things that would draw me away. A noise in the background, the mechanics of it, the clenching of whichever body part his wandering hand might browse. But in my dream, all I can sense, all I have, is this kiss.

He is warm, and even in my dream, I think of his breath against my ear the night we met and there's an exciting and comforting déjà vu surrounding it.

Here, there is no rush, no passing of time.

He rolls on top of me and his eyes dart back and forth between mine. From this angle, his features jump forward and I can see every spot of him. The dark speck in his right eye, a beautiful detail that makes him. The light stubble on his chin, cheeks, neck, how it's perfectly gruff against the brush of my thumb. The soft freckles that mark the tops of his shoulders, thin and faint. I wonder if those freckles truly exist. I believe with all of myself they do.

"Show me your tits," I say as his chest suspends atop mine, because even in my dreams I'm still a creeper. He smiles (the goofy, adorable, sexy one) and sits up, on his knees at my waist. He's already shirtless, so he sits there, his inner thighs pressed against the outside of mine as I marvel over his naked torso. I run my hand along his abs again, zigzagging along their edges.

"I don't have any beads for you," I breathe.

"I don't want beads," he whispers back as he stretches out over me again.

"Then what do you want?"

Our eyes race back and forth again.

"Show me yours and I'll show you mine . . ." He tugs at the thin white T-shirt bunched just below my otherwise bare chest.

"I've already seen yours," I say, closing my eyes to savor the feeling of his fingers brushing my bare stomach.

"You have. Twice. It's time to make things fair." He lifts the thin tee over my head with one hand and throws it to the ground. I admire him as he admires me. His eyes follow his pointer finger as it runs down the side of my neck, as it swirls around my nipple's edge. I cock my head back.

"I looked for you," he says as he continues his motion. That voice. It's distinct. Smooth and rumbly at the same time. A voice that could lull me to sleep with a bedtime story or drive me wild saying dirty things. Either way, it most certainly belongs in the bedroom. This bedroom.

"You did?"

"Yes," he says, cupping the side of my face as he looks down at me. "That next morning. I went back to the bar . . ." His voice trails off because we both already know the rest.

He leans down for a kiss, and as that kiss moves deeper against me, I push back into him with equal force. I've never had the opportunity to touch his lips in real life, but here they are a sweet, savory combination. Butter and jam on toast. I press so every possible inch of me is touching him. Skin on skin; he is an extension of me. I feel his attraction against my leg and instinctively align myself to it.

His eyes race back and forth over mine again as he hovers above me and I raise my hips in response to the question they are asking. I reach between us, curl my hand against his erection, and watch as his eyes slowly roll then close. Beneath my hand, he is solid, pulsing. I squeeze gently and he moans, just barely, in approval. I slide my hand up, position it just below the head, and align myself again, motioning him steadily, up and down, against my swelling clit.

I clench his flexed bicep with my free hand. He breathes into my neck in short bursts, anticipation ruining us both.

When I can't take the tension any longer, I slide his erection down me, then hold it against my entrance before letting go. We make eye contact and I will him forward, daring and pleading in equal part. He gives me an errant half grin and we lay still a moment, suspending pleasure, testing which of us will break first.

Finally, obediently, he responds, crashing into me with force and precision. Instinctively, I tighten around him, hugging him in. I throw my head back, wanting to stay connected like this, forever still, but equally desperate for him to begin the motion I'm yearning for. His hips respond. Back and forth they go and we find our dance. We both move, forward and away, hammering into each other forcefully, ensuring I take all of him in at each coalescence.

Just as momentum builds to its maximum, he pulls out. I experience the emptiness with an intensity that tugs at me from the inside. Before I can voice my objection, he slides down me, his mouth making contact between my legs. He gives me one, strong stroke of the tongue that forces a loud moan from my depths, then stops. He lifts his head to face me. "I've wanted to do this since the night we met," he huffs before his tongue connects again.

His mouth is . . . magic. He's somehow sucking from the top of his mouth while, simultaneously, his tongue caresses in a slow figure eight just below. I beg him not to stop, sometimes out loud, sometimes to myself. He is a machine, never faltering or changing motion, the rush toward climax never broken.

When I'm on the edge of orgasm, he halts abruptly again. He rises to his knees and, before I can fully take in the view of him from this new angle, his hands press into the top edge of my hips and in one brisk motion he flips me over, presses me facedown against the body-warm sheets. His hand spreads across the back of my head as he sits over me, fingers drawn wide as he palms my skull before he drags his fingers in, tugging my hair into his fist as he does. I cry out in pleasure and he rewards me with his full weight atop me. I dig my fingertips into the mattress as he enters me from behind, his open mouth pressed into my right temple as he curves into me over and over again.

Down we fall into a crater of seismic activity. It's not so much that we are moving together, but the whole bed, the whole room, the whole earth is moving with a succinct motion to give us pleasure.

His mouth finds the side of mine and I climax with him still pressed inside me, one final thrust pressing that elusive button somewhere deep within.

"Julian," I gasp into his mouth.

I roll over to face him and he collapses on top of me. His heart beats against my chest, his ribs pressing out with each sharp breath. He lifts his head and smiles. At this angle, his hair hanging forward as he hovers above me, with so much color in his face, he looks so delicious I want to snap a picture. We stare at one another for a long while in silent satisfaction and it takes nothing more than the look on his face—a decadent mix of pleasure and want—for my body to slide from contentment to yearning once more. I need him again. And again and again.

And then, as I'm about to claw at him for more, he points to the nightstand as his presence begins to fade. I follow his finger to find a basket filled with Bourbon Street beignets. I inhale, practically tasting the fried dough from the scent alone. Feeling the moment fading, I grab a beignet and shove it into my mouth, warm dough melting against my tongue as the last sensation before it all disappears. Before he disappears.

I awaken with a jolt, unable to move. I relive every detail, running through it all again, committing it properly, before it can rescind itself from my memory. I can't let that happen. I recount the feel of his kiss. The detail of his skin. I replay the vividness of his hands against the jut of my hips, how his fingers wrap nearly all the way around. The feel of his warm, taut body pressed against mine. This dream—no, *dream* seems too trite a definition—this event—will undoubtedly stay with me for months, if not forever.

I lay there, sweaty and trying to catch my breath, unsure if I'll ever recover from what Julian just did to me.

There's something almost sinister about my life now, this living without a plan. It almost makes me think anything is possible.

My phone dings and, still breathless, I reach for it on the nightstand. A six a.m. text to the Happily Everett After group chat from Melody. *Serena, I NEED Danny's last name to finalize the seating chart!!!*

Welp. That killed any residual orgasmic effects still fizzing around inside me from the Julian dream.

15.

It's my last day of work at WAP. The one time last week Autumn asked me about my plans, I simply told her, "I've got things brewing."

There's nothing brewing.

I've spent these last two weeks volleying between terror and liberation, confusion and back to terror. There hasn't been much mental space for things like deciding what to do with the rest of my life.

I went so far as to email Dr. Murphy yesterday to try to back out of the "Life at Thirty" feature. I'm fairly certain he'll be relieved to choose someone else after what I outlined in my email: *I have no job, no boyfriend, no future plans. I'm sort of drifting at the moment. I'm certain mine's not the type of story that would do anyone any good.*

I've yet to hear back.

I am no closer to finding Julian from Bourbon Street either. Beyond my list of the four things I know about him and wandering his neighborhood, I haven't figured out where to start. Now that Danny and I have parted ways, it's no longer nefarious—the determination to find him. And after that dream, I can hardly think of anything else besides what he would feel like pressed inside me.

Odette and I built a plan on the plane, but when I scroll through the note on my phone, it looks like nothing more than a plan hatched by two drunk ladies on a plane, because there is nothing specific I can use. It's mostly one incoherent, run-on sentence that says things like *go to Chamber Hill* and *find him no matter what*. It also says *find and lick his tantalizing abs*, which I specifically remember Odette insisting I add. I basically just typed whatever generally encouraging or raunchy statements made their way out of Odette's filthy mouth.

This morning, I pulled up last quarter's "Life at Thirty" feature of the *UW Daily* because I like feeling fresh, throbbing pain across every inch of me. It's a hell of an article to have to follow. The alumnus featured is Travis Dorsey, a graduate of the business school. He founded his window-cleaning business in his dorm room his junior year. Now, eight years later, he has built it to a respectable forty-million-dollar-a-year business with sixty employees.

The photo on the front page of the edition is of him and his insanely hot wife who was a single mother of a two-year-old when they met. The now-four-year-old stands in front of them in the picture, his blond curls hanging in his face and looking like a cross between the Stay Puft Marshmallow Man and the Gerber baby in overalls over a miniature white dress shirt. There they stand in front of their waterfront Lake Sammamish home, the lake a piercing blue in the background. I scroll down to the story I have practically memorized.

School of Business graduate Travis Dorsey knew from an early age he was an entrepreneur.

Good for you, Travis.

At the age of fifteen, he founded a micro-lending platform for teenagers with business ideas, which ultimately ended up funding his now forty-million-dollar company, ViewClear Window Cleaning.

I've never met Travis Dorsey. I imagine him like many of my clients at WAP, arriving at each appointment with some new vacation or toy to boast about.

Why do I do this to myself? I think as I stare at the picture again. Travis Dorsey is the exact type of person who secures selection for the "Life at Thirty" features. He's handsome, accomplished, well-rounded, enviable. He's someone these graduating seniors should aspire to be.

The article goes on to describe the meet-cute between him and his now-wife. How her toddler son spilled milk all over Travis's pant leg on some gorgeous waterfront restaurant patio in Kirkland. *"I looked up and she had rushed over. She was apologizing profusely, and I just knew: I want to marry this woman."* I used to scoff at this line.

A last day of work is generally pointless, so at nine fifteen a.m. Autumn suggests I can go ahead and pack up my desk, then head out. I've been taking things home one or two at a time over the last two weeks, though there wasn't much to begin with. My desk isn't cluttered with sports bobbleheads and a stash of candy like Joey's. He's been distant the last two weeks since I told him of my impending departure. He has even abandoned his usual upbeat humming, replaced by ballads like "Wind Beneath My Wings" and "My Heart Will Go On." It seems as though he believes we were meant to sit across each other forever. A few weeks ago, I did too.

I give Joey a loaded smile over the wall, though he likely can't see it.

I run through my mental checklist. I've closed out tax prep for all my clients. I've notified them all of my departure, several of whom responded with best wishes in my (extremely vague) next steps. Sutton Dickson even sent me a long, heartfelt email telling me how much she and Carson have enjoyed working with me over the years. She included a sunset photo of Craig, shirtless with his hands stuffed into the pockets of his bright yellow boardshorts, feet in the ocean. It's not lost on me that she intentionally chose a photo of him pre the facial hair she despises so much. *Whenever you're ready,* she captioned it.

It would seem there's nothing left to do except leave.

I brought a big purse today, and the few remnants left on my desk—my UW coffee mug, a few accounting books, the framed picture of me and my mom—easily fit within it. I won't have to make the jaunt to my car holding a box with a fern inside for everyone in the lobby to wonder if I was fired while calling out things like, *"Everything happens for a reason!"* and, *"This too shall pass!"* There was enough of that when my mom died. I have an overflowing pocket full of unsolicited words of generic wisdom.

Whenever I see someone in the elevator holding that box, I wonder if they were walked out by HR for making a scene. It plays better in my head that way—picturing them throwing old awards, shattering glass conference room walls and yelling things like, "Suck it, Michael," or "I've always hated you, Jan," to their coworkers as they are escorted out.

My exit will be tame, though I don't know what it says about me or the last eight years I've dedicated to this firm that I am most sad to say goodbye to Carl the security guard.

Autumn walks over from her office and props her elbow on the separator wall. She's smiling, though I see the concern. It's as if she's just left her child at preschool for the first time and can't bring herself to leave.

"You're all set then?" she says.

"I am." I place the strap of my bag over my shoulder. "Autumn, I just want to say thank you again. I appreciate how big of a risk you took on me, hiring me right out of school. I hope I haven't disappointed you in any way."

She exhales. "Not at all, Serena. I applaud you for being honest." *I applaud you for being honest.* I look at her, then Joey. Is this a thing to praise someone for? Quitting one's job with no plan? "I can't wait to see where you end up. And please, please reach out if you need anything. I'm always here. Literally."

We hug—an embrace that lasts far longer than I would except from Autumn. She returns to her office and closes the door, and I wonder what type of person she will hire to replace me, to sit across from Joey, staring at him from the nose up. With little fanfare, there will soon be someone new housed at this desk, in my chair, daydreaming out the same window at the same downtown Bellevue view. It's humbling, the ease with which she will be able to replace me.

As soon as Autumn has left, Joey comes around to my desk and takes his one-butt-cheek perch atop it.

"It's bewildering you won't be here at this desk next door tomorrow," he says. I smile. Who knew I'd be so heavy-hearted to leave him?

"It's been great working with you, Joey. Take care, okay?" I lean in for a hug and he places his hand against the back of my head as we embrace. An odd, odd choice.

As I turn to leave, he jumps in front of me, pulling two tickets from his shirt pocket and holding them out. "Wait! I was wondering if you would attend a concert with me? I have these tickets and, well, maybe we can determine it your departure hurrah?"

"Oh, that's nice, Joey, I—"

"It's nothing big, like not a big star. It's this Nirvana tribute band called *Teen Spirit*. I've seen them before, they're wondrous. It's tomorrow night." He holds the tickets up higher in front of him.

I pause. *Nirvana tribute band? There's such a thing?* And simultaneously: *Julian.*

I should say no. I know Joey wants to take me to this concert because he has a crush on me. I know he's been waiting patiently for Danny and me to break up so he can shoot his shot. He's invited me to things before. Trivia night at Forum Social House across the street or an after-work beer at Tavern Hall. I've always politely declined. I know if I say yes now that I'm single, he'll think it's a date. I know I'll be leading him on. I know I will be using him.

"That's very kind, Joey. I just don't know if I'm ready to, you know, date quite yet."

"Oh, yes of course. This is not a date. I mean it as a coworker goodbye gift." He looks so hopeful that I feel bad for leaving him alone with the empty seat across the wall, that I didn't consider him in my decision.

"Sure," I say. "Let's do it."

His face brightens so distinctly, I am disgusted with myself.

I know how ridiculous it is to say yes with the hopes of running into Julian. Moreover, it's absurd to think that just because he was wearing a Nirvana T-shirt the night we met he would go see a Nirvana cover band. It's a pretty extreme correlation to make. Nonetheless, I make it. Because it's the first real step I've taken in the three weeks since meeting Julian to actually find him. Going to this concert shows my dedication more than anything, really; the determination in me that Autumn so appreciates. It does not at all make me a desperate sociopath.

I say yes, feeling a little awful about myself for doing it. But also a little delighted.

I make my way down to the building lobby for the last time, hug Carl, and ride the elevator to the parking garage, wondering if I've made a series of detrimental mistakes in the last few minutes.

16.

Now that I am unemployed, I have time to do things like google "tech companies in Seattle" for the millionth time. It's no surprise I find pages and pages of results. I click on one of the first, which highlights a list of the most successful start-ups of the year and I navigate to the links for the company websites. I go to their TEAM pages and scroll through the pictures. None of them are Julian, though I do see a general lack of diversity in their leadership teams, which I find distracting.

A problem for another day.

Using Google Maps, I search tech companies in and around Chamber Hill, clicking sporadically on the ones whose names sound interesting that I haven't already looked into. Mostly, though, I find myself reading articles about how some of these companies came to be. How they launched, the background of their founders, the messy mistakes they've made. I know this particular rabbit hole isn't drawing me any closer to finding Julian, but before I know it three hours have passed and my eyes are sore.

Before I close my laptop, I go to my banking website and check my balance. The charges jump out at me like punches to the eye: the plane ticket to New Orleans, a slew of Bourbon Street drink tabs, and, of course, the hideous bridesmaids dress. The thought of living off of my savings for the foreseeable future makes my pulse throb at every point. It's tempting to go running back to Autumn, as Danny suggested. But I can't do that. I quit for a reason. And I can't just take another job, I've decided, because I quit a perfectly good job, which I didn't do just to take another perfectly good job. I have to find something meaningful, and I have to do it soon or before I know it, I'll be living under the bridge with The Fremont Troll.

I close my laptop.

I pull out my phone and look over the note I've been adding to over the last several days just to, you know, see . . . If I *were* to post to one of those chance-encounters pages: *To the guy who flashed me his tits at Mardi Gras—you: Nirvana T-shirt, hot bod, there celebrating your friend's thirtieth birthday, left with my strand of purple beads and a soaking-wet drunk friend. Me: pink crop top, dark brown hair, with the drunken bridal party dancing (them, not me) on the bar. Let's talk. I just need to see if I get all the feels again in your presence.*

I delete the note.

Obsessing over a random guy I met at a bar who works for a tech start-up. I can't think of anything more unstable or undoubtedly unsatisfying to my mother if she were still here.

After several days of Google searches like this one that don't amount to much other than to pique my curiosity about start-ups generally, I cross *He works at a tech company* off the list.

Clarence's face pops up on my screen. He rarely calls, only texts.

"What's the emergency? Are you hospitalized for dehydration due to excessive diarrhea?"

"That was one time!" he screeches. "Look at what I just sent you. Though I don't know why I bother when you are so wretched . . ."

I place Clarence on speaker and open the image he texted me.

"Why are you sending me a picture of Melody? A highly retouched one at that?"

"Look closer," he says.

I zoom in on the photo of Melody standing on the bar of the last stop on Bourbon Street from the bachelorette party. She has one of her strappy-heeled feet pointed forward and the photo is taken at the precise angle from which you can see right up to the edge of her hot pink mesh underwear. Her face is turned to the side, laughing as though this were a candid moment she didn't demand seventy-five retakes of to ensure the right amount of candidness.

It takes a moment to notice my blush pink crop top in the background. Standing next to me, leaning against the wall of the bar, looking at me, is Julian.

I sit forward on the couch. "Holy shit, where'd you get this?"

"Is it him?"

"Yes, it's him! Where'd you get it?"

"Nice work, Serena."

"C—where did you get this?" I slow my words so he knows I'm serious.

"Melody posted it on her socials. She's been posting a picture a day from the trip since you guys got back. She captioned it *No ugly coyotes here.* So desperate."

I zoom in even closer on Julian's face. It's only two-thirds of it, mostly the right side. Across from him is the left side of my face as I smile up at him. Though it's a bit grainy, he's looking down at me with a concentration that's out of place in the middle of all the chaos around us.

I feel the tug in my belly.

"I think I know how I may be able to leverage this to get some answers," Clarence says.

"Really? How?"

"Too much to explain over the phone. Meet me for dinner tonight?"

"I can't, I have a . . ." I can't say date. It's not a date. ". . . a coworker goodbye thing tonight. Tomorrow?"

"Actually, I'm gonna need you to apologize first. For bringing up The Event."

I smile. "I'm sorry you got such bad diarrhea from the oysters at Shell Bar that I had to show up at your place two days later with a stack of towels layering my back seat to drive you to the emergency room."

I feel his glare through the phone, though he knows if the situation was reversed, he'd never let me live it down either.

"Tomorrow. I'll tell you everything then," he says finally.

"Why are you being so mysterious?" I wonder if this has anything to do with the secret he's been keeping since I got back from New Orleans. He's lucky I've been too distracted lately to press him on it, whatever *it* is.

"It's sexy, isn't it? The mystery? Isn't that why you want this guy?"

I want to argue but the words don't come. "It's not the *only* reason. I'll see you tomorrow," I tell him.

In the meantime, I have to believe the concert with Joey will help solve some part of the mystery of Julian from Bourbon Street.

17.

I TELL JOEY I'LL MEET HIM AT THE DOWNTOWN SEATTLE VENUE BECAUSE I want to ensure this night is as clearly platonic as possible. As I park and make my way toward the entrance, I'm generally unhinged at the thought I may find Julian.

The show is at an old-timey theater in the heart of the city with a traditional, brightly lit marquee made up of little yellow bulbs and rimmed with gold accents. It sends a general wave of nostalgia over me. I'm eager to admire what promises to be a fancifully detailed lobby and main hall as I make my approach.

Joey is waiting out front. He's easy to spot because he's the only person standing right under the marquee facing the street as groups of people move past him toward the entrance. He's wearing jeans, Vans, and a black Nirvana T-shirt with a plaid corduroy jacket over it. I've opted for the watercolor dress Tatiana chose for me, on the off-chance Julian is in fact here. I realize the delusional quality of my thoughts and actions.

"Serena, hey!" he yells as I approach. He throws a hand in the air and waves with unnecessary force. "Glad you've arrived. Wow, a beguiling dress." When I reach his side, it's apparent Joey has added more gel to his hair than usual. He's smiling so big it makes me feel worse than I already had. "Shall we?" he says. He holds his arm out for me to grab on to.

"Yes, let's do it," I say, leading the way into the theater as if I haven't noticed his offered elbow.

Inside, the lobby does not disappoint. It's grand, covered in burgundy fabric and gold accents everywhere I look. The ceiling is high and painted with angelic details that make me imagine the Sistine Chapel. The ornate doorframes and crown molding juxtaposed against all the flannel, knit beanies, and Nirvana T-shirts makes me smile.

I spot several people wearing the same gray band T-shirt Julian did the night we met, and each time my heart flutters a bit at the chance it might be him.

Our seats are balcony level; it's the perfect spot to admire the exquisite details of the auditorium. The whole theater is dome-shaped and dimmed except for the lights directed toward the stage. The ceiling bears deep blue paint that's reminiscent of an open night sky.

I'm grateful to be up here because down below us, the crowd is dense and I anticipate a mosh pit once the concert begins. And a bonus: at this height, I can survey the crowd fairly easily. As we take our seats, I wonder if I would be able to recognize the top of Julian's head. Though I've technically never seen it, I'm certain I would.

I've been looking so intently over the crowd I realize I'm ignoring Joey. I look over and he is smiling at me expectantly.

"I'm sorry, what was that?"

"I said, fancy a beer?" Now I wonder if Joey is British. I know he is not.

"Sure, yes, that would be great," I say, reaching into my purse.

"No, don't worry I've got it." Before I can argue he has jumped out of his seat and is off toward the lobby. I sigh, feeling the guilty weight of Joey's excitement. But I'm also relieved he is gone for a few minutes. I can gawk at the crowd unabashedly until he returns. I hope for a long line at the bar.

I've surveyed the bulk of the crowd down below twice now and am fairly certain Julian is not there, though I concede it's hard to say for sure at this angle. It feels important to reiterate—there are so many beanies. I turn in my seat and begin evaluating the patrons around me on the balcony.

Directly behind me is a group of men who look to be in their forties, two of which have hair just like Kurt Cobain's—blond, to their shoulders, kind of stringy. They don't pull it off the way Kurt had. In my research of all things Nirvana last night, I found that Kurt Cobain was particularly handsome. Another justification for my budding interest in Nirvana.

Scanning each face farther and farther back, I realize the highest few rows are shaded and I can't make out any of the faces in those seats. Undeterred, I focus on those I can see. It's mostly folks older than me, many of whom look like the group seated directly behind me, excited and a little greasy. My eyes have reached the last row I can see and they stop oscillating like they've run into a wall. In the middle of the far row, taking a sip from a clear plastic cup, I see Julian.

I wheeze.

Joey returns, sidestepping his way to the middle of our row with two beers, hands me one. "Thank you," I say, taking an immediate sip. It's foamy and lukewarm, though it could be bathwater and I wouldn't have an opinion about it at this moment. I look back just as the lights dim and immediately the crowd erupts. The excitement is palpable. Now everyone is on their feet and I've lost sight of him completely.

The stage is illuminated and the decibel of the crowd crescendos to an impressive height. Joey is screaming beside me in a high-pitched wail. His octave jars me further. It's then we get our first look at the band; like the guys behind me, the lead singer also dons a Kurt Cobain—reminiscent hairstyle. And it's not just his hair. He's wearing a graphic tee of some kind underneath a chartreuse mohair cardigan that immediately makes me think of my bridesmaid dress.

I turn and look back a long while, trying to decipher if the man pumping his fist in the air is in fact Julian. *The* Julian.

It's got to be him.

The band opens with "Smells Like Teen Spirit." The first strums hit and the crowd loses their minds. I keep looking back to catch glimpses of Julian through the crowd of bopping heads and thrashing arms. He's about ten rows back, and though I can't see him fully, I catch a flash of teeth and my heart bounces wildly like a kid in a wave pool.

I look over at Joey, who is shooting me smiles between song lyrics. I need a plan. There are too many people and there's too much activity for me to attempt to approach him now. I wouldn't be able to get to him anyway. He's seated in the middle of the row and I'd look like a maniac climbing over people to get to him. I'd likely take a flailing elbow to the face. And I can't stand at the end of the row and yell his name; he wouldn't hear me over the noise. I keep glancing back, ensuring he's still there. If he pops out of his row to go to the bar or bathroom, I'll follow.

For this moment, though, I am strangely satisfied. Julian and I are in the same room again.

Joey is having a blast beside me. He mouths every word to every song and bangs his head forward and back as he does. Most of the time, he's got one arm raised in the air with his thumb over his two middle fingers in a rock-on sign. I can't help but smile when I look over at him, and then back over the crowd, realizing this experience is as much an homage to Seattle as it is a concert. It's a reflection of a time in our history that defined the city, and as the venue lights swirl around me, I respect it.

Joey, for his part, is a great platonic date. He's so engaged and excited it's hard not to be overtaken by some of his bubbling energy.

The concert ends with an encore of "Love Buzz," leaving me feeling tender and sentimental as Kurt's words echo around me: *Would you believe me when I tell you you're the queen of my heart?*

When the lights come up, I'm actually a little sad it's over. I enjoyed myself, at a concert with Julian. I can pretend we're here together, I decided halfway through. I look up and see he's begun making his way to the aisle. I'm overcome with the terrorizing thought I may lose him in the crowd. Again.

Joey turns toward me. He's expecting me to file out of the row in the same direction as the people beside me. It's the obvious thing to do—the row has split down the middle with each half filtering out on either side and my side is closer to the end. But Julian has gone the opposite direction. So I just stare at Joey.

"After you!" I say eventually, shoving my hand forward and past him, indicating the row behind him is clear. He shrugs then turns and makes his way to the aisle. I follow closely behind.

As we exit the auditorium, I spot Julian in the crowd a few feet in front of us. I say a silent thank-you for his height, which has made him easy to locate. Before I can edge my way toward him, he ducks into the men's room.

"Shit," I say aloud. Joey looks over at me as we are ushered forward by the crowd. "Hey, let's use the bathroom!"

Joey gives me a confused look and I realize he may think I've just invited him to share a stall with me. "I mean, I'm gonna go to the restroom. You should too!" He shrugs again and I'm grateful Joey is so agreeable. He disappears into the men's room and I hover outside the door. I'll be casually standing right outside the men's room exit when Julian comes out.

No big deal. Totally natural.

Several men journey in and out of the restroom and I am clearly in the way, standing in the middle of this high-traffic zone. Sure enough, when I turn my back on the door, I feel the bump of an arm against me. *This is it.* I steel myself as I turn around.

"Oh, sorry," the deep voice says as we make eye contact. He's tall like I remember, wearing the same gray Nirvana T-shirt from Bourbon Street. He's got barely-tamed brown hair. He's the guy I've been watching since the concert began.

But he's not Julian.

Up close, I can see his bone structure is similar, though they don't share much else in terms of features. Fake Julian's eyes are black, like my heart at this moment.

Fake Julian scrunches his eyebrows at me and I realize I'm staring at him with an open mouth. I close my mouth.

"Excuse me," he says, his face crinkled in clear annoyance. He shuffles his way around me and trots off without looking back.

I am contemplating scheduling a vision test when Joey appears at my side.

"Wow, you pee fast," he says. "I've never had a girl make it out of the bathroom before me."

I don't respond because there doesn't seem to be an appropriate response.

We follow the crowd out of the theater and people begin to disperse. Joey walks me to my car a few blocks down, still riding his Nirvana high, jabbering excitedly about his favorite moments of the show. He doesn't seem to notice the walking, blood-drained corpse beside him.

"And how good was 'All Apologies'? I got chills," he gushes as we walk. The air is brisk and I fold my arms around myself. "Oh, here," he says, beginning to remove his corduroy jacket.

"No!" I say, a little too loudly, and he stops walking. "I just mean, no thanks. I'm fine, really." He stands there for a second, trying to determine what to make of my behavior it seems, then shrugs and begins humming "All Apologies" as we keep walking. If he would allow himself to see it, he'd realize I've acted like a lunatic all night. I think of Coral as we walk, the defeat having taken me over. She would know what to say, what to do, to make it all okay. It's in moments like these I long for her once-abundant assurances.

We arrive at my car and Joey lingers.

"Thanks a lot. This was fun," I say, opening my car door. I shuffle my hands in my purse and pull out a fifty-dollar bill. "And look, I'd really like to pay for my ticket."

"What? Serena, no. I invited you," he says, shooing my hand away. There's no one around and the late-evening mist is swirling under the streetlamp beside us. We stand there awkwardly, as I wonder why he isn't turning to leave, to head to his own car.

Then, the worst-case scenario happens.

Joey takes a step closer. He's got this spacy look on his face and his sand-colored eyebrows are twitching up and down. I back up into my open car door. I watch in horror as he licks his lips, closes his eyes, and leans in. I panic, reflexively ducking and sliding around him. When

I do, he falls forward—literally falls—into the driver's seat of my car.

"Ow!" he says, and he sounds like a toddler cursing the ground they just tripped over.

"Shit, are you okay?" I grab his arm to help him up.

"Yeah, fine," he says, looking more embarrassed than anything. He's holding the bridge of his nose. I think it broke his fall against my emergency break. And perhaps I'm imagining it, but his nose seems to have taken on a slight right slant.

"Joey, I just broke up with my boyfriend," I remind him.

"I'm sorry," he says, still holding the bridge of his nose, so it comes out quite nasally. And though we are lit only by streetlamps, I take in the redness in his face. "I just thought, perhaps this would be my only chance now that you are leaving."

I sigh. It's tough to be mad at him when he might have a broken nose and I've misled him about my intentions too.

"I thought you knew this was friendly. That we are friends." He smiles and I am pleased to find he seems okay with this. That he's happy to hear me say I consider us friends. I'm also pleased there doesn't appear to be any blood spewing from his nostrils.

"Please, take it," I say, shoving the money into the breast pocket of his jacket. He's too busy fussing with his nose to notice. I start to climb into my car, then stop midway. "Can I do something for you? Drive you to your car? Take you to the hospital? I think I have a tampon in here somewhere."

"What?"

"For your nose, Joey. I heard somewhere if you stick tampons up your nose it'll—"

"No!" he says with a nasal yelp. "I'm fine. Bye, Serena."

I can't blame him for not wanting this night to end with my tampons shoved up his nostrils. I oblige. "Thanks again, Joey. I really did have a good time. I'll miss you."

"WAP will never be the same without you," he says just before I close the car door, and I figure it's as fitting a goodbye as any.

18.

I CROSS *HE'S A FAN OF LIL WAYNE AND NIRVANA* OFF THE LIST. NO LIL WAYNE TOUR dates are coming to the Seattle area in the next six months (I've checked, of course) and there are seemingly no Lil Wayne tribute rappers in existence. I can't determine how else to leverage this specific list item in my search.

To make matters worse, I settled into bed post-concert to find an email response from Dr. Murphy.

> *Serena,*
>
> *I'm sorry to hear you have no job, no boyfriend, no future plans. A hopeless state of affairs, indeed. I have confirmed to Sadie you will be the interviewee for my last feature, just as we've planned all these years and just as you stated you desired as a testament to the time you and your mother spent reading the features together over the years. I imagine that desire has not changed.*
>
> *Best,*
> *Dr. Murphy*

I should have known better than to email Dr. Murphy and try to back out. There's no way he'd let me slink away. And, of course, he's leveraged the kryptonite I find it so hard to fight against—my mother's wishes. Now I just need to come up with something to say in the interview that doesn't humiliate me forevermore.

The next evening, Clarence and I meet at the Chamber Hill restaurant we scoped on our previous Saturday expedition, which is just around the corner from the boutique where I bought the Monet dress. I should have explored the menu at Wine & Thyme before I suggested it. Because now, as I wait outside the front entrance for Clarence, I'm looking over menu prices on my phone and feeling ill. The entrees cost more than I've ever been willing to pay on a night out. It'll be water and a starter salad for me tonight.

"Hey, stranger," Clarence says as he steps up beside me. Since the concert with Joey was a bust, I'm filled with anticipation at Clarence's revelation he might be able to leverage Melody's bar top photo to find Julian. A new lead means my hope of finding him is not dead in the Bayou water.

I wrap my arms around him. Tonight, Clarence is dressed in a button-down shirt with a long trench coat over it and a scarf laying neatly around his neck, lying flat and serving no other purpose than to provide a pop of color and charm.

We step inside Wine & Thyme and I reflexively close my eyes and inhale. The scent alone promises the food is going to be extraordinary. The restaurant is not particularly grand or noteworthy upon first view, but it's got an authentic charm, like most everything on Chamber Hill, I'm finding. It smells of garlic and rosemary, and of course, the earthy aroma of thyme, and my stomach moans in response. There's freshly pressed pasta draped across a beam that hangs over the bar. In the back, a spiral staircase circles up to an indoor second story. We are seated at the last two stools at the far end of the bar.

It's nice, being out and experiencing places that are meant to be experienced. The idea that any time I step out of my apartment I could run into Julian or have an encounter even a bit as thrilling makes me feel the call for adventure strongly. Dinners out are a small but mighty step forward.

We both peel out of our jackets and layer them over the back of our barstools. Under his coat, I can see Clarence is wearing the familiar red-and-gray-plaid shirt I gifted him this past Christmas.

"Can we get a bottle of the Caymus Cab, please?" Clarence says to the bartender almost immediately.

"Oh, no, I was just gonna stick with water tonight," I tell him. Out for adventure? Yes. But expensive bottles of wine? That'll take time.

"It's on me," he says, and I'm immediately annoyed and relieved. Clarence has picked up many a tab over the years when I've retreated into my fear of spending.

"Thank you," I say with an unintentionally forceful exhale.

"So I talked to Danny," he says when our wine arrives. He takes a sip as he gauges my reaction.

"Oh?" I knew it was only a matter of time before Danny reached out to Clarence. It's a natural next step, to test the waters and see if they'll have a friendship now that I am not the connecting strand. He's clearly underestimating my relationship with Clarence though. "Please tell me his take on our breakup," I deadpan.

"He told me you're having some sort of existential crisis, that you quit your job and broke up with him out of absolutely nowhere. Oh, and that you have a collection of dick pics on your phone. Anything else you want to share?" he asks with a wicked smirk.

"I do not have a collection of dick pics on my phone . . . anymore!" I profess. The bartender flicks his eyes at me.

Clarence raises an eyebrow. "Whatever. And you should see this." He scrolls through his phone then hands it to me. It's the picture of Danny and me at Snoqualmie Falls, the one he asked me for, posted to his social media. It was a freezing February day and my face is poking out under my puffer jacket hood. I can see why Danny likes it though. The sun jutted its way out of the clouds at just the right moment and it highlights the perfect skin of his face in a way reminiscent of golden hour light.

I look at the date. He did post it the day after our breakup, the day I sent him the picture (also the day he texted me three times asking for it again). The caption reads, *Serena and I are no longer, my search continues* with a string of several emojis including a mermaid and a needle and thread, which I find confusing.

My decision to break up with Danny is confirmed when I look at the photo and feel nothing but a little squirmy. But then I do the thing I shouldn't do. The thing I know will send me into a spiral of self-loathing. I read the comments. The first one, from his mom.

His mom.

The woman who's served a charcuterie board complete with salami slices bent to resemble flower blossoms for each of my many visits to her home. The one who cried tears of happiness when Danny and I got back together. The one who, just two months ago, referred to me as the daughter she's always wanted. Well, it's a real throat punch, her comment on his breakup post, front and center for all our mutual friends (and all his urban foraging followers) to see. *You deserve better.*

I can't dwell on it long, because there's a slew of other comments that jump out at me. *Her loss,* says one of his UW friends who tagged along with Danny to my apartment every Thursday night in college for my budget homemade spaghetti Bolognese. *You are such a catch! You'll find someone who appreciates all that you are,* says another from a female coworker of his, which I find rather inappropriate. And then there's *See you at the Weeds and Wild Foods Walk Saturday.* Okay, that last one's not about the breakup (I don't think) but it somehow still pokes at me.

It occurs to me then—my life these last eleven months with Danny, and perhaps all the way back, wasn't my own. It was a dollhouse designed to make my mom happy. It's evident now though: I've grown a head too tall and no longer fit inside its walls.

Clarence takes his phone from my hands and shoves it in his pocket.

"I hope his continued search ends in happily ever after. He'll make someone very happy," I say.

"How diplomatic."

"It's true. I want him to be happy. We just weren't the right fit any longer."

"Yes, well, I can't keep collecting your castaways as you cut people out of your life."

"Harsh."

"Tell me I'm wrong," he dares.

Clarence is referencing Coral, of course. He is, after all, a bridesman. It was the three of us together for much of our childhood, not just me and Coral. They have continued a friendship he purposely keeps separate from ours because of our (mine and Coral's) complicated relationship. His words are a deep cut nonetheless.

"Still. Ouch."

He raises his eyebrows at me in response.

"Coral and I are talking again. I'm in her wedding. Same as you."

"You know what happened has stayed with her," he says in that soothing tone reserved for rare conversations about my fallout with Coral and Auntie Lakshmi.

"She was never meant to know!" It's my reflexive reaction when Clarence brings up what happened back then. Thinking about the past, about my part in where I am with Coral, it's more than I'm willing to face.

He gives me another surly look and I throw my hands up in defeat. He refills our wine glasses and I'm grateful for the merry nature of the patrons around us. It's hard to feel weighted when you're sipping Caymus and smelling these smells and sitting in incredibly flattering lighting.

"Can we please change the subject?" I plead. I can't transfer my Danny guilt to renewed Coral and Auntie Lakshmi guilt right now.

"Fine. How 'bout this? How could you *ever* leave WAP?" he says, his jovial nature returning. "Did they want you to start cleaning up after people, is that it? Did they give you a bucket and a mop?"

"Not funny," I say. "So are you gonna make me beg for the details of your plan with Melody's picture?"

He smiles mischievously, enjoying having a secret I desperately want to know. "I guess I should start at the beginning." He takes a long sip of wine for dramatic effect.

I stare at him, then motion with a swirling hand that I am losing my patience when he doesn't immediately continue. Finally, he blurts it out. "I met someone."

"Really?! Who? Is it Chris Hemsworth?" I lean in.

"Funny."

His smile is infectiously giddy.

"Wait. Is *this* the secret you've been keeping from me?"

"Perhaps."

I lean in. "Who is he?"

Clarence has dated in the past, of course. He's the type of guy who's always in some kind of relationship, though they are usually casual and undefined. He's never prefaced anything with "I met someone."

"It happened in the craziest of ways."

I realize I've been so caught up in my own mess, too self-absorbed to acknowledge perhaps things were going on in his life I should be aware of.

"I got in a car accident," he begins.

"Oh my god, Clarence, what happened?"

He flicks his hand in the air and rolls his eyes. "It was nothing, just a fender bender. This Karen cut me off on Pine downtown and when I couldn't slam on my brakes fast enough, she had the nerve to jump out of her car and start yelling at *me*. And meanwhile, her Lexus bumper barely had a scratch." The way he says *Lexus*, drawn-out and his voice deepened with his eyes rolled to the top of his lids, makes me almost spit out my wine.

"So, what happened, you figured out at that moment you're straight and fell for Lexus Karen?"

"She had the nerve to call the police on me! And then *he* showed up." His face brightens and my heart tugs in his direction.

"You fell for the cop?"

"I did," he says, a sly smile invading his face. I decide I want nothing more than to drain my bank account to treat Clarence to this meal. "His name is Terrance."

"Wait, Clarence and Terrance? You've gotta be kidding me."

"I know, right? It's the only negative thing I've found so far. It was amazing, Serena. He gave *her* a ticket and when she started filming him, yelling she was going to post it online and expose him as a dirty cop, he smiled and talked directly to the camera, gave his full name, his phone number, even flashed his badge to the screen. All with this charming smile on his face, which just infuriated her even more. It's gone viral and you should read the comments, virtually all in support of him. #LexusKaren was even trending for a day. It was incredible."

My mouth is agape as he regales me with the details. We shake our heads at each other in disbelief. I underestimated my best friend, I realize, as I stare at him in awe. I assumed that because he's logical and rational, he couldn't also be a romantic.

Clarence met someone. And by the look on his face, I know this someone is special. I stare at him, feeling deep, sincere happiness for my best friend. But also a low, grumbly pain at the base of me.

"Was it love at first sight?" I ask in almost a whisper.

He evaluates me before answering, cocks his head to one side. "No," he says. "No, not exactly. But it did hit me like a slap to the face. Like, it was the last thing I was expecting, especially with Lexus Karen serving as witness to it all."

I take his hand in mine. "I am *so* happy for you, Clarence."

We stare at each other for a moment and I believe he's thinking of the same things I am. Of all of our history together, of all the relationships we've been through, about all the wrong people we've allowed in.

It's hard to relive my history with Clarence and not think of my mom, Auntie Lakshmi, and Coral most of all. It feels wrong, the big things happening in all of our lives, Coral not here. That it's not the three of us cheers'ing Clarence's new relationship tonight. *It has stayed with her.* His words from earlier envelope me like a dense fog.

"You're in love," I say as I evaluate his softened face, and it's not a question. It's a full-blown statement.

"I am," he says, and we giggle like we haven't since we were kids.

"When was this?" I wonder how long he's been sitting on this information and exactly how bad of a friend I've been.

"When you were in New Orleans. So not only did I have to miss the bachelorette trip, but then I got in a car accident on my way home from finding my superpower, which apparently isn't driving, and was pretty pissed overall until, well, you know."

My shoulders fall. "This happened when I was in New Orleans? Why didn't you tell me earlier?"

He shrugs. "I was gonna tell you when you got back, but you had your own things going on. Besides, I wanted to ensure it was . . . real."

I plead *I'm sorry* through my eyes to my best friend. He met someone too. Someone he's actually with and he didn't tell me because I was so caught up with my own antics. But it also explains why he's been allowing topics like true love and The One as I've rambled on about Julian.

Our food arrives and Clarence immediately forks the first bite of his exquisitely plated gnocchi then tells me more about Terrance. He's from a huge family, most of whom Clarence has already met. I marvel at the speed at which this has all happened. Terrance has met Clarence's parents as well, and I can only imagine how incredibly happy Marky is.

"So, all this to tell you how I think we can leverage that Face-Tuned picture of Melody." He leans in.

Right. I had almost forgotten about the bar top photo in the details of Clarence's new love.

"I'm thinking, we ask Terrance to investigate. Leverage his copper skills. Use facial recognition software or whatever else he might have at his disposal to help find this guy."

"You think that'd work? That Terrance would do that?"

Clarence runs his thumb against his bottom lip thoughtfully. "We can ask."

"You keep saying *we*."

"Yeah, you think I'm gonna ask him to do this without him meeting you and seeing your desperate face?"

My smile grows wide as I lean toward him and squeeze his hand. "I get to meet Terrance," I say in a tone reminiscent of Cinderella talking to birds.

"And he may be able to answer all your questions about this guy Julian." I only have a moment to think wistfully about his words because then Clarence adds, "He'll be here soon."

"We're doing this *tonight*?"

Clarence nods wickedly. Putting me in uncomfortable situations is his favorite pastime.

19.

He looks down at his phone. "He's here. I'm gonna go grab him." Clarence is out of his seat before finishing the sentence. I'm about to grab his arm, follow after him, but the vibration of my phone against the mahogany bar hooks me. Another text from Melody to the Happily Everett After thread. *SERENA! I NEED DANNY'S LAST NAME FOR THE PLACECARDS!!!* Wow, all caps. She's really mad. And it's not lost on me that she keeps texting the group instead of me personally to ensure they all know I'm a fuck-up. I replace my phone. I'm not dealing with the wrath of Melody tonight, nor can I deal with the idea of not having a date to Coral's impending wedding.

"This is Terrance," Clarence says, suddenly back, holding his hand out as if he's a magician who's just made a gorgeous man appear from behind a sheet.

"So great to finally meet you, Serena," he says in a voice even deeper than Clarence's. He flicks his eyes at Clarence and they smile at each other in a way that makes my face bend in adoration.

I expected Terrance to be handsome. Everyone Clarence dates is really, really good-looking. And Terrance does not disappoint. I muse that they have virtually the same skin tone, both deep and rich. Terrance is taller, bigger than Clarence with a presence that's hard to miss, and I think about how distracting his build and good looks would be should I come across him in uniform during a crisis. The most noticeable thing about him is the light green eyes, so pure they look like contacts.

His green eyes make me think of Julian. They are different shades—Terrance's a light, fine sage while Julian's are more hazel moss. I instinctively search Terrance's for a speck of black—in the right one just below the pupil—but his are even.

"I can't believe it took this long for us to meet. I'm so sorry," I say as we sit, Terrance taking the empty barstool beside Clarence.

"Clarence says you've been going through some things lately."

I look at Clarence and he's gazing at Terrance as he speaks, smiling. *Wow.* Clarence is so damn smitten. I can feel their handhold under the bar.

"Yes, well, that's no excuse," I say.

"You're right, it's not." Clarence takes his eyes off Terrance and looks at me for the first time.

I realize then Terrance likely knows everything about me. Maybe not things like who my first kiss was (Sawyer Hartley in the seventh grade in front of Clarence and Coral outside the Bellevue Square mall). And he likely doesn't know Clarence held my hand through my mom's funeral, giving it three squeezes each time a loud sob escaped me. But he probably does know most things about me—my mom, my recent breakup, my recent career shift. I know this because of the way Clarence is looking at him; this astonished, eager look, like he's stepped into the pages of a fairy tale and can't believe his luck that he ended up in the role of the main character who has the potential to get his happily ever after instead of as the troll trapped in the dungeon for eternity. That is the look of someone who has spent hours sharing all parts of themselves with their other half, and I am a big part of what makes up Clarence.

Every time they look at each other like that, the hole inside me grows, small embers eating away at singed edges. I feel as though I may combust.

"We have news," Clarence says.

"Ok, diving right in, are we?" Terrance says, moving his arm to rest along the back of Clarence's chair.

Clarence goes on, undeterred. "We're moving in together. Well, Terrance is moving into my place."

I know I should be thinking something protective, like *it's too soon*. They only met a few weeks ago. I know I should plan to later warn Clarence he could just be swept up in all of this and encourage him to think logically. I should be taking on Clarence's usual role as the logical one. But seeing what love has done to him, and knowing what Julian has done to me, I can't manage to say any of these things.

"Now we just need to find *you* someone, from what I hear," Terrance says.

"I met someone a few weeks back," I tell him. Terrance's lips part, his eyebrows raise. It's rather adorable. Clarence gives me a thin smile because he knows what I'm about to say.

I tell Terrance everything about Julian—about our initial encounter, my quest to find him.

"I know it's ridiculous. I don't even know this guy," I say, succumbing once again to the reality of the situation.

"More ridiculous than falling for the cop who shows up after a fender bender to give you a ticket?" Clarence says, and they are gazing at each other once again.

"Was it love at first sight?" Terrance asks, his head pressed up by his palm, elbow resting on the table, as if the weight of the question might make him topple over. The same question I've been pondering since I met Julian. The same question I asked Clarence just moments ago.

"I don't know. Maybe? Or maybe he was just the conduit to a feeling I've never felt that was not about a romantic connection. One that set me on this path to make some big decisions in my life."

"Don't give him that much credit," Terrance says. "You made those decisions for yourself because you wanted them, not because of some guy."

I decidedly adore Terrance.

"Is there any way you could find him that you haven't explored? There's gotta be something," Terrance says, and Clarence and I exchange a look.

"What?" he asks, following our exchange.

"There's this picture," Clarence says, pulling out his phone. "And we thought, perhaps you'd have a way to use it to find him."

"Me?" Terrance looks back and forth between us.

"Yes. Don't you have facial recognition software or image databases or something that you could run this photo through and find a match for?" Clarence asks, holding out the phone so he can see the picture.

Terrance looks to me and I hunch my shoulders and smile pensively.

"You know I'm just a beat cop, and that I don't work for the CIA, right?"

I raise my eyebrows at Clarence. This was a bad idea. He presses anyway. "Right, but you have access to stuff like that, don't you?"

Terrance looks back and forth between us again.

"I'm sorry," I mouth to him. I'm asking a cop to use facial recognition software to find the guy I met for thirty minutes in New Orleans. I want to slap my palm against my own cheek. Hard.

Terrance looks between us a beat longer.

"Lemme see what I can do," he then says. I exhale as Clarence clasps his hands around Terrance's shoulders. "But if I get fired, I'm comin' for both of you." He points and squints at each of us and I see the sexy cop Clarence fell for so easily.

Over chocolate cheesecake and another bottle of wine, Terrance tells me more about how he became a cop (his best friend convinced him to join the academy with him), his family (four brothers and two sisters, many of whom still reside in the Renton home he grew up in), and his general love of Michael B. Jordan (and his movies). My cheeks hurt from smiling as I learn about this man who has won my best friend.

"Well, you guys are perfect." I throw my hands in the air as if I've given up trying to find a flaw.

"There is the one, obvious thing," Clarence says, leaning in conspiratorially and in a low, ominous tone. "We *cannot* be Clarence and Terrance."

"We're not. We're Terrance and Clarence," Terrance says, and I laugh.

"What about Terry? TerraClare? T'ran?" I suggest.

Terrance makes a face.

"Or, Clare," I say, smiling at Clarence across the table.

"He calls me C, like you do, Serena," Clarence says, gazing again at the man by his side.

"T and C. Perfect. So, what are your terms and conditions?" They both laugh at my cheesy joke and I feel like I may be gaining another brother. Sometimes, you just know these things. They peer at each other some more. My heart melts and from it spews boiling lava. Their love hurts.

We close the restaurant, drinking and laughing, and I couldn't be more enviously happy for my best friend. And, also, a tad hopeful Terrance may be the lifeline I've been waiting for.

20.

NEARLY A MONTH HAS PASSED SINCE MEETING JULIAN AND I HAVE MADE NO progress in finding him. And even more pressing, I am over a week unemployed and have made no advancement toward finding a new job either.

I consider telling Coral about it all—Julian, my job, Danny. She's the person I would have gone to about this kind of stuff before my mom died. Despite growing up with similar financial circumstances and single-mom sisters, we became very different people. She has always been the romantic one. The one with love and marriage at the forefront of her dreams. She expected a life full of grand gestures and easily-won orgasms.

My fairy tales consisted of enough money to be able to eat at restaurants (with an alcoholic beverage and my own entrée) and to buy peanut M&M's each time I checked out at the grocery store. A man beside me in those daydreams? A shadowy figure perhaps, but nothing more. It wasn't until meeting Danny that I truly considered it.

"You'll be my maid of honor and you'll be engaged to the best man," she once told me with the certainty of a fortune-teller. It was a Saturday afternoon, which meant family dinner and our moms shuffling and spinning around the kitchen, whipping up a scratch meal with whatever ingredients were left from the week. Coral and

I sat on the little round woven rug in the center of my bedroom and waxed on about what our lives would be. Even then she knew, despite being two years younger, she would likely be the first to be married and my wedding would come later, if at all.

She could picture it all so clearly—what she wanted out of life with positive affirmation it would all happen. When I would try to do the same—picture my life—I saw a blanket of fog. It's been years since we've really talked, though. Besides, she's already overwhelmed with all things wedding planning and I fear her brain might explode if I ask her for any mental energy.

It's another Saturday morning and I once again find myself on Chamber Hill. It has become a bit of a routine, grabbing a coffee at the spot on the corner downtown, the one nestled between all the shops, then spending the day exploring the neighborhood.

It's an overcast, drizzly late March day and I'm in a parka and boots despite it officially being spring. I know we've got two solid months at least before Seattle shifts to summer and the green all around turns a few shades brighter and the sun glints off the Sound like it's a sea of diamonds. The city—the whole state rather—will make way for its well-kept secret: that Seattle in summer is one of the most beautiful places in the world, or so I imagine. Summer here almost makes the ashen, wet skies, adversarial traffic, and proliferating cost of living worth it. On days like these, I try to remind myself of the breakthrough weather upcoming.

With my coffee still steaming, I find myself again at the entrance of The Flatterie.

"Serena, hi!" Tatiana says, and I am impressed she remembers me. The shop is full of customers, roaming racks with clothes piled in their arms. Despite the bustle, she makes her way over to greet me. "How's that dress working out?"

"It's my favorite thing in my closet," I tell her. I've worn the dress three times so far. On my Cheesecake Factory date with Danny, the rare Sunday last week when the sun came out (though I only ran errands in it), and at the concert with Joey. I decide wherever my career takes me next, it has to be to a place where I can wear The Dress.

"Excuse me, can I try these on?" Two women whom I presume to be mother and daughter approach us, both with fiery red hair and hips like mine. The older of the two is holding the same dress Tatiana chose for me. My smile is immediate. I think to tell her she's going to love it, but hold off, deciding she should have that glorious first-look-in-the-mirror experience in its purest form.

"Of course," Tatiana says. Then, to me, "Sorry, it's a little chaotic. I'm short-staffed."

"I can help," I say reflexively, taking the dresses from her arm. "Follow me, ladies." I make my way to the dressing room. I do it to help Tatiana, yes. But selfishly, I want to see their faces when they experience the magic of this dress. Tatiana smiles and nods then makes her way to another customer.

As I wait outside the dressing room, I think of the agony of shopping with my own mother. We never would have set foot in a store like this. The discomfort of shopping still raises the hairs on my neck at the price tag roulette that would occur each time I'd eye something on a secondhand rack then graze my hand down to the tag and flip it over, wondering what I would find. A disappointing number, usually. I'd know before I could register the actual number. Double-digits were for sure a no. I picture Coral and I, as preteens, rummaging racks, on a treasure hunt for anything high-end that had been discarded. Once, deep in a clearance rack at Value Village, she found a black Madewell low-high dress with the original three-digit Nordstrom tag still attached. It was two sizes too big and a far more mature style than what those around us typically wore, but we begged Auntie Lakshmi to buy it. I still have that dress in my closet, unworn, because there was never an actual occasion to wear it to before it became two sizes too small.

"It's incredible." The older of the two women bursts from

behind the curtain of her dressing room in the Monet dress and twirls gleefully.

"Isn't it?!" I squeal back.

When my aid in the dressing room is no longer needed, I peruse the store some more. Several women are flipping through hangers on each rack marked *Butt, Hips, Tummy, Bust*. I walk along the perimeter of the store, reading the sayings on the walls. There are a few in the back I hadn't previously gotten to. One is the lyrics to the song "All About That Bass" by Meghan Trainor. Another reads: *Work out because you love your body, not because you hate it.*

As silly as it may sound, despite the chaos of a bustling retail store on a late Saturday morning, I am calm inside these four walls.

I've once again made my way to the front of the store when Tatiana returns. At the entrance, there's a sign I hadn't noticed before. *Help us flatter!* it reads. *Join our team.*

"Sorry," she says, out of breath. "As I said, it's crazy today. Every day, really."

I evaluate her as she stands there smiling, catching her breath. She's happy. Seemingly perpetually happy. Happiness arrives in my brain as a pursuit-worthy goal, and I wonder what it means that it never occurred to me as an acceptable objective before.

"I want to work here," I say. I'm not sure what's happening anymore. Apparently, I just blurt things without thought. It's clear I've broken my filter, the part of my brain that should control rational thought and speech. But I've also never been more sure of anything.

There is no logic in any of it. For me to drive forty minutes down here every day, to have quit my perfectly stable accounting job (which I went to school for four years to get), to work retail in a boutique on Chamber Hill. I don't know how to explain it other than it's what I want. It feels good to want something.

The pursuit of happiness is now a goal.

Tatiana's face lights up. "Oh, great!" she says, motioning for me to follow her to the sales counter in the middle left of the store. "Do you have any retail experience?" she asks when we get there.

"No, well, I did work at the university bookstore in college."

"That counts." She smiles. "Do you have a résumé with you?"

"No, I . . . I didn't plan to apply for jobs today," I say, realizing I make for a very poor candidate.

"That's okay. I'm a big believer in the person, not the paper," she says, and I think of Autumn. "Why don't you just tell me about your-self?" I start babbling and can't seem to stop because, again, the part of my brain that is supposed to control speech no longer functions properly. I tell her how I left my accounting job after realizing it's not what I want, and I'm still not sure what I want, but something about this little store feels right and I'm trying to do that more—chase what feels right. I even tell her I'm turning thirty soon and have that "Life at Thirty" feature coming up and I'm probably having a mental breakdown somehow associated with that.

I'm more surprised than anything when I leave The Flatterie, the boutique in Julian's neighborhood, with a job.

21.

I TRY TO RATIONALIZE ACCEPTING A RETAIL POSITION AT A BOUTIQUE ON Chamber Hill as a logical thing to do. One, I need a job. And this is a paying job. It certainly doesn't pay as much as my accounting position though. In fact, I realize when I leave the store I haven't even asked what it pays, and I have to call Tatiana to find out what I'll be making. This "new" me seems to delight in shocking the old me, who never would have accepted a job without knowing what it pays. Then again, old me wouldn't have sought out a job in a boutique either.

Once I learned the wage, I reviewed the numbers and realized I will still be eating into my savings each month, so unfortunately The Flatterie has to be a temporary fill. My dining menu for the fore-seeable future will include Totino's instead of Pagliacci to offset the discomfort I feel of pulling unnecessarily from savings. I certainly know how to grocery shop on a budget, though something inside me still winces at the thought.

But the number two reason, the obvious, is I now work on Chamber Hill. While I don't particularly expect Julian to wander into a women's boutique to riffle through the items on the *Bust* rack, it does mean my chances of running into him have increased substantially.

It's a win/win, really.

It's been a week, five days of work, and I have yet to regret my decision. It turns out Tatiana is one of the coolest people I've ever met. My favorite part of the day has quickly become when we are prepping the store to open. No customers yet, just the promise and hope of a good day, when we talk about life.

"I wish I was as well-traveled as you," I tell her as she regales me with accounts of her globetrotting. She has trekked the world and has stories about living that make me realize I haven't done much of it myself—living, that is. "What was your favorite place?"

"Man, that's like picking a favorite child I think, or at least, what I imagine that would be like." She smiles as she straightens clothes against their hangers on the *Butt* rack.

"I spent a year in my early thirties serving as a mahout at an elephant sanctuary in Thailand to an elephant named Mae Mai. That was pretty special."

"Wow," I breathe. "Tell me everything about it."

Tatiana smiles greedily. "I prepared her meals and made sure she stayed healthy. We grew so close I could recognize her trumpeting and know it was her instead of one of the others. It was marked, like a voice. She was saved from street performing for tourists. Don't ever pay for an elephant ride," she warns me. "They treat those animals so poorly."

I nod, wondering if I'll ever be in a position to turn down an elephant ride in the streets of Bangkok or Phuket.

"Where else have you been?" I ask with a kidlike enthusiasm. This life of Tatiana's might as well be magical—straight out of Harry Potter or *The Polar Express*. Just hearing about her travels opens my small world to a realm of new possibilities. It's exciting in a terrifying kind of way.

"Porto, in Portugal, was pretty incredible. I fell in love with the bookshops and pastries on every corner. I ended up staying three months when I fell in love with a local baker. Tomás. His chocolate croissants were . . ." She rolls her eyes back and tilts her chin to the ceiling. "We're still in touch."

I stop folding T-shirts on the front display table to stare at her, mouth agape.

Tatiana did it all earning a meager income, hopping from one job to another to support her nomadic lifestyle until she decided to settle on Chamber Hill and open her shop. And it's why she was looking for help. "There's still a lot for me to see out there," she tells me.

Tatiana has quickly proven to me that you can enjoy life without a trust fund. You just have to want it, be creative, unconventional, and a little fearless. The pursuit of happiness runs deep in her.

And the clients adore her and this boutique. She knows at least fifty percent of them by name. They are loyal and some shop exclusively with Tatiana. Seeing them walk out with an expertly chosen item of clothing that makes them feel spectacular makes me truly believe we are helping women go out into the world as the best versions of themselves: confident and empowered. Before walking into this little shop, I didn't fully realize clothing could do that.

I much prefer these types of clients to my previous ones.

The more Tatiana tells me about the shop, and her life, the more I feel like I am meant to be here. It doesn't hurt that Tatiana has taken me under her wing, already treating me like a trusted partner, in this together. To Danny, I would have conveyed this job as something to fill my time, not offering him the truth: I am happy here.

I am also finding ways to be useful, which neither of us had anticipated. Her books are a mess because, "I'm a creative," she tells me, and apparently, that means you can't accurately manage accounts payable. I make quick work of organizing it all. I even find some areas where she is wasting money (three online subscriptions for redundant accounting software), and her intuition of hiring the girl with no direction proves worthy.

"Why do you not have a website? An online retail option for the store?" I ask her one day as we are preparing the floor after closing for the following morning. It's quite shocking to me to learn there are still businesses out there that don't have an online presence. Especially ones as special as The Flatterie.

She shrugs as we fold sweaters on a display table. "Customers have asked me, a lot actually. Especially those who find us when they are visiting from out of state, or who want to share The Flatterie with a friend or something. But I don't know how to do any of that stuff."

"Is it something you'd want to do though? Have The Flatterie online, where it could reach millions of people instead of just those who can visit this one store?"

She smiles delicately and it's apparent it's a dream of hers to expand this business.

I don't particularly know how to build a website either, but I am confident I can help her figure it out. Maybe we can increase the revenue and my paycheck can grow a little eventually. Besides, women outside of Chamber Hill need to know about The Flatterie. I have a problem to solve, one I want to solve, and I feel a dormant muscle inside me come alive. A muscle seemingly in close proximity to the one Julian roused.

I'm working on a Saturday, which I haven't done since college (except overflow work I used to take home with me on weekends each tax season at WAP). It's an unseasonably warm spring day and everyone who walks by has a smile. More customers wander in than usual because, with the mood-lifting weather, people give themselves permission to wander and peruse rather than just get where they are going.

I've missed my lunch break by almost an hour by the time I step out to grab an afternoon coffee at the shop on the corner. I've decided to allow myself one day a week to indulge in lunch out, otherwise I pack homemade sandwiches and salads. Checking my phone as I go, I see another text from Melody. *You ARE bringing a plus one, and I need to know WHO! Danny DOES know about this wedding, RIGHT!? I don't need to tell you how difficult it will be to make adjustments so close to the date!!!* I shove the phone into my pocket so her words can't harass me further. I can't tell her about Danny, not until I figure something else out.

I place my usual order at the coffee shop then head across the street to grab a sandwich at the deli before circling back for the coffee. As I make it to the curb across from the coffee shop, it happens. The moment I've hoped for, the one I've fantasized about for weeks now, since Bourbon Street. I spot Julian. *Real* Julian.

22.

I BLINK HARD, BEGGING MY BRAIN TO REGISTER THE TRUTH. I CONCEN-
trate my eyes on him and this time, I am sure. It is *him*.

He walks into the coffee shop on the corner. The one I've been
frequenting for a week and have already monikered *mine*. I saw his
face, though, before he disappeared into the shop. His whole face in
the sunlight, no strobing lights and waving limbs to obscure my
vision. I saw clearly the same brooding eyebrow ridge and dark hair.

I look for the Nirvana T-shirt through the glass but he's wearing a plain gray V-neck instead. This makes sense as I explain the
situation to myself more; he likely doesn't wear that same Nirvana
T-shirt every day. I walk in after him and watch as he engages with
the barista. Though I can't hear his order, I'm now dying to know
what his go-to drink is. I move to the side while he awaits his caramel macchiato with extra foam (I've decided his drink order is the
same as mine).

I try not to leer, though I am overjoyed to see he is just as handsome as I remember and I haven't romanced his face with time and
fantasy. My eyes flick over his nethers as I get a flash of my dream. My
armpits begin to sweat and I once again feel like an ogling pervert.

I worry momentarily about the strain this situation is placing on
my hammering heart.

Making my way over to the same stretch of counter and grabbing my waiting drink, I set down my paper-wrapped sandwich because I don't want to be holding a hoagie when he sees me.

For as many hours as I have dedicated to thinking about this moment, I can't believe I don't have some sort of plan. Some kind of intro to time warp us back to that night. I scurry through a list of possible options in my mind.

I could ask the barista to play "Back That Azz Up" over the speaker system but I venture a guess that they have a song rotation on repeat in the store and thus the request would prove logistically problematic.

I could bump into him. Just a gentle nudge of my elbow into his as I walk past. I quickly rule this option out as well because I am holding hot coffee and can't bear the thought of burning his beautiful stomach.

Out of ideas, I stare at him, hoping he'll notice me first. That he'll get that Spidey Sense tingle up his spine, forcing his eyes up.

Eventually, it works. He looks up. Though it doesn't go quite how I hope it might. He doesn't run up to me and bend me backward and kiss me. He doesn't scream, "Serena from Bourbon Street!" making all the other patrons stop and stare. He doesn't burst into tears and say, "Thank god I've finally found you." No, what he actually does is quite the opposite.

I've stationed myself right next to him, as though I am waiting for my order though my order is already in my hand. He's looking down at his phone while he waits, and when he senses my presence, he glances in my direction. He looks at me, his eyes lock on mine. He smiles laxly and then shifts his focus back down at his phone. One barely registered sideways glance.

That's fucking it.

Okay. He doesn't recognize me. While the thought is momentarily soul-crushing, I'm undeterred. After all, my hair is in a ponytail today. The night we met it was down. And I'm wearing less makeup. It's the ponytail and less makeup. Of course.

That's when I decide I need to do something grand—jar his

memory and take him out of this normal, daily circumstance and back to that once-in-a-lifetime night on Bourbon Street.

Before I can talk myself out of it, I put my hands to the sides of my mouth like a megaphone and yell, with all my might in the middle of the bustling coffee shop, "Show me your tits!"

Unsurprisingly, this garners his attention, as well as that of every other patron in the small shop. I have everyone's full scrutiny, including the pink-faux-hawked barista with whom I've become friendly. A teenager standing in line angles his phone at me, likely filming to ensure he captures what this fool (me) might do next. TBD, kid.

But the worst is Julian, who's staring at me, his brows furrowed—but not in a flirty, reminiscent way. No, they're pressed together in a fight-or-flight kind of way like he's trying to decide if he's gonna need to make a run for it or jump on top of me to hold me down like I'm a knife-wielding psychopath.

And, I may have just gotten myself blacklisted from my new favorite coffee shop.

"Hi," I say, taking a cautious step toward him.

"Hey," he says, straightening and looking around the room for help. Most of the patrons have moved on from my outburst, safe because I've seemingly chosen my victim: not them.

He looks down at his phone after the exchange of hellos.

I take a step closer. "Do you remember me?" I ask. At this, he places his phone in his back jeans' pocket and focuses his attention on me fully. He shoves his hands into his front pockets, evaluating me for a thoughtful moment as I try to suppress the visible heaves of my chest.

"I'm sorry, I'm afraid I don't. Do we know each other?" he asks, and it seems as though his mind has been stripped completely of our time together on Bourbon Street. *But you ate me out and left a basket of beignets*, I want to say, but quickly remember that part was a dream. I'm sure there's a simple explanation for his memory loss. The security guards who threw him out of the bar that night must have shoved him to the ground and he clearly suffered a concussion when his head hit the germy pavement. Perhaps there was even a coma that he's just come out of. *Poor Julian.*

This is when I turn into a bumbling fool. "Yes, I mean, no, well, kind of. We met—"

"Hey, babe," I hear from behind me, and before I can react there is a woman by his side. She's got a sheet of straight blond hair and these unreasonably shiny pink lips. She's significantly taller than me. She snuggles into his side and I can't help but notice she fits against him perfectly. I observe her slender hips because it's the first thing I notice on other women. I feel like a child in comparison to them as a pair, short and pony-tailed. She has grabbed a hold of his arm and she plants a peck on his lips. I feel the jolt of it on my spine.

"Who's this?" she asks, looking at me expectantly.

My theory could still be true, I remind myself as we all stare at each other awkwardly. Maybe the concussion only wiped his short-term memory and this is an old girlfriend he went back to afterward because she was the last person he remembered. Things like this happen! It happened in that Channing Tatum/Rachel McAdams movie and it was based on a true story.

"Serena," I say quietly, my eyes darting between them. I can't decide who to look at.

I've never been in love. His words to me that first night.

My eyes finally land on Julian, wondering if perhaps I've gotten it wrong again somehow. My drunkenly euphoric, Julian-induced love buzz that I've maintained over the last several weeks instantaneously transitions to a wicked hangover.

His face registers something then, like my name has triggered the memory, and his eyes grow a little wider. He looks at the girl beside him, who's coiled around his arm like a snake. A long, shiny, slender snake that probably smells like apple turnovers or some other baked good she likely doesn't eat to keep her hips that slim.

His eyes are wide, his palms upturned.

I can almost feel the panic rising inside him.

"Okay then," I say, and turn to leave because I can't take it anymore.

"Serena, wait!" I hear him yell after me, and I turn to see the girl clinging to his arm look up at him with confusion. I bump a table and a customer on my way out the door. Their faces—hers of confusion, his of disbelief—are seared into my brain like they've been pressed into my skull with a branding iron.

I am practically running, hot coffee in hand, less one Italian sub hoagie, when I enter the store. I head straight to the storeroom in the back without making eye contact with anyone, including Tatiana, closing the door before she can follow me in. I don't want her to see me cry.

Everything I've believed about Julian—about myself as a result of meeting him—have been ruinous lies.

Part Two

Of Eight Billion

23.

I MAY HAVE FOUND HIM, THE EMAIL FROM TERRANCE READS. THAT'S ALL IT says, with a document attached.

"Yeah, so did I!" I yell to my empty apartment as I delete the email and slam my laptop closed. I don't need to be reminded that the guy who led me to upending my entire life is a fraud.

Not knowing what to do with myself, wishing I had my mother here beside me, I call Odette.

"Are you calling to tell me you've found Juicy Julian?"

"I found him," I tell her, then burst into tears. I'm crying, yes, but mostly because I'm angry at myself for having put so much time and effort into a stranger when our entire encounter was a lie.

"Oh, dear, tell me," she says.

I'm pacing the path from my living room to my bedroom door, plodding the same five steps over and over again.

I tell Odette everything—that he didn't remember me at first, that he has this gorgeous girlfriend who kissed him and clung to his arm like a panda in a bamboo tree, and that he panicked when the memory of me finally came to him.

I tell her how conflicted I am, my brain and heart colliding like opposing players in a rugby match. I hear my brain (*you can't be mad, you had someone else too*) and I feel my heart (*but it hurts anyway*).

"Did you feel the pull? Not the one between your legs, but the other one?" she asks.

I'm wondering why it even matters now. "I don't know," I say, as I think back on the encounter. "I was overwhelmed by the fact I ran into him. Even more taken aback by the fact he didn't remember me. And then, seeing his girlfriend . . . I don't know if I felt it." I say *girlfriend* with all the venom I can muster. Odette doesn't respond and I continue after a heavy silence. "Maybe I just thought he was something special because I was, I don't know, unhappy in my life."

"Perhaps," she says with drawn-out regard.

"It was just so organic, the way we met, our interaction, our connection that first night."

"Organic in an inorganic time," Odette muses.

"Maybe it wasn't meant to be with Julian." I close my eyes, wondering how I could have gotten it so wrong. How my head, my heart, my lady parts could have all come together in a single, united effort only to lead me to a man I can't have.

"Serena," she sighs into the phone. "I've had three loves of my life. Well, two, actually. That middle one, Corbin, turned out to be a dick. The point is, this idea that you get one true love and there's only one chance at happiness—it's a crock of shit. Love at first sight, who says it can't happen more than once? Havin' it happen to you even once is simply proof it *can* happen. There are no set paths, Serena. Only choices."

I roll my eyes. "You sound like a self-help book."

"You're damn right I do. And you wouldn't've called me if you didn't want my words of wisdom."

The tears stream in a steady procession. If there are no set paths, only choices, it seems pretty evident I'm making the wrong ones. "I'm more lost than ever."

She sighs. "I'll be right there."

I sniffle, my tears temporarily subsiding out of confusion. "What?"

There's an aggressive knock at my apartment door.

When I open it, there stands Odette, suitcase at her side, phone pressed to her ear.

"No way," I say, thinking now more than ever that Odette has magical powers. We both hang up our phones in unison. I throw myself against her thin frame, practically knocking her over. "What are you doing here?"

"D'you think I'd help you build a plan then not be here to see it through? Besides, my daughter and I were sick of each other after forty-eight hours. No more month-long visits for me. Figured I'd stop by here on my way out, see you."

"How'd you know where I live?"

"My daughter figured it out, she's got some internet skills. Amazing what she can find on that internet."

I hug her again.

"Okay, okay, enough of that. Now, pour the good stuff, sounds like you need it," she says, entering my apartment.

We sit on my couch, vodkas in hand, and I'm quickly withdrawn.

"Don't get discouraged, dear," Odette says, as if she can feel Julian churning inside me once again. "Have you tried the internet sleuthing yet? Want my daughter to help google the things? How many tech companies can there be in the Seattle area?" I appreciate her dedication to the cause, but also Odette is doing the thing my grandmother does, which is to think "finding things on the internet" is much easier than it actually is. Like, *fling, flong, flang,* I press a few keys and I've just learned quantum physics.

"I've tried. But it doesn't matter. He has a girlfriend. I'm not interested in pursuing things with someone who told me he's never been in love but has a girlfriend."

"Remember, these things—that feeling you had when you met him—it's special. And if it can happen once, it can happen again."

In my conversations with my mother, she is logical, practical, as she was in life. But Odette. Odette allows whimsy and pursuit. I like who I am with Odette. Just as I liked who I was with Julian. She rings the same bell inside me and it activates some latent piece of who I am supposed to be. Perhaps none of these recent developments in my life would have happened without meeting Julian, sure. But I now also wonder if perhaps they wouldn't have happened without Odette and her gentle reassurances that pursuit of these things my mother would have found silly is okay; rightful even. She gives me a small bit of hope that all of these things, which on the surface feel disconnected and destructive, may actually be merited. I don't quite know what to do with it yet, that hope.

I think about what I will be like at Odette's age. About what I will have to look back on. "Odette, did you have a career?"

"I did work, but not in the first half of my life. I had my daughter and Marv and that was enough. But when my marriage was coming to an end with that second one, I took a job at *The Advocate*, the largest newspaper in Louisiana." She sips her vodka slowly, staring into the memory.

"Were you a writer?" I try to picture a younger Odette, typing away at a desk in a tight pencil skirt with a long, slim cigarette dangling from her mouth in an office filled with bar carts and sexual harassment. Then I realize I've summoned a scene from *Mad Men* and I'm very much in the wrong decade.

"No, no. I had no experience with that. I fetched coffee for all the reporters who thought they were smarter than God. Every once in a while, they let me take notes in meetings or order lunch. But I loved it."

"What did you love about it?"

"I loved havin' something all my own. And Corbin, he couldn't stand it, that I took that job, which made me love it even more. It reminded me of when I was a kid and I stole the neighbor boy's bike, hid it in the garage, then told everyone I wrangled it away from a burglar. Then, I wrote a news story about it and posted it to my front door for the neighborhood to read." She lets out a laugh that sounds like *he, he, he.*

"I took a job at a little boutique," I tell her.

"Well, aren't you full of surprises. Tell me why."

I shake my head. "I felt a tug toward it, I guess. It's the opposite of rational. I'd like to think it was brave, but it can't be brave without a plan, can it?"

Odette is quiet for a moment, staring into space, and I think she may fall asleep with her eyes fixated on the wall. Just as I'm about to ask if she's still listening, she speaks. "When you were a kid and teachers or adults used to ask you what you wanted to be when you grew up, what was your answer?"

"I didn't have a good answer then either. It always changed and it varied from doctor to dog walker to magician." The correct answer, I came to understand, was whichever job offered decent money and opportunity, which was why I pursued an accounting degree.

"You'd make an excellent magician," Odette says with a mischievous giggle. "Well then what did you love to do when you were younger?"

I think about it for a moment. It's hard to assess my childhood and see *me*. I rarely find memories anymore that aren't of my mom—of interactions with her, of watching her. I wonder if some loss response inside me prioritized the memories of her because they were deemed most critical to retain. But in salvaging her, I've lost myself a bit.

"I used to dress my cousin Coral up a lot. I loved choosing outfits for her and styling her, I guess." I reflect on my relationship with Coral again and there's a longing similar to the one I feel with my mom.

I think back to the one and only Diwali celebration Auntie Lakshmi and my mom took us to as kids. Coral and I wearing matching too-tight pink-and-green saris sent from our grandparents in India, accessorized with excessive amounts of gold jewelry. Between the four of us, we wore every piece Auntie Lakshmi and my mom owned, brought with them when they came to the states. I stood Coral in front of the mirror, positioning bangles along her wrists and the maang tikka against her forehead.

Turns out, there wasn't a lot of love from the community for two broke single women with daughters in ill-fitting saris. We never attended another cultural celebration again.

"Sounds like you took that job because it's something you've always loved. Perhaps you *are* doing the things you're meant to and your damn brain is just getting in the way."

I sip my vodka. It's too much, Odette's line of thinking.

"Enough about my miserable life trying to act like a grown-up. How are *you*, Odette?"

"I'm fine," she says, batting her hand into the space between us. She stares blankly at the TV before adding, "Being a grown-up is overrated, you know. Getting older is an odd thing. The world makes you feel like . . . you matter a little less each day. That you should *need* a little less from it as time ticks on." She sighs. "My daughter is a lovely host, though I can't help but think I'm in the way a bit, comin' into her space, using her things, testing the balance of her life." She flicks her eyes toward me briefly. "This has been fun, mattering to you."

I stare at Odette. I open my mouth to speak but can't seem to find a response. Odette's words strike like an open palm to my cheek.

I wonder if it's how my mom felt as I started college and made plans for a long-term future outside her home. If she felt me needing her a little less each day. If only she knew it wasn't true. That I needed her then. Still need her now.

I wrap myself around Odette.

"Okay, okay, enough. I didn't come here to heap more sadness on top of your already pitiful state." When I release her, she scoots herself deeper into the couch. "Wanna hear somethin' a bit more interesting?"

I nod.

Her face brightens while her eyes take on an unruly sheen. "My daughter ordered this electrician to come fix the broken ceiling fan in my bedroom at her house the other day," Odette says. "He was a dish. Juicy Justin! Let me tell you, I sprawled out on that bed and watched him work that screwdriver."

"Odette!" I faux scold.

"Oh, don't you worry, there was no afternoon delight in the cards for me." She sighs, then tells me she's got a bad hip anyway.

I smile, appreciating Odette for being the type of person I met just once, who became invested in my success, whatever it may look like.

There are no set paths, only choices. I chose to quit WAP and take the job at The Flatterie. I broke up with Danny. And so far, I don't have one ounce of regret.

Though I'm still guilt-ridden and heartbroken, Odette has done what I've come to rely on Odette to do in the short time I've known her. She's made me a little hopeful again.

"But it would have been nice to get to run your hand along those abs, eh?" she says into the silence wistfully, as though she's been thinking about it this whole time.

After Odette heads to sleep (I insist she take the bedroom), I settle into the couch with my laptop and take a look around my apartment as the light moseying in the living room windows shifts to deep blue.

Before our breakup, Danny offered that I could move in with him, and I momentarily stopped breathing. I picture a little Pomeranian bouncing excitedly to greet me at the door, all fluff and squeal. The thought makes me clench everywhere.

I've made the transition very clearly from *Is there something wrong with me?* to *Yes, there is definitely something wrong with me.* This swirl of indecision within me has caused a constant pinch in my airway.

I scroll through my emails before turning in and there it is. A message from UW, from my interviewer, Sadie Bridges, asking to schedule a time for the "Life at Thirty" interview. FUCK.

24.

I CAN SEE MY "LIFE AT THIRTY" FEATURE NOW. *SHE WAS HIRED RIGHT OUT of school to a prestigious accounting firm only to "resign," and when she couldn't find anything else, she ended up working retail. Oh, and her personal life? A few close friends, but she broke up with her almost-fiancé so she could spend her time pining for a guy she met for thirty minutes who was so drunk he barely remembered. She does this a lot, isolating herself. And did we mention that guy has a girlfriend? A shiny, WNBA-tall one at that.*

They won't feature me as a success story; it'll be a cautionary tale. I'll be the carnival freak show exhibit.

Now, I have only four weeks. Four short weeks to get my life in order to prove to these impressionable college kids (and myself) that I know what the hell I'm doing. And now that I've been proven wrong about Julian, I've got even more work to do.

I barely sleep, my brain riddled with these thoughts.

"I have an idea," a rickety voice whispers into my ear. I open my eyes and jerk at the sight of Odette leaning over me on the couch.

"Whaa?" I sit up and wipe the drying drool from the corner of my mouth.

"I have an idea," she says again, still standing over me, her face disturbingly close to mine.

"What time is it?" I ask, the sky outside still dark.

"Don't know, six something or other. I'm an early riser." She sits beside me as I rub my eye with my palm. "I was thinking. You should join one of those dating websites. Now that you know there are promising connections, let's find you one that's not a liar pants."

I finally open my eyes fully. Odette is smiling at me, those dentures (veneers, maybe?) on full display. She's proud of this idea of hers and by the gooey look on her face, she's been thinking about it all night.

"I've been on dating apps before, they don't work. Not for me."

"There are eight billion people in the world . . ." She pauses, looks up to the ceiling. "Yeah, I think that's right. Almost eight billion people. To think you can be struck alive by just one, well, those are way too poor of odds."

The thought of reinstalling my Dater Baiter app makes me want to throw a pillow over my face and hold it down. I've had it, deleted it, reinstalled it several times over the years, depending on my feelings about dating on any given day or week or year. The last time I deleted it was six weeks before I reunited with Danny after an incredible date with a golden-haired phlebotomist named William, only to see, two days later, his mug shot on the news as the serial carjacker terrorizing the Hilltop neighborhood in Tacoma.

He had pulled out my chair and bought me tacos. It was a huge loss.

Clarence is constantly telling me I would have better luck finding the love of my life on Grindr. Yes, Grindr.

"It's time you meet Clarence," I tell Odette, dialing his number.

"Why are you calling so early when you're unemployed?" It's clear Clarence is out of bed, likely already worked out, showered, and dressed.

"I'm reinstalling my Dater Baiter app. I've hit a new low."

Odette squeals and clasps her hands together in delight beside me on the couch. She looks rather cute engulfed in my purple UW T-shirt. Despite her full suitcase, she eagerly rummaged my T-shirt drawer last night.

"I'll be right over," Clarence says, then hangs up. Working from home serves him well.

Fifteen minutes later, I open my apartment door to find Clarence with a bottle of champagne in each hand.

"Nice," I say as he brushes past me.

"Nice," Odette echoes as she stands from the couch.

"I thought the low point was quitting your job and dumping your boyfriend on the same day. Nice to see there's even farther to fall," he says as he enters. "Who's this?"

"Oh, hi there, I'm Odette. Lovely to meet you."

"Serena?" He bends his eyebrows into a wavy line.

"It's too much to explain right now."

Odette makes her way over to Clarence's side. "What a dish you are," she says, squeezing his right bicep. "Serena, dear, please tell me why we're searching for some rando when you've got all this right here." She squeezes again, noticeably harder.

"I prefer the male variety," he says with a wink.

"Shame," she responds with imposing eye contact.

"It's wrong how excited I am about this." He immediately makes his way to the kitchen and goes to work on opening the first bottle of champagne.

"That we agree on," I say, pulling three flutes from my cupboard and orange juice from the fridge.

He takes the glass from my hand and fills it nearly to the brim, then does the same to Odette's, then his. I fill the slit of room left with OJ.

"Tell me it's a waste of time, that there's nobody of quality on there. Tell me there's a high likelihood of falling for a carjacker again so I have an excuse to be alone forever."

"God, and here I thought I was the dramatic one," he says.

"I know I need a date to Coral's wedding. But it feels too soon." He knows I'm referencing the recent updates with Julian, which I shared with him immediately after. Seeing Julian with a girlfriend has trumped any residual discomfort I had about the breakup with Danny.

"Well, considering Danny posted the breakup news the next day, I guarantee *he's* already dating."

Odette puts her finger and thumb in the shape of an L on her forehead and I'm distracted by the Smash Mouth song playing in my head.

"Oh god, what if I come across Danny's profile?" My entire body puckers at the idea.

"Does he have one?" Clarence asks with a little too much enthusiasm.

"I don't know, but if he does, it would be my luck that we would be suggested as matches."

Clarence laughs and Odette mouths *I like him*, pointing in his direction.

"I'm glad my pathetic life is so amusing."

"Stop it. Actually, I don't think it's a bad idea. I mean, like you said, you'll need a date for Coral's wedding now anyway. And I know you don't have any prospects of your own." Clarence takes a long sip from his glass, then points it at me with conviction. "Let's find you another College Danny. He was a catch. I thought you two would be married, for sure."

"Who's College Danny?" Odette says, eyes wide with delight.

"Same Danny she just broke up with, technically. They dated in college first and had this sort of perfect love back then."

I press my eyes shut at how swoony he's being.

"She met him at a frat party. She thought she would marry him." It's rather amusing that Clarence is willing to share details of my life at seven a.m. with some elderly stranger in my apartment named Odette whom he has never heard of. Yet, here we are.

"He was not *in* a frat. He was just there," I clarify. Danny would never frat. "That entire first night convinced me STDs are airborne and I would catch one just from being there. And the bathroom had stalls with no doors on them, which I wholeheartedly believe was so the brothers could watch female guests pull their pants down. And the whole place smelled like dirty gym socks and stale sex," I tell her. I might as well lean in at this point.

"I can only imagine what that place would look like under a black light," Odette muses.

"Anyway, Clarence collects strays at parties, it's what he does. He introduced me and Danny that night. He was an environmental studies major at the time, which I found attractively noble."

Odette snickers.

"It was hard to meet people in college who had a passion for anything other than drinking," I say defensively. "I thought college was where you met critical thinkers and dreamers and people who were building the foundation to change the world. Instead, I found stoners and trust fund babies who didn't know how to do their laundry."

"Perhaps you were hanging out on the wrong side of campus," Odette offers.

I realize it now as I recount that first encounter with Danny. He once held inconvenient dreams too. He once wanted to save the world. Somewhere along the way, we both succumbed to practicality. I feel a brief closeness to Danny once again.

And, he liked Star Wars, which allowed for a layer of familiarity since I'd seen every movie thanks to Coral's obsession with the franchise. I don't offer this part to Odette; the rest of the details of that night feel like they should be just mine, like Danny's round brown eyes, which sort of popped off his face, reminding me of when I used to stare at those Magic Eye illusions as a kid.

"He got my number that night and we were immediately inseparable," I do share with Odette.

That first meet-up with Danny was one of the best dates I've ever had. He took me on a day date to wander Pike Place and, at first, I wondered why he'd choose something so cliché when we were both natives to this state.

"We take it for granted, how fun the touristy stuff can be," he told me as we strolled the open-air market. It was one of those perfectly sunny spring days in Seattle that made you feel the kind of rolling happiness that accompanies gratitude.

We took our time, revering the buckets of fresh flowers and ice beds of halibut cheeks and jumbo lobster tails. We stood entertained by the spectacle of men in waders tossing fish as they made a full street show of it, all with the Sound glittering just beyond. We snagged pieces of gum from a family visiting from South Carolina and stuck them on the gum wall. We crossed Pike Street and fought the bustling crowd to grab a paper cup of mac and cheese from Beecher's, taste-testing at least a dozen fresh cheese samples before we did. We drank Mac & Jack's beer on a bustling sidewalk using my freshly minted of-age driver's license. He picked up a bag of truffles from a little candy shop a few yards down I didn't know existed and we ate them on the grassy hill overlooking the water, surrounded by dreadlocked hippies and street musicians. He made me laugh, a lot, which was painful for my overstuffed belly, and it was there I got my first look at the dolphin-shaped birthmark under the neck of his Seahawks T-shirt. I wanted to see the whole thing.

I slept with him that first night, at his Ballard studio apartment, where I learned it was his first first-date sex too.

We talked a lot about "getting" each other in a way no one else ever had. We spoke fancifully about who we wanted to be, both individually and together. We'd lie in bed, staring at the dark ceiling, making fantastical plans for our future, saying things like, "When we go to Spain . . ." and "When we both have our high-powered jobs . . ." It was the "when we are married" statement that came out of his mouth often and it, more than all the others, felt like a promise.

I realize now I mostly missed who I was in my life during that time more than I actually missed him when we got back together.

Over the next seven months, he was kind, loving, clever, and I was hard-pressed to find anything negative to say about him. We had the freedom of not knowing that this, in many ways, was the best it would ever get.

That is, until my mom died.

To be fair, expecting a twenty-two-year-old college senior a few months shy of graduation to know instinctively how to be there, how to care for their partner, through the unexpected loss of their only parent is an impossible task. I realized that, even then. Especially when he had changed majors to accounting and was overextending to graduate on time.

When it first happened, he was there. He showed up with obscene floral arrangements, pizza from Pagliacci, and honey lavender ice cream from Molly Moon's. He'd offer to take me out to movies, for walks. He tried to pull me back into our normal life as quickly as possible, thinking that was how I would move on. He had never lost a parent though. He didn't understand it would take more than a week to feel better. He didn't know the person he was getting on the other end of it was never going to be the same one he fell in love with. There was a crack in the vase. I would always be refurbished at best.

College Danny thought my sadness was something he could love out of me. And when he realized he couldn't, he withdrew.

The odd thing about it all was we never even broke up, technically. We never had the sit-down talk where we said we loved each other but needed to go our separate ways. No, it just ended, slowly, like the last drips from an upside-down bucket meandering their way out. And soon enough we hadn't spoken in more than three weeks and on a Thursday in deep winter, I left a box of his things at his front door when I knew he'd be in class. I found a similar box on my front mat when I arrived home from my shift at the campus bookstore a few days later.

Was there one specific thing that turned Danny flat over these last eight years? One incident or moment that stomped the audacious hope right out of him from the time we first met to the time we came back together? Though I don't know for certain, I assume he was nicked away over time, that he was rounded and softened of his sharp edges as he ran into expectation's whetted corners and society's shrewd boundaries.

I fear we were too much the same, Danny and me.

And, I'm starting to see a trend in how I handle it when people disappoint me. I think of Coral and Auntie Lakshmi, and my shoulders round.

Odette nods in appreciation.

Flanked by Odette and Clarence on the couch, I open my Dater Baiter app and begin to scroll. The options are more abysmal than I remember. I sigh, telling myself I should give it a chance. After all, I'm now dateless to Coral's wedding, as Clarence has reminded me. And Melody is breathing down my neck for Danny's last name. I can't tell her he's not coming, not without a replacement name, or she may poison me at the rehearsal dinner to keep the numbers for her precious seating chart even. Besides, I'd take a decent-looking mannequin rather than having to show up and face Coral and Auntie Lakshmi alone.

"Okay, first up," I say when I've scrolled to my first suggested match. "John, thirty-three. Personal trainer. Why are they all personal trainers?"

"Because gyms are where all the man whores hang out," Clarence says. "Keep reading."

"John's bio: 'If you're thick, move along. Newsflash, being well-traveled is not a personality trait and your nose piercing makes me want to barf. Don't slide if you're not ready to ride.'"

An unfortunate place to have begun. I'm concerned about what exactly on my profile screamed "good match" to this guy.

"Leading with hostility is not a good look," Clarence says.

"I don't know, his arms are quite lovely," Odette offers. She reaches over and presses her index and middle fingers to the screen and expands the photo so John's tribal-tatted bicep takes up the entire screen.

I grab the phone back and pass on John the personal trainer.

"Next up: Judd, twenty-six. Pharmaceutical sales rep. His bio reads: 'Guns, buns, and sexy puns. I don't want to come across as cocky, but I want to be your dick-tator. Ethically non-monogamous.' *Ethically non-monogamous?*"

"Hard pass," I proclaim just as Clarence says, "Hell no."

"Wait, not so fast. Is there a picture of his buns? He says buns in his profile, I wanna see said buns." Odette reaches for my phone and I swat her away.

I shake my head, moving on, wondering if I have the fortitude to continue much longer.

"Abraham, thirty-two. Abraham is a Lyft driver. His bio reads, 'Looking for someone to bring to family events so they'll stop trying to set me up. If you can't laugh at yourself, I probably will. My ex-girlfriend scarred me. Literally. She threw a vase at me and it punctured my arm.'" I release the phone into my lap. "Welcome back to the dumpster fire that is online dating," I say.

"I don't know, I kinda like it." Odette cocks her head and licks her lips as she evaluates Abraham. "When we're done with you, can we set up a profile for me? Maybe label me something like Bayou GILF."

Clarence gives me a saturated, heavily approving smile. I don't bother asking Odette how she knows what GILF means.

I go to the kitchen to refill our mimosas and Clarence follows.

"I still can't believe Julian has a girlfriend," I say.

"Maybe she came after you guys met?" Clarence holds his glass out while I refill it.

"I don't know which would be worse."

"I know it sucks he has a girlfriend, but why haven't you looked at the information Terrance sent over?"

"I deleted it. I can't put myself through that. What if he *is* amazing? It'll just hurt that much more. Have you seen it?"

He shakes his head. "No. Terrance refuses to tell me anything. He says you should be the first person to see it, then decide what to do with it from there."

We both sigh.

"The One is out there for you, I know it."

"Did you, Clarence Clement, just say The One? You're the most cynical person I know."

"Yeah, well, love has changed me." He shrugs then grabs his and Odette's glasses and heads back to the couch as I follow.

"Odette, what are you doing?" I ask as Clarence hands her back her glass. She's holding my phone, typing.

"You have a date with"—she squints and presses the phone close to her face—"Craig Dickson. Tomorrow night."

She holds the phone up to show me and somehow, she's had a full conversation with him already.

"Odette! No," I say, grabbing the phone.

"He's a fox. I'll go in your place if you're not willing." She crosses her legs and leans back against the couch, flummoxed.

"Lemme see," Clarence says, taking the phone from me and plopping down next to Odette. "Wow, good work," he says.

I grab the phone. "I know him!"

"You do?" Odette exclaims, though she seems more thrilled than shocked by this new detail.

"I don't *know him* know him, but he's the son of one of my old clients." I look at the phone, review Odette's conversation. "You said I'm into lumberjacks with big axes!"

Clarence shrugs. "Who isn't?"

"You two are not allowed in the same room together ever again."

They high-five and Odette ends the discussion with, "Eight p.m. tomorrow, at a place called the Flowerbox. Maybe things will end with him . . . in *your* flower box." They both say the last bit in unison and high-five again.

And that's how my first date in over a year came to be.

25.

After Clarence leaves, Odette entertains herself, binge-watching some show with an awful lot of sex scenes while I scour job boards, catching on those that are for brand management or e-commerce. I read through the descriptions, jotting down notes about position requirements and my gaps in correlation to those requirements.

I have a hard time thinking about these types of skills and roles in new companies though. As I take these notes in the margins of my notebook (the same one that still holds the list about Julian) and on the back of unopened pieces of mail, I can only seem to think of Tatiana and The Flatterie. About how I want to do these things for *it*, for *her*.

Midday, I look up to find Odette rewinding a kitchen counter love-making scene, the woman slapping the man's bare ass with a spatula, and I wonder what Netflix hole she dove into, how out of whack my recommendations list is going to be.

Reviewing my work again, I realize I know what I want. Through the notes and random lines scrawled about on various items at my desk, I've essentially built the job description for the role I crave. I want to help Tatiana take The Flatterie online, open its doors to the world.

I wish I could sign up for marketing classes at night so I can learn how to launch an online business, but I can't justify the spend. So instead, I take advantage of every free resource I unearth. And I'm surprised to identify a plethora of options, once I begin looking. There's more information on the first page of Google results than I can objectively classify, and I am quickly convinced I can obtain a full bachelor's degree worth of information on my own.

And, I'm starting to wonder if soon The Flatterie will be considered a start-up like Julian's company.

Julian.

My memories of him are all tainted like someone poured gasoline over them and lit them on fire. Because now I can't see our first interaction with the abandon I initially had—as this kismet-type encounter that I believed he felt as deeply as I did. Because now I know that, to him, it was just an indulgent conversation with some random girl on vacation. Because now I know he flew home to his glossy girlfriend, and I was gone from his mind the second he left that bar on Bourbon Street. Because everything he told me was a lie.

But, back to work.

For the past two weeks since taking the job at The Flatterie, I've been filling my time absorbing as much information as I can about what it takes to run an online business, specifically to launch and run an online boutique. I've started building a presentation for Tatiana. She doesn't know I've been doing any of this. That I think I can help her expand The Flatterie in big ways. I've been cramming as much information into my brain as I can so we can get a site up as quickly as possible once I convince her it's the logical next step for her business. And that I am the one who can help her do it.

If my article in the *UW Daily* won't feature me as a successful accountant at a prestigious firm, and certainly won't profile an almost-fiancé, then perhaps I can show them some road-less-traveled version of success in my career.

Craig Dickson lives in a Ballard waterfront home (paid for by Sutton and Carson per their taxes) with his two French bulldogs named Algorithm and Outlier. This is the only information Odette is willing to share with me from his profile, as she deleted her conversation with him (as me) before I could read through it fully. She did show me one picture—him at a park with his two Frenchies—and I will admit, he's outdoorsy handsome. Far "woodsier" than I would have assumed from Sutton's sales points and my own imaginings of a wealthy Dickson offspring pushing forty. He looks far more laid-back in his profile pictures than the one Sutton sent me during my last week at WAP.

"If you need me, I'll be right here," Odette whispers, taking a seat at the bar. She has a holiday-red silk scarf wrapped around her silver pouf of hair and thickly-rimmed black sunglasses covering her eyes in the darkened restaurant. It's also seven forty-five p.m. and already largely dark outside.

"You're hardly discreet," I tell her before asking the bartender for an extra dirty martini, the drink she preemptively asked I order her on the drive over. It's clear Odette believes she is in a Russian spy movie.

"Nonsense. Nobody pays attention to an old lady." She bats her hand and eagerly accepts her drink from the bartender. "Now hurry, go outside and arrive again."

"You better hope this goes well, or you'll be out on the street," I tell her, before slipping back into my jacket. A young man at the bar looks up at me with a harsh expression. "She's not as sweet as she looks," I tell him as she points a lush smile in his direction.

Back outside, I steel myself for dinner with Craig Dickson. It's been over a year since I've been on a real date—one that wasn't at The Cheesecake Factory or with a gift card or on my couch. I cannot believe my first one back is with Craig Dickson. From what Sutton has told me about him, I find it surprising he would be on the apps at all, elusive as he is (per his mom) when it comes to love.

It's just dinner. The wind gusts and I pull my jacket tighter around me.

"Serena?"

I turn to find a guy standing behind me, who looks to be Craig Dickson's more weathered, less exercised brother. He's leaning into the Pacific Northwest backdrop of it all with a plaid shirt and the wiry beard his mother hates so much and I wonder if he's chosen his shirt because of Odette's comment about lumberjacks.

It's not a good start.

"Yes. Craig?" I say, extending a hand to this Dater Baiter n' switch.

He nods, smiles, and shakes my hand aggressively, a mouthful of many, many teeth staring back at me.

"I wasn't sure it was you."

He's unperturbed by my comment.

"After you," he says, pulling open the thick oak door.

At the bar, Odette is ordering her second martini.

"This is a cool spot," I muse after we are seated and we both unfold our napkins into our laps and look around, me pretending I wasn't previously inside moments before we met outside.

We are seated in the back corner of the restaurant, thankfully, far away from the raucous bar. As far as wing women go, Odette is by all accounts a pretty shitty one, having forgotten about me completely, it seems. She's chatting up the guy at the bar who likely believes she's my verbally abused white grandma.

"Yeah, I dated the bartender's sister once," he says, pointing in that direction. "So, are you vegan?" he asks when he's turned to face me again.

"No."

"Cool, cool. Last Dater Baiter date I went on, the girl was vegan and it was not cool." He says the *not cool* part with his eyes stretched wide.

"Right," I say, taking a sip from my water glass. I set it down and he then picks it up, taking a sip from the same glass, despite having a full, separate glass on his side of the table. *Why?*

"Do you think rabbits are appropriate pets?"

"Huh?" I say, still distracted by the fact that he just drank out of my glass.

"Rabbits." He says, then looks at me expectantly. When my face seizes with confusion, he repeats, "Do you think rabbits are appropriate pets?"

"Oh, I uh, I don't know, I guess?"

"Mmmm," he says, then leans back in his chair and folds his arms. Then almost immediately, he leans forward and pulls the bread basket toward him. There's a variety of offerings inside, and I watch in horror as he grabs each one in his palm, pulls it out, examines it (even smelling a few), then puts it back, eventually choosing a block of sourdough.

I push my bread plate aside.

"This girl I went on a date with last week, she had a rabbit." He takes a bite of bread—rather he moves his mouth to the piece in his hand, crashes his teeth down around it and pulls until a morsel separates, then sucks it into his mouth.

"Sounds like you go on a lot of first dates."

He nods as he chews. "Yeah. It's all a numbers game, right?" He smiles, open-mouthed, so I can see the mangled piece of bread on his tongue, atop his bottom row of molars. I wonder how Carson and Sutton ended up with a son like this. It's further validation that money doesn't solve all. And that it indeed doesn't buy class.

It's evident I feel nothing toward Craig Dickson. Well, not nothing. I feel annoyance about the tiny breadcrumbs stuck to his beard and his lack of social hygiene etiquette.

"So in your messages, you said you collected a lot of beads down at Mardi Gras." He gives me the most unsubtle wink imaginable, mouth open and all.

"Did I say that?"

He nods.

"What I meant was, I avoided getting beads." I wink back at him as I say "getting beads."

"Likely better off, those things are probably full of lead." He laughs and my heart plummets to my stomach. Even now, after knowing Julian lied to me, has a girlfriend, and as I'm on a date, I think of him with painful longing.

"Do you like uncircumcised penises?"

"I'm sorry, what?"

"Some girls don't like a hood, I'm finding."

"I think I'm gonna vomit," I say, rising from the table.

"Oh, you're sick?"

"Yes. That's it. I'm sick." I cough delicately into my fist. I thought I would tell him over the course of our meal that I know his parents. That it would make for a charming anecdote. Hardly matters now.

At the bar, Odette is holding court, the bartender and three other young men surrounding her. She says something, slaps her palm against the bartop, and they all burst into obscene laughter.

"Yeah, you should go then. Imma eat," he says, pointing both burly thumbs toward the table.

"You do that," I say, then I make my way to the bar.

"Oh dear," Odette says when she sees me, then downs the remainder of her martini with an audible "Ah" as she sets the glass back down. "That bad?"

"He's a Corbin, not a Marv," I tell her through gritted teeth.

She nods in understanding and scoots out of the bar stool.

"Odette! Leaving so soon?" the guy next to her says, emphasizing his disappointment.

"Gotta run, honey. You go get that ring. She's not gonna wait forever," she says, wagging her finger at him. He puts his hands up in acceptance and defeat.

We both look back at Craig as he rips at another piece of bread. "I once read beards carry more germs than toilet seats," Odette says as we step into the brisk evening air.

Somehow, Odette and Clarence convince me to go on three more Dater Baiter dates. Odette, Clarence, and Terrance hang at the bar for the other three, drinking and laughing while I sit through more wretched dinners. There's John, the personal trainer (Odette's choice), who is in fact a man whore who sleeps with all his clients. There's Theo, an ER nurse who is a little too excited to talk about the dead bodies he's encountered. And Paul, a barista (also Odette's choice) who, before our meals have arrived, rattles off a long list of qualities he hates in women, which included making more money than him and not possessing a deep-rooted love for Jimi Hendrix.

We four fall, exhausted, onto my couch after the last one.

"It's a sad state of affairs out there," Clarence says, his forearm pressed to his head dramatically as if *he* were the one enduring the horrid encounters. I watch him squeeze Terrance's hand. "Coral would absolutely, masterfully spin this misfortune that is your new dating life."

I want to argue, but I know he's right. In times like these, my cousin who used to be like a sister would have lightened the hopelessness with her fairy-tale view of the world.

As I sit, head slung over the back of the couch, I worry I may never feel that pull toward another person again. But if these dates have proven anything, it's that I'm not willing to settle.

The evening is made worse by a text from Melody to the Happily Everett After chat: *Wedding emergency!!!!! Meet @ Hang Glider Bar at 8 pm tomorrow night!!!!!* Melody uses exclamation points like star ratings. Her use of five exclamation points means whatever is going on, it's five-out-of-five-stars dire. I just hope it's not a ploy to pin me down in person to extract details of my nonexistent wedding date.

26.

By the time Clarence and I find parking and trek the half mile to the entrance of the Hang Glider Bar, we are the last of the bridesmaids to arrive. Odette flew home this morning and, without her here planning horrid dates and supporting my pursuits, a little of the wind in my sails is gone.

"I assume this was Melody's choice of locations," Clarence says as we enter. It's some trendy new spot with alcohol bottles displayed on floor-to-ceiling shelves like books on bookshelves and a specialty cocktail menu that does not include a drink under twenty-five dollars. I checked beforehand.

I smooth the dew from my hair and wipe the wetness against my black jeans. I question, as I always do, why I bothered to straighten my hair, as I can already feel the frizzy outer layer that has emerged.

The group is easy to find, seated at a table in the middle of the action, the best spot in the house. I imagine Melody demanded it when she arrived.

The other five bridesmaids are all huddled around the table, Melody next to Coral with her arm around her shoulders.

"Okay, they're here. Now can you fill us in?" Melody says when we approach. I can hear the disdain in her voice that we are (glances at my phone) six minutes late. I want to point out that she chose a location without ample parking, but I refrain.

"Hello, everyone. Sorry we're late," I say, removing my jacket and taking the empty seat across from Coral and Melody.

"Yes, dreadfully sorry," Clarence quips, eyes on Melody.

Coral looks up at me with big, watery eyes that look a lot like mine, and I feel a pang of loss sharply in my belly. I miss her. I miss having a family.

"Thank you all for coming, I know I've asked a lot of you guys lately," she says, sniffling.

"Nonsense, it's our absolute honor! Now tell us what is going on," Melody says, hugging Coral in closer. I observe their interaction as Melody moves Coral's hair off her face and rubs circles into her back. My throat clenches in response. It's jealousy I'm feeling. Absolute, unfiltered jealousy. If my mom hadn't died, if things hadn't happened the way they did after, it would be me who is maid of honor. But Melody is the person, outside of her fiancé, Everett, who Coral now turns to in moments of distress or joy.

"Should we order drinks?" Coral asks, sniffling and holding back tears. "I hear they have a drink called a Paper Plane that's good."

"Coral, yes, we will order drinks. Lots of drinks. But first, tell us what's going on." Melody's tone is firm and I'm wondering if they teach empathy in law school. If they do, I'm certain she got an F. I've been up at all hours of the night working on my presentation for Tatiana, yet I'm not acting like an impatient turd.

Coral looks around the table, making eye contact with each of us, lingering on me. "I just, I don't think I can do it," she squeaks out. Her eyes are brimming with tears and she's still looking at me when she says this. I feel my heart pull toward her, an ache and longing to be the one with my arm around her offering consolation.

"What happened?" Melody asks.

Coral blots at the corners of her eyes with a napkin. A waitress arrives.

"Three bottles of chardonnay please," Melody says to the waitress without asking anyone what they want.

Clarence beside me scoffs.

"And a Paper Plane, please!" I yell. The waitress gives me a nod and Melody shoots me a dirty look. *It's for Coral,* I tell her with my eyes.

When the waitress leaves, we all look to Coral again, awaiting the bomb she is inevitably about to drop about why she has decided she may not be able to go through with the wedding. If Everett cheated on her, I'll do something. I'm unsure what it is that I will do exactly, but it will be vengeful.

I don't know Everett well, but I have ascertained a few details about him, thanks to the engagement party and the bridal shower, which predated the bachelorette trip. Coral and Everett work together at a rubber manufacturing company. He's a sales manager, though not hers. She explained to me after a few drinks at one of the Bourbon Street bars what it means to be a *global materials science company that focuses on fluoropolymer technology,* though I didn't manage to grasp it. Anyway, they make and sell rubber.

Coral and Everett kept their relationship a secret for over a year before finally coming out. By *coming out* I mean they were caught making out in a TacoTime parking lot during the lunch hour by one of the sales reps on his team.

At the bridal shower, Melody regaled us all with the story of how they fell in love. How Everett would find excuses to walk by her desk on the far side of the building. How he finally worked up the nerve to ask her out. How their first date was a day of wine, exploring the Woodinville tasting rooms, where he learned of the ease with which Coral vomits. How after that first date, after Everett dabbed wet paper towels at the hem of her white shorts to clear the puke stain, they became exclusive. To her credit, Melody masterfully wove in several jokes about rubbers.

I had to exit the room that day, taking solace in one of Melody's many bathrooms, so Coral or my Auntie Lakshmi wouldn't see me cry. I've missed so much in Coral's life. But, missing her fall in love with her future husband, this one tugs at my insides like the pressure of a taut rubber band. A rubber band Melody likely stole from the rubber company Coral and Everett work for and had implanted in me while I slept in New Orleans.

Coral blows her nose into her napkin then rubs at it aggressively. "Everett doesn't want to go to India for our honeymoon!" she cries.

Clarence and I exchange a look. Is *this* the crisis?

"Is India a honeymoon destination?" Melody scrunches her face in confusion. "And wait. You haven't booked your honeymoon yet? Your wedding is a month away."

"We haven't booked it because we can't agree on where to go. I want to go to India, visit family, but he wants to cruise the Mexican Riviera! He says it's too much and too far, a trip to India." She sobs as if she has just told us Everett has been cheating on her their entire relationship. Or that he's dying. "What does it say about us, about our relationship, that we can't even agree on where to go for our honeymoon, a trip intended to be a celebration of our marriage!"

Melody looks at me as if I should know what to say. I don't. I don't because I no longer know Coral, not the way I used to. I try anyway. "Coral, have you explained to him why you want to go to India? That our grandparents are there, that they are getting older, and that you haven't seen them since we were little?" Melody has a perplexed look on her face. "Our grandparents," I repeat, feeling a renewed kinship to Coral. We share grandparents. Grandparents who were too elderly to fly across the world to bury their daughter. We are family.

Coral sniffles, swipes at her nose with the soggy napkin in her hand. "I did. I mean, I mentioned it, yes."

I make my way around the table and shove myself between her and Melody. I stroke her long, dark hair that looks like mine. "I'm sure if you try again, if you really explain it to him, he'll be more open to the idea." The vein in my neck is pulsing and I start to sweat. I, of all people, am trying to console Coral because someone she loves is not understanding the importance of family. Without this wedding, it's unclear when Coral and I would have ever spoken again. I tried to give them the benefit of the doubt, that everyone handles grief in their own way, but Coral and her mom are my only family, local at least, and they left me to figure it all out on my own once my mom's funeral was over. Or at least, that's how it felt at the time.

The opening in my heart's memory slams closed again.

"I'm sure it will all work out," I say, making my way back around the table to my seat.

"Have you ever felt this way? With Danny?" she asks across the table. It's ironic she's saying this because she never actually met Danny. Coral's only knowledge of Danny is that he was to be my plus one to her wedding, and that he's the guy from college who, whenever she asked to meet, I insisted we wait until graduation so it would be momentous. She doesn't even know his last name, as Melody has eloquently pointed out in her many group texts.

"Danny and I broke up," I tell her. She looks like she may cry again, and I think perhaps she feels it too. The loss of these last eight years between us. Of being a bystander to a life you were once a main character in. I look into her eyes and it's like a flashing billboard: *You've Missed Big Things*, it screams. I want to tell her now, as we share this scarce moment of connection, that I would take back my part in all of it. That I would burn that letter before she ever saw it. In a heartbeat, I would, if it meant we could have this time back.

"I'm sorry. What happened?" she asks in a childlike tone.

What happened? I contemplate this. What did actually happen? I met Julian at her bachelorette party. I felt what might have been love at first sight, though I'm still trying to determine if I believe such a thing exists. I then proceeded to completely upend my life because of whatever spell he put me under. I've spent the time I should have been looking for a new job looking for him, only to succeed in finding him *and* his girlfriend.

"I realized I need more."

She presses her eyebrows together and I notice how over groomed they have become the closer we get to the wedding, severely straight-edged, which looks quite odd as she frowns.

I feel like I've said the wrong thing.

It makes me wonder again, albeit for a sliver of time, if I've made a mistake in letting Danny go.

"Maybe that's it," she says, a single tear gliding down her blushed cheek. "Maybe I need more than what Everett and I have." Though we are sitting across the table from one another, it feels like an intimate conversation. The other ladies and Clarence have all dispersed. Only Melody remains at the table, though she's got her back to us, chatting with some random guy who looks like Chris Evans, if Chris Evans were fifty pounds heavier with zigzagging teeth.

I don't know what to say to Coral. It's certainly not something I can answer for her, just as Odette couldn't answer it for me. Our drinks arrive and as the waitress pours the wine, I slide the Paper Plane in front of Coral. She gives me a weak smile of appreciation.

"Can you picture your life without him?" I ask her. She sighs, presses her eyebrows together again, and I can see she's likely gotten Botox on her eleven lines because they don't press together the way they used to. Even so, it's apparent she's putting real thought into the question.

"No," she says, and I swear there is relief on her face. "No, I can't imagine my life without him."

We both smile and she jumps from her chair and in an instant she is next to me, throwing her arms around my shoulders. I've missed her and the connection I feel to my mother through her. I let her hug me, let the warmth seep into my deepest, most impermeable parts.

When she releases after a long while she looks at me and asks, "Can you picture your life without Danny?"

I don't need long to answer. "Yes, I absolutely can," I tell her as Julian's face flicks across my mind like the glint of a coin in the sun. Perhaps I've given up on Julian too quickly. I too had a significant other when we met, so how can I judge him so harshly? Perhaps he's been contemplating a breakup of his own since meeting me. Or, perhaps seeing me again even triggered one. Who knows? What I do know is that Julian is still out there in Chamber Hill, the neighborhood I've come to consider my own.

"Oh my gosh, I don't know why I didn't think of it before!" Coral says, her voice now electrified and shrill.

"What?"

"Well, I know why I didn't consider it. Because you had Danny, but now . . ." Coral's tears are gone and she looks as though she was never crying, never contemplating calling off her wedding.

"What are you talking about, Coral?"

"This is perfect. You and Pete!"

"Pete? As in Everett's groomsman who I'm walking down the aisle with?"

"Yes! He's single. He asked Everett *a lot* of questions about you after the engagement party."

I attempt to recall what I know about Pete. I spent most of the night of the engagement party anxiety-ridden about being in the same room with Coral and Auntie Lakshmi. Coral introduced me to Pete that night, we chatted for a moment, he joked about what type of entrance we might make into the wedding reception, and that was about it. I can hardly recall his face, though I'm inclined to believe it was pleasant. He didn't seem to have any particular oddities when we met. I wonder if I am ready to start dating after the Dater Baiter debacles, if Pete is a potential prospect, or if I want anyone at all if his name is not Julian. I do need a date for the wedding though. I'll need someone to distract me from the burden and unease of the day.

"Can I give him your number?" Coral is bouncing in her chair, something she does when she's excited dating back to when we were kids. It makes me think of an eight-year-old Coral, ten-year-old me, sitting at the counter of my childhood apartment, sneaking shredded cheese out of plastic bins from the refrigerator as she described in detail the type of wedding she would have. "Outdoor, next to the water. A big tent for the reception with chandeliers and moss. I wonder if I could rent fairies to fly around," she said, and we both giggled.

You'll be engaged to the best man.

Pete is not the best man, but he is a groomsman and my escort down the aisle. Perhaps some version of her childhood dream can come true. And if it does, perhaps it will erase some of the time we've lost.

Coral is looking at me so hopefully, I can't seem to say no.

"I'll think about it," I concede, and she squeals with delight.

This night, for all its complexities, leaves me lighter.

I think I'm about to make a clean escape, when Melody catches Clarence and I at the door. She squeezes my elbow, pointed fingernails pressing into my skin. "Wedding date details. Now." She squeezes harder. "I heard you tell Coral you broke up with Danny. Who's your new plus one? There's going to be one, right? I do not have time to redo the entire seating chart . . . again." Melody's eyes are bulging and her neck is strained and she looks on the verge of something popping—a vein or a disc perhaps. She glares at Clarence when she says *again*, which I assume is in reference to Terrance as Clarence's recent wedding date addition.

"I'll get right on that," I tell her as Clarence ushers me from her vise grip and out the door.

27.

I ENTER THE BOUTIQUE FIFTEEN MINUTES EARLY, LAPTOP UNDER MY ARM and a nervous twitch in my left eyelid. It's funny, really. I've never been this intimidated for a presentation, ever. Not in college in front of a lecture hall full of human calculator classmates. Not each time I walked into the conference room at WAP to meet with my wealthy, formidable clients. But somehow, presenting to Tatiana about taking her business online has me jittery.

"Morning, thank you," she says as I hand her coffee, part of my new morning routine.

I roll my shoulders back, clear my throat. "I'd like to meet with you after we close today."

She raises her eyebrows at me. "Oh?" she says, then sips her coffee. "Please tell me you didn't find a real job already and are leaving me, because I will be devastated."

"No, but I appreciate the devastation it would cause." I pause and take a sip of my coffee to build suspense or nerve, unsure of which. "I've been thinking about ways to expand the business, as you've mentioned you'd like to do. I have some ideas I'd like to present to you."

She raises her eyebrows again. "Oh," she says. "Okay, then. I look forward to it." She squeezes my shoulder then makes her way to the front of the store to greet the first customer of the morning.

The day goes by surprisingly fast. It typically does nowadays. I barely notice hours pass when I'm helping clients here. At WAP, I would sometimes glance at the clock to realize only two minutes had clicked by since the last time I looked. I know most people won't consider my job at The Flatterie "more" than what I had at WAP. But I love it. And I didn't even know I wanted it, or perhaps needed it, until it revealed itself to me.

There's a steady stream of customers throughout the day and I have become confident in my recommendations to clients. Tatiana has spent significant time with me, teaching me how to dress the many forms of the woman's body. I've already reorganized my closet at home, featuring first any items I own that could end up on the *Hips* rack at The Flatterie. Some regular clients have even referred to me as Tatiana's protégé. She is the most expert stylist there could possibly be, so it's a sublime compliment.

One of our last customers of the day is a teenage girl with a brown bob haircut in a baggy sweatshirt and ragged jean shorts. When she tells me she's never been here before, I excitedly describe the store and our mission, the way Tatiana had to me the first time I stepped in. "Is there an area you'd like to flatter or feature?" I ask.

"I'd like to hide my chest," she says, eyes cast to the floor. *Then don't ever go to Mardi Gras,* I think to tell her.

My best guess is she is about sixteen. Sixteen and well-developed, and I can only imagine what it must be like for her. I think of the girls who developed early when I was in school—ogled by both guys and girls and almost always unfairly labeled *sluts*.

I spend twenty minutes with the girl, whose name, I learn, is Bella. I load her up with a wrap dress, camis for layering, a square-neck smocked crop top, silk blouses, a twist-front crop in navy blue *and* yellow and thick-strapped tanks.

She buys almost all of it and is so happy she's practically bouncing out of the store when she leaves. But not before hugging me. I feel more satisfaction than I ever have at work.

As closing time draws near, I think of one of my conversations with Odette. How she asked me what I enjoyed doing as a kid. I look around the store. Maybe she's right. Perhaps I didn't just fall into this. This notion gives me an extra boost of confidence as my presentation draws near.

When the sky outside has turned to purple, the air goose-bump inducing, Tatianna closes the front door, turns the lock, and slaps her hands on her thighs.

"Okay! What a day!" she says. "Now, I'm dying to hear what you've been working on."

We head to the back room and huddle together around my laptop screen. I wish we were doing this over cocktails. I wish I had a collection of Odette's airplane bottles shoved into my purse to calm my nerves.

Tatiana watches eagerly as I open my laptop.

"When I first began working for you at The Flatterie, you told me your goal was to hire more help so you could continue to travel, to go on adventures. And you also shared with me your ultimate vision for this brand was to take it online, though the thought of doing so was overwhelming. But, taking this business online will allow you the freedom you need to do the things you love. You can serve other women while also serving yourself." I click on the first slide after the cover page. It includes a picture of an elephant at a sanctuary in Thailand, a mahout standing next to her elephant. Next to it, the face of a bookshop in Porto. I've even thrown in a picture of a chocolate croissant for good measure.

Tatiana smiles. I smile. I've got her attention.

"Your sales from this one store location are impressive, Tatiana. In fact, from a revenue standpoint, this one retail location does better than eighty-eight percent of stores of its kind, although we both know The Flatterie is in a league of its own. And your word-of-mouth and referral business, while largely untracked, I estimate to be roughly seventy-five to eighty percent of your new business. Imagine what that could mean for sales if we expanded beyond one store location to online."

I scroll to the next page of my presentation, where I have built a mockup of a homepage for The Flatterie website. It looks like the pages of old fashion magazines, updated with diverse women. The women I wish I'd seen growing up. I never saw Indian models with big hips. But she's there, on this homepage archetype, mixed in with many others.

Tatiana's face is fixed on the screen, her eyes moving slowly across every image, every word. She smiles as she reads the tagline aloud: "The Flatterie will get you everywhere."

"I realize this is a huge undertaking, and there's a lot that has to happen, but I've been reading up nonstop. I've found a hosting platform with a beautiful template with the bones of the site already built. I've scoured over the financials and have set a budget for the additional inventory, shipping costs, website hosting, all of it." I scroll to the next slide, which runs through the financials. "As you can see, you can do this without a loan of any kind, but it would take some investment on your end." On the screen, I point out the key budget points.

"Now, you're likely wondering if *I* am the right person to do this. If I'm capable of this huge undertaking of expanding your business online. I know I don't have the experience, but I have conducted a significant amount of research. And as you know, I can expertly manage the financial component."

Tatiana is nodding along.

The next slide is the one I'm most nervous to present. It's a job description for an e-commerce marketing manager position. For me. I'm not so brash to suggest she just hand me this newly created role today with no experience after working for her only a handful of weeks. But I am just brazen enough to suggest I earn it once the site is live and certain benchmarks of sales are hit. Benchmarks I have put considerable thought and research into and have outlined in detail in my presentation.

"So as you can see, I would have a significant, interested stake in ensuring the business's online success."

I walk her through the remaining slides, which include more bullets about why I am the right person to lead this charge.

By the end, Tatiana is still smiling, though her arms are crossed tight against her chest. "I knew I hired you—someone with very little retail experience—for a reason. Well done."

"So what do you say? Are you ready to move forward?" I ask.

Tatiana hesitates.

There's a nagging inside me. My heartbeat sounds like a ticking clock in my ears. I have a little over two weeks until the *UW Daily* "Life at Thirty" feature. And wouldn't it be impressive to be able to say I took this one location, this one store to a successful online launch in that time?

That would be a feature-worthy story.

"What about this?" I say. "I'll work on it on my own time, after hours. I'll get the site up and running. I'll work with our vendors, set this room up for temporary shipping, and hire temporary help as needed. I'll work in the store by day and stuff shipping boxes back here by night if I need to. I know we can do this."

Tatiana gives me a thoughtful stare. After a long while, she sighs. "Okay, Serena. I'm going to let you test this."

I wrap myself around her.

"But it's a test. This is a huge undertaking in which neither of us has real experience. And, I can't let you do it for free, so please use your time wisely."

"Thank you, thank you! I will ensure this is a success, Tatiana. Thank you."

It's the only time I've left the store not thinking about Julian. I rush home to start building my first website. There will be no room for much else these next few weeks.

28.

I'VE BEEN HEADS DOWN WORKING ON THE FLATTERIE WEBSITE FOR THE past week with barely any sleep and absolutely no social life. I've uploaded pictures and written descriptions of the clothing pieces Tatiana has chosen to launch with. The item description I just finished is for a magenta tunic for the *Butt* section. *The long, flowy fit of this blouse falls just below the backside. This, along with the three-quarter-length sleeves, serves to flatter the Butt section of the body. Pairing suggestion: the Georgia black leggings.* By the way, those leggings are named after Georgia O'Keeffe. After I told Tatiana my favorite dress reminded me of a Monet, we decided to name all the clothing pieces after famous artists.

In the daze and pace of work, Julian still torments my thoughts. I don't know Julian.

I don't know his favorite movie, his favorite food. I don't know his goals or dreams. I don't know if he wears socks to bed or flosses regularly. I don't know if he invests in mutual funds. I don't know if he tips well. I don't know if he wants kids or how many. Hell, he may already have some. This other, much longer list about Julian, goes on and on.

My stomach burns with a radiating sting.

I shuffle around in my bed that night, unable to shake the feeling that something's not right.

When the dull morning gray begins to emerge, I sigh and grab my phone from the nightstand. I have a Dater Baiter notification. *You up?* Says the message from Craig Dickson, from 12:45 a.m.

I just got *You up'd* by Craig "uncircumcised" Dickson. It's almost as low of a dating moment as seeing the serial carjacker's mugshot. I let out a guttural growl.

As I'm about to throw my phone against the wall in disgust, it pings with a new Dater Baiter message. An awaiting match. I open the app and find a familiar face.

Pete, 32

Civil Engineer

Bio: NSYNC over Backstreet. I own a vehicle with a roof rack. I like long walks and I cannot lie. Emotionally available women to the front.

"Wait, what is that smile?" Clarence says, standing in my doorway.

"You scared me! I forgot you were here," I say, palm to chest. Clarence has taken to sleeping on my couch on the evenings Terrance works late. It's a bit incomprehensible, how quickly he's grown accustomed to having a partner in bed beside him, and how uncomfortable he now is when that comfort is absent.

"First you wake me up with your growling, now you're smiling." Clarence grabs the phone from my hand. "He's cute."

"It's Pete. The groomsman I'm walking down the aisle with at Coral and Everett's wedding. The guy Coral wants to set me up with."

"Yes!" I met him at the engagement party. Good hair."

I take the phone from Clarence and hold it up for inspection. Pete has a cute photo. He's not wearing a ski mask at the top of a mountain or a tacky Halloween costume. It's not a shirtless selfie in the bathroom mirror. There's no dirty-as-a-toilet-bowl beard. There's nothing repulsive about the picture at all. It's just him, looking at the camera, smiling. He's sitting on an outdoor restaurant patio from the looks of it, though it's hard to tell exactly. He's got this floppy, dark curly hair that hangs to one side and a bright smile with kind eyes that for a moment make me think of Danny.

I click the heart on Pete's profile.

"There's nothing more romantic than falling in love at a wedding," Clarence muses groggily.

"What has happened to you?" I ask, fighting a smile. I fail and we grin sleepily at one another for a moment, taking in the magnitude of the answer to my question.

I go back to reviewing Pete's profile picture. He's more handsome than I remember and I hope the picture hasn't been photoshopped. As I am examining his photo, I get a message from Pete in response to my heart of his profile. Apparently, he's an early riser, or maybe he also can't sleep because he's reeling over a recent revelation about a once-thought soulmate.

Go Huskies, his message says, likely in reference to the UW T-shirt I'm wearing in my profile picture. I wonder for a moment if he realizes it's me, his default wedding date, but then he follows up with: *Coral let me know you are recently single. I'd like to say I'm sorry, but that would be insincere.*

I smile. Is this flirting?

"What is happening?!" Clarence says, scooting closer to look over my shoulder, catching up on our interaction. "Respond with something funny. But flirty. But not too out there to where he thinks you're not serious. Something like, *It's too early to be insincere*, with a winky face emoji."

"Those are way too many rules," I say, shaking my head.

I reply: *How do you think the other members of NSYNC felt about having to be backup singers to Justin on the "Gone" single? Do you think they knew it was the beginning of the end?*

I think Joey Fatone was just happy to be there, he responds and I laugh. A second later, Clarence laughs from over my shoulder. If I'm going to show up dateless to this wedding, perhaps Pete and I can at least be in a pseudo coupling.

Within a few more messages, we've made plans for coffee early next week. One small break from working on The Flatterie site is reasonable.

"Please don't say bye, bye, bye to this one," Clarence muses, and I hit him in the face with a pillow.

My phone dings again and this time it's an email from Sadie Bridges, the editor of the *UW Daily*, expressing her excitement for our upcoming interview, confirming the logistics.

I should probably just stop looking at my phone altogether.

29.

Pete and I meet for coffee on a Monday afternoon because my schedule is now a retail one and not a corporate one. Pete works a nine-to-five but obliges and agrees to sneak out midday, our compromise being I meet him at the coffee shop on the ground floor of his office's Seattle high-rise.

Pete is a civil engineer who designs roadways. So, when the 405 is backed up during peak rush hour due to a road expansion project, it's likely Pete's fault. I try not to hold it against him.

When I walk in, I find Pete has already arrived. He's standing close to the door, smiling as I enter, wearing a plaid button-down shirt over dark jeans and tan dress shoes. It's an easy, attractive style, and I place his fashion sense in the pros column of the list about Pete I've started in my head. I'm hopeful Pete's list will push Julian's out of my heart completely. There are only two additional items on the list so far, both in the pros column: 1) he's friends with Coral and Everett, and 2) he's a fan of NSYNC. Now that I've seen it in person when I'm actually paying attention, I might add his floppy curly hair to the pros list as well.

"Serena," he says when he makes his way to my side. He leans in for an embrace and I note he smells like a lemon sugar cookie, and I wonder if some old girlfriend got him hooked on Bath & Body Works lotions.

We place our orders (a caramel macchiato for me, cappuccino for him) and we choose a table in the back corner against the windows. There are skyscrapers in all directions, and I can't see much except Fifth Avenue and the lobby floors of the buildings around us. They are gray to match the early May showers of the afternoon sky.

"I want to apologize," he says abruptly once we've sat down.

"What could you possibly have to apologize for?"

"If I came off as rude when I implied I was happy about your breakup."

The truth is, I haven't missed Danny. It's jarring, how little he's been on my mind, except to realize that in the second go of it with us, the magic was all but gone, replaced by pure practicality. "I don't think you were rude."

"Okay great. I also feel like I should apologize to Joey Fatone, but I don't have his number."

I smile and he seems to enjoy it.

"Seriously, though. I'm glad we're doing this, Serena." Pete smiles back and I take note of his nice teeth and crooked smile that rises higher on the left than the right. The sound of my name echoes against the panes of the raindrop-beaded windows and the square metal table between us long after he's said it.

I do the thing I know I will. I anticipate it before it even happens. I compare Pete's silly grin to Julian's. I listen intently to the tenor of my name from his crooked lips and await that zing up my spine. The one I felt when Julian spoke my name. As much as I will it along, it doesn't come. Pete has lost a competition he doesn't even know he's in. I'm growing annoyed with Julian and his relentless takeover of my thoughts.

"I'm glad we're doing this too," I say, determined to give Pete a fair shot.

He leans forward, crosses his arms on the table in front of him. "So, tell me all things Serena."

It becomes immediately obvious Pete is an excellent listener. I place this on my pros list as well. He asks me several questions about my interests, how I grew up, and it's decidedly a genuine inquisitiveness. When we talk about my breakup with Danny, his response is, "Well at least you figured it out before you wasted any more time." I leave out the part about him planning to propose at Coral's wedding. When I tell him about my recent job change, he finds the positive: "As long as you're happy, that's all that matters, right?"

I spend quite a bit of time regaling him with insights on The Flatterie because I find myself giddy to share all I have been working on. I wonder if he notices the bags under my eyes from my four a.m. fits of inspiration.

"I can't believe you're building an entire online retail business in just a few weeks with no experience in e-commerce," he says, shaking his head. His eyes are wide and his disbelief makes me momentarily question if I've done everything right. I feel a flutter of panic that perhaps building this website for The Flatterie is a bigger undertaking than I realize.

"I've spent countless hours researching, double-checking the links, ensuring the payment features work properly . . ."

"Wow. Shoot me a text when it goes live. I'll buy my sister a shirt or something." The left side of Pete's mouth pulls upward and there is nothing but support in his face, his tone.

"I'll do that," I say, letting my smile linger.

"So, Coral tells me you're going to be the next alum in the 'Life at Thirty' feature in the Udub *Daily*. That's incredible! I've read those features since I was in high school."

I slump in my chair. Whenever I convince myself this article is not a big deal and that nobody reads them the way I do, I am reminded it is, in fact, a huge deal.

"Yes, that's right. I'd forgotten all about it."

"It's a pretty extraordinary accomplishment to get that feature," Pete muses, mostly to himself. *Yeah, I know, buddy.*

"Enough about me. Tell me all things *Pete*."

It turns out Pete and I have a lot in common. He lost his mom too, though he was much younger than me when it happened: at thirteen to a hit-and-run while on her evening walk just a block from their home. He says things that immediately bind me to him in understanding. That it hardened him in some ways, made him oddly tender in others. That the loss is largely quiet, then leaps forward at unsuspected times. That he experiences a burn in his chest when he sees a family at a restaurant that includes a mom and a young teenage kid. Especially when that kid stares at their phone or scowls through the meal, oblivious to how lucky they are. Pete offers the comfort of commiseration. It's not that electric surge I felt with Julian, but he does, in a short time, slightly warm a previously stiffened layer of my matter.

He too was a free-lunch kid, and we bond over our ingrained memories of the weekly menu.

"Fridays were pizza squares with the little pepperoni bits," he says, smiling. "My favorite."

"Same, the obvious favorite. The worst, though, were those mushy green beans that came as a side with everything. Like it was the only vegetable available."

"Yes! I had the same. Every elementary school must have used the same food vendor. I'm sure they came out of those big watery cans." He shakes his head and we both make a face.

Pete quickly worms a tunnel to my soft center.

"Tell me about Everett," I say, rolling the edge of a napkin between my thumb and forefinger against the table.

"Have you not spent much time with him?" he asks and I'm embarrassed to have to admit I know very little about the man who is marrying my cousin.

"No, not really. How do you know him?"

Pete leans back in his chair. "Everett and I have been friends since middle school. We got close in high school on the baseball team. We all dated around back then but Everett was always a relationship guy. He had the same girlfriend all through high school.

Then another girlfriend pretty much all through college. He's a Big Brother to an eleven-year-old kid whose dad took off a few years ago . . . Why are you looking at me like that?"

I slowly lower my eyebrows and soften the purse of my lips. "Because it sounds like you're telling me what you think is appropriate to share with his fiancée's cousin. I don't need you to sell him to me, I just want to know who he is."

Pete leans forward and smiles bashfully. "Okay, I get it. What do you want to know?"

I inhale sharply. "Does he love her? I mean, I know he loves her, he wouldn't have asked her to marry him if he didn't, at least I hope he wouldn't, but does he really, truly love her?"

Pete gazes at me with a bit of a squint in his eyes. I appreciate he doesn't rush an answer of yes. After a moment, he says, "They're great together. Sure, they have their occasional tiff or pet peeves about one another. Like Everett finds her love of all things Star Wars a bit bizarre, but they are really solid. An aspirational couple, even. He will love her well, Serena."

I don't tell Pete that Coral's Star Wars obsession stems from our childhood, when a neighbor left a table of free goods in the courtyard of our apartment building when he moved. Coral and I watched as he set up, then tumbled down the stairs to be the first to explore the treasures. I snagged the book on natural remedies I thought my mom would appreciate and Coral, the collection of Star Wars DVDs.

My belly warms, and I am unsure whether it's in response to Pete, Coral, or Everett.

Pete looks at his watch and indicates he'd better head back up to his office in a few minutes.

"So, are you bringing a date to the wedding?" he asks as we make our way to the door. He jerks his head back to whip a dark floppy curl of hair from his forehead.

I rub my lips together. "I don't have one, no."

"Good."

"Man, you really root for my failures in life," I tell him.

Pete gives me that crooked smile. "Then I won't bring one either, a date that is, if it's okay with you?" He raises his eyebrows at me to ensure I catch his subtext.

"Great," I say.

"Great."

I think of how pissed Melody is going to be when I tell her not only have I not come up with a plus one for the wedding, but I've just likely kept Pete from bringing one too. The thought makes me smile.

We part with plans for dinner over the weekend.

Pete has not exhibited any psychopathic tendencies so far, smells like sugar, and seems genuinely interested in getting to know me. Are these reasonable items to base the exploration of a future on? I decide they are. As I watch Pete walk away, I find I am actually a little excited about Coral's wedding.

Eight billion people, I think as I make the walk back to my car.

30.

I HAVE JUST A FEW DAYS UNTIL THE INTERVIEW, AND I STILL FEAR THE ONLY thing people will take from my feature is that I am thirty and work a shitty retail job.

The irony is, I've built an entirely new appreciation for retail workers. This job is hard. It's physical—I'm on my feet all day and they, along with my back and neck, ache when I get home each night. Customers can be incredibly rude. And I will now *never* walk into a store again without refolding anything I pull apart to look at. That shit takes time to fix.

Over the last two weeks, I've built the entire website for The Flatterie. While it took hours and hours, it was less complex than I had expected since I used a customizable template from a website building and hosting platform that held predesigned, beautifully modern templates—no coding required. I found one template in particular that fit the brand perfectly—black and white with a sandy wood background that instantly reminded me of the sign above the storefront. It looks as though I moved the store onto my computer screen in a way that is homey and personal but also grand.

We've hand-selected the pieces to launch with, the ones Tatiana feels best represent the brand. I've uploaded pictures of all the launch products, written descriptions for each, all named after artists as an homage to how color and design can change the shape of a canvas. We've incorporated the words of self-love from the walls of the store to the pages of the site, which pop up softly in the background when a customer clicks from one page to another. Tatiana has adjusted the storeroom to allow us to prep shipping packages. I've convinced Tatiana to allot a marketing budget so we can advertise on social media. We have captured it all.

I've brought a bottle of champagne with me so when we lock the doors to the store at the end of the day and meet in the storeroom/online-order prep room, we can toast in celebration as I hit the button to send the site live.

The day drags in a way I haven't experienced since my time at WAP. I am ridiculously exceptional at my job during these few hours. I practically attack each new shopper with enthusiasm when they enter the store. I am full of compliments to every person I see because they all look especially lovely today. Not only have I refolded and rehung items within seconds of minor disarray, but I could also be accused of stalking customers to preemptively attend to their discarded items.

I'm a mess of nerves as the clock ticks closer to the launch. Tatiana has a lot riding on this, and now, so do I.

"I can't believe this is happening," Tatiana says breathlessly as I pull out my laptop. The storeroom was already a tiny square with no windows and one single-bulb light overhead, but now it's crammed full of three months' worth of product to account for our estimated first online orders. Tatiana takes a seat on a too-low stool that pushes her knees to her face, and I reposition a few boxes so I can sit on one that holds several dozen of my Monet dress. I figure we should squeeze every ounce of luck we can out of this launch, and my ass on a box of my favorite dress can't hurt.

"Maybe we should wait a few weeks, test things out a little more. This seems so fast," she says, spinning her pointer fingers in little circles in her lap.

I think of the feature, the upcoming interview.

"Tatiana, everything is ready. Why put off your future? The future of The Flatterie?"

She smiles pensively, releases her breath.

"Are you ready?" I ask Tatiana once my laptop is open and propped on the small desk in front of us. We are both seated far too low, and I imagine we look like little kids huddled in front of the TV on their living room floor.

Tatiana closes her eyes, takes another deep breath. "No," she says. "But let's do it anyway."

I squeeze her arm. The adrenaline rush I'm encountering is beyond most anything I have ever experienced. It's as if I'm raising the 12th man flag at a Seahawks game or saying, "Gentlemen, start your engines" at the Indy 500.

I already have the pages we need pinned open including the site's admin page and our Google Analytics to track site traffic from our social media advertisements once we run them.

Glancing over at Tatiana, I see her stress is apparent in her drooping shoulders, her tapping foot.

I intend to pull up each page, walk Tatiana through what we can expect to see over the next few days. I've kept her up to date every step of the way and she has approved every piece of content on the site, every layout. She knows how all of this is meant to go, but I want to prepare her as much as possible nonetheless.

I open the analytics page first, ready to explain to her how here we will track visitors from each of our online ads. But before I can get the words out, something stops me. I see numbers. There should be no numbers. We haven't sent traffic to the site yet, because the site is not yet live. We haven't hit the button to send it live, we haven't even opened the champagne yet! I refresh the page and see the numbers again. *Shit.*

"What's going on?" Tatiana asks, examining my panic-stricken face. I try to contain my expression and am thankful my heart is buried under my skin and ribcage, or its pounding would give me away.

"I . . . I don't know. It looks like the ads went live before the site is officially up." My eyes dart around the screen, begging it to tell a different story.

"And that means what, exactly?" I can feel Tatiana's unease, heaped on top of my own.

"It means . . . well . . . that our paid ads on social media sites went up with links that didn't link to anything because the site wasn't up."

"Oh, shit." Tatiana stands.

"No, no, it's okay," I say, trying to mask my desperation. "Look, we can launch the site now, and . . . problem solved. We won't have lost that much money on the advertising . . ." I turn the site live, but there is no fanfare or celebration as I had intended between us. Instead, we are now both standing, our faces close to the screen as if our proximity will solve all.

"Okay, that's fixed but . . ."

"But what?" Tatiana asks, undoubtedly seeing the dry cranks in my head turning harshly.

"I just want to check something . . ." I switch screens and pull up The Flatterie social media pages, finding what I feared. Tatiana doesn't need me to explain this part, it's as clear as my inadequacy. My best guess is the ads were up only a few hours, but there are already negative reviews posted about the "fake" site.

Tatiana gasps, places a hand over her mouth as she reads them. *Not a real business,* one reads. *Don't click the link, your information is probably being sold to internet pirates,* reads another.

I look away from Tatiana's horrified face and fight back tears as I try to dig to the bottom of the problems, plural.

As it turns out, I've made several mistakes. I chose a hosting platform for the site because of the beautiful template but didn't look into the negative reviews of their actual hosting services. The site runs incredibly slow and within hours we've received several complaints about the cart timing out when customers go to make a purchase. Despite having tested and retested them several times, I somehow misidentified some of the product links because when you click on the picture of the periwinkle maxi dress that aims to flatter one's butt, you're directed to the camo print V-neck in the *Bust* section.

Bust is right. It's all a big bust, and not the kind we aim to flatter. I shouldn't have rushed this. I should have understood my limitations. And, clearly, we should have had a quiet launch first with no advertising so we could work out any kinks before we sent traffic to the site. Anyone who knows anything about building a website would have likely advised Tatiana of this.

It's past midnight when Tatiana and I finally determine there's nothing else we can do this evening.

"I'm sorry, Tatiana," I tell her as we slump in the barely lit room, surrounded by the boxes of preordered inventory we may not sell as a result of my abhorrent failure. "I guess we weren't ready. I mean *I* wasn't ready. I thought I knew what I was doing. I thought I could do this. I'm so, so sorry."

She sighs heavily and it's as if the weight of her breath blocks my airway. I know what this means for her. For her business. I've wasted thousands of dollars of her money. She has negative reviews for a business that didn't previously have a single one. She has floated a ton of resources to birth this thing, all because she believed in me. Because of her belief in the dream I sold her.

And I rushed it, so selfishly, because I wanted to have something to boast about in my feature in the *UW Daily*. I can't help but think if only I had taken my time, done it right, without a rushed deadline for myself, this would have turned out so differently. I used Tatiana and her store for my gain. I don't deserve the beautiful dress Tatiana chose for me that first day I walked into her store. I deserve the crumpled pink crop top in the back corner of my closet that, despite several washings, still smells like Coral's puke and Bourbon Street.

"I should have paid more attention, made sure I knew how everything worked," Tatiana says, speaking largely to herself. She can't even look at me. I don't blame her. "It's my fault."

"Tatiana, of course this is not your fault! *I* did this."

"It *is* my fault. This is my business. I should have known better. I should have done more research, ensured I understood the risks."

I wipe at the tears pouring down my cheeks because I can't cry in front of her and make this about me even more than I already have.

My legs are wobbly, so I plop back down on the box of Monet dresses. The cardboard collapses under my weight, sending me careening to the cement floor. I lie there on my back atop a pile of plastic-sealed dresses, legs and arms in the air like a dead cockroach. *Fitting.*

I know I have to fix this somehow. Not for myself; there's little hope of salvaging anything before the interview anyway. No, I have to do it for her and for the mission we set out to accomplish of making The Flatterie accessible to women everywhere. Somehow, someway, I have to correct this mess. It's either that or go crawling back to my old life so Tatiana can try to recover from my destruction.

31.

"I'M NOT LETTING YOU DO THIS," CLARENCE SAYS, SHOVING HIS WAY INTO my apartment. "Ugh, look at you."

I do as he suggests and look down. I'm unshowered, braless, wearing sweatpants and a holey Katy Perry T-shirt I've had since high school from a concert Clarence, Coral, and I attended together, the tickets a gift from him for my seventeenth birthday. My scrunchied hair is flopping to one side atop my head.

"I already told you, I don't want to celebrate. There is *nothing* to celebrate." I plop down onto the couch emphatically. I have already planned out the first night of my thirties. I'm going to watch old episodes of my favorite comfort shows and order pad Thai. Oh, and drink wine. Lots of wine. And if I'm feeling adventurous, I may even run to the Rite Aid on the corner and purchase whatever leftover Easter chocolate remains in the discount bin.

As I said, I have plans.

"How about the fact that you are alive and made it to your thirtieth birthday when so many people die young and don't get to this point? Or that you have a best friend who cares enough to deal with this?" He motions his hand up and down me. Clarence has a knack for calling out first-world problems. "I'm not letting you spend your thirtieth birthday wallowing in self-pity. Don't forget, you did all these things to yourself." He stands between me and the TV so I cannot see the *One Tree Hill* episode that's playing. Exasperated, I click it off, the remote directed at his midsection.

"Is this supposed to be a pep talk? Because if so, it's the worst one I've ever heard," I say, hugging a throw pillow to my chest.

"It's not a pep talk. It's real talk."

"Wow, looks like you did learn something at that self-help conference after all."

This displeases him. "Get up, get dressed."

When I don't move, he grabs the pillow out of my hands.

"What the hell, Clarence? I thought Terrance had made you nicer," I say, standing.

"You don't need nice right now, you need some tough love. Get dressed, I'm taking you out."

Only Clarence would identify forcing someone to go out and have a good time on their birthday as tough love. I relent, knowing he won't, trudging animatedly to my bedroom and closing the door.

"Wear something hot!" he yells from the couch.

The first item in my closet, hanging intentionally in the front, is the Monet dress, and I fight the urge to cry. It's what I want to wear, what I should wear, but I can't bring myself to take it off the hanger. It makes the reality of the mess I've created at The Flatterie all too depressing. I settle for my go-to: black skinny jeans and a billowy V-neck silk top. I brush my hair, my teeth, I swipe on mascara and lip gloss. I shrug at myself in the mirror, realizing on this milestone birthday, I have no idea where I go from here, no idea what I'm doing. Part of me wishes I had never met Julian. I could have gone on in my perfectly contented ignorant bliss. How dare he poke holes and let the sunlight in?

When I emerge from the bedroom twenty minutes later, Clarence is sprawled across my couch. He has moved the bowl of peanut M&M's from its usual place in the middle of my dining table to his lap and is sipping a glass of wine, watching the pot-brownies episode of *One Tree Hill*. *Jerk!*

"There she is," he sings, voicing his approval when he sees me.

"Yeah, yeah," I say, grabbing the glass from his hand and taking a long sip.

"Why don't you just drink from the bottle? That seems like something this new you might do."

I roll my eyes again, grabbing the wine bottle. "Okay, Clarence, I get it. Let's celebrate! Let's cheers to the end of my relationship with the man I thought I was going to marry, the end of my accounting career I worked so hard to get, and, oh, probably the end of the job I love at The Flatterie. Did I forget anything?" I hold the bottle up in a cheers'ing motion.

"Don't forget the death of your twenties," he adds, clinking his glass against the bottle.

"Cheers." I go ahead and take that swig from the bottle because why the hell not? It's my birthday and I'll spiral if I want to.

Clarence takes me to a rooftop bar a few blocks from my apartment. It's a cold night, and the chilly breeze on the street is an occasionally vicious gust up here. But the sky is clear so I consider it a small win on this day I can soon thankfully turn the page on.

"Thank god this is not a surprise party," I say when we are seated at a small two-seater table against the glass. I pull my jacket tight around my neck.

"I know you better than that. Coral did reach out, wondering if I had anything planned. I convinced her you wanted to do something quiet."

Coral did reach out to me today too. As did Auntie Lakshmi. There are people who care about me, I remind myself. Even Danny sent me a text. *Happy birthday*, it read. Straightforward. Not even an exclamation point or cake emoji. At least it wasn't a dick pic, which I half expected from him out of spite. Then again, Danny would likely never do anything so unbound.

"Where's Terrance tonight?" I ask, settling into the idea of being out. If I push aside the fact this is my birthday, all the things that have happened as of late in my life, I can enjoy a cocktail on a beautiful rooftop with my best friend. The humble city lights all around us remind me how small my problems really are.

"Working. His schedule is all over the place. He says a few more years and he will have enough seniority and he can work a more standard schedule."

"Look at you, talking about things like 'in a few more years.'"

I swear Clarence is blushing. Even in the dim evening light, against his umber skin, I can feel it.

"I'm really happy," he says, smiling. "I was terrified that moving in so soon would ruin things. But now, I can't even remember what life was like before him. It's like he's always been here."

I agree. Love has changed him, conclusively for the better.

Our waitress wheels over a bucket stand with a bottle of champagne chilling inside.

"Happy birthday," she says as she uncorks the bottle.

I look to Clarence.

"Regardless of what you think, this day requires celebration," he says as the waitress fills our glasses. When she has replaced the bottle in the stand and left us, he holds his glass up.

"To you, my beautiful, inspired, shit-show of a friend, on her thirtieth birthday. We've seen each other through so many things. I truly cannot wait to see where life takes you next. May all your dreams for this year and beyond come true." He clinks my glass and the tears fall so easily I barely notice them.

"I'm sorry, I'm such a basket case. I don't know why I'm crying." I blot at my eyes with my napkin.

"Try to explain it," Clarence says, taking a sip from his glass.

I stare at him, though the simple sight of my best friend's face makes me want to keep crying. "I miss my mom. I miss her so intensely right now. I don't know if it's because of this birthday, or because of quitting my job, which I know she would disapprove of, or because I've reconnected with Coral, but I miss her so much." I make no attempt to stop my tears. We are seated in a shaded corner on a dark night, and I'm grateful the other patrons hardly know we are even here. "And I think about Julian, all the time. It's this weird obsession almost, like I'm starting to believe I didn't meet him and I just made him up. I think I'm having a mental break."

"Serena," Clarence says in a deep, grounded tone. He's leaning forward, looking at me like only someone who really knows me could. "You are not having a mental break. But even if you were, that's okay. We'd deal with it. You're figuring out how to live your life the way you want to."

"Yeah, but I'm making a mess of it."

"Do you regret breaking up with Danny?"

My answer comes so reflexively I say it before Clarence has even fully finished his sentence. "No."

"Okay, then how is that a mess or a mistake?"

I gaze at my champagne glass, watch the bubbles rise.

"Why won't you look at the info Terrance came up with on Julian? Just to see! Aren't you dying to know? I am."

I stare at him across the table, then shake my head. "I can't put myself through it. Not again. It hurt too much seeing him with another woman." I shut my eyes. "He told me he's never been in love. There's no explanation he could possibly give that makes that lie okay."

"But what if you're wrong? There are a million things you could have missed. What if she was some crazy stalker he broke up with that keeps showing back up? What if he comes from a really affectionate family and that was his sister? Or what if he got a concussion and it only wiped his short-term memory and this is an old girlfriend he went back to afterward because she was the last person he remembered, like in that Channing Tatum/Rachel McAdams movie."

Clarence is also a Channing Tatum fan.

"Odette was right. I have to focus on the feeling. If there's someone out there that could make me feel like that, I have to believe it can and will happen again. With someone else."

"Okay, you'll move on. But can we at least look at Terrance's findings, just to see?"

I dab at my face, though my tears have dried. "Fine. But let's just enjoy this night first." Clarence raises his glass and I down mine.

I reach for the champagne and pour another. The bottle empties into my glass and I am surprised by how quickly it's gone.

Clarence sighs. "Let's get you something to eat."

The day comes to an official end but instead of pained relief, I feel nothing but euphoria; five glasses of champagne bliss.

"Okay, c'mon," Clarence says, scooting me onto my bed. He's working to remove my boots but I am scissor-kicking my legs and laughing hysterically. "Serena," he says in the same parental tone he uses with me often.

"Clarence," I say, pressing my chin to my neck and deepening my voice to mimic him.

He manages to wrangle off one boot.

"Yay, Clarence!" I shout as I clap my hands, because everyone deserves praise for their accomplishments.

He smirks and I can see he is not hating me as much as he is pretending to and I take it as a sign I'm at my best. The room begins to wobble and I wonder why my ceiling fan is spinning so incredibly fast. *I'll call a fan doctor tomorrow*, I tell myself. Maybe Odette can send Juicy Justin.

I tire from all the flailing and when I stretch out on my back like a starfish to catch my breath, he whisks the other boot off and exhales after the task.

I roll over on my stomach. "I love Juicy Julian," I confide to my pillow. I pretend it's his cheek my face is pressed into instead of cotton and feather.

"I'm starting to believe that you do actually love him. But please tell me he did not introduce himself as Juicy Julian when you two met," Clarence says, pushing the hair out of my face.

"No, Odette gave him that name."

"I do enjoy Odette."

"She's my soulmate."

"I thought Juicy Julian was your soulmate?"

"I don't believe in soulmates."

Clarence gives up and pulls the comforter to my shoulders. He softens his tone. "You said you were moving on from this guy."

"I like who I was with him. I was . . . carefree," I say. "Even if it only lasted a few minutes."

Clarence sighs. "I know that feeling," he says in almost a whisper.

I spring up and Clarence jerks backward in surprise. "You do! You do know the feeling because you are in *love*! You *love* the cop! Clarence and Terrance foreva!" I hold up four fingers when I say *foreva*.

I throw my arms around his neck. He's shaking his head at me as he tries to hide his smile. "So you, of all people, should know how I feel." I release him and fall backward into bed, curling into the pillow again.

When Clarence turns out the light and exits my bedroom, I close my eyes and grin as I fantasize about Julian having a girlfriend . . . who is me. I quickly fade into an alcohol-induced slumber, the last thought in my mind before I do: *I will never get over the guy from Bourbon Street.* In my euphoric state, this notion doesn't feel as hopeless as it likely is. It just feels good.

"It's probably for the better, that we don't look at Terrance's email," I hear vaguely, unsure if Clarence's voice comes from my bedroom or a dream.

32.

I keep trying to make things up to Tatiana, though I know I can't fully. I've come in early, stayed late. When one of her part-time sales associates called out sick, I took her shift. I've personally responded to all the negative reviews online. The site is still live, though we pulled all social media ads after my snafu, so online sales have trickled in. I've offered to pay Tatiana back from my paycheck for the money she's lost, though she won't accept.

"It's our mistake, not just yours," she continues to remind me, though we both know it's not true. Because I've been so overwhelmed with the aftermath of the site debacle, I've barely thought about the feature until the morning of the interview.

The "Life at Thirty" interview is taking place at a coffee shop near the center of campus, and as I park my car and make my way across the Quad, I take in that it's the first time I've been back here since graduating eight years ago.

As I walk, the memories of this place carve into me like the blade of a dull sword. Everything about my college campus is bittersweet. I had amazing times here, but it's also where I lost my mom, and I can't think of my last few months of school without feeling the loss of her. I think about sitting in classes in a haze, about pressing forward to graduate on time, despite everyone around me permitting me to put it off for a semester, or however long I might need. Dr. Murphy even went so far as to get grief leave approved.

Believe me, I wanted to. I wanted to take three months off to cry. To go through her things and decide what to keep and what to hand over to Goodwill. To take final moments smelling the clothes in her closet. To shower with her shampoo, lather myself in her baby powder–scented lotion. To say goodbye to the physical remnants of her life. But I didn't have a choice. Grief couldn't pay my rent or give me a refund for my classes mid-quarter if I didn't finish them. So, while people around me said things like, "Wow, you are so strong," and "Good for you for pressing on," it wasn't out of choice or healing. It was out of necessity. My mother had already paid for my final semester before it happened, thankfully, and so if I didn't finish, that money—and that one final act of investment in me and my future—would have been wasted. An approved leave may have covered it; I never inquired fully, though I knew my mom would have hated me putting off graduation. The loss was so raw, I couldn't heap the thought of disappointing her to the already crushing weight.

I think about the graduation I didn't attend. Despite the distance that had already grown between us, Coral and Auntie Lakshmi insisted I should go, that they would scream louder than anyone else there, but somehow it wouldn't have been right. Being back here, feeling her more closely than I have in these years since her death, I now wish I would have gone. Perhaps it would have kept Coral, Auntie Lakshmi, and I together.

I've thought a lot over the years about what it would have been like had things happened differently. I think about what it would have been like if my mom were still around, of course, but I also find myself thinking a lot about her in terms of how people die. At the time, I'd only known one other person my age who had lost a parent: Katy Peterson, who grew up down the street and with whom Coral and I played neighborhood kickball games as a child. Her father died of cancer. I can't recall which kind, because at the age of ten, there was no distinction between one type and another. For Mr. Peterson, it was a slow, progressive end. Katy told me once, a few years later, that dying is worse than death. That waiting around for someone to die, anticipating an inevitable end, was a far too heavy construct. I often wonder if my mom (and I) got lucky when hers came suddenly.

It's the best time of year to be back on campus, though, making it decidedly more pleasant. The cherry blossoms in the Quad are in full bloom, late this year as if they waited for me, and the delicate pink petals cover the trees like spinning cotton candy. The long branches reach out over the walks, like the extension of the umbrellas that scurry by. They are protectors, these trees. I've always thought so.

It's hard not to feel nostalgic as I walk alongside the triangles of grass, reminiscing about sitting here on this lawn enjoying a coffee and reading from a textbook. This setting could make reading from a textbook lovely. These are the moments I want to relearn, the ones that make the memory of this place friendly.

I think about Danny as I stroll. It's hard not to. As much as this place is tied to the loss of my mother, it is also tied to him. I could have married him, probably would have by now had my mom not passed, and if the inadequacies of who we were as twenty-two-year-olds didn't shove themselves between us. I think now, as I make my way to the center of campus, that timing does matter. I know Danny's parents are healthy, but that he will eventually lose them, like we do. I know he will think of me when it happens, however briefly.

As I enter the coffee shop and take in the bustle of activity, I consider what it would be like to be this age again. To be oblivious to the fact that in less than a decade, I'd be an utter failure.

My interviewer, Sadie Bridges, is a twenty-two-year-old college senior, graduating next month with a degree in journalism. She walks into the coffee shop just a few minutes after I do and though I expected it, still I am struck by how young she looks. She's got her hair split into two matching French braids, and I think of a toddler. I can't decide if her youthful appearance makes me more anxious or less.

She beelines to me. "Serena?" she asks, her voice high and light.

I'm easy to spot, I realize, as the others in here have the same baby face she does. I'm the only one who looks worn with life.

"Yes, hi," I say, taking her hand. Sadie's smile is big, and it turns her eyes to slits. It makes me think of Julian. I hate that I still think of Julian.

After ordering our coffees, we sit down at a table in the corner and I'm grateful there is no one seated around us to overhear any of the disappointing words about to come out of my mouth. For now, I try to think about just disappointing Sadie. I will think of the other 46,000 students and countless alumni later.

Sadie peels off her jean jacket, and under it is a black Nirvana T-shirt. Of course.

"Dr. Murphy has wonderful things to say about you," Sadie begins, and my heartbeat immediately sounds like a turn signal in my ears, suggesting I off-road it and make my getaway. "It seems you really made an impression on him during your time here. He's not particularly complimentary of many people." Sadie smiles again and I infer Dr. Murphy has not told her about my mother.

"We grew close my senior year. I don't know if I would have made it without him."

"I know what you mean! Senior year is, like, *so* brutal!" she says.

I give her a tight-lipped smile.

Sadie places her phone on the table and sets it to record. A verbal account I cannot contest later. I stare at it, feeling the urge to shove it to the ground when she's not looking. The seconds on the screen are already ticking ahead and it makes me feel like it's a race to the end, and while I don't quite know where the finish line is, I picture it off the edge of a cliff.

"I like to keep these things informal, so let's just talk like girl-friends," she says, and I wonder if this is some interview tactic she learned in one of her journalism classes.

I give her another forced smile. "Great." My cheeks hurt from the pressure of holding this face.

"So perhaps to start, you can tell me a little about why you chose to pursue an accounting degree."

I lean in, grateful her phone screen has gone dark, though I know it's still recording. "I was raised by a single mother who worked as an office assistant at various companies. She never really had stability with one particular company. Much of that was my fault. She had to take time off work anytime I was sick or if a babysitter fell through. We didn't have much help. My grandparents are elderly and live in India. It was just us." I think of Auntie Lakshmi and Coral, of Clarence's parents, and realize we did have support. I think to correct myself, though something holds me back. Sadie is listening intently, each nod of her head urging me along.

"The one thing she valued, wanted for me, more than anything was stability. A stable career that would ensure I had long-term job security. I've always been good with numbers and accounting came as a natural fit. My mom used to say if you have a job that deals with money, you'll get used to having it. Like being financially stable could be gained via osmosis or something." Sadie smiles and her eyes disappear again.

"And as you navigated your four years here, did you ever question whether you had made the right decision? If you had, like, picked the right major?"

I can't seem to make eye contact with Sadie. The short answer is no. I believed I was doing the right thing. I had watched my mom struggle her whole life, always one paycheck away from uncertainty, never able to get in front of her life. Always reacting to it. I knew pursuing the degree I did would help to ensure I didn't struggle the way she had. But there was something else too. An obligation to do the right thing—to achieve the things my mom wanted so badly but was never able to attain for herself.

"I got what I wanted out of it—a good, stable job," I say.

"And you were hired right out of school at Watson Ackerly Pierce, which is pretty incredible!" She releases a childlike giggle. "What's it like working with all those wealthy clients?"

Sadie has this look on her face like she is admiring a shiny gem. I contemplate pulling my sweater over my face, pretending I'm somewhere else. In the bathtub, sitting on a beach running my hands along the sand, in a walk-in freezer because it's so damn hot in here.

It's like meeting Julian tilted me sideways and now the straight line I'm walking leads to a different end. One that's not laid out, one I'm uncertain of. But the nagging feeling—the one that's my mom's voice in my head telling me to value stability above all else—is fading. I'm terrified to lose it, but now equally terrified to follow it.

"I quit my job at Watson Ackerly Pierce a few weeks ago," I say. Sadie stares at me. "Yup. I quit my perfectly great accounting job with no plan. And then, I was wandering around Chamber Hill and found this boutique, and I took a job there! A retail job that pays less than half of what I was making at WAP. A job that offers virtually no dependability and makes no promises for a stable future. I chose a brick-and-mortar retail shop when about ten percent of retailers permanently close each year due to online shopping. It's the opposite of stable. Oh, and I broke up with my boyfriend, who I thought I was going to marry, for no particularly good reason. Not one I can define at least. But please don't print that part because he will die of embarrassment of his association to me if you do."

Sadie is looking at me like I am a madwoman, and I feel like one as I ramble on as though poor, twenty-two-year-old Sadie Bridges is my therapist.

"And you know what the most absurd thing about it is? I'm happy! That's the strangest part. I'm *happy* about these preposterous, irrational decisions. Because *I* made them. I made these decisions. For myself. Not for my mom or based on what my friends would think or whether it was generally acceptable. Don't get me wrong, though. I'm also really scared. I don't know how I'm going to pay my bills. I've perhaps ruined the chances for The Flatterie's online business because I thought I had something to prove. But the store, it's really, truly amazing. One of a kind! And I wanted people to know how wonderful it is. I still do. I don't know what I'm doing with my life. But it feels like it's mine."

I stare at Sadie, unsure of how she might react. Will she get up and walk out? Will she laugh in my face? Will she call Dr. Murphy and ask him what the hell he was thinking choosing me for this, his final feature?

Sadie doesn't do any of these things. Instead, she does the thing I perhaps expect least of all.

Sadie begins to cry.

And it's not that her eyes have accumulated little pools or one single tear glides down her baby-round cheek. No, the twenty-two-year-old editor of the *UW Daily* with French braids starts *bawling*.

33.

I JUMP OUT OF MY SEAT TO GRAB NAPKINS FROM THE COUNTER AND BRING them back to Sadie to wipe her leaking face.

"I'm so sorry if I said something to upset you." I place a hand atop hers from across the table.

She sucks the snot back into her nose with impressive force. "No, I'm sorry. I can't believe I'm acting like this. It's just that, you are like, so right!" She heaves and sobs again and now people are watching and giving me dirty looks as though I am the cause of Sadie's outburst. I'm still uncertain if I am.

"Talk to me, Sadie," I say, my voice gentle and light, the way I would speak to a toddler in French braids.

"It's just, I'm the editor of the Udub *Daily*, you know? I'm getting my degree in journalism. I'll graduate magna cum laude." She stops to blow her nose and I can't seem to determine how anything she just said should be causing her tears.

"That's great," I say gently, unsure if I am helping or hurting.

"Yeah, great for my parents. My mom was a weather girl in New York before she met my dad. Back when they were still called weather girls. She still sits us all in the living room whenever I'm home to visit and plays us her old on-air tapes." Now I am the one nodding and urging her forward. "And I thought this was what I wanted. I did. To be on-air like her. To be the next, like, Hoda Kotb. But I'm just . . ." She trails off and sobs again.

I venture a guess. "You're not passionate about it?"

She shakes her head. "I'm not nice enough!" she blithers, and I have to bite my lip to hold in my surprised laughter.

"You're nice, Sadie. You are *very* nice."

"Yeah, but Hoda Kotb is like, *nice*. Like, genuinely nice. I'm not. I can be a real bitch. Like I watch her uplifting stories about kids who make dolls to raise money for cancer or moms who pursue a new career at forty and I think, I don't want to tell those kinds of blathering stories. And not to mention, my broadcast journalism professor says I say 'like' *way* too much to ever be on-air!" And she is sobbing again. Her eyes are red and she's run through most of the stack of napkins. She's dabbed at her face so many times that tiny bits of tissue are stuck in her eyelashes, around her nostrils.

I hand her a new napkin because I don't know what else to do.

"Do you want to be a journalist?" I ask her. It's a complicated question, one I wish more people had asked me about accounting. My instinctual reaction, my answer to the first ninety-nine times someone might ask me, I'd likely have said yes. But perhaps for the hundredth time, I'd have broken down like Sadie.

She's sniffling, trying to catch her breath. "Yes, I mean, kind of. I'm the editor of the *UW Daily*. Do you know how hard that was to get? And do you know what former editors of the *Daily* have gone on to do? Writers at the *New York Times*, news anchors, documentary filmmakers. They're all changing the world."

"Do you want to be a journalist?" I ask again.

"Kind of," she repeats, staring out the window. There's a lot of activity out there—a bustle of students headed in all directions, some with purpose, some chatting and laughing seemingly without a care. The light swirl of rain has descended, creating a gloomy gray tenor. And a little black bird is waddling around on the sidewalk just outside the glass, pecking at the asphalt. Sadie doesn't seem to be taking any of it in, though; she's staring at all of it and none of it. "But not the kind my mom wants me to be. I don't want to be Hoda Kotb." She shakes her head defiantly.

"Who do you want to be?" I ask. I imagine her answer will be something profound, or, at minimum, something intentional, like "I just want to be myself." Instead, she surprises me again.

Sadie moans as if we didn't just meet a few minutes ago and I should instinctively already know the answer of her heart. "I want to be the next Wendy Williams!" she practically yells, and it's not the answer I am expecting. I place it right up there with "Tits are definitely my thing" as one of the most oddly timed sentences I've ever heard. Sadie goes on, her tears largely dried. "I want to talk about celebrity gossip and be able to say horrible things about horrible movies and call out old actors who hit on nineteen-year-old influencers on social media!"

She's put some thought into this. The pout on her face makes her look like she's just smelled something putrid.

"I'd watch that," I tell her.

"You would?" Her eyes go wide, and I am almost certain this is the first time she has said any of these things out loud. That before today, they were exclusively inner thoughts that tugged at her each time she moved closer to pursuing a traditional broadcasting career. I feel a kinship to Sadie.

"Hell yes," I say.

She smiles like I'm a parent who just told her they are proud. She straightens in her chair. "I am so sorry about this. I don't know what has come over me." Her red, blotchy skin glows pink anew.

"It's okay," I say. I pat her hand across the table again and we take a moment to just be.

I look around the shop. All these young people, about to go out into the world and have their failed plans smack them in their cherub faces. I turn back to Sadie. And then, I tell her the thing I wish someone had told me as I stood on the precipice of the rest of my life. The thing I've only recently begun to understand. "Sadie, nobody fucking cares." She stops sniffling and looks up at me. I realize I sound crass.

"What I mean is, nobody is paying attention the way you think they are. It's your life. Do whatever you want. Deep down, none of us knows what the fuck we're doing." Sadie gives me a weak smile and surprises me when she turns off the recorder on her phone.

"How can you possibly have enough to write the feature from this?" I ask her.

"I don't know," she says, looking defeated.

While I feel relief for Sadie about her own life realizations over the last hour, I can't help but still care about this feature in my deepest parts. And I now fear the article is going to be an unmerciful roast of me in the masterful vein of Wendy Williams.

34.

THE DAY AFTER THE INTERVIEW, I HAVE AN EMAIL FROM DR. MURPHY. IT'S succinct and definitive, just as I've always known him to be.

> Serena,
>
> Sadie debriefed me on the interview. Let's meet for lunch, my treat. How's Friday at noon at the ramen spot on campus? I assume you remember the place. Looking forward to seeing you again.
>
> Best,
> Dr. Murphy

I stare at the screen. While Dr. Murphy and I have exchanged a handful of emails over the years, I have only seen him once since graduating. I could say all the things people say, like life got busy or we could never seem to find the right time, but if I'm being honest, I know I have avoided him because of how much he reminds me of losing my mom. I think he's known it too, because he's always kept the door open, let me know he was there, though he never pressed. But I've decided not to do that anymore, shut people out at any sign of discomfort.

Booking the "Life at Thirty" feature all those years ago was not only an intended gift for me but for my late mother. A stake in the ground that could ease some of her fear as she moved farther away from her last breath. That to be featured meant I was to be okay. I had something holding me accountable still.

I'm back on campus for the second time since graduating and there's far less discomfort than the first time just a few days ago. It's a wet spring day and I'm shaking myself off as I enter the ramen place on campus that was always Dr. Murphy's favorite.

I find him easily, seated at a table in the middle of the small space, facing the door. He gives me a wave and a hardened smile. Seeing Dr. Murphy transports me back to his office two buildings down where I once spent so much time. I recall the dusty floor plant in the corner built of cheap plastic and so poorly constructed I wondered if he'd built it himself in some ill-advised middle-aged hobby. I'm curious if he still has the same pictures on his walls. The one I used to stare at from his leather couch, a whimsical nature scape by Thomas Kinkade. I learned to identify the time of day by how the light reflected off the glass frame of that piece of art.

"Serena," he says now, standing to greet me.

"Hi, Dr. Murphy. It's good to see you," I say, and it is. It doesn't make me sad as I had feared for so many years.

"Likewise," he says. He looks older, though his features are very much the same. The jagged lines across his forehead are deeper, wider set than before. His fluffy hair is now almost completely gray. He's retiring in just a few weeks, I recall as I evaluate him.

"Shall we order?" he asks. He hasn't looked at his menu and my anxiety about this meeting softens, remembering his usual order as if it were *my* favorite. I nod and he flags down the waitress. He requests his standard bowl and I order the same because today his comfort food is also mine and nothing sounds lovelier than a bowl of something warm on this soggy day.

"You spoke with Sadie," I say, though I know he of course has.

"I did." He takes a sip from his water glass, holds it in his cheek for a beat, then swallows. "Not what I was expecting."

I take an intentional breath in and out.

"I'm sorry," I say, because I am. He's one of the only people left in my life who could exhibit sentiment that resembles parental disappointment. I imagine I'm here today because he wants to tell me in person he will not run my train wreck of a feature. I am hopeful he does, in fact, tell me this. That I get let off the hook, am saved the embarrassment.

"Sorry for what?" he asks.

"For making your last feature . . ." I'm uncertain how to finish. Not what you hoped? An unsatisfying culmination of your work over the last almost forty years? Weird?

"For making my last 'Life at Thirty' feature honest?"

Our food arrives and I can't help but close my eyes as I inhale the scent, feel the warmth of the steam against my still dampened skin.

"Honest, yes. But also messy."

"Life is messy." He says these types of things often, I remember. Clichés or observations of life that are commonplace but somehow they sound new and inspired when spoken by him.

"Tell me, how's your family?" he asks. I'm about to say I have no family. "Your cousin, aunt?" I purse my lips. *I know what you're doing,* I want to tell him. I want to talk about the article, not my personal life. I need to know what Sadie is writing, how bad it will be. I need to know if he approves of any of it. But also, I'm afraid of what he might say.

"They're good, fine. Coral is getting married. In a couple of days, actually. I'm a bridesmaid."

"And do you get on well with her soon-to-be husband?"

I swallow hard. "I don't know him all that well."

He leans back in his chair. This is something Dr. Murphy used to do a lot. Sit back silently, which somehow makes the words spew out of me with a force akin to Coral's projectile vomit.

"I haven't seen much of her until recently. For the wedding. Not since, you know."

"Remind me," he says, still leaning back in his chair.

"Since my mom died. Since a few weeks after, when . . ." I stop, unsure how to explain it, though I know he already knows.

"Since you pushed everyone around you away?" Dr. Murphy's words are a blow to my chest. He's supposed to be on my side.

I correct him. "Since they weren't there for me."

He leans forward, his hands clasped, forearms resting on the table, spritely white hairs poking from them in all directions.

"How were they not there for you?" Dr. Murphy knows the answer to this question. He was present through it. They were there for me in the beginning, when it first happened, but then they went so quickly back to their normal lives, barely spoke of her, seemed to want to forget her completely.

When I don't answer, he moves along for us both. "Serena, you were twenty-two at the time, just trying to get your footing. Make it to graduation. You were in survival mode. But you're thirty now. It's been eight years. Why have you not resolved this? This is the only family you have left, in the states at least. And you know what they say. There are three sides to every story. Perhaps your truth—your memory of how things played out—was and is skewed by your own grief." He says this last part as a statement, not a question.

I stare at Dr. Murphy from across the table as he sucks ramen broth from his spoon again. I'm an adult now—no longer fragile from loss—and he's speaking to me like one.

When my mom died, I have to admit, Auntie Lakshmi, Coral, and I, we managed our way through together. I'd even be inclined to say we all felt it equally deeply, though in different parts of ourselves. Auntie Lakshmi lost the sister she'd grown up with and raised daughters with. Her best friend. Coral lost her Auntie who was her second mother, having spent equal time at our apartment as her own home.

Something about my connection to them disintegrated shortly after. Like a fraying cord that finally snapped. But why? I told myself it was because they moved on too fast, too aggressively. Now I wonder if perhaps my expectations were too high. That it was misguided and selfish to assume everyone should handle their grief according to my terms. That letter was my doing, our familial undoing. And as has become abundantly clear over the last several weeks, I have a bad habit of pushing people away at the first sign of trouble.

"Thank you, Dr. Murphy," I say.

"We've barely had a complete conversation."

"I know, but I hear you. It's time to grow up."

He curls his hand around his water glass. "Before you know it, you'll look like this, wondering where it all went. Isn't that what I'm supposed to tell you?" he says with a thin-lipped smirk. His comments make me think of Odette. *The world makes you feel like you should need it less as time ticks on.*

I take in the sight of this version of Dr. Murphy from across the table. He is still a place of comfort.

As we wrap up our meal, I work up the nerve to ask, "Are you going to run the feature?"

He wipes at the corners of his mouth with his napkin, places it in the empty ramen bowl. "I am."

"What's it going to say? I didn't give Sadie anything feature-worthy."

He stares at the table thoughtfully for a moment. "I'm going to leave that up to Sadie."

I have no choice but to leave it up to Sadie as well.

As I say goodbye to Dr. Murphy, I have no idea how this feature will turn out. And though I thought I'd leave with clarity about the article, I have very few questions answered. Nonetheless, it's a happy goodbye because I know exactly when I will see Dr. Murphy again. In three weeks at his retirement party. And at least I'll get a first look at the article a few days before publication and thus will have time to digest what everyone in my world will be reading about me.

And, for the first time, I see a bridge toward making amends with Auntie Lakshmi and Coral.

Perhaps Julian is not the answer to the love I've been searching for all these years, I think as I make my way back to my car. Perhaps that love is already here, and just needs to be tapped again. And if that's the case, I may be okay with not finding him. Better than okay.

What if Odette is right? Maybe Julian is a reminder that I can be struck by another person. And if it can happen once, it can happen again. With someone else. Someone who would search for me with the same yearning urgency I did for him.

35.

JULIAN

MY BROTHER IS ENGAGED. BRENDAN ASKED KOURTNEY TO MARRY HIM AT their favorite spot on Chamber Hill, Wine & Thyme, just two nights ago. While I'm truly elated for him, there was a surprising stab of loss when he told me the news. I can only assume it has to do with *her*.

Serena.

I can't stop thinking about Serena. Her dark brown hair that smelled of jasmine or lavender or something brimming with floral and comfort. Her dark, almond-shaped eyes that reminded me of the soft, mesmerizing glow of candlelight, that seemed to look right into me. Her pink cropped shirt that showed off a few inches of her stomach. I had tried not to stare at her stomach.

Unable to sleep, I roll over and eye the string of shiny purple beads on the nightstand. The ones she gave me. I am lying in the dark, thinking about this girl I met more than two months ago. And I'm still reeling from the things I shared with her.

I told her I've never been in love.

Who does that within minutes of knowing someone? I almost

went so far as to suggest what was going on between us that night was the closest, by far, I've ever been to something like love.

But that would have been crazy.

It's as though I was stripped bare in front of her and the only thing that made sense was to stand there and let her see me. I shake my head at the absurdity, though the feelings hold firm.

Despite the magic of that first night with Serena, I now find the memory marred by her run-in with Brendan and Kourtney. Serena thinks I have a girlfriend. I haven't been able to sleep well since, agonizing over how it must have looked to her, seeing "me" with another woman. I want to find her. I always have, but mostly now to be able to tell her: I'm not that guy.

If she only knew.

If she only knew I showed up at the bar the morning after we met, looking for her. I've never chased down a girl, let alone one I don't even know.

I don't know what I expected to find. When no one came to the bar door, and I realized there was no hope at that early morning hour, I slumped into the back seat of my Lyft and returned to the hotel before Brendan or Kurt could notice I was gone.

When I landed back in Seattle three days later, I was still thinking about Serena. The memories of her are not fading away. No, they were still there long after I had unpacked and washed my clothes, rewashed them because they still carried the mud-swamp odor of Bourbon Street. They are still there after I've recovered from all the beignets and beer.

She's taken hold.

I should have let Brendan get Kurt back to the hotel room on his own that night. I should have immediately snuck back into the bar when security wasn't looking and gotten her number, her social media, her last name. But by the time we got Kurt settled at the hotel and I made my way back to the bar, it was too late. She was gone.

After a few days home, I met Brendan and Kurt for a Saturday lunch at Wine & Thyme.

"I met someone on our trip. A girl," I told them. I shared how, when.

"So, what's the deal, have you met up with her?" Brendan asked.

I told them the story that I hadn't spoken aloud and expected razzing in return. I know how silly it sounded, longing for this girl I barely met. But I was heartened when that's not what happened.

"Let's find her," Brendan said, as if it were the most normal thing in the world. Kurt even agreed.

Proving his dedication to the cause, Brendan invited me to dinner that evening, just him and I, so we could build a list of everything I know about her. Since he met Kourtney, our time *just us* is rare. He even suggested the Cheesecake Factory we used to frequent as teens, for old times' sake.

Two weeks went by and I thought incessantly of ways to find her. Kurt and Brendan have taken very different approaches in their support. Brendan made suggestions I'd already thought of, like searching all the accounting firms in Bellevue or scouring social media. Kurt, on the other hand, randomly texts anytime he comes across someone named Serena. He has sent me LinkedIn profiles and news articles if they include anyone with her name. He's even sent me a picture he snuck at a restaurant of a woman seated at a table beside him when he heard her dinner mate call her Serena. None of them have been her though.

I stroll Tribute Park during the sunny afternoons, stepping out of my office that's not far away, thinking of ways to track her down. I don't know much. She's an accountant in Bellevue. She has a cousin named Coral who's getting married. That's about it.

I googled "bachelorette parties on Bourbon Street" thinking, I don't know, maybe there would be a picture of her friends dancing on the bar at the place we met and I could leverage it somehow. I stopped at the koi pond, watched the orange fish flutter around, wondering if she was thinking about me too.

By evening I fell ill and had to cancel on Kurt.

"You love seein' these guys," he said.

"Sorry, I think I've come down with something," I told him as I crawled into bed at seven p.m. "I'll catch 'em next time."

"You sure this isn't just you pining for this girl? You've gotta live your life, man."

I shook my head though he couldn't see it. "No. I really am under the weather."

Kurt sighed through the phone and I hoped he could find someone to give the extra ticket to last minute. It's a particular type of person who enjoys a Nirvana tribute band.

I tried to forget about her. I settled back into my routine of the gym and work, when on a Saturday in early April, when I once again found myself in the office on the weekend, Brendan called. He typically only calls if there's an emergency. I answered immediately.

"Brendan?"

"Hey, I um, I think I just . . ." He trailed off and my anxiety built.

"You just what? Are you okay?"

"Yes, sorry, I think I just found that girl you met at Mardi Gras. Serena, right?" My heartbeat stretched to my ears and I questioned whether I heard him correctly.

"Serena? Where are you?" I said, grabbing my keys off my desk. Was I really about to go chase after this girl?

Yes. The answer is yes.

"I'm at the coffee shop around the corner from the Bloom Market with Kourtney. But Julian, she's gone." My heart sank. No, it didn't sink. It crashed to the floor like a dropped dumbbell. He relayed the story. How she clearly thought Brendan was me. How she saw Kourtney kiss him. How she fumbled her way out the door and by the time he explained to Kourtney and they tried to follow, she was gone.

We're not twins, Brendan and me. We are Irish twins, though, born twelve months apart. And though we've been mistaken for one another throughout our lives, I've never particularly seen it myself. It probably doesn't help, though, that we have a similar style and go to the same barber. Or that we live in the same neighborhood.

I fell back into my chair. Serena thinks I have a girlfriend. If she was hopeful about us, the way I have been, she likely isn't anymore.

The next day, I went to the coffee shop. I sat for hours with my laptop to work, though I mostly stared at the door, willing her through it. She'd been there at least once, just the day before. It's more than I'd had to go on since we met.

When I was finally ready to give up, I strolled the Bloom Market around the corner, wandering, though I didn't have the fortitude to enter any of the shops.

The next time Brendan called rather than texting, it was to tell me he's engaged. He'd been planning the night for weeks. I even helped him pick out the ring. He's been with Kourtney for three years and she balances him, grounds him, challenges him to be the best, most present version of himself. These were not the types of characteristics I would have thought to look for in a partner until I saw the two of them together. And though it may be pathetic to admit, the first thing I thought of when he said the words "She said yes," was Serena.

It's a Tuesday in late May when my phone vibrates on the desk beside me. A text from Kurt. *Dude, I think I found her!*

I sit up in my chair. There's a link to an article. I click the link. It's *actually* her. Serena. He really did find her! I shuffle around the room looking for someone to share this news with, though there are no appropriate options. I look back at my phone. It's an incredible photo. She's sitting at a table, at a coffee shop I believe, dressed casually, smiling. She's wearing this yellow flowery top that pops against her tanned skin. She looks hot and my body begins to tingle.

I start scrolling. It's an article from the *UW Daily*, my old college newspaper. Apparently, it's hers too. It's certainly not a standard "Life at Thirty" feature like the ones I've read over the years, I realize quickly.

Actually, it's quite shocking, the article.

Nonetheless, I can't stop smiling. I now have everything I need to find Serena, the girl from Bourbon Street. A soon as I finish reading, I gather my things to go. Now I know where I might find her.

A notification on my phone stops me.

It's an email from someone named Melody, with the subject: *Trust me, you'll want to read this.*

36.

ALL I KNOW IS THE ARTICLE WILL BE POSTED SOMETIME TODAY. THE PAPER copies will be distributed on campus and at various spots around town tomorrow morning, available for the rest of the quarter. As I wait, I remind myself that when the quarter (and school year) ends, the online version will get unpinned from the homepage and shoved down under the weight of new stories as time goes by.

I was supposed to receive a first look—have the opportunity to mentally prepare myself for what was to come of this certain catastrophe of a feature. But as I feared, Sadie couldn't find the words easily thanks to my hopeless rant during our interview. In fact, both she and Dr. Murphy, when pressed, informed me she was working to pull something together right up until their publishing deadline. So I will find out my fate with the rest of the readership.

Nobody actually cares about this article, I tell myself. *Nobody fucking cares.* It's the odd mantra I've been reciting silently since Sadie notified me the article would be posted today. I want to scribble it in lipstick on my bathroom mirror. In fact, I think I will.

I've read every "Life at Thirty" feature in the *UW Daily* since before I graduated. I've read about alumni after alumni—seen their perfectly posed family photos, read about their successful careers and their proudest professional moments. I read about where he proposed and where she said yes (and every other possible combination).

I remember sitting at the small kitchen table of our apartment in high school with my mom, her pointing the features out to me, telling me the importance of getting into a school like UW. That it would be the first step in ensuring my success. "These are people who have it all," she would say. What I have never seen them feature in all this time, in the forty-plus "Life at Thirty" articles I have read over the last decade, is a single woman who gave up her accounting job at a prestigious firm to work in a clothing boutique and made her interviewer cry.

This will be a first. And not like Amelia Earhart as the first woman to fly solo over the Atlantic Ocean or Marie Curie as the first woman to win the Nobel Prize in physics. No, this will be like the richest man in the world spending his money to build the first private, phallic-shaped rocket to outer space.

But I digress.

I've refreshed the *UW Daily* homepage at least fifty times and it's only nine a.m. I sigh, close my laptop, get dressed for work. My phone beeps and I nearly give myself a concussion lunging to the dresser to pick it up. It's Clarence. *Whatever happens with the feature, it will be okay.*

Immediately, I text back, *I love you.*

I get ready in an adrenaline-induced rush and arrive to work twenty minutes early. I will myself not to look at my phone while I am on the sales floor as I'm still trying to earn my way back into Tatiana's good graces. But when my break comes, I rush into the storeroom, sit carefully on the new box of Monet dresses (there's gotta be some luck in there somewhere), and refresh the *UW Daily* homepage. It looks different than the page I've refreshed so many times already.

The feature is up.

My skin ignites and my breath goes shallow. The first thing I see is a picture of me that Sadie snapped across the table at the coffee shop with her phone. It's already a significant departure from the professional presentation of the previous feature cover photos. This one looks as though I may have hijacked the site and photoshopped my picture on top of someone else's. I'm sitting across from her in the coffee shop, smiling and looking pleasant enough, though I can't help but think I look a little sad. The saving grace is that Tatiana chose a yellow floral blouse that pops out of the frame and lays perfectly atop my tanned skin. *Thank god for Tatiana.*

I hastily scroll to the content of the article. I was hoping there would be just one sentence, a statement that consisted of something like, "Sorry, due to extreme loser behavior, we've canceled Serena Khan as our featured alum. Printing nothing was the far better choice," in the middle of a big white empty space.

But no, there is an article. There are so many words I need to put into my brain and construct meaning from.

The door to the storeroom squeaks open and I let out an "Ah!" of surprise. "Tatiana, what's up? Do you need me for something, because I think I have"—I look down at my phone—"Like five minutes left of my break and—"

"Serena," she says, taking the phone from my hand.

"No! I—"

"I'm not going to let you read this alone," she says. "Sienna's got the floor covered for a bit."

I exhale, feeling utterly idiotic. What I've done to Tatiana, to her business, is far worse than anything that could be in this article.

"You don't have to do this," I tell her. And I don't just mean support me through this article. I mean act as though we are friends or that she forgives me.

"Serena, stop being so hard on yourself," she says firmly and I want to cry again. There's something in her voice that sears the corners of my heart. This damn storeroom's dungeon-y walls have seen so many of my tears.

I adjust myself on the box of Monet dresses, take a deep breath, eyes closed. When I open them, I say, "Okay, read it."

Tatiana nods and runs her finger across the screen of my phone. She clears her throat, tucks her hair, and finally begins.

"'Serena Khan is not the typical alum we've profiled in the past,'" it starts. Damn. This is going to be bad. I helped Sadie embrace her inner Wendy Williams talents and now she's going to roast the shit out of me.

Tatiana glances at me to see how I'm handling things. I look at her through one peeking eye, the other pressed tightly shut. My face is braced for a fist to the chin. The lone lightbulb flickers ominously above us and it's as though we're prisoners in an underground bunker.

Tatiana continues. "'But she is, in fact, typical. And I don't mean typical as in average, boring, or predictable. What I mean is, she is all of us.'" I open my other eye. The article is written in the first person—a departure from every other traditionally journalistic piece I've read over the years. I lean forward to hear the rest.

"'You see, I've realized in my time here as editor of the *UW Daily*, I've done you a disservice. As have the editors who came before me. We've written these features in the past with subjects who have had it all figured out. Who have built impressive lives by the time they hit thirty. And sure, they deserve recognition for that. By no means do I intend to take away from any of their accomplishments or suggest they should not have been featured. Far from it. But it is important to note, all those successful alumni previously featured—they are the exception, not the rule. We thought we were giving you something to work toward. Something aspirational. But after meeting Serena Khan, I realize what we gave you, and ourselves, was very much the opposite.'"

The box of Monet dresses collapses under me, and I fall screaming to the floor. Why do I keep making this mistake! Tatiana outstretches a hand to assist, but I wave her off. "Leave me. Read!" I demand.

She hastily obliges. "'I've interviewed other alumni for this "Life at Thirty" feature. And each time, I've regarded that person with awe. I've wanted what they have, wanted to be them in some way, whether because of their career accomplishments, their philanthropic work, their family, their love life. But the bridge between where I stood and what they had achieved seemed unattainably long. Longer than just eight years. And then I met Serena.'" Tatiana looks up at me and smiles before continuing.

"'She graduated from the Foster School of Business with an accounting degree and was hired right out of college at Watson Ackerly Pierce, a prestigious accounting firm that manages the personal finances of wealthy clients. A coup, by all accounts, given how many applicants they received at the time, most of whom brought more experience than her. Serena's former boss at Watson Ackerly Pierce, Autumn Kaplan, had this to say: "I saw a lot of promise in Serena. She was smart, determined. She had pressed through to graduate on time despite a personal tragedy. Someone who can do that, I just knew, was full of grit. Grit can take you a long way."'"

I didn't know Sadie interviewed Autumn for this article. I smile, grateful to Autumn for being willing to sit down for it even after my departure. That Autumn is still who I want to be in many ways.

"'Up until now, this sounds like a typical profile. You would not be surprised that we picked Serena Khan for our feature. But then, you find out as I did during our interview, that just weeks before our sit-down, Serena quit her job at Watson Ackerly Pierce with no plan. The only thing driving her: that little voice inside telling her there was something else out there. A better match. And where did she land? A women's clothing boutique on Chamber Hill called The Flatterie.'" Tatiana recites the store name in the same singsongy voice as when we first met, and while I didn't realize what I was doing at the time, I am so grateful the shop's name came out of me during the interview and made it into the feature.

"'When I researched The Flatterie, I found an amazing mission. You see, Serena didn't take a job at any old boutique. No, she saw the potential of an incredible calling to help women go out into the world as their most confident selves. Why? Well, the answer to that is something I believe we can all relate to. Up until a few weeks ago, Serena Khan lived her life for other people. She pursued a degree that was smart, practical. She took the job she thought she was supposed to take. She built a solid book of business at Watson Ackerly Pierce. She did what her single mother expected her to. And it was all with good intention. Her mother didn't know she was pushing her down a disingenuous path. She thought she was saving her from the hardships of her own.

"'But something was missing. What I learned from Serena, that I hope you will too, is that thirty is not a magical number. It's not a litmus test for when we should have our lives in order. And what does "in order" really mean, anyway? I've redefined success as a result of Serena Khan. And this new path begins with pursuing passion.

"'So, keep fumbling your way through. That elusive thing called passion is out there, waiting. And remember: deep down, "None of us knows what the fuck we're doing," as Serena reminded me.'"

Tatiana drops the phone to her lap and beams at me. "I think what you have here, Serena, is a glowing article!" She hands me my phone and I read the last few sentences a handful of times. I scroll back to the top of the page, wondering if this is some sort of prank. But no, it's the real article, posted to the homepage, right in the middle, above the fold, of the *UW Daily* site.

It's time to get up off the cold concrete floor.

I hug Tatiana, squeezing her with every ounce of strength I have. "I'm so sorry," I tell her when I release.

"Stop it, now's not the time for that," she says. "Where's that bottle of champs? Let's open it now."

I start to breathe again, slowly, looking over the homepage of the *UW Daily* again. As I marvel—a headline in the TOP NEWS sidebar catches my eye. A boat crash on Lake Washington. It happens from time to time—boating accidents in our waterlogged state—but the thing that draws me in is the name of the boat involved. *Sutton*

Love. I quickly skim and find that Craig Dickson took his parents very expensive boat out on the lake and managed to crash it into the backyard dock of a Microsoft executive.

I am so very glad to be here with Tatiana instead of at WAP dealing with the aftermath of Sutton and Carson's bearded spawn.

My phone beeps and I jump. *Sadie Bridges is a badass bitch. And so are you!* Clarence's text reads.

Eight years of fear about this article; so much anxiety over the last few weeks as my life shifted to something virtually unrecognizable— all released thanks to Sadie Bridges. And a little thanks to me. I've got to do that more—give myself credit.

I text Sadie, *Thank you!!!* and she texts me back almost immediately.

*Thank YOU! Promise me you'll be a guest on my talk show one day! Maybe I'll call it Nobody F*cking Cares.* I laugh out loud and Tatiana laughs at my response.

There's another text, this one from Pete. *Cool article.*

Finally, a third text that momentarily forces me to stop breathing. A message from Dr. Murphy, which I reread four times. *Thank you, Serena, for making an honest mess of my last feature. I couldn't be more proud. And I can't think of a better way to go out.*

It seems I was right, nobody really fucking cares, except to see that I am happy.

The pop of the champagne cork echoes in the little room and Tatiana pours into two paper cups.

"To you," Tatiana says, tapping her rim against mine. "You'll probably have all the job offers you want after this."

"To The Flatterie," I say, pressing my cup against hers, because I can't imagine being anywhere else.

37.

It was surprising to receive an immediate positive response from Coral when I texted her asking to get together days before her wedding. When I pull up to the address and see the expansive two-story home, I double-check to verify I have it right. Coral moved in with Everett shortly after their engagement, and this is the first I'm seeing of the place she now calls home, with its hipped dormers and sizeable grassy front yard. Apparently, rubber manufacturing sales is a lucrative business. It's a difficult association, picturing Coral now living in a house like this considering how we grew up.

I make my way up the front walk, shuffling my feet along the widely spaced steps. The bark lining the walk is wet and there are perfectly groomed bright yellow flower bushes all the way up. I wonder if Coral has taken up gardening. I picture her sitting on her knees in a sun hat with a garden hoe and it's a comforting visual.

I ring the doorbell and it is a long, chiming chorus. As I stand waiting, I move the tub I'm holding from one hand to the other. It was unclear to me what makes for an appropriate hostess gift on the occasion of visiting your cousin's new home for the first time after an estrangement. I look down at the tub. I took my best shot.

"Serena, hi," Everett says when he opens the front door. "Come in."

When I enter the foyer, I can't help but scan all the details of the room. There's a giant chandelier that hangs down from the pitched ceiling, casting vivid light across the open space. The stairs that lead up to the second story curl as they go and are framed with a modern railing of metal rods. There's a round oak console table tucked against the stairway with a bouquet of what appears to be real white flowers—hydrangeas, garden roses, and snapdragons— and just above it, a large canvas printed photo of Coral and Everett. I recognize it as one of their engagement photos, also printed on their Save the Dates.

I observe the flowers once more. We never had fresh flowers on display growing up. *Good for her,* I think as the corners of my mouth raise appreciatively.

"Coral's out back," Everett says.

"Oh, I brought you guys this. It's silly, just something Coral and I used to like."

I hand him the tub of Neapolitan ice cream and appreciate that he smiles as if it's a perfectly normal gift.

"Thanks, I'll get it in the freezer." I follow him down the short hallway that opens to a grand space that includes the kitchen and living room. It is beautifully decorated and has exquisite features like rustic wood floors and stainless-steel everything. Coral's collection of Star Wars memorabilia is prominently placed on a display table in the corner, and it confirms she does in fact live here. The collection has grown considerably since I've last seen it. It's odd, the seemingly innocuous thing that can give you a pang of longing.

On my way out the back door, a framed picture placed atop the kitchen counter catches my eye. It's from my high school graduation. There I am, in my royal blue cap and gown, flanked by my mom and Auntie Lakshmi on either side, with Coral bending her way into the frame.

It strikes me how much my mom and Auntie Lakshmi looked alike. I didn't particularly notice it growing up, but evaluating this picture, they look as though they could have been twins. Coral made a huge, glitter-covered sign that read, *We love you Serena!* She held it up during the ceremony as she screamed like it was a concert.

My chest aches.

"Coral loves that picture," Everett says from behind me, and I realize I've made my way over to the frame, have scooped it into my hands.

I set it down and head out the back door.

Coral is seated in a wicker chair, one of four positioned around a fire pit at the end of the patio, which overlooks a large spread of grass. She has her bare feet perched atop the edge of the firepit and is holding a glass of what I guess to be iced tea in one hand, a book propped open in the other. She is the picture of calm, which is quite impressive three days before her wedding.

"Hey, babe, she's here," Everett says as he follows me out the door.

Coral closes the book, sets the glass on the ground beside her, and stands to greet me. We embrace and I take the seat beside her.

"Can I get you anything to drink? Or eat maybe?" Everett asks. "I'd offer you cookies or something, but Coral won't allow anything that tastes good into the house." He winks at her.

"Don't worry, after the wedding you can go back to a pantry full of sugar." They smile at each other the way I've noticed couples do sometimes, where everything they say seems like an inside joke.

"But now we have ice cream. Serena brought it." He nods at me appreciatively then looks back at Coral. "Neapolitan. Can I bring you a bowl?" he asks.

Coral smiles and her eyes are glassy.

"I'm fine, thank you," I tell him.

"I'll give you gals your privacy then." He leans down and gives Coral a peck on the lips before heading back into the house and closing the door, leaving me alone with his fiancée.

"Your home is beautiful," I tell her.

"It's Everett's home, technically, but it's starting to feel like mine." She smiles as she looks around.

"Get your name added to the title," I tell her.

"Of course," she returns, and we smile, knowing it's what my mom would have said if she were here.

"Thanks for suggesting we get together."

"Of course," I say, now wishing I had accepted Everett's offer of a drink so I had something to do with my hands.

The late-afternoon sun is glinting against the small shards of sea glass that fill the fire pit jutting between us. Coral looks up to admire the clear blue sky and I follow suit.

"I hope this is a sign the weather will cooperate on Saturday," she says.

"I'm sure it will."

She tilts her head back down and stares at me for a long while and my throat clenches.

"What is it, Coral?"

She pulls the book from her side into her lap, and I recognize it immediately. It wasn't a novel she was leisurely reading when I arrived. It's a diary. *Our* diary. Our shared diary from when we were kids.

"Oh my gosh, where did you find that?" I say, leaning forward.

"In a box of stuff from when we were kids. I've been slowly going through old boxes as Everett and I get this house in order."

I shake my head and exhale amusedly. "That book should never see the light of day. Please tell me Everett has not read it."

She hugs the hardcover to her chest protectively. "Absolutely not! This is for our eyes only!"

"Can I see it?" She hands it to me, and I run my index finger across the cover, plain teal with a purple-and-gold-butterfly sticker placed on the bottom right corner that has partially peeled off. The book is so thick the cover doesn't lie flat. I flip through and find my childhood glued to the parchment pages.

The first page that forces its way open holds a picture of me, Coral, and Clarence huddled together on a bench in our middle school cafeteria. I have bangs. Awful bangs. Clarence has this floppy grin on his face that is all teeth, his eyes scrunched closed. I don't remember the moment this picture was taken or the day, but I do vividly remember the tie-dye sweatshirt Coral is wearing that switched hands between us so often I cannot recall who it actually belonged to.

The next page that flops open has Green Day concert tickets glued down on one side with text on the other. *Tonight was the best night of our lives. I will never, ever doubt Coral again when she wants to spend hours entering contests.*

Coral won us those tickets in some online raffle, I remember now. I was fifteen, Coral thirteen. We snuck out and took our first cab ride, paid for from our collective savings. I wonder if our mothers ever found out about it. I think of that night with Julian, how this was not the thing that came to mind when he asked if I had ever lied, cheated, or stolen. I somehow never considered anything I did with Coral to be mischievous. Somehow, our actions were always justified if I was with her.

I flip again and find a picture of Coral's senior prom. In the photo, we are standing outside the front door of Coral's house (Coral, her date, me), crammed together in the small entryway. Coral is wearing my old teal prom dress, which she preferred to the burgundy one Auntie Lakshmi and found. Coral's date, Robbie Moynes, has his arm stretched behind Coral and she later told me his hand grazed her butt as the picture was taken.

I gently close the diary and look up at Coral, who has been watching me flip pages.

"Thank you for sharing this," I say.

She nods. We both look at the ground, at the grass, at the shimmery glass in the cement fire pit. Anywhere but at each other. Music begins playing, muffled from inside the house, an aggressive rap song. This is what makes me finally look at Coral.

"He listens to gangsta rap while he cooks dinner," she says. "It's his thing."

"At least he cooks dinner."

"He knows how to make three things. Chicken alfredo with jarred sauce, spaghetti with jarred sauce, and grilled chicken."

"With jarred sauce?" I offer.

"No, jarred salsa." We both make a face of disgust.

Coral smiles, then her features quietly fall again. "This is nice."

"It is," I concede.

Coral scoots her chair closer to mine. "Serena, I'm glad you wanted to meet. It's been great, having you around again because of the wedding. I knew I missed you, but I didn't realize how much until I started seeing you again."

I know the exact feeling.

She stares at me for a moment and when I don't respond, stands and walks into the house. As she disappears into her exquisite home with the Star Wars display in the corner, I sit in the silent sunshine wondering what comes next. Am I being kicked out? Am I meant to leave? I look around, wondering if this is all a setup and Melody is going to jump out of the bushes and place a hood over my head in some sort of Handmaid of Horror master plan to get rid of me once and for all.

As I contemplate my next move, Coral emerges from the house, holding a bottle of tequila and two tumbler glasses. I hear a string of curse words from the kitchen and see Everett's head bopping as he twists the lid of a jar.

"Here," Coral says, handing me a glass after she has poured two fingers into both. "Sorry it's not Don Julio."

"That would have been an impressive detail," I muse.

We sip in unison and it's as though our mothers have taken over our bodies. I think of all the times we saw them sitting on our little apartment balcony, feet kicked up on the railing, or at our kitchen table, sipping tequila together. *That will be Coral and me someday*, I'd think as we looked on secretly from around the corner.

"I've been thinking a lot about what happened to us." Coral looks at me expectantly, as if I hold all the answers.

I shift in my seat. "People handle grief in different ways, I suppose."

"I'm sorry you thought Mom and I weren't there for you. I know Mom feels the same. But it seemed like you wanted nothing to do with us after it happened. And that list was . . ." She chews at her bottom lip, searching for a word—any word—that could sum up the complication of us. ". . . heartbreaking."

I physically flinch. The list she's referencing, the one that caused our division, doesn't exist anymore. It never should have existed at all. Just before college graduation, when I expressed my anger to Dr. Murphy at Auntie Lakshmi and Coral for moving on so quickly from my mother's death, he suggested I write them a letter. Not to send. But to express the hurt, get it out of me, then set it on fire. I scoffed at the idea that day he mentioned it over ramen. But two nights later, overcome with the sharp loneliness of feeling like my mom's life no longer mattered to anyone but me, I wrote the letter. I listed it all out—twelve reasons and ways they had failed me, failed her. Twelve reasons Coral and Auntie Lakshmi had disappointed me in their lack of what I deemed appropriate grief.

"You guys just . . . disappeared." My voice is as thin and frail as my resolve to maintain this divide between us.

"Serena, you shut us out. Every time we invited you over or stopped by or suggested outings, you turned us down. After a while, it seemed like it was hurting you that we were even there. And seeing that list made it clear, we couldn't do anything right."

I want to say that's not true. I want to argue and tell her how alone I felt. Somehow the words don't come. Perhaps I did channel my grief into anger toward them. Anger was an easier emotion than grief.

She was never supposed to see that list. I only tucked it into our shared journal because it was a safe place. The safest space I had ever had.

"We lost her too," Coral says quietly. The tears have formed swiftly in her eyes.

Seeing the vulnerability in Coral's face, I feel like an absolute ass. Eight years gone because of ineffectively managed pain.

It's odd—I no longer remember a single item I wrote on that list.

And because I still don't have the words, I jump up and hug my cousin who's more like a sister. "I'm sorry too," I whisper into her hair. "I'm so sorry I ever made that stupid list. I'm sorry I pushed you guys away. It was never about you guys. It was about me. Missing her."

She presses into me, and I feel a release as we embrace. Not eight years' worth of release, but some bit of lightness returned to me.

The list about Auntie Lakshmi and Coral. The list about Julian. I've done this thing my whole life—reducing people to lists of facts and details, moments in time or blurted words or mundane details, and built a world of truths around them. I turned my family into everything I wrote down the second Coral opened that journal and unfolded that piece of paper—withdrawn, absent, lost. The problem is, people can't be reduced to lists and deductive reasoning based on the components of those lists. We are far too intricately tangled of humans for that.

The string of curse words grows louder. Everett has opened the door and is making his way toward us.

"I don't mean to interrupt. I just wanted to see if you're staying for dinner," he says. "I made chicken. With salsa."

I look at Coral and we share a smile. It's kind of like the smile she shared with Everett earlier. The kind you share with people you really love when virtually everything is an inside joke.

"I'd love to stay," I tell him.

It turns out Everett's jarred-salsa chicken is much worse than Coral could have prepared me for. I eat every last bite.

38.

Coral's wedding day feels like the culmination of one hundred and fifty years of bridesmaid duties. Technically, it's been twenty-eight years of knowing Coral, her whole life. Those years have included adventures, wistful conversations, and life goals all building to this day that Coral has wanted for as long as she has known how to dream.

I arrive at Melody's house at eight a.m., still unsure why, considering the ceremony doesn't commence until four p.m. I review Melody's emailed list once more before exiting my car.

Don't forget to bring!

Dress
Shoes
Undergarments
Makeup for touch-ups
Extra bobby pins
Breath spray or mints
Lint roller
Clear nail polish
Hair spray
Sewing kit
Bottle of champagne

I look to my back seat, confirm I have everything on the list, though I'm confused why each of us is required to bring a bottle of champagne when later in her email she was sure to state we are allowed no more than two mimosas per bridesmaid. This part of her email was bolded and underlined.

Before I make my way to Melody's door, the familiar message notification from my phone dings. It's a text from Tatiana. *Look at this!* It says, with a screenshot attached. I open it and find yesterday's online sales. A new record. *Your article has blown up. I've gotten dozens of messages from potential new clients saying they saw your feature in the UW Daily and want to shop with us, share the site, get the word out about our mission!*

Wow. Admitting I don't know what the fuck I'm doing is paying off in more ways than I could have ever imagined. One more text from Tatiana comes through, which fuses me to my seat. *You believe in this thing and I don't care if we fumble our way through. I want you by my side as we do it. Let's talk Monday about what your future with The Flatterie looks like. Enjoy the wedding!*

I shove my phone back into my bag out of fear that if I read Tatiana's words again, they will change. I know how absurd it is to be discussing a possible promotion after just a few weeks and after my massive site launch failure. But Tatiana sees something in me. Just like Dr. Murphy had. And Autumn at WAP had. I'm starting to see it too. And I will work harder for The Flatterie than anything else in my life, past or present.

I can't wait for Monday.

As I make my way to the door, I think of how Danny had planned on proposing tonight. Before the day was over, I could have been engaged. I am beyond grateful this won't be the case.

"Serena! So great you're on time!" Melody says when she opens the door. She is already wrapped in the silk floral bridesmaid's robe Coral gifted to each of us. She shoves mine at me before she has closed the front door. "Here, you can change in the guest bedroom just through there, then feel free to come upstairs." She raises her shoulders and makes an "Eek!" sound. She's positively jittery. Perhaps her email should have limited coffee intake for the day too.

I follow her directions and once in my approved attire, head upstairs. The room is packed, abuzz with the same restless energy Melody bestowed upon me downstairs. Auntie Lakshmi is standing with the other bridesmaids, all laughing and squeaking like ducks. Coral is seated in the bathroom, in a chair placed by the window. She's in her silk BRIDE robe, mimosa in hand. Her hair is being curled by one of a handful of beauty gurus hired for the day.

My heart hammering at the sight of Auntie Lakshmi, I approach Clarence first. He glances up from his phone at my approach. "Good, you're here," he says, then pulls a flask from his matching floral robe's pocket and hands it to me. I don't ask what's in it before I take a swig, grimacing as it goes down. Bourbon. "Melody is already driving me crazy. She demanded I shave my chest when I arrived so there wouldn't be 'little pube hairs' poking out the top of my robe in the getting-ready pictures." He rubs at his chest dramatically.

"Keep rubbing," I tell him. "The only thing that'll piss her off more than chest hair in the photos will be weird razor burn marks."

His phone beeps and he pulls it from his pocket. He laughs, types a response, then replaces his phone into the other pocket of the robe.

"Terrance?"

"No, Odette. She's giving me her play-by-play takes while she watches *Serendipity*. She wants me to accompany her to New York to 'meet a stud and have frozen hot chocolate.' Her words."

"You two have a text chain without me?"

Clarence presses his lips together and pulls his phone out, types quickly, then replaces the phone again. "Not anymore."

I glare. He smiles.

"Serena," Auntie Lakshmi says, having joined us. She acknowledges Clarence then gives me her full attention. Tentatively, she grasps each of my arms, just above the elbow, then pulls me in. She smells just the same as I remember, notes of baby powder and cooking spray. Her body has the soft, round familiarity of my mother. As I close my eyes, for a brief moment I believe they are my mother's arms wrapped around me. The sensation makes my feet unsteady and I release her.

"What an exciting day," I say to her, and she smiles, though I can see there's plenty behind her eyes. Regret, I imagine. Or at least that's what I'm feeling.

"Come with me," she says, patting my hand that rests atop hers. I follow her to the bathroom and she shuts the door, so it's just her and me, Coral, and the woman curling Coral's hair. I say hello to Coral, give her the appropriate level of enthusiasm for her big day, and Auntie Lakshmi pulls me back to her.

"It makes me so happy for us to be together again," she says, holding my hand in hers. "I'm sorry your mother can't be here." This last part feels like a punch to the diaphragm.

"Me too. She would have loved to have been here to support Coral. And you."

She pats my hand as her eyes get misty. Mine do too. "I have something for you," she says. She bends down to retrieve her purse from the floor in the corner, fishing out a small package.

"What is this?" I ask as she hands me the pink heart-shaped box.

"Open it."

I do as she says and lift the velvety top. Inside is a silver necklace with a pearl at the center of the pendant, surrounded by the loose silver shape of a mother hugging a child. My tears are immediate.

"It's from your mother," she tells me, patting the tears away from her clean face with the napkin folded neatly in her hand.

I shake my head.

"It is. When you girls were younger, your mom and I found these at a jewelry store at the Factoria mall. I know that's not a special place, but when we saw this necklace in the window, we both bought one and said we'd give them to you girls on each of your wedding days."

I don't notice Coral has risen from her seat by the window until she is standing beside me. She has her thumb and index finger gently pulling a pendant back and forth across her neck. The same as mine.

"I was going to wait until your wedding day to give you yours, but I thought your mother would have loved for you girls to get them on the same day. And, I don't know, from what Coral has been telling me, it seemed like perhaps you needed a sign from your mamma."

I fall into her and begin to sob. It's a full-on, Sadie Bridges bawl onto my Auntie's silk floral robe. "I'm sorry," she whispers into my hair and then kisses it. She's hugging me tighter than anyone ever has, other than my mother, and I, for another aching moment, pretend it's her. They have the same height, same thick, coarse black hair, same soft middle. It doesn't take much effort to imagine.

I know I'll still carry the weight of disappointment and loneliness from my mom's death. I know it's a much more complicated family burden than can be fixed with one apology. But her acknowledgment (and I know this is what she is apologizing for), is, for today, enough.

"I'm sorry too," I whisper into her neck.

"Okay, enough. I can't have swollen eyes for my photos!" Coral says, wiping the tears from her cheeks. We stand there in a small circle, wiping at our faces, and I feel that thing I felt with Julian and haven't felt since. A pulsing vein connecting me to another.

I soon realize why we were summoned at eight a.m. Hair and makeup for the bride, five bridesmaids, and mother of the bride takes hours. We laugh and make jokes to calm Coral's nerves and I milk my two mimosas, though they are still gone too quickly. Clarence and I polished off his flask and I am eagerly awaiting the reception, where Melody will have a variety of distractions to prevent her from keeping track of my activities or drink count.

A little before three p.m., we travel to the venue by three car-loads. Coral has chosen a plush green winery with views of the Sound. The picturesque scene is perfectly her, wholly matched to her childhood dreams. The weather has indeed cooperated and it is nothing short of a Pacific Northwest miracle. I still won't believe this clear sky coup until the ceremony is over and we've retreated into the reception tent.

Our group takes over a back room of the main building for the last minutes leading up to the ceremony. I shove Melody out of the way to be the one to position Coral's veil. She smiles at me through the tulle and I am happy. So very happy for her. She looks like one of the Mexican wedding dolls we used to play with as kids that Auntie Lakshmi found at a yard sale. I realize as I observe her now, she very well may have chosen this dress because it reminded her of our childhood idea of what a bride should be. She's covered from neck to wrist to ankle in ornate lace that I feared might look prudish, but her curves make her somehow look like a cross between a matron saint and a bridal suite–ready pinup. Her bright red pout and spar-kly snow-white lids pull her look together incredibly. The necklace from Auntie Lakshmi lays atop the fine lace as if part of the dress itself.

Coral is a bride.

"This is it," I tell her, taking her hands in mine. She releases a breath and smiles, her teeth and eyes sparkling through the veil.

"This is it," she repeats. She turns to line up for her entrance, then spins back to me. "Serena." She takes my hands in hers once again. "I just want you to know, I love you. And I loved your mom, so much. I wish more than anything she was here. And I wish—"

"I know," I tell her. Because I know she wishes she could take back these last eight years. I do too. I stop her because it's her wed-ding day and she deserves to feel nothing but excitement and love at this moment despite her anxious energy throughout the day. Coral is calmer than I have ever seen her. It's clear she wants this with all of herself. Love suits her.

As I stand there holding her hands, I can't help but hope she'll get to return the favor someday. But I'm willing to wait for someone who makes me feel like Everett does Coral.

Music begins to play and there's a collective gasp of excitement from the bridal party. "Line up, everyone!" Melody yells in a whisper. The groomsmen have joined us behind the reception tent and Pete is by my side in an instant. He's impartially handsome, cute even, in his black tux.

"Hi," he whispers as he holds his arm out for me to grab on to. "You look beautiful. Save me a dance or two tonight?"

I smile, squeeze his arm in agreement.

As the string quartet sparks long, crisp notes into the spring breeze, Pete and I inch forward. The couples before us make their way down the aisle to the string quartet strumming a stripped-down version of Coldplay's "Yellow." I bend to sneak a peck around the tent at the scene as Clarence makes his solo walk. Guests are seated in transparent chairs on a flat of grass overlooking the water, mighty evergreens just beyond. A sizeable wooden arch stands at the end of the white-rose-petal-decorated aisle, where Everett stands awaiting Coral.

Soon, it's our turn. I look back to Coral and give her a thumbs-up before Pete and I begin to walk. The piercing cadence of the strings and their notes against the open air and evergreen trunks makes the moment nothing short of magical. I am smiling, at peace, and ready to enjoy this night that is as much a family reunion as it is the union of Coral and Everett.

Pete and I are almost halfway down the aisle when one of the wedding guests shoots up from his seat. He's smack dab in the middle of the rows on Everett's side. He has this incredulous look on his face like a ghost is using him as a punching bag. And he's standing there, staring right at *me*.

I can't help but stare back. Dark brown hair. Hawaiian Punch—red lips. Green eyes like hazel moss. Julian from Bourbon Street has interrupted my walk down the aisle.

39.

I think I'm still walking down the aisle and I think I still hear the strings releasing something resembling music. Pete beside me is eyeing Julian now, as are most of the guests. At the arbor, Everett has a bewildered look on his face; he's also wondering what the hell is happening. I think it's pretty safe to say this is not some kind of flash mob surprise for the bride. Several thoughts and emotions run through me as Julian and I stare at each other. They range from *Fuck my life* to palpable exhilaration.

My eyes are wide and his are too. He certainly remembers me now. And I think I'm making the same disgusted face I did the first night we met when I thought he said "Chest for beads," because he seems to finally realize what is happening and promptly sits back down, though he doesn't take his eyes off me as I pass him. He's got this feral cat–type look in his eyes and I wonder if he's going to do something desperate. But why?

By the time Pete and I have separated in front of the arbor and I've taken my spot ahead of the other bridesmaids, it looks as though Julian has composed himself. He's back in his seat; his face has softened, though his eyes are still glued to me. I try not to look in his direction, though it's like telling myself not to think of the color blue because I can't seem to keep my eyes from darting in his direction. *Blue, blue, blue!*

Clarence leans forward and whispers in my ear, "Who's that weirdo? Wait, he's the guy from the picture, isn't he? Julian. Shit! He's here!" I don't respond because Clarence is having this conversation largely with himself.

Melody has made her way down the aisle and taken her place in front of me. I try to slink behind her. Her Handmaid of Horror senses are keen though. She knows there's something wrong with me, more than usual. She turns, glares.

The music changes and everyone rises. I sharply recall we are in the middle of a wedding. Coral's wedding. A wedding where I must maintain some semblance of composure.

The sound of the quartet strumming a slow, stripped-down version of "When Doves Cry" gives me chill bumps. Coral looks as if she is floating as she starts her way down the aisle of freshly shaved grass and white rose petals and she is a vision of delicate lace. I can't help but look to Everett. His eyes are red, full. He's run his hand down his cheeks to his chin several times and the way he's looking at her—like he loves her so much it hurts—it breaks me. No matter their problems, no matter Coral's momentary doubts, this man loves her with all of himself. There is nothing more evident to me than this. I understand Everett deeply in this moment. The greater the love, the greater the phantom pain of potential loss. Despite this, I can't think of anything more worthy of pursuit.

My vision blurs and I suck in air, tilting my head upward to keep the tears from falling. The exact moment Coral steps to the spot that blocks my view of Julian (and his of me), I bat at my eyes to clear the tears. And when Coral steps forward, it is once again Julian and I staring at each other. There's no exhilaration left, just pain. It hurts to look at him, to know he's taken.

The men I've had in my life circle around in my head like a carousel. Danny. The Tacoma carjacker. Joey. And Pete recently. None of them have ever made me feel like this. The way Julian did. And still does. It is confirmed. This thing with Julian was (is!), without a doubt, absolute, torturous, soul-crushing love at first sight. He's made me a believer and this acknowledgment leaves me gutted.

"Please be seated," the officiant says and the guests reposition themselves. I look at the woman beside Julian and it's not the woman he was with in the coffee shop a few short weeks ago. She looks at him and smiles. I want to vomit. If I do, it would land on Melody's back, her bare shoulder blades specifically. It makes for a pleasant daydream in an otherwise painful moment.

Why does this dress have to be chartreuse *and* mermaid *and* tulle? I itch everywhere. Perhaps I'm breaking into stress-induced hives under this thing. I try to focus on Coral and Everett. On what is, from the bits I've caught, a lovely ceremony. I don't get to see Coral's face, but I do see Everett's. The way he looks at her doesn't change as the ceremony goes on. He is proud, hopeful. I can't help but believe that at this moment, he does fully intend to spend the rest of his life trying to make her happy. It sends a sharp pain through me each time I look at him and so now I can't look at him or Julian. So I stare at the back of Melody's head, watching as the occasional bursts of wind loosens one of her bobby-pinned curls.

When the officiant (Everett's high school baseball coach who became ordained online for the occasion) says "You may kiss the bride," applause and whistles ring out and the spell over me is broken. Everett bends Coral backward for an extravagant first kiss.

They make their way back up the aisle as the Star Wars theme song plays (Coral's choice). When they are halfway gone, Melody and her husband, also the best man, come together in front of the arbor. Melody grabs his suit jacket and pulls him forward in an aggressive kiss. She kicks her leg back into the air and I see her eyes flicker toward the photographer as she's accosting her husband with her mouth. Once the photographer has snapped what I assume she deems to be an adequate number of photos of them, she releases her husband, takes his arm, and continues their exit up the aisle. I join Pete, my heart pounding. I'll have to walk past Julian, in pretty close proximity. Pete smiles at me and places his hand atop mine on his arm.

"Don't even think about it," I joke, knowing he has also just witnessed Melody's extravagant display. He laughs and we make our way out of dodge, but not without the weight of Julian's eyes on me every step of the way.

The bridal party huddles together outside the reception tent, chattering excitedly about the lovely ceremony. Melody expresses gratitude that none of us messed up. Someone mentions the guy who stood up and there's a response of "That was weird" from another before the conversation moves along to gratefulness that the sunshine held up the whole ceremony. Clarence gives me a knowing look. Coral and Everett head off to sign their marriage certificate and take their first pictures as husband and wife.

The guests are exiting the ceremony area and I inadvertently make eye contact with Julian. He beelines toward me. I look around for someone to talk to, something to hide behind, but everyone, including Clarence, has broken away and I am a vulnerable gazelle the herd has left behind.

"Serena," he says in a voice higher than I remember. "Hi."

"Hi," I say, then turn to run, er, walk away.

"Wait." He grabs my arm and I feel it again. That strike of lightning that pierces its way through me. The same as the first time we met. It's still there. Part of me is thrilled I feel it still. The other piece of me is distraught. "Wait," he says again, softer this time as he releases my arm with an apologetic look in his eyes. "Where are you going?"

"Wedding duties. It is a wedding, after all. A day of love. Don't you just *love* love?" I break our gaze because I can't get sucked into those green eyes. "Where's your girlfriend?"

He narrows his brows and I realize I've never seen back-on-his-heels Julian. Goddammit, I'm drawn to this version of him too.

"Serena," he says, and I feel the heat of the sound of my name from his mouth again.

"Look, you don't owe me anything. Whatever you have going on in your life, it's none of my business." I turn to make my escape.

"Serena, I can explain!" he yells after me and all I can think is I didn't get to see his adorable smile this time.

If I wasn't part of the wedding party, I would leave. I would steal a truck à la a Julia Roberts rom-com. Instead, I have an entire wedding reception to get through, avoiding Julian. Why is he even here? Is he an invited guest? Is he crashing? Does he know Coral somehow?

I have no answers, but my eyes continue to find him, of course they do. He's so handsome, in his navy slacks, white button-up shirt, and navy-and-pink-checkered tie. Dressed-up Julian is equally as adorable as Nirvana T-shirt Julian. I have to consciously try to ignore the heat rolling between my legs.

As the guests file into the reception tent, I retreat to the bathroom. There are two things I realize as I stare at my reflection in the mirror, pressing a coarse paper towel against the sweat on the back of my neck. One is that Julian just saw me in *this* dress. The chartreuse monstrosity. How could he have possibly taken me seriously? And two, I now have to make my entrance into the reception in front of him. This second item wouldn't be a particularly painful point in the grand scheme of the situation I find myself in until I remember my entrance is a choreographed dance with groomsman Pete to the Flo Rida song "Low," aka "Apple Bottom Jeans."

It was Melody's idea, that each couple choreograph a dance to one of Coral and/or Everett's favorite songs as their introduction. Melody is the gift that keeps on giving. I am mortified as I play the choreography in my head, trying to determine if there is a way out of this. The answer is no, not without disappointing Coral on her wedding day. The one day that can't be turned sideways.

Shit.

I clench my jaw and make my way out of the bathroom, half expecting to find Julian waiting for me and feeling a twinge of disappointment when I find he is not.

The bridal party is already lining up outside the reception tent.

Pulling one of the thick white flaps aside, I take a peek. It's stunning as I knew it would be with Coral and Melody at the helm of the decor and detail. There's an ethereal quality inside, with string lights and chandeliers hanging across the top of it. There are tall vases all along the white-cloth-draped tables filled with moss and cream flowers of all kinds. I almost expect to see the fairies floating around, the ones she always wanted. It, like the ceremony, is everything she dreamed of as a kid. She did it. She made her dreams for her big day come true. The beauty of it makes the chartreuse bridesmaids' dresses all the more unreasonable.

"Hey!" someone says and I jump. Pete is standing beside me, his crooked smile wide.

"Pete, Jesus," I say, my hand pressed against my chest.

"Sorry, jeez."

Julian has me unhinged. "Sorry, Pete. I'm just . . . nervous about our dance, I guess. What if we change it? Maybe we could just walk in and wave or something instead?" I'm desperate, both of us sensing it.

"What? Serena, we're starting introductions, like, now. There's no time to change it." He places a hand on my shoulder. "Our dance is epic. Everyone's gonna love it. Especially Coral and Everett." *Shit.* He said the thing that reminds me I have to do this. I exhale forcefully and nod.

We are the fifth entrance, with only Melody and her husband behind us before Coral and Everett make their grand entrance. We inch closer to the entryway of the tent as each couple makes their way in and I can hear my heart in my ears. It's so loud I'm unsure I'll be able to hear Flo Rida. I'm bending this way and that, trying to sneak a peek inside to locate Julian, hoping he's tucked in a corner somewhere behind an extremely tall person where he won't be able to see any of it.

But of course, he's not. The universe is finding this all too amusing to give me that dignity. Julian, instead, is seated at a table close to the opposite end of the room, stationed just on the other side of the dance floor. The dance floor where the grand finale of our choreography will take place. I lean into Pete, trying to see the seat beside Julian. It's the same girl who was beside him during the ceremony. Perhaps his girlfriend was too busy washing her silky blond mane to be his date. Or perhaps he's a big fat cheater.

Pete looks over at me like I've lost my mind. *I have, Pete. I have.*

In front of us, the third bridesmaid and groomsman pair has made their entrance, dancing some viral dance to Megan Thee Stallion, and the crowd is roaring. The guests are getting more into it with every dance.

Clarence is next. He enters solo, having refused to dance with one of the straight groomsmen who would have cramped his style. Clarence instead is a one-man show, strutting to The Sugarhill Gang's "Jump on It." He's a crowd favorite, of course. Especially when he rips his shirt open at the end to reveal his hairless, razor-burned chest. Melody scoffs behind me.

His song is over before I am ready. Immediately, the first beats of our song, mine and Pete's, begin to play and I know what I have to do.

There is no other option but to lean in.

I take a deep breath, certain the air hasn't reached my lungs, and on the beat, Pete and I dice-walk into the tent.

In some ways, we've gotten lucky with our song choice. The lyrics pretty much outlined the choreography for us. We start with a reverse running man, which I must say is quite impressive in my heels and the tulle of the dress skirt that sweeps the floor.

The song billows across the tent and the crowd's energy is feeding me. *Shorty got low, low, low, low* (you can guess the moves here). I can't look over at Julian without losing my place, so I don't. I consider this a blessing. But I can feel his presence, his eyes on me. I don't see him laughing, his goofy smile, but I imagine it's there.

She turned around and gave that big booty a slap (again, pretty straightforward). I have to give it to Pete. He has slapped his own behind with such force I can hear the smack over the music. The crowd roars in approval.

Despite only practicing the choreography a handful of times and mostly last night after the rehearsal dinner, we are incredibly NSYNC, pun intended. When we turn to the side and chest pop, I feel us hit on the beat in lockstep.

We've gyrated our way to the center of the dance floor and it's time for our grand finale. Here goes nothing. I jump into Pete's arms, my legs wrapped around his waist (which is particularly difficult in a mermaid dress) and when the beat hits, I lunge my torso backward. The crowd goes wild, and I can see from my peripheral, upside-down vision, that we have even earned some standing ovations.

In my direct line of sight, though, is Julian. He is standing, clapping forcefully. He takes his thumb and pointer finger into his mouth and whistles.

I. Am. Mortified.

Pete grabs my arms and pulls me up to face him before I release my legs from his hips. We scurry to the side of the dance floor before Melody's song begins. I am standing directly in front of Julian now, inches from him.

"Serena," he whispers and wraps his fingers around my arm gently as the crowd awaits the next entrance. I shake free of Julian and turn around only long enough to give him a look that presses him back in his Chiavari chair.

The next song starts and by now, most of the patrons are standing and dancing. I feel Julian behind me, also standing. He has inched incredibly close. It sends a rush of heat through me.

"I need to talk to you," he whispers in my ear from behind me and my eyes flutter. Pete turns toward us from beside me to evaluate the situation.

"Not now," I whisper-yell and exchange places with Pete. I refuse to ruin Coral's wedding day with my nonsense.

Melody, who got to walk with her husband, has of course ensured her choreography is incomparable, and it rivals her moves from the bar top on Bourbon Street.

She has chosen "Crazy in Love" by Beyoncé, and I am uncertain if this is in fact a favorite of Coral and Everett's or if Melody simply chose it for herself. I'm surprised she hasn't brought in her own wind machine for her performance. Perhaps there's one hiding somewhere.

Melody and her husband begin to dance, and she is living out all of her exhibitionist fantasies. Someone may have to break it to her after these sixty seconds of pleasure are over that she is not actually Beyoncé and this tent is not filled with members of her Beyhive.

She is once again able to gyrate with unencumbered mobility because, did I mention, Melody's maid of honor dress is not mermaid? No, she somehow ended up with a one-strap cocktail dress that, while still chartreuse, is quite flattering. And much easier to kick her legs up in. I realize at this moment Melody is likely responsible for choosing the chartreuse mermaid eyesore me and the rest of the bridesmaids are wearing so she could shine in comparison. Well played, Melody. Well played.

Melody and her husband end their concert with a kiss and the tent erupts in approval. She takes in her applause for almost a full minute before joining the rest of the bridal party along the perimeter of the dance floor.

As the room recovers, my vulnerability builds. It was easier to avoid him with all the noise and distraction. But now, Coral and Everett are entering the reception and the crowd of people grows silent as they transition into their first dance. This is my opportunity to get out. I sneak out the back of the tent and gulp the crisp air. Being near him, knowing I can't have him, it's too much. He's already hurt me in ways someone I don't even know shouldn't be able to.

Before I can fully catch my breath, I turn to find Julian has followed me outside. I spin on my heels to escape him again.

"Dammit, Serena, would you just stop for a second?" he says. But I can't stop. I can't give him more power over me than he already had. Than he still has.

"I don't have a girlfriend!" he yells as I am walking away. This stops me. I turn and walk back to him, trying to avoid a scene right outside the tent doors.

"Sorry to hear it didn't work out," I say.

"Serena, I didn't have a girlfriend when we met. I don't have one now." He shakes his head for emphasis and places his hands under my forearms crossed in front of me. The strike hits me again. It hits him too. I can see it, moving back and forth between us, spreading through him the way it is me. I can see it because he lifts his eyes so slowly it seems to be a mighty effort against the distraction of what is happening in his body, in mine.

"I don't understand," I whisper, still fighting the wave of force that feels like taffy in my veins.

"My brother, Brendan. *He's* the one with a girlfriend. Well, fiancée, now," he says, his hands still cupping my arms. I release my hands so his also fall, needing to concentrate on the words we are exchanging instead of his touch.

"Your brother," I repeat.

"Yes, you ran into my brother at that coffee shop, with his then-girlfriend, Kourtney."

I shake my head. "No, it was you. I saw you."

"You saw my brother, Serena. *He* was at the coffee shop." He repeats this as if he will continue to repeat it for as long as it takes for me to receive it.

I shake my head again. "Is that what you say whenever you need to get out of something?" I ask. He shakes his head and releases a heavy breath, then reaches into his pants pocket and pulls out his phone. He taps at the screen a few times, scrolls. My eyes trace the outline of his quads through his pants as he does.

He holds the phone out at me. He's pulled up a picture on the screen. It's him and someone else, whom I presume to be his brother. A selfie of the two of them standing on a cliff somewhere, ocean behind them. Their faces take up most of the picture. At the close angle, I can see Julian is the one on the right. He's got the black speck in his iris. His brother, Brendan, to his left in the photo, does not. Other than this one detail, they look incredibly similar.

"Well, fuck," I say, because I can't think of what else to say. The corners of his mouth pull, and I feel myself flush out of embarrassment, attraction, connection. I observe the straight line between his insides and mine and I can feel it pulling, firm but gentle.

40.

"My brother, he was there with me the night we met," he says. I think back to the end of our encounter on Bourbon Street, security holding his friend up by the armpits. I had been focused on that guy. But there was another, the one who said they had to go. The one I looked at and saw Julian's face on and thought I had imagined it.

I wince. I've been my own obstacle all along—with my career, with my family, with finding Julian. Had I just stopped to listen to his brother that day at the coffee shop. Had I not pushed Auntie Lakshmi and Coral away. Had I been brave enough to live my life for myself instead of what I thought I was supposed to do, perhaps my entire adulthood thus far wouldn't have felt like I was swimming against the current.

"Did you look for me after New Orleans?" he asks as he replaces his phone in his pocket. I press my lips together, wondering if I want to admit it. Have I made enough of a fool of myself when it comes to Julian? But then I think, *I've wasted enough time.*

"I did," I say. He smiles. It isn't that big open-mouth smile I've thought of so often over the last several weeks. This one is different. It's thin, his lips pressed together. This one also makes me melt. I immediately wonder how many different smiles there are and if they will all make me liquify. "Is that charming or douchey?" I ask him.

He reaches down and takes my hands in his. "It's charming," he says. "Very, very charming." Then he smiles with his whole face. I don't have to tell you what it does to me.

Somehow, we've inched closer to each other and are swaying to the music wafting from the tent, in some semblance of a slow dance. One song flows seamlessly into the next and I am grateful there is no pause in music that could ask us to separate.

Roberta Flack's sweet, mesmerizing voice fills the tent and billows to us in the outside air and this moment is ours. I close my eyes, attuned to the sensation of his body next to mine. Of how each part of me feels against him. My hands, small and protected. My waist against his upper thigh, hot and bothered. The side of my head against his chest, peaceful.

I pull away to look at him as we continue to sway. "What are you doing here?"

He grins. "Melody and Terrance invited me. Actually, more like demanded I come. And Melody insisted I bring a platonic plus one so I wouldn't mess up the seating chart?" I think of Pete and I and our last-minute decision not to bring dates, leaving two empty seats Melody desperately needed to fill.

"You know them?"

He shakes his head softly. "I don't. But they reached out and said it would be worthwhile for me to come today. That I wouldn't be disappointed."

"So you just accepted the invitation from complete strangers to attend the wedding of more complete strangers?"

He shrugs. "Melody is a little scary. I was afraid to say no. But really? I was hoping somehow, in some little part of me, that the worthwhile part of coming today would mean finding you."

I stare up at him. "So Terrance really did find you with facial recognition software?"

His face twists. "I have no idea. They gave me no details. But after Bourbon Street, after meeting you, I felt like I needed to say yes to the . . . indulgence."

We continue to sway softly as the party continues on the other side of the tent.

Somehow, Pete has found us. He is suddenly standing beside me, looking perplexed. "Can I cut in?" he asks, his arm already raised to wrap around me.

When I don't immediately answer, Pete looks at me, then at Julian, back at me. Julian gently squeezes me in like he doesn't want me to go, and I appreciate it more than he could possibly know.

"Give me one minute," I tell Julian, before stepping out of his embrace. "Stay *right* here." He gives me that just-a-little smile he did that first night when I left him to escort Coral to the ladies' room and there are Pop Its firing in my gut.

I pull Pete several feet away. "Hey you," I say first, because this is all so profoundly weird.

"Hey." He gives me his own special smile—that crooked one, and my heart puddles. I didn't mean to, but I realize now I've led Pete on. Even when I thought this could be the start of something with Pete, my attention, my affection, and perhaps even my whole heart was with Julian. I now know there was never actually any room for Pete. Not really.

"You're such a great guy, Pete."

"Oh, fuck," he says, that crooked smile returning to his face, though this time it feels more brave than silly. "A conversation that starts with a compliment."

"I'm sorry, it's just—" I turn and look over my shoulder at Julian, who has stepped back even farther at the tent's edge to give us our privacy.

"I think I get it," Pete returns, looking back at Julian then to me again. And, even with so few words and no real explanation, I know he does. We have that type of link, Pete and I. The kind where, after loss, you know you've got to grasp on to connection wherever you can find it.

I make a mental note to find some means of a more wholehearted apology later. But I cannot let Julian out of my sight again.

Pete returns to the reception tent, head high.

Julian is waiting, just where I left him. Without words, and with no hesitation, my body sinks right back into its place against his. It's bold and effortless all at once to fall into him. It's a combination I'm not particularly used to, though am certainly fond of.

We sway.

Until I pull away once more. "Wait, if you don't have a girlfriend, who's the woman you were sitting next to during the ceremony, and inside?"

Julian flushes. "A family friend," he says. "I brought her as a favor to my mom, who's been trying to get her out there after a bad breakup. But there's nothing there." I realize we'll have to figure a way to get him out of that.

But for now, we sway some more.

I lean farther into him. A Savage Garden song streams its way to us, which normally I would have made fun of—the obviousness of a song like this one on a wedding playlist. But today, today I love everything about it.

I pull back from him again. "Just so I'm perfectly clear, you don't have a girlfriend?" He shakes his head. "Or wife, or boyfriend?"

"No significant other of any kind. And just so *I'm* perfectly clear, tits are still definitely my thing." He scrunches his face as he cringes at himself.

"Did you look for me too? After New Orleans?" I ask. I want to savor this endless dance with him, but I also need answers.

He smiles, kisses my hand, and I almost lose my mind at the feeling of his lips on my skin.

"After we got kicked out of the bar that night we met, Brendan and I got our friend Kurt to the hotel and then I came back, looking for you. I snuck back in, looked all around. But you and your friends were gone."

"Coral threw up again," I say.

"Yeah, I figured it was something like that. And when I saw you were gone, I can't even describe to you what that felt like."

"Try," I say, desperate to hear it.

"It was like . . . this overwhelming loss. Or miss. I don't know. I'd never felt that way before."

I nod.

"I went back the next morning. Super early because I couldn't sleep. I don't know what I was thinking, like you would have been there that early—"

"I was."

"What?"

"I was there. I saw you. We were driving to the airport and I saw you. I tried to get to you, but you got in the car so fast."

"Wow," he says on an exhale as we relive our near miss. He squeezes my hand.

"When I got back home, I tried to find you on social media, but I didn't have much to go on. Then I saw you walking down the aisle, and then Melody, and the bride . . ."

"So you recognized Coral without her BRIDE sash between her legs?"

"I did, somehow." We smile and then his face grows serious with an intensity that makes me lose my stomach. "I did look for you, Serena. I thought about doing all kinds of things to find you. I thought about posting about our meeting to one of those chance encounters boards. I thought about posting a video searching for the woman from Bourbon Street, hoping it would go viral."

"Why didn't you do any of those things?"

He hasn't broken eye contact with me yet. "Because we met for one night. I thought, it's crazy for me to feel this way. And what if she doesn't feel the same?"

The music shifts to something upbeat and we slowly separate. It feels like Velcro being ripped apart.

"I have one more thing to ask you," he says as he takes my hand and leads me back into the reception. "If you had to choose: lead-filled beads or this dress?"

"Lead-filled beads, all day. No question."

He smiles that goofy, adorable, too-wide smile, and I squeeze his hand.

"Lucky for you, I still have mine," he says.

I stop walking and face him. "You do?"

He nods, that thin smile back on his face. This one looks proud.

"Why'd you keep them?"

He stares at me for a moment, his eyes darting back and forth over mine and I chase them with my own. "I think you know why," he says.

We are facing each other, in the corner of the tent, away from the crowd of people. It's just us two, everyone else too busy flopping around on the dance floor to "Uptown Funk" to notice us. Everything about it feels just like the night we met. A sweep of wind catches us from the open tent doors, and as my skin raises, it's as though a bit of the magic of Mardi Gras has whisked itself all the way to the Emerald City. To us.

I glance over and find Melody in the crowd. Even she looks happy. Her arms are outstretched around her husband's shoulders and she's throwing her head back laughing as he nuzzles against her neck. They vary between this and mouthing the words of the song to one another.

She did this, helping to get Julian here. Even if it was mostly to save her seating chart, I have to think perhaps it was, just a little, for me. We make eye contact across the tent and I mouth *Thank you*.

She whispers something into her husband's ear then makes her way to the corner Julian and I have taken ownership of.

"Julian," she says, holding her hand out to him when she's reached us.

"Melody." He shakes her hand, a knowing look with matching hints of a smile across both their faces. "I feel like I should hug you."

She shakes her head once. "I'm not a hugger."

The final trumpeted beats of "Uptown Funk" hit and when they do, Clarence and Terrance make their way over to us.

"This is him!" Clarence yells, throwing his arms around Julian. He *is* a hugger.

The three of them exchange greetings.

"I need to know how this happened," I say finally.

Clarence looks to Terrance while Melody points in his direction.

"Turns out we didn't need facial recognition software," Terrance says. "A simple drag and drop into Google images was enough." He takes hold of Clarence's hand. "I wanted to leave it alone, let you look at the information when you were ready, but Clarence enlisted Melody's help when he couldn't sit on his hands any longer."

"To persuade him to come to the wedding. I'm highly persuasive," Melody adds.

"Melody didn't require much convincing, shockingly," Clarence says. "Turns out the ice in her veins is neighbors with a tender, beating heart." Clarence strokes Melody's arm and she recoils.

"This is getting a little too Hallmark movie for me," Melody says. "I'm dancing. Julian, be good to her or I'll nut punch you." And with that she's off to the dance floor.

We watch her grab Coral's waist and sway her back and forth as a sing-along breaks out to Journey's "Don't Stop Believin'."

"She'll forever say her willingness to help was for the sake of her beloved seating chart," Clarence says. "But when I explained everything to her, she confessed to meeting her husband during a drunken night at Señor Frog's in Cabo and that when they met, 'he struck right through' her. She helped because she knew what it could mean for you two to find each other again."

Julian takes my hand in his, squeezes it tight. I had all the information I needed on Julian for weeks, sitting in my computer's trash folder. While I wish I would have looked at that document from Terrance, stayed and listened to Brendan at that coffee shop, I have to believe things worked out the way they were supposed to—messy and meandering—because it all led me here.

My list about Melody, up until five minutes ago, would have

included one seemingly toxic trait after another. It would have reduced her to a one-dimensional paper doll. I am wholly reaffirmed:
no more lists.

Clarence and Terrance return to the dance floor, their eyes
stuck on one another. The buttons of Clarence's shirt flew off during
his reception entrance dance, so his razor-burned chest is still displayed proudly. I want a love like theirs.

Julian and I are alone again and my eyes go back to his. I can't
seem to make anything else matter.

He cups the side of my face with his hand, his thumb under my
chin, leans down, and brushes his lips against mine. I'm not even
certain I can call it a kiss, this graze that is so soft and controlled
it's like a warm gust of wind against my mouth. It's enough for me to
come undone.

I've imagined this kiss for three months. I've wondered what
those Hawaiian Punch lips might feel like on mine. How soft his
tongue would feel in my mouth. How the dance of our lips would
come together. It's better than I imagined, truly. Because what I
couldn't adequately live in my dreams was his warmth, his taste. The
tickle of his breath against my skin. I feel like a cat who's found a
strip of sunlight to bask in. "What's your last name?" I ask urgently
once we've parted, in case I lose him again.

He smiles. "Gentry. Julian Gentry."

"Julian Gentry," I repeat, savoring the way *his* name sounds
from *me*.

We stand in the corner, holding hands and just sort of staring at
each other, taking turns leaning in for another kiss as a soft, instru-
mental version of Nirvana's "Love Buzz" hums us.

Epilogue

THERE'S STILL A LOT TO LEARN ABOUT JULIAN GENTRY. SINCE RECONNECT-
ing with him almost a year ago at Coral and Everett's wedding, I've
learned the tech company he "works for" is *his*. He founded it and
is the CEO. The company is an app that matches sick children with
donors.

Yeah.

It's small, barely profitable, and he's fumbling his way through,
but it's his and he loves it and he's been largely single the last several
years because he's been treating his business like the love of his life.
And it is. I love that about him.

The best part about it is, now that I'm managing The Flatterie's
online presence, he's offered a myriad of suggestions and solutions
that have not only made The Flatterie that much more successful but
has made me attracted to the way his brain organizes thoughts. I've
never had that before. And of course, I've fixed the mess that was his
company's finances, which he was managing himself.

I've also learned he's incredibly humble. That his employees
adore him and he has no ego around them. This part I didn't learn
from him, rather it was uncovered when I was *actually* able to stalk
him online.

He has this incredible ability to be present in a moment. He
kisses like there's no rush at all. Like he could just kiss for hours

with nowhere to go and nothing to do. His attunement in the bedroom is the same and I am happy to report that his mouth is, in fact, magic.

He's not perfect, though. I found that out three days after the wedding when he took me to his place and I discovered he has an entire room dedicated to Nirvana. It's not a Nirvana-themed room, which perhaps I could wrap my mind around. No, It's a shrine. A room that serves no other purpose than to display Nirvana memorabilia. Band member bobbleheads and framed band T-shirts, the prized possession being a *Nevermind* album cover, signed by Kurt Cobain himself, obtained from an eBay auction, though he refuses to tell me how much it cost.

I pictured Julian home alone, in the Nirvana room for hours at a time, picking up each item to survey it and then delicately replacing it in its thoughtfully picked location. The secondhand embarrassment I feel for him is married with adoration for his dedication to this piece of his identity.

This quirk has made him and Joey fast friends.

His musical tastes don't end there. I received a glimmer of his vast knowledge of useless musical trivia the night we met, but there's more. So much more. His playlists are like a glimpse into a kaleidoscope. They leap from Chris Stapleton to Britney Spears to, of course, nineties' and early two thousands' hip hop. He knows so many facts about these artists and their songs. A new track will begin and there's a "Did you know?" statement that follows. Every time.

I've learned he loves to travel. He's far better traveled than me, having visited every continent except Antarctica (though it's on his list) and over thirty countries. It's impressive and I can't help but daydream about traveling with him, about cruising down the Seine or sharing an authentic village dinner in a hut in Peru. These new people in my life—Odette, Tatiana, Julian—they've taught me that beyond just surviving, life can be full of exploration and adventure.

But then he tells me his favorite thing to do on these trips, especially those in the US, is to take ghost tours. He pays money and reserves a spot on guided ghost tours in virtually every city he visits. He stands at the front of the group next to the guide, asking questions and keeping his phone stationed in his hand, snapping dozens of photos as he goes, stopping to evaluate each of those pictures to see if he's captured any orbs or perhaps something even more otherworldly. He even forced Brendan and Kurt on a tour in New Orleans, which he claims was "the best one ever." I'm not sure what to make of this particular interest of his quite yet.

I've also learned he likes to watch classic black-and-white films like *Casablanca* and *Citizen Kane*. On the surface, I consider it charming, but I also find myself scrunching my nose each time he suggests we watch one together. I inevitably fall asleep less than halfway through every time, though I rarely object because observing him watching these movies with intensity, it's downright adorable. For now, I'm content being in his world, finding out what he likes; and feeling his growing passion for mine. I'm even more content falling asleep to the classics when he tells me watching these old films is something he used to do with his grandfather, whom he simply called Pap. *The Maltese Falcon* was Pap's favorite. It's Julian's too.

But like I said, there's still a lot to learn.

It's my thirty-first birthday. It's been over a year since Julian and I first met and so far, the reality of him is better than I could have imagined.

It turns out thirty-one is the milestone birthday I hadn't expected. If you'd told me a little over a year ago I'd be celebrating tonight with the man I met on Bourbon Street, reveling in the success of The Flatterie's online business, which just hit two million in sales last week, I would have told you it was someone else's life you were talking about. I'm certainly glad I was wrong; and I'm certainly glad it's mine.

I stand in the middle of the crowded bar, surveying my group of friends. Clarence and Terrance. Coral and Everett. Tatiana, Joey, Carl, the building security guard from WAP. Julian's brother, Brendan, and his soon-to-be-wife, Kourtney. Pete and his girlfriend, Jules, also known as Julian's family friend at Coral and Everett's wedding. That's right. They were an instant match once Julian and I were out of their way that night. Even Melody and her husband are here. Though our road to friendship was pothole-filled, she would cut someone who wronged a loved one. I respect that.

And, of course, there's Julian.

I look around at them all, feeling the one thing I spent so much time chasing. Passion. That, and thanks to Julian's and Tatiana's tales of adventure, a bit of wanderlust.

"If you puke on me tonight, I swear I'm going to throw you in the Sound," I tell Coral as she comes back from the bar with several shot glasses pressed together between her hands.

Everett places his arm around her lower back and hugs her in. They did end up honeymooning in India and he loved meeting our grandparents. Julian and I plan to visit them next summer.

Clarence grabs a glass and holds it up. "To my shitshow of a best friend," he says, then clinks his glass to everyone's, Terrance beside him last.

"For fuck's sake," I hear behind me and I smile in recognition before I can turn to see her face. Odette is standing there, removing her coat and intentionally elbowing the people around her to make space as she does.

"Odette!" I yell and then wrap myself around her, her body feeling like a mess of knives inside a trash bag. She hugs me back in a remarkably tight grip.

"This him?" she asks, batting her hand toward Julian with her flimsy wrist, her hand bobbling in the air.

"It is," I say, holding on to her arm. "What do you think?" I ask her, loud enough for Julian to hear. He's smiling at us, waiting to introduce himself.

"I've gotta see something before I can make up my mind," she says. Odette reaches for the bottom of his T-shirt and lifts it so high it covers his face and she is staring at his torso, her eyes at nipple height. I laugh, as does everyone else, and I can see they are already as enamored with Odette as I am. Still holding his shirt up with one hand, she reaches out and runs her free hand across his abs.

"Oh!" he says and reflexively pushes his waist backward. I'm unsure if he's done this because of the surprise or the cold of her hand. Probably both.

"I'd fuck him," she says with a shrug as she releases his shirt.

I make a mental note to discuss the problematic nature of Odette's behavior with her later.

Odette stays for one drink, her signature dirty martini. She says the shot she took in addition to her martini doesn't count. Then, she Lyft's back to her daughter's home with the promise of drinks each time she is in town. And of course, she is the perfect excuse for an eventual return to Louisiana.

I wrap my arms around Julian's neck and rise to my tiptoes to kiss him. We sway gently despite the upbeat music and I realize it's the first time we have danced since Coral and Everett's wedding (if you can call either dancing). Pressing into him and resting my ear against his chest, I feel the thing that has always eluded me. I feel safe. And it didn't take a certain bank balance to get me there.

A familiar song comes crashing down, the beat of the drum and the beat of my heart in perfect rhythm.

"It's our song!" he says emphatically as "Back That Azz Up" renders me almost deaf. The music is so loud it requires yelling to hear one another. I'm wondering what we are doing here, knowing both of us would prefer being back at his place on his couch, even if it means watching an old black-and-white.

"Chest for beads!" I yell into his ear because this is all too familiar a scene.

And then he does the thing I am not expecting. The thing made-up Julian—list Julian—couldn't do, wouldn't do. The thing only real Julian can do because real Julian does unexpected things. He releases me and reaches into his jeans pocket. He pulls out a strand of shitty, probably lead-filled, purple plastic beads.

My mouth flies open. "You really kept them, all this time!" I shout. He nods. I lean forward and he places the strand around my neck.

"I did," he says.

It's the perfect birthday gift.

A year ago, I would have said an engagement ring would have been the thing I wanted most of all. But today, on this thirty-first birthday, I am content with this new relationship, unsure of where it will take me but excited for the surprises ahead.

I've shared him with my mom often, in all the little and big moments over this past year. Most recently, as I curled my hair in the bathroom mirror getting ready for tonight.

"This is the birthday I'm most excited for, more than all the others," I told her.

"I know," she said quietly in response.

"I'm sorry," I told her. *"For disrupting it all the way I have."*

"I know. But you don't have to be. Seeing you, with him, you did get everything I never had after all. Your life—this life—it's everything I never knew I always wanted. Enjoy it, amma."

After getting ready, I pulled open the drawer to my nightstand, looking for my new journal—which contains no lists, only thoughts and hopes—and found instead the mojo bag I bought in New Orleans, once meant for Danny. It had been shoved in that drawer in my bedroom the whole time. Perhaps it stayed with me on purpose, surrounding me with New Orleans magic even when I didn't believe.

When I broke up with Danny, there was a visceral, betrayal-like sensation coursing through me tied to losing the last guy my mother would ever meet. But Julian has gotten to know her in ways I never expected. Getting to share her with him—how we grew up, the special moments, the conversations I still have with her—her memory is evergreen, reborn through the eyes of someone experiencing her for the first time. It's allowed me to get to know her again too.

While there was an unmatched strike of lightning between Julian and I that first night and when we came back together at Coral's wedding, I know that love is, more than anything, a choice. And after everything I've learned about Julian Gentry over the course of this past year, all the things that have made him whole, I purposefully choose him.

Maybe he'll disappoint me someday in the future. We will likely disappoint each other in minor and perhaps major ways all along this relationship. But, for the first time in my life, I'm okay with not knowing. With letting this journey take me where it may.

As I said, there's still a lot to learn.

"I love you," he whispers into my ear, and I still feel the same deep pleasure as the first time, knowing I'm the only one he's ever spoken those words to.

I whisper the words back, still in disbelief of all that aligned for us to come together. That of eight billion people, I found one who feels like home.

Acknowledgments

I GREW UP in the suburbs of Seattle in the Pacific Northwest. Like many hometowns, the area lives in my mind in a perpetually idyllic state: the unsullied air, the epicurean eats, attending Salmon Days each year as a child. I found it virtually impossible to choose one town, one small corner of focus. Instead, I collected places and feelings, memories and pastimes, from the area as a whole to build the fictional city of Chamber Hill. Those familiar with the area may see parcels of Ballard, Issaquah, Seattle, Kirkland, Bellevue, and Capitol Hill nested within it.

In the New Orleans portions of this book, you will find much of the same—a combination of real and fictional descriptions, all in an effort to capture the overall feel of a place. Though liberties were taken, the folklore and mysticism of New Orleans continue to entice me to learn more about this distinctive place.

This book wouldn't have been possible without the support of many, many dear people in my life and that support often goes back long before any words hit the page.

To my brilliant agent, Elisabeth Weed: You have championed me and this book from day one. Thank you for your unwavering support and clear vision that at times blew my mind. You plucked me from the query trenches, and I will be forever grateful. Thank you DJ Kim and The Book Group team for your endless help and support.

The entire team at HarperCollins and specifically my editor at Harper Perennial, Micaela Carr: Our first call will forever be a defining moment in my career. Your genuine excitement for this project and our alignment on pretty much everything still makes me feel wholly unworthy. Thank you for pouring all of yourself into this book. Thank you also to Heather Drucker, Joanne O'Neill, Amy Baker, Lisa Erickson, Megan Looney, and Emily Griffin for your support along the way.

Sawyer and Sienna: You teach me something new every day. You are constant reminders that there are no limits except those we place on ourselves. I aim every day to see the world as you do—one vast, endless possibility for exploration and joy. I did this to make you proud.

My parents: This need to create came from both of you.

Dad: Your will to push the envelope and not give a damn what anyone else thinks is something I admire. It has helped me be more fearless and indignant in the best possible ways.

Mom: Your strength is unmatched and you are a constant reminder that it is truly never too late to go after what you want. You started your own business in your forties, bungee jumped in your fifties, and walked the Great Wall in your sixties. You are an inspiration and a fighter. Thanks for being the model of a strong female character.

Raj: Thank you for answering all my random texts about random things and being my human Google while never questioning the sanity of my questions. I look forward to a book signing at Forum Social House.

LaTrenda Lawson: I knew you would provide unconditional support and you did not disappoint. If I have one hope for anyone pursuing a dream, it is to find someone who will cry happy tears for you the way LaTrenda does for me.

Christelle Lujan: You spent countless hours geeking out with me over writing details nobody else would have cared about. Your dedication to the craft is inspiring and you are in part responsible for me starting *and* finishing this thing.

Thank you to my writing group members Lindsey Ray Redd, Eden Wilder, and Allie Gravitt: I couldn't have done this without you. We've been together since word one of this book. You were my first readers and your feedback was invaluable. You've cheered me on at every step. You are what women supporting women means, through and through.

My additional critique partners, Teddi and Madhu, thank you for the sense of community you have provided. And Teddi, for your *two* reads of this book. There are big things ahead for both of you and I'm lucky to get to play witness.

Thank you to my *many* additional beta readers: Jill Beissel, Hannah Stone, Genny Carrick, Laura Hartley, Erin Thomson, Lauren Searson-Patrick, and more. You each provided a unique view of the reader's experience and there is some imprint of each of you on these pages.

Grace Shim: You were my first traditionally published author friend and it made me feel real cool to call you a friend. Thank you for believing in me when you didn't have to.

I'd be capable of very little if not for the circle of powerful and achieving women in my life who supported me well through this process. Raelene Plant: You were an early supporter, beta reader, and encouraged me like nobody's business. Thank you for ensuring I got Seattle right. Amelia Walsh: For The Flatterie—we'll build her someday. Wendi Cox: Thank you for the Star Wars inspo you didn't know you provided. Michele Vierra and Melissa Campbell: Thank you for letting me peruse your dating profiles. I am truly sorry for, as Clarence points out, the sad state of affairs out there. What I found on your apps was so much worse than what made it into this book.

Jane Alexander, Beth Lebowitz, Erin Mahoney, Alyssa Lawson, and so many more: Thank you for being examples that everyone should aspire to hustle like a woman. You inspired the bold women in this book. I built their strength from your examples.

My husband, Kris: Without you, there would be no book. You supported me endlessly with the gift of time. You showed me grace when I was "in the zone" and not fully present, staring into space thinking about something in these pages. I will be forever grateful for your unconditional love and belief in me, but mostly for proving that real, lasting love can come from a drunken meeting in a bar. We did this.

NEELY TUBATI ALEXANDER is the author of women's fiction with rom-com feels you can escape into with a smile. Originally from the Seattle area, she currently resides in Arizona with her husband and two elementary-aged children. If she's not tucked away at the little desk in her bedroom writing, you can find her at some kiddo activity, drinking wine, or watching reality television, usually the last two together.

Neelytubatialexander.com
Instagram: @Neelyalexanderwrites